LEKE APENA

SECURE
THE BAG
NOT
THE HEART

URBAN
INTELLECTUAL
BOOKS

First published in Great Britain by Urban Intellectual Books UK Ltd, 2024

Copyright © 2024 by Leke Apena

Paperback ISBN: 978-1-7398939-2-7

eBook: 978-1-7398939-3-4

Printed and bound by Amazon KDP.

❀ Created with Vellum

ABOUT THE AUTHOR

Born and raised in east London, Leke Apena graduated from the University of Brighton in 2011 with a degree in English Language and pursued a career in communications.

Leke writes unconventional, challenging and entertaining stories about the modern Black British experience and wants to challenge the idea that black men do not write or read romance.

instagram.com/urbanintellectualauthor

ALSO BY LEKE APENA

A Prophet Who Loved Her

Flavours of Hackney

Flavours of Black

As always, for you, Issy.
May you become a fierce woman.

CONTENTS

Love is whatever you can betray. Betrayal can only happen if you love.

JOHN LE CARRÉ, *THE LOOKING GLASS WAR*

PROLOGUE

THE BOY WOULD BEGIN his day with love. But it would end in death.

"Why do we have to keep our relationship a secret?" the boy asked the girl, narrowing his eyes at her. "Don't you like me?"

They were walking together in the blistering heat on the dry savannah terrain in the rocky capital of Ogun state in southwestern Nigeria. Returning from another arduous day of high school, the boy and girl, both age twelve, were still in their threadbare school uniforms. The boy wore a plain, polyester white shirt and green slacks, while the girl wore the same shirt but with a green, high-waisted pleated skirt. At their young age, the poverty and tribulations that blighted millions of Nigerians' lives were insignificant to the most crucial question in their youthful existence—do you fancy me?

Grinning at the boy, the girl poked him on his left shoulder. "You know I like you," she said, her eyes resting on the boy's lips. "But I don't want everyone at school to know. If Mr Akedu finds out, he will flog us."

The boy chortled and kicked a small rock across the rough,

sandy-coloured path as he and the girl walked past a local church. The building was made of concrete, which was already cracking; the green paint on its walls was peeling, and its tin roof was dark brown with rust. An old dark-skinned woman, wrapped in a long white dress almost blinding in the sun's heat, stood by the church's entrance.

The boy's attention was drawn to the old woman, and he saw in her bony right hand a brown leather Bible she held against her breast. She then closed her eyes as if in a trance and raised her right hand upwards. The boy watched, slightly unnerved, as the old woman called to her creator above.

"God will cleanse Nigeria of corruption, deception and bloodshed. These diseases which blight our nation. Only Yahweh can purge our lands of the greedy, the liars and the gluttonous."

The boy forced his eyes away from the raving woman and turned his attention back onto the young girl.

"Mr Akedu does not even know what is happening behind that big head of his," the boy said, with a cheeky smirk, "or what is even happening in front of his fat belly."

The girl chuckled, but the boy could sense something bothering her. She let out a deep sigh filled with sadness for someone so young. "That is not the only reason. *Baba mi,* I think my father is getting sick." She cast her eyes down and looked at her black, shabby plimsolls. "He told me that if he gets too ill, I will be sent to London to live with my auntie."

Now, the boy tightened his face with panic, and the lightness in his voice evaporated. "Your father is tough, one of the toughest men in Abeokuta", the boy said, beaming at the girl. "Even the area boys and bandits piss their pants when they see him. He will get better soon so you can stay in Nigeria forever and never have to go to that cold country."

The girl laughed aloud. She looked at the boy as they trodded along their rocky and dry pathway. In the far distance was the shimmering silhouette of the famous Olumo rock basking in the sun's glare.

"I hope you are right, but I still have to take care of my father while he is still sick, so I don't want him to know about me and you. Your mother and my father are best friends. My father still sees me and you as siblings. I don't want that to change for him, not while he is ill. Please understand."

The boy and the girl stopped at a dusty crossroads and turned to face each other. On each side of their path were thick shrubs and small, concrete bungalows built on steep, rocky hills. The boy stretched out his arms and took the girl's hands into his palms. "It is alright, I understand," he said. "But tell me that you love me at least. I need to hear you say it."

The girl shook her head but chuckled. "Yes, I love you."

"And do I have your heart?"

"Yes, you have my heart. It belongs to you. Forever."

The boy smiled. Satisfied. Joyful.

"I need to think of a nickname for you," the boy said, still holding the girl's hands. "That is what boyfriends do for their girlfriends in those American high school movies your father watches."

The girl bit her lip and stifled a short laugh into a hiccup. "I know you will think of something nice. You have a good imagination."

Hearts ballooning with the air of young love, the boy and girl leaned forward and kissed each other softly. Then they leaned back, let go of each other and bid farewell as they began to go in opposite directions. Three times, they looked back to catch each other's smile, savouring the last few moments they would see each other for the day until they had disappeared from each other's view.

With a spring in his steps, as he skipped home, the boy had a broad smile. When had he started liking the girl? He could not say. But it did not really matter. All he knew was that the girl had given him her heart and he would forever cherish her. Never would he betray her.

As the boy approached his mother's house, a small, detached two-bedroom bungalow made of poured brownish concrete, he saw a tall, slender adult man he did not recognise standing by the front porch. He was staring at the boy's mother's house. Parked on the road was a sleek, black Range Rover. Only some people in this part of Abekouta could afford such a luxury car. The boy figured it must be a government vehicle. A sense of unease crept up the boy's spine.

The unknown man on the porch wore an oversized, plain black agbada that reached all the way to his heels. His shiny black shoes were so pointy at the tip that they reminded the boy of a penguin's nose. But it was the man's golden rings on each of his fingers that held the boy's attention. Each ring contained a dark, circular black stone. The boy would never forget the sight of those rings.

When the man turned away from the bungalow to face the approaching boy, who now took timid steps towards him, the boy saw that the man wore dark sunglasses and in his right hand, he was clutching a small brown box.

The man flashed the boy a smile, but there was something untrustworthy and dangerous about him. Words from the raving woman by the church earlier suddenly echoed in the boy's head.

"God will cleanse Nigeria of corruption, deception and bloodshed. These diseases which blight our nation."

"Hello, young man," the tall man said as the sun reflected on his dark sunglasses. He extended his free hand, and the boy stared at the man's long face. Something was frightening about this man.

"Do not be afraid, young boy," the tall man said.

Although he did not trust him, the boy decided to shake the man's hand.

"Is this your mother's house?"

The boy nodded.

"Please give this package to your mother," the man said as he handed the brown, square parcel to the boy, who cautiously took it and looked at it with equal intrigue and suspicion. "It is important that she opens it as soon as possible."

"Yes, sah," the boy said, studying the envelope. He could feel something circular, rigid and loose inside but could not guess what it could be. He looked at the man. "Sorry to be so forward, sah, but who are you?"

The man patted the boy on the base of his head. "I am a friend of your mother's. That is all you need to know." The man smiled at the boy like an uncle would at his nephew. "You are a *good* son."

Something in the man's tone, the way he said "good son" from his cracked lips, rattled the boy, but he could not pinpoint what troubled him about the strange man with the golden rings.

With a strangely satisfied look, the man gave the boy a curt nod and then walked back to the Range Rover, pulling his black agbada over his shoulder. The boy stood on the front porch until the man entered the vehicle and drove away.

The boy entered his mother's bungalow two minutes later, holding the parcel. He walked into the foyer and shut the front door. Immediately, his nose caught the strong and unpleasant whiff of egusi stew, which became more potent as the boy entered the living room.

"My handsome prince, is that you?" the boy's mother said in a cheerful voice from the kitchen.

"Yes, mummy, *e kasan*."

"Come to the kitchen, I am cooking. Let me see your wonderful face."

Still gripping the parcel, the boy strode towards the kitchen, passing the glass dining table in the living room where his mother had piled books, scattered white document sheets and had left her laptop on. Knowing his mother, the boy figured she was busy writing another article for the newspaper.

When the boy entered the kitchen, his mother stood by the rusting oven stove. She wore a long, yellow cotton apron with a red turban wrapped around her forehead. There was a big, cylinder-shaped metal pot on the stove where his mother stirred the tender meat mixed with egusi stew using a wooden cooking spoon.

As if she had sensed her son's presence, the boy's mother turned away from the cooking pot to face him. Not a day went by when his mother's beautiful, chestnut brown oval face and big, dark eyes did not fill the boy's heart with joy. For him, his mother was the embodiment of an angel.

"How was school, my prince?" the boy's mother said, placing the wooden spoon on the kitchen top.

"School was fine, mummy," the boy said. He considered telling her about what the girl had told him about her father being sick but decided it was not his place to say.

"I saw your teacher, Miss Sumi, at the market. She tells me your essays are beautifully written."

The boy's lips widened into a big smile that raised both cheeks. "I want to be a reporter like you, mummy. When I grow up, I want to write stories about the bad guys in Nigeria like you do."

The boy's mother smiled tenderly at her son. "You can be whatever you want, my prince." Her eyes then fell on the brown parcel the boy was holding. "Is that for me?"

The boy nodded. He presented the parcel the strange man with the dark sunglasses and golden rings had given him to his mother as if it were a gift. "A man was standing in front of our house, and he told me to deliver it to you. He said he was your friend."

The boy's mother took the parcel from her son and examined it. She flipped it from side to side. It was not addressed to anyone, and there was no indication of who the sender could be. She pressed her lips together and narrowed her eyes.

"Do you know what it could be, mummy?"

"Let's find out."

Gripped by an eager excitement, the boy watched as his mother peeled the seal of the parcel. Once it was torn open, the boy's mother looked inside the package, and her eyes widened. The boy saw the unmistakable flash of dread in his mother's eyes.

A deafening bang followed by a fierce heat and a blinding light were the last moments the boy would remember as his mother's beautiful face was blown to pieces by the exploding letter bomb.

18 YEARS LATER

PART ONE

LOVE AMONG THIEVES

Secure the bag
　　Idiom

Definition:
　　An expression used to describe the act of taking advantage of a situation to obtain something of value – usually, but not exclusively, money.

1

IF EVERYTHING WENT AS PLANNED, in the next thirty minutes, Yinka Saraki would have successfully blackmailed 200 million naira from one of Nigeria's wealthiest CEOs.

Until then, she still had to stay in character. Wearing a synthetic wig, flare eyelashes with contact lenses and applying her make-up differently from usual, Yinka had convincingly transformed herself into the fictional Carla Ifeyemi, a business management graduate from UNILAG who worked as a PA. The roleplay had proven effective. And now, the allure of sex was her greatest weapon, and Yinka was dangling it in front of her victim, Adekunle Bankole, who sat slumped and intoxicated beside her in the silver Mercedes-Benz C-class saloon currently cruising through Berlin.

Outside, the night washed Germany's capital in a bright glow. The blinking lights from the city's vintage lampposts illuminated Charlottenburg's regal facades and grand boulevards.

As the car drove past Charlottenburg Palace, its baroque architecture rutilant with golden light, Yinka took a moment to admire western Berlin. It was her first time here, and she understood why the Charlottenburg district was a beacon for wealthy European socialites and elites. The region's famous boulevard, Kurfürstendamm, known to locals as KuDamm, was lined with every upmarket boutique brand, from Chanel to Louis Vuitton. But it was not the district's luxury retail offerings that interested Yinka; it was its numerous restaurants, jazz cafes, and art galleries. She was a sucker for highbrow cultural entertainment. After this blackmail mission was complete, Yinka hoped that she and Oge, her boyfriend, could visit Monkey Bar, a popular rooftop bar she had read about online, and admire the burning sunset over the city.

The romantic moment Yinka was fantasising about ended when she felt Adekunle's massive hands squeeze her exposed thigh. Tonight, she wore a dark green, slit-thigh dinner dress that Adekunle had bought for her from one of the upmarket boutique shops in Ikoyi, the most affluent neighbourhood in Lagos. Still drunk from the alcohol he had consumed at the conference afterparty, Adekunle clumsily slid his fingers across her dark brown thigh towards her crouch. Yinka held his wrist before he could reach there.

"Just how much did you drink tonight, Mr Bankole?" Yinka said. She slowly moved Adekunle's hand to where it belonged – on his lap. "Your hands are very adventurous tonight."

"You know how much I grave your body, Carla," Adekunle slurred in his Nigerian accent. "And please, Carla, my name is Adekunle. Or Ade. Mr Bankole is far too formal for what we have."

Yinka grinned at Adekunle with pathetic amusement. Seducing him had been almost too easy. Adekunle Bankole, the first child in one of the most powerful families in Nigeria, was the CEO of Bankole Healthcare Group, which offered private healthcare to the very few Nigerians who could afford it.Blackmailing a puissant business person like Adekunle Bankole meant knowing everything about the man and exploiting any discovered weaknesses for financial gain. But Yinka and her team were maestros at subterfuge by now. After months of character reconnaissance on Adekunle, a few bribes and calling in some favours, Yinka had successfully implanted herself into Adekunle's inner circle - and his sexual fantasies.

As part of an initiative by the Nigerian government to bolster the country's reputation in the trillion-dollar private healthcare market, Adekunle travelled to Berlin to speak at a conference focused on developing the medical industry across West Africa. A few hours earlier, at the prestigious Charlottenburg-Wilmersdorf museum, Adekunle had been a keynote speaker and had given an impassioned speech about bringing the most advanced healthcare technology to benefit the Nigerian people. It was, of course, all grandstanding and bullshit. Adekunle Bankole, like the rest of his lionised family, were categorically corrupt.

Adekunle was now leaning into Yinka. The earthly, woody fragrance from his Tom Ford aftershave tickled her nose, and the stench of alcohol reeking from his big mouth made her want to gag. "Tonight, we will finally do the role play. It is all I have been thinking about," he said, breathing hideously loud from his nostrils. "Even during my speech, I was picturing you tying me up in our hotel."

Doing her best not to roll her eyes and break character, Yinka playfully tapped Adekunle on his fleshy nose, which resembled a hog's snout, and gently pushed him away from her. Adekunle sat slumped on the backseat, his hands by the side of his black Emporio Armani dinner jacket. He now had a childish grin on his face.

"I will punish you tonight," Yinka said in a hushed voice. "Then afterwards, you can have your way with me. Anyway, you want." Yinka bit her lip to add some zing to her seductress roleplay.

"I cannot wait," Adekunle said, staring at the car's interior roof with glazed eyes, no doubt fantasying about Yinka's dark-skinned, naked body and all the ways he would twist her. The very thought of Adekunle, with his heavy pop belly, laying on top of her made every cell in Yinka's body shudder. But if everything went smoothly tonight, she would not have to endure that horrifying experience.

It was 9.45 pm when the driver pulled up outside the B&B Hotel Berlin-Charlottenburg, where Yinka was staying with Adekunle. Located in the heart of the Charlottenburg district, the hotel looked as expensive as you would expect from a five-star hotel. Adekunle had deep pockets and loved lavishing money on young women he went to bed with. Knowing this, Yinka had booked the hotel using Adekunle's Amex credit card. Yet Adkeunle's opulent tastes were not the only reason she had chosen the hotel - its location made it the perfect getaway.

Adekunle was now fiddling with the door lock with an agitated look on his round, fatty face. "Driver, will you open this bloody door," he said aggressively, throwing a scornful glance at the driver, who kept his attention on the windshield. "You cannot see me struggling? Idiot."

"Sorry about that, sir," the driver said with a drop of cheekiness. The driver, a black man with a light complexion in his late twenties, had thick, shoulder-length dreadlocks and spoke with an unmistakable inner London accent. Yinka held back a chuckle. The driver's name was Jaali and unbe-knownst to Adekunle, he was, in fact, one of Yinka's closest friends and allies. Jaali's trademark sarcasm always came out when playing around with people. He would always say it was the north London in him since he had grown up in Tottenham.

Adekunle kissed his teeth and muttered something unin-telligible but rude. The lock on the rear door on his lefthand side made a clicking sound. Impatiently, Adekunle pulled the handle, and the door swung open. A cool breeze filled the vehicle and swept over Yinka's skin.

"Let's go," Adekunle said. He had exited the car and was now offering Yinka an outstretched hand.

"Give me five minutes, baby," Yinka said, putting on a softer tone when she said 'baby' to placate Adekunle's over-eagerness. "I just need to make a quick call, please."

As Yinka hoped, Adekunle did not insist and nodded at her. "Ok, no problem, my tantalising beauty. I'll go check in and see you in our room very soon. You know our room number, right?"

Yinka flashed a smile. "Baby, I booked the room. I am your PA, remember? It is my job to make your life as smooth as possible." She then licked her lips. "And pleasurable, too. We are in room 505."

God, it was too easy with this foolish hippo of a man. Adekunle winked at her and then staggered towards the hotel's reception, passing an old, fancily dressed white couple who gave him a curious stare as he wobbled past them.

With a sigh, Yinka stretched her torso over the backseat of the car and shut the rear door that Adekunle had forgotten to close. Jaali turned around from the driver's seat and gave Yinka a playful smirk.

"Damn, girl," he said, clearly enjoying Yinka's masterful display of seduction. "I always knew you were good, but not *this* good. You have this idiot dribbling like he has never seen a woman before. When I say you are the melanin reincarnation of Aphrodite, I mean that. The beautiful destroyer of men."

Yinka shook her head and kissed her teeth playfully at Jaali's teasing. Ever since she had known him from their days as undergraduates at the London School of Economics almost a decade ago, he had become a brother to her.

"Ok, on a serious note now," Yinka said, observing the

time on her gold Michael Kors watch. "Have the security cameras been disabled? And what's Oge's and Kisi's ETA?"

"The Engineer has successfully accessed the wireless network the hotel's outdated security cameras are connected to and disabled them temporarily." A ping sound came from Jaali's phone. Someone had sent him a text message. He took out the burner phone from inside his blazer's breast pocket. He looked at the screen. "Well, look at that. Montana has just texted me. She says Oge and Kisi will arrive in the getaway van at the hotel's parking lot in the next five minutes."

Even as the follow-up question materialised in Yinka's mind, Jaali had already anticipated what she would ask. "I resent the details about the hotel suite you booked to Oge and Kisi, and The Engineer has already cloned the keycard to access the room. Your boyfriend has it."

Yinka nodded with satisfaction. After many years of successfully pulling off high-stakes blackmailing operations on Africa's most corrupt elites, the team now functioned like clockwork. "And I am guessing I have about 15 to 20 minutes before the hotel's night staff realise their security cameras are compromised?"

Jaali smirked at her. "Yep. So you better not waste too much time doing up foreplay with that drooling fat donkey."

Yinka reached out her right hand and patted Jaali on the shoulder. "Sounds like everything is accounted for. Great work, as always. You better get out of here."

"Will do." Jaali turned the car key in the ignition, and the sleek car's engine rumbled to life. He looked at the rearview mirror and winked at Yinka. "Go secure the bag, Yinks."

Yinka stepped out into the cool evening air and closed the car door. After Jaali had driven off, Yinka walked towards the hotel's fancy reception, straightening her evening dress as she did so.

Now was the time for the hard part. And the fun part.

2

WHEN YINKA OPENED the door to the luxury double room she had booked on the hotel's fifth floor, Adekunle had already stripped off his clothes until he was only in his boxer shorts. It was a pitiful sight, and Yinka was sure it would become a staple of her nightmares.

Summoning every willpower and acting believability she could muster, Yinka ogled admiringly at Adekunle's semi-naked body. The Nigerian businessman's rotund belly resembled a slightly deflated beach ball, sagged over his Calvin Klein boxers like a lump of hardened and melted chocolate.

"Come here, you fine, delicious woman," Adekunle said, gesturing for Yinka to approach him with his outstretched arms.

"Of course," Yinka said with a tight smile as she took measured steps towards Adekunle's repulsive body.

When Yinka was close enough, Adekunle eagerly pulled her into him. "Kiss me," Adekunle demanded in a brutish voice. He squeezed Yinka's right bum cheek from underneath her dress, biting his lip as he enjoyed the curvy shape and volume of her derrière. Yinka winced in discomfort.

Closing her eyes, Yinka thought of Oge's soft, red lips as

she leaned forward and connected with Adekunle's thick mouth. *My God, why is he moving his tongue like a wild rattlesnake?* Yinka thought as she allowed Adekunle to envelop her whole mouth with his own and then drive his tongue down her throat. *This will be the worst of it.*

After half a minute, but what felt like an eternity of mouth torture for Yinka, of Adekunle's wet and sloppy tongue trashing in her mouth, Yinka withdrew from him. She was grateful for some air and the unpleasant ordeal to end finally. Adekunle, on the other hand, was now leering at her and drooling from the mouth. It was detestable, but Yinka cast aside her disgust. The team depended on her.

"Get on the bed," Yinka said, wiping Adekunle's salvia residue from her lips and keeping her eyes on him. "I am going to punish you first. Then it will be your turn to punish me."

Adekunle flashed a devilish smile, like a greedy child about to gorge on a cake he knew he wasn't allowed to eat. He threw his considerable body weight onto the double bed, causing the mattress to sink like a huge boulder had landed on it. He rolled onto his back and spread his arms and legs like a fat starfish on the bed. "Please. Punish me."

Last week, back in Lagos, when Yinka had been planning Adekunle's trip to Berlin, she had ordered bed restraints, handcuffs, and a leather whip to be delivered to the hotel in Berlin. From the intel that Yinka's team had garnered from former mistresses and Lagos prostitutes that Adekunle had slept with, Yinka had learned that Adekunle had a fetish for BDSM and dominatrix sexual activities. It had been a recent character trait for the businessman who, having bedded many women, was now in search of even more intense sexual pleasures to satisfy him. Privy to his sexual proclivities, Yinka had expressed to Adekunle a month ago, when they were alone in his private car and chauffeured through Victoria Island in Lagos, that she was a practised dominatrix. Adekunle looked like he was going to explode with joy at that moment. In a beautiful act of fate, the discovery of Adekunle's kinky sexual desires provided the perfect way in which to blackmail him.

Now, in this hotel room in Berlin, Yinka was going to give Adekunle the BDSM experience of his life that she had boasted about – or so he thought.

At the left corner of the bed was a sealed cardboard box. Yinka walked over to it, bent down and sliced the tape with her green acrylic nails. Inside the box were handcuffs, bed restraints, a bondage hog tie and a blindfold. Yinka had spent an hour last night on YouTube watching tutorial videos on how to set up a bed restraint for kinky lovers into BDSM.

Yinka took the items from the cardboard box and turned to face Adekunle, spread across the bed. Glancing at the clock on the wall, Yinka knew she had five minutes to strap Adekunle down. Oge and Kisi would be arriving shortly.

"I cannot wait for you to punish me. Whip me. Hurt me."

Adekunle closed his eyes, with a ridiculous grin on his face, as Yinka began to restrain his arms and legs with the straps. She used the handcuffs to hook his limbs onto the four corners of the bed frame. Lastly, she tied the blindfold tight across his eyes. When Yinka had finished the BDSM setup, she stood over Adekunle by the end of the bed. All four of Adekunle's main limbs were bound and stretched across the king-sized bed. In a way, it looked like he was about to be tortured by some sadistic individual, but Yinka figured that was the whole excitement behind BDSM. Some people reached a point in their sexual lives where humiliation, submission and dominance were the only way to get off sexually.

Yinka took another glance at the clock. It was precisely 10 pm. Oge and Kisi would open the door any moment now.

"What are you waiting for?" Adekunle said, tilting his head forward. "I am tied up and ready. The anticipation is killing me, Carla."

Yinka curved her lips into a sinister grin. "I may have forgotten to mention this, but we're going to have some company."

Adekunle raised his eyebrows. "Company?"

The room's door handle turned before the door swung open. Oge and Kisi marched into the private suite dressed identically in black combat trousers, military-style pullovers, and black, thermal lightweight balaclavas. They both looked like militant insurgents. The two of them came to stand beside Yinka.

Detecting that other people had entered the room, Adekunle turned his head frantically, quickly realising that he was in the deepest of shits. "Carla, what is happening here? Who else is in the room?"

"This must be very embarrassing for you, Mr Bankole," Oge said, his Nigerian-accented voice dripping with sarcasm and scorn. Yinka knew her boyfriend had the biggest smile, even with his covered mouth. After all, he concocted this blackmail scheme with precision and determination being the competent strategist and leader of the team.

"Who are you?" Adekunle demanded harshly. He twisted his neck as if trying to detect where Yinka stood in the room. "Carla, what is happening here? Who are these people?"

"My name is not Carla, you stinking baboon of a man," Yinka said. She had dropped the faux pretence of attraction from her voice and replaced it with her genuine contempt for Adekunle.

"Stinking baboon of a man," Kisi said, smacking Yinka lightly on the shoulder. "That's a good one. How do you come up with these creative insults?"

"What the bloody hell is going on here!" Adekunle was now shouting. Fear gripped his voice as tightly as the restraints on his wrists and ankles.

Oge cleared his throat to prepare for Adekunle's condemnation. "Mr Adekunle Bankole," he began dramatically as if he were a judge delivering a sentence, "you are guilty of misappropriating business loans provided to you by Zenith Bank and encouraging physicians at your medical laboratories and health clinics to rob from poor and sick Nigerians."

"Are you stupid!?" Adekunle said, seething.

Oge continued to speak as if Adekunle had said nothing. "In 2018, documents that we have obtained reveal that you were given a 500 million loan from Zenith Bank to procure MRI equipment from a German manufacturer for one of your health clinics in Ikeja. However, I have evidence that the equipment was never ordered or delivered to your clinic, yet there is no explanation for where the bank loaned money ended up. But I imagine you sent the money to one of your private offshore bank accounts instead."

"You pig! Who do you think you are?!" spat Adekunle.

"Secondly," Oge continued, once again ignoring Adekunle's outbursts, "I have documents which reveal how you have been encouraging your medical labs to hike the cost of medical tests by 50 per cent, and you've been instructing doctors at your clinics to prescribe tests and medicines that patients don't need so you can make extra profit to line your pockets."

Now Adekunle was violently struggling on the bed as he wiggled and thrashed as if possessed by an evil spirit. Tried as he might, he was tied onto that bed and going nowhere. Yinka had to admit she was enjoying all this.

Oge walked over to the front of the bed and looked down at Adekunle. Sensing Oge's proximity, Adekunle stopped flailing and looked up at Oge as he delivered his final rebuke. "And lastly, Mr Bankole, I now have photographic evidence of you about to engage in marital infidelity."

Kisi raised her iPhone towards the bed where Adekunle lay strapped, spread out, and took at least a dozen photos.

"Can you imagine these very incriminating photos appearing on social media and Vanguard news," Kisi said, scrolling through the photos. "It would further embarrass the already humiliated, once great Bankole family."

As soon as Kisi said that, Adekunle again began angrily and fruitlessly struggling on the bed he was bound to. "So it is you bastards who have done this," Adekunle said, his voice thick with hatred. He swore in Yoruba loudly. "Do you think you will get away with what you have been doing to my family? When we find out your identities, I promise you that I will personally slaughter each of you like cattle and feed your carcasses to my dogs. You bastards!"

"Look at this *oloshi*," Oge said in a snarky tone, which made his Nigerian accent more pronounced. "You are the foolish man so carried away by a woman that you find yourself tied to a bed in nothing but your underwear."

Adekunle fell silent and seemed to bow his head in defeat and shame. "Those pictures cannot be made public," he said, his earlier ferocity replaced with a pained hopelessness. "What do you people want from me? Money, I am assuming?"

Oge chuckled. "Ah, so your brain is as sharp as your prick."

Yinka glanced at the clock in the room. It was 10.10 pm. The security staff would soon realise the hotel's CCTV had been tampered with. She tapped Oge on the shoulder, who turned to look at her. "We have five minutes, my love," she said. Let's finish this."

Oge nodded and turned his attention back to Adekunle. "Listen very carefully, Mr. Bankole, because the instructions I will give you are vital to protecting your reputation. Firstly, you will order the hospital equipment you were originally supposed to procure with the 500 million loan from Zenith Bank. Secondly, you will immediately offer your clinic patients a 70% discount on all medical tests. Lastly, you will wire 200 million to a bank account, whose details you will receive from an encrypted message sent to your WhatsApp shortly. This money should be wired into that account by 8 am tomorrow. Any questions?"

Bizarrely, Adekunle began to chuckle. "I have understood your instructions and will deliver on them as long as you do not release those images." Adekunle's thick lips formed into a twisted sneer. "But you think you've won, don't you? *The Robin Hoods?* Isn't that what the media is calling you? You people, you terrorists, have personally attacked members of my family, and you will regret it. And you, Carla, or whatever your name is, you *ashewo,* when I found out who you really are, I will personally rape you myself before sharing you with my house boys. Bitch."

Adekunle's head was knocked back violently against the mattress as Oge's right fist plummeted into the bottom of Adekunle's nostrils. Blood gushed out like an exploding cheery as Adekunle howled in pain.

"Poor Nigerians are forced to take out obscene loans from banks to cover hyper-inflated medical costs while your family fattens their bellies in your mansion behind your guarded gates," Oge said, with a burning rage inflaming his fierce voice."Your father and his entire family are a cancerous tumour growing in the heart of Nigeria, and I am the cure to the disease. Your pitiful old man will be next."

Even as blood trickled down from his nose, Adekunle managed a chuckle. "My father is one of Nigeria's most powerful and well-protected men. You will need an army to touch him."

"Oh, we'll see about that." Oge raised his fits to strike another blow on Adekunle, but Yinka grabbed his arm with her right hand before it could land.

"Enough," Yinka said in a concerned voice. It was not the first time she had seen Oge's explosive, unpredictable and violent rage. In the past, he had killed a man because the red mist had consumed him. She softened her voice as she gently lowered Oge's clenched fist.

"We have accomplished what we came for. We did not come here to beat a man to death. We're not murderers, my love."

Oge opened his mouth to say something but was interrupted by Kisi, who looked at the screen on her iPhone with a concerned look. "Guys, I just got a message from The Engineer. The security cameras are back on. It's time to go."

"Wait! You cannot leave me here like this!" cried Adekunle, who had restarted his futile struggle against the bed restraints.

But Yinka, Oge and Kisi did precisely that. As soon as Yinka opened the room door with her keycard, all three of them bolted out of the private suite, leaving the battered, bloodied and disgraced Adekunle to scream in anguish.

After galloping down the hotel's stairwell, dismissing the use of elevators to avoid running into hotel staff, Yinka, Oge, and Kisi emerged from a fire exit into the hotel's car park.

Within minutes, they were inside the black Volkswagen van that served as their getaway vehicle. By the time it was 10.20 pm, Kisi was speeding through the lit streets of West Berlin, dodging the traffic and swerving past the cars driving through the roads as the city's nightlife came alive. Yinka and Oge sat at the back of the van, adrenaline rushing through their veins.

The Robin Hoods had done it again. Another successful blackmail operation. *But how long do we keep living like this?* The question dominated Yinka's mind as she rested her head on Oge's warm chest and felt her boyfriend's heart rapidly beating.

3

"CHEERS, FAMILY, TO ANOTHER SUCCESSFUL MISSION."

Jaali, with a triumphant smile, uncorked the bottle of Prosecco in front of Yinka and the rest of the team as they convened in the living room of their rented apartment in Kreuzberg. The sparkling wine gushed and fizzled out of the bottle and streamed down the length of his forearm.

The team had rented the three-bedroom apartment to serve as their temporary headquarters for the teams' operation to blackmail Adekunle Bankole. It was a comfortable, fully furnished apartment with modern furnishings and a fully equipped kitchen. The Wi-Fi was the most critical component of the apartment, allowing the team to access the security networks at critical venues that needed to be breached and carry out undetected virtual reconnaissance of essential locations. Even now, strewn across the floor were several laptops. Plastered on the front wall of the apartment was an A1-sized map of Berlin. Earlier, Kisi, using a red felt tip pen, had traced the fastest getaway route from Charlottenburg to the Kreuzberg district. Scattered on the dining table were dozens of surveillance photos of the hotel Yinka had booked for Adekunle, the conference's venue, and a few expertly forged German IDs and passports. Pulling off a complex operation such as the one the team had done tonight required an almost pathological level of organisation and precision. One miscalculation could cause the whole operation to collapse.

Still in her evening gown but with her synthetic wig and fake eyelashes now removed, Yinka sat on the leather couch beside Oge. Her boyfriend had removed his balaclava and had his right arm across her shoulder. Kisi, also maskless so you could see her heart-shaped face and low-cut, dyed red hair, sat cross-legged on a pink egg chair. Sitting by the glass table was Joshua, nicknamed 'The Engineer' by the team because of his aptitude for IT and hacking, wore oversized, full-rimmed spectacles that looked too big for his tiny head. As always, he wore a passive expression as if not much interested him. Montana, the bubbly team member whose voluminous, brown, frizzy afro was a testament to her big personality, sat beside Joshua. She looked up admiringly at Jaali, her fiancé.

Jaali went around the living room, pouring the Prosecco into everyone's wine glasses. He started with Joshua, who was eyeing the wine bottle as if it were secretly poison.

"Are you aware that Prosecco contains high amounts of sugar and carbonic acid?" Joshua said, adjusting his spectacles as Jaali held the wine bottle before him. Yinka chuckled as Jaali rolled his eyes. "Which is to say it can cause corrosion in your teeth."

"For God's sake, bro," Jaali said, as the rest of the team began to laugh, "we've all just made a shitload of money. For once, will you shut down your big brain and enjoy life's pleasures."

"Come on, engineer. Don't be a killjoy now," Oge said with a cheeky grin.

Joshua sighed before his mouth curved into a conceding smile. "Fine, very well."

Once Jaali had filled everyone's glass, they all reached out and clinked their glasses together in a toast to another successful mission. Afterwards, each took short but satisfying sips of the sweet sparkling wine. Yinka noticed that Jaali was still standing before everyone and had not taken a seat next to Montana. He cleared his throat loudly, and everyone in the room focused on him expectantly.

"Now that this bloody mission, which has taken months of planning and long nights to pull off, is thankfully over, now is a great time to make some personal announcements." Jaali turned his head towards Montana and gestured for her to stand beside him.

Montana, dressed in a pink floral cami dress that Yinka had purchased for her as a birthday gift last year, leapt out of her chair and hurried over to Jaali to stand by his side. Joy radiated from her plump figure. As Yinka looked at Montana and Jaali standing together, she could not help but smile happily for them. They were Yinka's favourite couple. She was overjoyed when they finally entered into an official relationship two years ago after being on and off for years, primarily because of Jaali's commitment phobia.

Montana squealed as she clung to Jaali's arm, causing Kisi to roll her eyes and shake her head. Kisi was the complete antithesis of Montana—detached, cold, and cynical. She was bisexual but treated romance as something quite childish and was more into casual flings and one-night stands. When it came to what mattered to her, Kisi was all about the money, but Yinka knew she still cared deeply about the team despite her aloof character.

"I don't think you can keep us in suspense any longer; Jaali or Montana over there is going to explode in that flower dress," Kisi said in her characteristically deadpan tone. She took a sip of her Prosecco.

"Ok, ok, ok," Jaali said, holding Montana's hand. "I'll let Montana announce the news."

"We're finally getting married!" Montana said in a high-pitched squeal that could have shattered the wine glasses in the room. She held the fourth finger on her left hand to reveal a white gold engagement ring encrusted with diamonds. "And that's not all - we're expecting a baby."

Yinka, who had just swallowed a gulp of Prosecco, almost choked as she coughed, Montana's monumental revelation hitting her gut. But her initial shock was quickly replaced a tidal wave of immense joy. She leapt from the sofa and gave Montana a big embrace. "Oh my god, Monty. I am so happy for you," Yinka said, her hands wrapped around Montana's waist. "You kept this not-to-so-little secret quiet."

Montana made a mock sad face. "Sorry, Yinks. We found out I was pregnant about three weeks ago, but we've been so focused on the Adekunle Bankole operation that we didn't feel it was the right time to announce it."

Kisi, who now stood beside Yinka, gave Montana a weak smile. "You'll be an amazing mother, I am sure, but I can barely care for a gerbil, so what do I know." Montana playfully pinched Kisi on the shoulder, who smiled warmly and hugged her.

Joshua was now standing beside Montana. He adjusted his spectacles as he observed Montana's stomach. "Folic acid, calcium, iron, Vitamin D, Vitamin C, some B vitamins and omega three fatty acids provide fantastic nutritional benefits during pregnancy," Joshua said, in the matter-of-fact tone of an obstetrician.

When it came to Joshua's offbeat social cues, you could only respond with a smile, and Montana did precisely that. "Thanks, engineer. I'll keep that in mind."

"We've got another announcement to make," Jaali shouted over the animated chatter. Oge now stood beside Jaali with his left arm around his shoulder. "Montanna and I will be leaving The Robin Hoods, and the Adekunle Bankole mission was our last one with the team. We'll move to Essex, buy a house and be a family." Jaali then beamed at Montana as if his whole world was contained within her. "I love this woman and want to spend the rest of my life with her. Working with you all, we've made a lot of money conning Africa's most corrupt assholes, but it's time for both of us to bow out now. Leave the game on a high."

Oge gave Jaali a pat on the chest. "My brother from another mother, what do I even say? It's been a pleasure having you on my team." Oge pinched Jaali's nipple as his mouth curved into a cheeky grin. "And you better be a good husband and father." Oge looked at Montana. "Monty, if this man acts up, just call me. I'll knock some sense into that Congolese skull of his."

Jaali playfully punched Oge on the shoulder, and the two 30-year-old men began to playfight like close brothers.

Yinka, who had felt nothing but euphoric happiness about Montana and Jaali's next journey into family life, was suddenly overcome with a sense of anxiety and foreboding. It crept up on her and gripped her. She turned her attention to Oge, now having an animated discussion with Jaali and Joshua.

Yinka had been devoted to her boyfriend's crusade against African corruption for nearly all her twenties. After graduating from her London university, she had followed Oge into this world of blackmail wholeheartedly, forgoing the future she had planned for herself. Yet after eight years of being by Oge's side, what did Yinka have to show for all her unwavering loyalty? There was no wedding ring on her dark brown finger. No expectant baby. She would be a thirty-year-old woman next year and be nothing but a wealthy thief.

Oge came towards Yinka and hugged her tightly. "I am so

happy for Jaali and Montana. You know they will be wonderful parents."

"Yes, no doubt. They will be a wonderful family," Yinka said, as she tried to bury the uncomfortable feeling of jealousy and unfulfillment that had suddenly come over her.

4

By 11.30 PM, most of the team were exhausted from the day's events. Kisi and Joshua retreated to their separate rooms in the apartment, while Jaali and Montana went to sleep together in the second double room.

To Yinka's surprise, Oge had booked a luxury hotel for their last night in Berlin for the two of them. Knowing how much she had wanted to see the capital, he told her this gesture was a way to show her one of the city's most beautiful views as they would have no time for sightseeing tomorrow.

The Hotel Indigo Berlin was located very close to the East Side Gallery, famous for its mural, the Fraternal Kiss, and the most extended surviving section of the Berlin Wall. Oge had booked a private suite on the highest floor of the hotel building, which gave them a spectacular view of the Spree, the main river that flowed through Berlin from north-eastern Germany.

Within minutes of arriving at their private suite in the hotel, Yinka and Oge had stripped each other of their clothes and made intense love on the soft, king-sized, upholstered bed. Several years of being intimate with each other had given them an intricate understanding of each other's bodies, and their passionate lovemaking had yet to wane.

Oge was a very physical lover who used his hands, lips and tongue like delicate instruments. With his tongue, he traversed Yinka's dark brown body, from her round breasts down to the opening between her legs. He used his two-digit fingers to enter her, gently playing with her clitoris and rubbing the walls of her vagina to her moisten her below, and with his mouth, he gently nibbled and sucked on her dark nipples.

Each touch from him transmitted waves of pleasure through Yinka's body. When Oge finally entered her, he drove himself as deep as he could inside her, and Yinka felt the power, strength and heat of his whole body as he thrust himself in and out of her with a rhythm that started slow but gradually became faster and fiercer until they both climaxed loudly.

Twenty minutes after making love, Yinka sat upright on the bed, reading her latest book on human cultures: 'Social Intelligence: The New Science of Human Relationships' by Daniel Coleman. For the evening, she wore a silky, green cami night dress. Feeling the lingering effects of post-sex bliss, which made her feel lightheaded, Yinka closed her textbook and placed it on the white polyester pillow beside her. She turned her head to the balcony where Oge was currently standing. He was wearing only boxer shorts and was gazing out into the night while smoking a cigarette.

For a moment, Yinka admired her boyfriend. At 6,2", Oge was athletic and toned like a sprinter. Having mixed heritage, Oge's mother was Nigerian, and his father was a white; Oge had a light complexion, like the colour of the sand in the Sahara desert. His hair, which Yinka had personally braided into cornrows and trimmed with a skin fade, was cinnamon brown, the same colour as his full beard. Yet the most distinct feature about him was the faded scar, which started at the top left of his forehead and ran horizontally down to his earlobe like a dried river. Despite the tragic story behind the scar, it gave Oge a hardened and rebellious aura that Yinka found irresistible. Yinka rolled out of bed and strolled to the balcony to join Oge.

"Why do you always smoke a cigarette after we make love?" Yinka said, pinching Oge's left bum cheek as she came to stand next to him. The view from the balcony was gorgeous, with the river Spree reflecting the lights from the surrounding towering buildings. In the distance, over the parapet, Yinka could make out the silhouette of what remained of the Berlin Wall.

Oge took a drag on his cigarette. "A cig after sex is satisfying," he said, staring out into the darkness of the sky. "When I was a journalist in Lagos in my early 20s, I used to have.."

"...five packs of Marlboros a day to deal with all the bullshit of Nigerian politics," Yinka said, knowing the short anecdote by heart now since he repeated it at least once a month.

Now Oge turned his whole body to face her. He had that familiar, playful smirk on his face, Yinka had seen it since their childhood, which bought out his boyish charm. "Exactly, and now I only smoke after making love to you, Coffee Bean."

'Coffee Bean' was a nickname Oge had given Yinka because her skin had the same tint as the coffee bean seed. If anyone else had given Yinka such a nickname, she would find it pathetically corny, potentially even offensive. But with Oge, the nickname made her feel incredibly validated that he admired her dark complexion. In the past, when she was a teenager living in London, few people admired her dark skin tone. She was even mocked for it.

Yinka wrapped her arms around Oge's V-shaped torso, but she began to feel the post-sex serenity fade. Now, the uncomfortable anxiety Yinka had felt after Montanna and Jaali had announced their nuptials and impending parenthood gripped her again. She could not hide this unease from Oge forever, and now was the time to communicate how she felt. Like healthy couples are supposed to.

"You know Montanna and Jaali are not the only ones leaving the team," Yinka started, looking up at Oge's face as she spoke. "Josh has told me privately that he is considering going legit and working for an IT software company in his native country, Uganda. And Kisi, as much as she loves money, she's told me before that she wants to take a step back from our operations and go back to Ghana. We've been black-mailing and scamming all these wealthy criminals for almost a eight years now now, my love."

Oge let out a deep sigh. He flicked the burnt-out cigarette over the parapet and rested his hands on Yinka's shoulders. "Yes, the team is splintering. But we'll lay low for a while, like we always do after a big operation, and then begin to find and recruit new members to join our cause. You know how persuasive I can be."

Yinka nodded, but this was not what she wanted to hear. "I know you're good at convincing people; you convinced all of us to become your Robin Hoods all those years ago, but how long are we going to keep living like this, my love?"

Oge gave Yinka a probing look. "You think our cause is no longer a worthy one?"

Picking up on the slight hurt in his voice, Yinka quickly shook her head. "You know, I don't think that. Yes, we are stealing money from the most corrupt politicians and busi-nessmen in West African countries and giving most of it back to the poor they've stolen from, but it doesn't change what we are."

"Which is what?" The defensiveness in Oge's voice was loud.

"We are highly qualified thieves, my love. We are like the criminals we steal from only with good intentions."

Oge shook his head. He walked away from Yinka and

moved to the balcony. "We're more than just thieves", he said in a low voice, and Yinka felt Oge was trying to convince himself. He then turned his whole body to face Yinka again and narrowed his eyes at her. "Our parents fought against corruption with their lives, or have you forgotten?"

"I would never forget what our parents fought for and died for. But they were journalists, not thieves like us. We are fighting corruption with corruption in an unwinnable war."

"You're seeing it wrong, Coffee Bean," Oge said, shaking his head. "Remember what I've told you before. To destroy your enemy, you must sometimes become like your enemy." Oge sighed. "You've always understood this. What's changed?"

Yinka let out a deep sigh. "I want to have a normal life, my love. Have you forgotten that I want to build a school in my father's village? That's my life ambition. And then I want to be your wife and have your children one day. I want to be a mother. Is that not a worthy cause to you?"

Oge sighed and walked away from the parapet toward Yinka. He placed his arms around her waist and pulled her into him. Yinka did not resist, although a small part of her wished she had the courage to.

"So this is about Jaali and Montana?"

"It's not about them," Yinka said, her frustration towards Oge rising considerably. *Why is he not listening to me?*

"Coffee Bean," Oge started, slightly condescendingly, as if he was soothing his spoilt daughter, "everyone has their time-line for marriage and children. We don't need to rush because our friends are starting families. Our time to have our own family will come. But right now, I have a purpose, and I cannot stray from it. And I won't."

Yinka felt her whole body sink with an all-encompassing tiredness. The day's emotions drained her of her usual combativeness, and she had no more energy or willpower to continue debating Oge's pathological desire to fight African corruption. "Ok, I am tired. I don't want to argue," Yinka said, rubbing her eyes. Can we go back to bed?"

Oge nodded and kissed her on her neck. "Yes. Let's go and relax."

Ten minutes later, Yinka had spread her legs for Oge to enter her once more. After their second round of sex, Oge immediately knocked out. But Yinka did not fall asleep so soon. Instead, she lay on the mattress and looked at the white ceiling decorated with elegant floral paintings.

For the first time in her relationship, Yinka had not thoroughly enjoyed making love. Something had changed tonight after their talk on the balcony. Oge was a warrior. He was also a killer. As much as she did not like to think about what Oge had revealed to her when he had reunited with her in London nine years ago, it still lingered in her mind, refusing to evict itself from her memory. Oge's rage and sense of purpose were so intense and so righteous in his heart that he would fight this war against African corruption even if it meant the death of him.

Yinka knew she would need to wait even longer for Oge to settle down eventually. But as she turned 30 soon, how long could she reasonably wait if she wanted children? Yet Oge was the only man she had ever envisioned herself with. He was the only man with whom she had ever made love. Besides, the dense jungle that was modern dating terrified her. At least there was the familiarity and reassurance of love with Oge, even if their relationship appeared to have reached a frustrating stalemate.

Conceding that they could be no one else but Oge, Yinka eventually wrapped his toned arms around her waist and fell asleep.

5

As INSTRUCTED, Adekunle Bankole wired 200 million naira into an anonymous offshore bank account the following day after receiving the details from Joshua's heavily encrypted message sent via a burner phone.

Using offshore banks was standard procedure for The Robin Hoods to conceal their stolen funds. Kisi, with her intricate understanding of how to launder illicit money, and Jaali, with his knowledge of how to set up dummy corporations as fronts, had worked together to create several fictitious companies across different parts of West Africa. All the money the team had swindled over the years was placed into business accounts belonging to these companies.

To pay themselves, the team had access to dozens of ghost accounts that acted as bank accounts for the non-existent employees at these fake companies. As to not arouse suspicion, the team had inside people at several West African banks - whom they paid a handsome fee – to deposit money into their accounts and protect their banking activity from any auditing. It was a complex and layered system for disguising the team's ill-gotten financial assets so their origins would remain hidden. Fortunately, the system had proved effective for years, and the team enjoyed and maintained a high standard of living. And with such a sizeable amount of money at their disposal, they could execute complex operations to steal from West Africa's most corrupt politicians, businessmen and businesswomen.

Yinka was sitting at the back of a taxi with Oge beside her and holding her hand. She was looking at her bank accounts on an app on her iPhone while dressed in a white sunflower split thigh dress and a Gucci Supreme mini handbag on her lap. In total, she had just over five billion naira. Although this sounded like an obscene amount of money, due to the outrageous inflation of Nigeria's woeful currency, it was just over two million pounds when converted to sterling. Yinka was not as rich as someone like Beyonce, but poverty was as far away from her as the Earth is to the moon.

With a satisfied smile, Yinka looked out the window and admired the view of the Kreuzberg neighbourhood. It was 10 am on Saturday, but there was already a lot of activity in this part of Berlin. Cyclists were peddling their road bicycles on the wide, paved sidewalks. The street vendors had set up their stalls, and many were selling Turkish kebab wraps, which smelt deliciously of cooked meat and grilled onions. Tourists and locals strolled along the pedestrian, passing the colourful and cartoonish graffiti that gave Kreuzberg its rebellious and bohemian personality.

It was a shame that Yinka could not spend more time with Oge here, but they had a midday flight to catch at Berlin Brandenburg Airport. Adekunle Bankole had no doubt gone to the German authorities after the events of last night, so the quicker the Robin Hoods left the country, the better. Using one of their many counterfeit passports, the team had each booked separate departure flights to Nigeria to avoid drawing attention to themselves. Yinka's and Oge's outbound flight back to Lagos was the first flight.

The taxi driver, a Turkish man named Emir, who looked

around his fifties and wore a black kufi, eyed Yinka and Oge from the rearview mirror. He smiled warmly at them. "You are a beautiful couple," he said in a mild German accent.

"Thank you, sir," Oge said, smiling at Yinka. She caressed his right hand and returned his smile with her own.

"Do you have children?"

"No, not right now," Oge said.

Emir waved his right hand while his left steered the wheel. "Ahh, ok. But you both look very young anyway, so you have plenty of time. Me, I have seven children!" There was immense pride in Emir's voice.

"Oh wow. That's a big family," Yinka said, turning away from the window.

"Oh yes, indeed," Emir said, nodding enthusiastically. "I was 27 when the Berlin Wall fell in '89, and I moved to Germany. I met my wife a year later, here in Kreuzberg, and I knew she was my soulmate. I married her in six months and gave her many children. It was the best decision of my life."

The way Emir spoke with joy about his wife and children made Yinka melt. If only Oge had this paternal desire within him to want to build a family with her. But as he had made all too clear last night, his crusade against corruption in the motherland was his focus right now. Yinka did her best to discipline her mind so she would not overthink. There was no point going back and forth on Oge's choice like a tennis game in her brain.

Emir took a left turn into a quiet residential street. A mixture of townhouses and graffitied commercial buildings flagged each side of the avenue. Parked vehicles, motorbikes and bicycles chained to lampposts lined the edges of the pavement.

The street looked so peaceful that Yinka was shocked when a white, full-sized cargo van pulled out from behind a parked silver Volkswagen and deliberately crashed into the taxi's nearside.

The loud sounds of shattering glass and crushed metal rang in Yinka's ears. Failing to wear a seatbelt, the force of the crash flung Yinka forward. She smashed her forehead against the headrest before slumping back on the backseat, her long, crochet braids whipping her face. A sharp and persistent throbbing quickly engulfed her head, and her vision became blurry. Though Yinka was in pain and concussed, she could still make out the sound of a van door sliding open. Then there was shouting from male voices. Gruff and aggressive.

"Oi, mate. That's him."

The coarse voices were British—Cockney. Yinka recognised the accents from living in Canning Town in East London as a teenager. Her white neighbours at the time had the same accent.

As Yinka began to stir, her eyes still half closed, and she rubbed her agonising forehead, she suddenly felt the warmth of the outside air. Someone had opened the passenger door on her side. Before she could react, Yinka was aggressively yanked from the backseat and thrown like a bag of rice onto the tarmac road.

"Fuck the bitch and the driver. He's the target. Pull him out."

With bruised hands, grazed knees and part of her sunflower dress torn at the bottom, Yinka strenuously got to her feet. Her head was still throbbing, but her vision had returned. Three men, all built like rugby players and all wearing balaclavas, were now standing a few feet from her. One of the men held a silver Glock 19, which he was now pointing at Yinka's face, while another man walked towards the left side of the taxi, where Yinka heard Oge groaning in pain. Behind the three men was the white cargo van with a dent in the front bumper where it had driven into the side of the taxi.

The first man who had walked off, wearing blue jeans and a navy parka jacket, was now dragging Oge, who was kicking and punching as he tried to fight off the man pulling him towards the van. The second man wore brown combat trousers and a black leather jacket and went to slide open the van's backdoor. The third man pointing the handgun at Yinka's face wore black combat trousers with a green army pullover.

Yinka, wide-eyed and too stunned to move, watched Oge suddenly elbow his aggressor in his left rib. The man grunted and stumbled back. Oge spun around to face her.

"Run!"

The man Oge had elbowed sprang forward and grabbed his right arm, twisted him around and then thrust his right fist into Oge's midsection. Instantly, Oge's eyes rolled backwards, and he collapsed onto the road.

"Leave him alone!" Yinka cried, stepping forward, suddenly ready to fight, adrenaline rushing through her as the man in the blue jeans lifted a now unconscious Oge from the ground.

"Don't try anything stupid, darling," said the man aiming the Glock 19 at Yinka's head. She noticed he had silver tooth. "Wouldn't want to fuck up that nice dress of yours even more."

Yinka took a step back. Her heart was beating so rapidly that she thought she might be having a panic attack. Trembling, she could only watch uselessly as Oge's abductor aggressively threw his unmoving body into the back of the cargo van and then jumped inside himself. Following suit, the man in the navy parka jacket leapt into the back of the truck and shut the back door. Fear tightened around Yinka's body. Where were they taking Oge? Yinka wanted to say something but had not recovered from the shock of the crash to properly articulate her thoughts into sentences.

With the hollow barrel of his gun still aimed at Yinka's forehead, the man in the combat trousers walked backwards to the van. Even as he opened the driver's door and stepped inside, his handgun never shifted away from the direction of Yinka's forehead.

Paralysed, like a deer caught in headlights, Yinka watched with a mixture of stupefaction and horror as the cargo van's engine suddenly rumbled. With a screech, the van made a 90-degree turn, streaked a few metres down the street, and took a sharp turn into a left road, disappearing entirely from Yinka's view.

For a few minutes, Yinka just stood transfixed. Her mind had not fully processed what had just occurred. It had taken just two minutes for the whole kidnapping to happen. Then, the sound of painful moaning coming from inside the wrecked taxi jolted Yinka back into her immediate presence.

Yinka stumbled to the taxi and peered inside the driver's window. A barely conscious Emir was still in the driver's seat, but his black kufi had fallen off, and there was a trickle of blood running down the side of his face from a gash on his forehead. But he was in a stable condition.

"Was it passiert? Geht es dir gut?" came a female voice in a soft-spoken German accent.

Yinka spun around. Behind her, a young woman in her mid-20s with pink hair, black leather pants, a blue crop top, and a spiky neck chocker stood with an understandable look of grave concern. Having just been involved in a car crash, Yinka quickly realised she must look utterly dishevelled, which would draw unwanted attention to herself. She needed to be out of sight from the public. Immediately.

As a social anthology graduate, Yinka learned multiple languages in her spare time, including German. While she could have been more fluent, she could speak German proficiently enough for simple conversation.

Yinka looked directly at the girl. *"Mir geht es gut, aber rufen Sie bitte einen Krankenwagen."*

As the girl took her phone out of her pocket to call an ambulance, Yinka hurried to the back of the taxi where she had been sitting. She opened the door and reached out to take her Gucci mini bag, which had been thrown to the floor by the force of the crash. It's not that she was precious about the bag, as expensive and pleasant as it was, but her iPhone was inside. Yinka needed to call the team.

After the girl with the spiky neck chocker had called the ambulance, she looked around to find that Yinka was nowhere in sight.

6

Forty-five minutes after Oge's terrifying abduction, Yinka found herself back in the Kreuzberg apartment.

Montana pressed a bag of ice on Yinka's head as she sat beside her on the sofa. At the time of the crash, Yinka had been so pumped with adrenaline-fuelled shock that she had not immediately registered the pain in her neck from the whiplash injury sustained from knocking her head forcefully against the armrest in the taxi. It was not until she was in the Uber that had collected her after the crash, with a tearful Montana and a tense Kisi beside her, that Yinka realised she had mildly strained her neck. Not only that, there was a small but painful lump protruding from her forehead - a by-product of mild concussion. Fortunately, none of her injuries were life-threatening, so thankfully, a visit to the hospital was not needed.

Now hopelessness and trepidation felt heavy in the apartment living room like an invisible smog. Everyone was so shocked by Oge's kidnapping and the violent nature of it that the only natural response had been stunned silence for a while.

Joshua was sitting cross-legged on the floor with five

laptops surrounding him in an arch. One of the laptops was connected to the television screen, displaying an enlarged Google map of West Berlin. Jaali was pacing around the kitchen, muttering to himself while Kisi sat on a ledge by one of the windows in the apartment in quiet contemplation. In their seven years as a team, no one had been caught, let alone kidnapped. Oge's abduction was a brutal gut punch.

"Were you able to verify the license plate?" Joshua said, looking up from his laptop at Yinka. "Using an advanced vehicle tracking software I've managed to hack into it; I could trace the van's whereabouts. It would take minutes."

Although it was logical question to ask, Yinka was still annoyed that Joshua had asked it. "A huge van deliberately drove into the vehicle I was a passenger in; I was thrown out of said vehicle by some man built like a gorilla, had a gun aimed at my head, and then I had to watch in fear as my boyfriend was violently abducted right in front of me and I could do nothing to stop it. Do you seriously expect me, through all that, to have verified the van's license plate?"

Josh lowered his gaze. "Of course not, apologies. I shouldn't have asked," he said, sheepish.

Yinka shook her head, which slightly hurt her neck. "It's not a stupid question, Josh. Sorry for my tone."

"No, it's understandable; I take no offence. Considering what you've just been through…" Joshua fell quiet. He looked away from Yinka and continued tapping at the laptops frantically.

Kisi suddenly looked at Joshua. "Could you not trace Oge's phone, engineer? That should be easy peasy, lemon squeezy for you."

Joshua shook his head with a solemn expression. "That was one of the first actions I took as soon as I learned of Oge's abduction. But his abductors have switched off his phone, most likely even destroyed it. Without the phone sending signals to cell towers, it's impossible to triangulate its current whereabouts. Even with the phone's IMEI number, I tracked the last location, but it was the street where the ambush occurred. Hence why I believe Oge's phone has been destroyed."

Jaali stopped pacing around the kitchen and turned to look at Yinka. There was a burning intensity in his stare. "And Oge's kidnappers sounded British, right?" he said, "like Danny Dyer types?"

Yinka removed Montana's hand from her forehead as the block of ice was now giving her a sharp and stabbing pain in her forehead. She looked at Jaali. "Yes, that's right. I recognised their accents. When I lived in east London in my teen years, that's how some English people around me sounded."

"But why would some British geezer types abduct Oge?" Montana said. She placed the bag of ice on one of the couch's cushions. "We've never gone after British businessmen or politicians before."

"Maybe they are mercenaries," Jaali said. He had restarted his pacing across the kitchen. "I warned Oge that we shouldn't go after the Bankole family. But he's been obsessed with them for the past two years. Mobolagi Bankole, the head of that family, is one of Nigeria's most powerful and feared men besides the president. The man has considerable resources at his disposal. Who is to say he did not hire these British thugs to carry out this abduction? It's more reliable than using Nigerian mercenaries, let's be real, innit."

"If Mobolagi Bankole or one of the Bankole family members is behind this, then why did these British mercenaries, if we're going with that, only take Oge?" Kisi said. She looked at Yinka. "How come they did not take you as well?"

"Yeah, I remember one of the abductors shouting to the others that Oge was specifically the target they were after. They called him the 'asset'," Yinka said, caressing her neck with her left hand, which still felt sprained and stiff. "It felt pre-planned, and I was never the target. So let's assume that the Bankole family is understandably after us and hired these British mercenaries to capture us; surely you would take two members of the team that are right in front of you instead of just one?"

Suddenly, with a potent force, Yinka felt dread creep over her. She began to feel her heat beat rapidly. In quick flashes, memories of the car crash, the gun in her face, and Oge's limp body being thrown into the back of the white cargo van engulfed her sensory perception. Yinka felt her breathing get shorter.

"Babe, are you ok?" Montana said, her voice thick with worry.

"Please, get me some water."

Moments later, Montana handed Yinka a glass of cold water and sat beside her on the couch's armrest. Yinka gulped the fresh, cold water in one go. The refreshing glass of water helped temper the severe panic attack she had just experienced. Now, she was focused and sharp again.

"We need to find out who Oge's abductors are, how they knew where to find us, where they've taken him and why," Yinka said. She gazed steely-eyed at everyone in the room. "We must use every resource we have, every contact we know and all the money we have to find him. We have to."

Jaali approached Yinka and tenderly placed his right hand on her left shoulder. "We'll find him, Yinks, don't worry. Whatever it takes."

Joshua, whose eyes behind his large spectacles were laser-focused on one of the laptop screens, suddenly spoke aloud. There was an audible alarm in his voice.

"Team, I am getting an incoming Microsoft Teams video call, and it's heavily encrypted, so untraceable. An unknown source is contacting us."

7

THE TEAM GATHERED before the living room's 62-inch Panasonic LED television screen. Joshua had connected one of the laptops to the screen. In a silence so intense it seemed to increase the room's temperature, they all stared at the incoming Microsoft Teams call, which had a blank profile icon. Yinka, who stood between Kisi and Montana, felt like she could hear everyone's heart beat as they watched with tense nerves as Joshua answered the video call.

The television screen went black. Everyone in the apartment eyed each other, perplexed, and then turned to Joshua, seeking answers. He pointed at the television screen, ignoring their stares. They all looked back at the television.

Where the screen had been black before was now showing a low-resolution image of what appeared to be a dimly lit storage unit with a single, dangling pendent light with a dim bulb. Metal cabinets filled the room and cardboard boxes stacked every shelf. In the middle of the storage unit, Yinka noticed someone tied to a black, metal folding chair. A long white sheet had been flung over this person, covering their whole face and their upper body with their arms tied to the back of the metal chair. Despite the low-resolution footage on the television screen, Yinka could make out the brand of footwear on the man's feet. Her heart somersaulted at the sudden jolt of realisation. They were brown Timberland boots. The same ones Oge had worn this morning.

"That's… that's Oge tied to that chair," Yinka said, the words limping from her mouth as if afraid to validate what her eyes could see.

"Oh my god…it is," said Montana. She instinctively held onto Yinka's right hand.

Even before the team could completely comprehend the horror of seeing their leader, companion and, for Yinka, her lover, tied to a metal chair in a dark room, a heavily built man in black combat trousers, a green army pullover and wearing a black balaclava walked into the frame, smiling a toothy grin and a sparkling silver tooth crown. Yinka immediately knew that this was the same man who had aimed the Glock 19 at her skull during Oge's abduction. Yinka controlled her breathing to settle her nerves. Now was not the time for another panic attack.

"That's one of the three kidnappers," Yinka said aloud, never taking her eyes off the man as he walked towards Oge, who remained unconscious. "The one who had pointed a gun at my head."

"Don't fret, you lot, your friend ain't kicked the bucket," said the balaclava man in his hoarse, cockney lad accent. His voice had a snarky tone, which irritated Yinka so much that she felt the agitation at the back of her neck. "He's just a little sleepy, is all. And it will stay that way as long as you carefully listen to my instructions and carry them out perfectly."

"Who the fuck are you?" Jaali said, clenching his fists as he glared at the screen. "Why did you kidnap our friend?."

"Firstly, mate, I don't like your potty mouth and lack of manners. And secondly, let's not bullshit here, I haven't kidnapped an innocent man over here. Stealing money from all these rich African types. You've made a lot of fucking enemies. But my employer is not one of them. He quite likes what you guys do and needs your services."

"And who exactly is your employer?" said Joshua, adjusting his spectacles as he studied the man on the screen.

"Yeah, because I am just gonna reveal confidential information. I ain't a twat, mate." The balaclava man produced a cigarette from his right pocket. He retrieved a distinct, golden polished brass lighter from his back pocket. With a calm attitude which made Yinka want to slap him hard across the face if she could, the balaclava man on the television screen casually lit his cigarette.

"Just so you lot know, the name's Bobby. I know all your names, so there is no need to go around the room. So let's get straight to it, shall we?" Bobby pocketed the golden lighter. "My employer would like your team to infiltrate the inner circles of three private bankers and convince them, by whatever method you deem necessary, to invest 3 million each into a crypto company called Afchain. Don't ask me what this means because I haven't got the foggiest. I am just my employer's humble messenger."

"A crypto company?" Joshua said, eyebrows raised. "Is this employer of yours aware of what we do exactly? We're not crypto experts or investors."

Bobby did not answer Joshua immediately. He took a long drag of his cigarette as if on a Monday lunch break at the office. "Yeah, my employer is not an idiot. Your team will use your neat infiltration and espionage skills to get close to these three private bankers whose details will be sent to you anonymously in a package along with a prototype of the Afchain technology. These should arrive at your address in the next ten minutes. Also, as part of your scope of work, you will recruit a crypto hedge fund manager onto your team, but one that my employer has preselected."

"Who is this crypto expert?" Yinka said. She was doing her best to concentrate on everything Oge's kidnapper was saying despite her heart going into overdrive with fear at the sight of her boyfriend slumped and unmoving on a chair.

"His name is Timon...Bakah...Bakah...re...one of those tricky African surnames you lot have. Anyway, he lives in London. You will find him and recruit him to your team. And you can't use any other crypto investor or expert for this mission. It must be him and him only. Comprendre?"

"And how are we supposed to recruit him? Furthermore, why would this Mr Bakare join us when he doesn't know us?" Joshua said.

"Because, four eyes, you'll offer him five million pounds to join your team."

Kisi scoffed. "Not everyone is going to leave their normal lives to join our cause—even for five million pounds, which sounds too good to be true anyway for most people." She snarled at the screen. "Looks like your employer hasn't thought this whole thing through."

"You know what, I'll give you that; it's a fair point," Bobby said. He took another drag of the cigarette. The smoke lingered in the gloominess of the dingy storage room. "But let's just say my employer has pulled some levers behind the scenes so that Mr Bakare will be very incentivised to work with your team for that five million offer. He'll practically jump at it."

"And how exactly will he receive this five million?" Yinka said. "It's not exactly a small amount of money, and we don't have that casually lying around."

Bobby sighed, clearly growing irritated by the barrage of questions as he took another pull on his cigarette. "As soon as your mission is successful and my employer has confirmation that the three private bankers will collectively invest nine million into Afchain, then the five million will be wired to your team to transfer over to him."

"But why is this Timon guy so important?" Jaali said, his

arms now folded. "Why does it have to be him we need to recruit specifically?"

"That's enough questions from you lot," Bobby said. He threw the cigarette on the ground and crushed it with the sole of his right boot. "So let's recap your assignment, shall we? Recruit the crypto guy from London into your team and then worm your way into the circles of three private bankers, whose details will be arriving to you shortly by courier, and convince them each to invest three million into Afchain. Read up on the company and familiarise yourself with it. Do this successfully, and your friend over here," Bobby waved his left hand at Oge, still slumped and motionless on the metal chair, "will be released back to you. But we'll contact you when that time comes, don't worry. Oh, and before I forget, you have two months to pull this shit off. Toodles."

Yinka and the rest of the team had dozens of other questions, but the Microsoft team call ended abruptly. Now, the television screen only displayed the plain navy background of Joshua's desktop.

For a few minutes, the team stood in silence as they digested the magnitude of their situation and the mission Bobby had assigned them on behalf of whoever his employer was. The image of Oge, the love of her life, covered in that white sheet kept playing repeatedly in Yinka's mind like a nightmarish movie stuck on rewind. She had to save her boyfriend's life by any means. That's all that mattered to her now.

The loud buzzer from the intercom jolted everyone. As Jaali stood closest to the door, he went to the intercom console by the apartment door and answered the call. After less than a minute, he placed the phone back on the front door panel and turned to the team, who looked at him expectantly. "There's a package downstairs for us."

"It must be the details of these three private bankers," Kisi said, scratching her head. "What the hell is crypto anyway?

I've heard of it. Isn't it like some new type of internet money or something?"

"I have a rudimentary understanding of crypto and its underlying blockchain technology," Joshua said. He sat back on the floor and began typing on one of his laptops. "At least we will be able to leverage this crypto investor who, according to that insolent man on our TV screens five minutes ago, will want to help us for a five million paycheque"

"What was this crypto guy's name again?" Montana said as she came to stand next to Joshua.

"Timon Bakare," Yinka said slowly. The name sounded familiar, and the more she thought about it, the more it tugged at a string of memories long buried in her mind's archives. "Engineer, can you please find his LinkedIn profile quickly?"

Joshua had Timon Bakare's LinkedIn profile up on the screen in less than a minute.

"At first glance, I gotta say, he's pretty impressive," Kisi said, who was analysing the LinkedIn profile as Joshua scrolled through it. "He graduated with a First Class in Economics from Cambridge, then worked at Werner Schmitt Bank afterwards, working his way up to a Senior Investment Analyst position before starting a small but successful crypto hedge fund, Secure The Coin Capital, five years ago. Judging from his last name, he's Nigerian, Yoruba from the sounds of it, so it could go either way regarding how agreeable he is." Kisi shrugged. "At least we're not recruiting a dim-witted idiot. Well, I hope not."

"Can you please scroll up Josh so I can see his profile picture again?" Yinka said as she stood in front of the television screen. Joshua did as instructed and scrolled up the LinkedIn profile, stopping at the top, where Timon's profile picture was visible on the right-hand side of the webpage.

Yinka studied Timon's photo. Holding a smug smile on his face, showing his immaculate snow white teeth, Yinka's first thought was that this was an insufferably arrogant man. In his profile picture, Timon wore a tailored, navy blue Italian-style suit with white cufflinks and a black tie. His skin tone was of a light brown complexion and he had short, black and well-trimmed hair. A noticeable stubble on his face added a ruggedness to his attractively angular face with a tight jawline and cheekbones. Shaking her head, annoyed that she found him quite good-looking, Yinka focused on Timon's dark, monoid eyes. It was those eyes which triggered a wave of terrible memories from her teenage years, memories which she had buried a long time ago. And to her utter disbelief, she finally realised who Timon was.

"I know him!" Yinka said aloud, horrified.

"You know him?" Jaali said, raising his eyebrows at Yinka. "From where?"

"We briefly went to the same secondary school when I lived in East London with my auntie."

"Really?" said Montana.

"Yes." Yinka clenched her teeth. "Him and his friends used to make my life a living hell, but I got my revenge."

"What do you mean by that?" Montana said, staring curiously at Yinka.

Yinka curved her mouth into a small but satisfying smile. "I tricked him and his friends and had them expelled from school," she chuckled. "A reunion with him isn't going to go down too well."

PART TWO

MR LONDON MONEY

8

TIMON BAKARE WOULD NEVER HAVE IMAGINED he would be proposing to his girlfriend twice.

The first time Timon proposed to Orisa Nnadi, a 23-year-old social media influencer known for her massively successful YouTube lifestyle podcast, 'Orisa In The City,' it was at Ikoyi, an exquisite Michelin-starred West African restaurant located in Temple, one of the most expensive districts in London.

Being a connoisseur of the finer pleasures in life, Timon spared no expense on the evening of the proposal, booking a private space at the lavishly furnished restaurant. At Timon's behest, the restaurant servers placed two white taper candles in the middle of their lacquer wood polished table.

The dishes from the £300 blind-tasting menu had been delectable: the standout for Timon had been the smoked crab and jollof rice, while Orisa had relished the cabbage egusi soup. After eating their food and guzzling almost half of the £170 bottle of Laurent Perrier champagne, Timon knelt on his left knee in front of Orisa. In the palm of his left hand was an opened black velvet case containing an engagement ring with a 19-karat white gold rectangular diamond at its centre. It twinkled in Orisa's eyes like the star of Bethlehem.

"Of course, I'll marry you," Orisa said, leaping from her seat to embrace Timon in a tight hug as he got to his feet, beaming with happiness. But no sooner had she wrapped her arms around him than she pushed him away. "But you can't propose to me like this."

Timon raised his eyebrows, bewildered. "What'd you mean?"

Orisa sighed ruefully as if Timon had somehow missed the point of proposing to someone. "Boo, you can't just propose to me privately. You know I have a global audience that follows my life, and this is a major moment for me that my fans would love to be a part of. Do you realise how much social media engagement I'll get if I turn this special moment into content? We have to do this proposal all over again."

"Oh..." was all Timon could uselessly muster as a response. He closed the velvet case with the engagement ring, feeling deflated.

They sat back down. Orisa stretched out and held Timon's hands from across the table.

"Don't look so upset, boo. I didn't say no. At least you know I will say yes, but we must make our engagement viral." Orisa's eyes lit up with a fevered excitement. "Oh my god, the TikTok views are going to be crazy! I need to let my social media manager know."

* * *

Two weeks after the first marriage proposal, Timon prepared himself for the extravagant, social media-optimised second marriage proposal. It was taking place at his riverside pent-house in Battersea, southwest London.

Timon entered the cylinder-shaped, open-plan dining room filled with dozens of guests. The seventh-floor riverside penthouse satisfied Timon's taste for life's finer delights. The penthouse, which overlooked the River Thames, was located in Lombard Wharf, an ultra-modern and ultra-sleek apartment complex shaped like an inductor coil and built at Battersea's edge. The penthouse's wraparound terrace, which offered majestic 360 views of the city, justified the property's eye-watering price tag. Fortunately, Timon had quite a few zeros in his bank accounts, so despite costing just under five million to take the property off the market, Timon had purchased the penthouse outright in cash six months ago.

Many of tonight's guests were Orisa's friends. A few of the invitees were Timon's former colleagues from Werner Schmitt, where he had started his career as an investment analyst. Others were his classmates from his days at Cambridge. Nearly everyone was holding wine glasses and engaging in conversation.

As soon as Timon entered the vicinity, many eyes turned to him and for good reason. He was dressed impeccably this evening in a velvet, two-button, single-breasted notched lapel blazer with flap pockets, tailored in Saville Row specifically for the occasion. Underneath the blazer, Timon wore a white shirt with an unbuttoned collar. Keeping with the crimson colour scheme, he wore burgundy chinos.

Timon stood beside the grand piano he had purchased last month, more for aesthetics as he couldn't play to save his life. He surveyed the room for Chikezie 'Kez' Ejikeme, his best friend and business partner, but he could see no sign of him.

Nearly all of Orisa's invitees, from the world of social media influencers and podcasters, were dressed identically, either wearing Crocs or Balenciaga's. Most of them had achieved fame and notoriety by talking nonsense on the internet - not down to any real skill or talent. But who was Timon to judge? In his view, if you're getting rich from it, then it's worth it. Always secure the bag was his motto.

Timon spotted Orisa standing by the temporary DJ booth

at the far end of the living room. When Orisa finally noticed Timon, her face sprung to life with a toothy smile, flashing her pristine veneers, and she waved at him. Keeping consistent with the theme of lovers, her idea, Orisa was wearing a curvaceous red bodycon dress with a deep plunge, showing off a seductive top view of her ample and round breasts. Her dress had a vertical split, tantalisingly teasing her long and toned legs. She wore red lace-up stilettos and dark red lipstick to complete her evening ensemble, which blended titillatingly with her skin tone - the colour of toffee sweets.

Timon had to bite his lip as he admired his soon-to-be fiancée. After tonight's soiree was over, he could not wait to be under the sheets with her, completely naked and making intense love.

Everyone mingling in the dining room stopped their conversations and wine sipping midway as the LED downlights built into the ceiling dimmed. Moonlight from the outside reflected from the terrace glass windows, basking the dining room and its IKEA furniture in an enchanted glow. The smooth melody of Whitney Houston's *I will always love you* played from the Bluetooth home speakers. Timon and Orisa were the only two people dressed in red - Orisa had told invitees to refrain from wearing anything red.

Standing at opposite ends of the living room, Timon and Orisa looked like two rose petals basking in the room's soft lighting. It was all very dramatic and all Orisa's idea. Timon took a deep breath and began the performance he had rehearsed with Orisa for several days.

He advanced toward Orisa with measured steps as if he were some noble prince claiming his princess. He could feel everyone's eyes and raised smartphone cameras tracking him as he approached Orisa, but it did not bother Timon. This was a show he was putting on.

As soon as Timon got close to Orisa, he went down on one knee, doing it gradually to heighten the tension. He produced the velvet box from the left pocket in his chinos, lifted the lid and presented the engagement ring to Orisa as if he were the first time. There was a collective gasp in the living room. Orisa cusped both her hands over her mouth, feigning surprise.

"Orisa Nnadi," Timon began, gazing upwards at Orisa, who was visibly crying now. When he proposed to her privately the first time, she did not shed a single tear, but Timon ignored this, knowing she had to ham it up for social media engagement. "My beautiful Orissy, my diamond and my soft cushion. From the day I saw you on my television screen on Singles Island two years ago, with your long, dark hair and those fluttering eyelashes, I fell in love with your beauty. Then, when God put us in the same Amapiano event on one eventful Saturday night at Embankment a year ago, I fell in love with your soul. And I haven't stopped falling in love. Orisa, will you marry me so I can keep falling in love with you like it's the first time for the rest of my life?"

Without holding back the waterworks, Orisa wept loudly as Timon got to his feet. Her eyes filled with tears; she took the wedding ring from the velvet case and slipped it on the fourth finger of her left hand.

"I do," she said aloud and flung herself dramatically onto Timon, giving him a full kiss.

The whole room erupted into thundering applause and whistles. Orisa detached herself from Timon's lips as the guests engulfed them, congratulating them. The DJ started playing WizKid's *'True Love.'*

From the corner of his eye, Timon caught Chikezie leaning against a bookshelf in the living room. Unlike everyone else, he had not filmed the marriage proposal. Instead, Chikezie had a diet Coke in his right hand and was shaking his head at Timon.

9

Fifteen minutes after Timon staged his second marriage proposal to Orisa, Chikezie joined him outside on the penthouse terrace. The two best friends, whose enduring relationship had begun when they were one of the few black students at Cambridge, were leaning against the glass balcony, staring at London's brilliant skyline in the evening's twilight. From this vantage point, Timon could see the white speedboats at the Imperial Wharf Marina bobbing slightly to the current of the Thames and the train bridge from Imperial Wharf station. Further out on the horizon, darkness blanketed Battersea Power Station.

"I cannot believe you actually did what you did in there, T," Chikezie said, shaking his head at Timon. Chikezie, who was built stocky and on the short side, being around 5"7, was dressed moderately in denim jeans and a grey overcoat despite having as much wealth as Timon. "So you're telling me you proposed to her for the second time just for social media? And all for what? To end up on *Shadesborough* or one of these other silly social media pages? Really, bro?"

"Kez, I've just got engaged to a beautiful black woman," Timon said, smiling wryly at Chikezie. "You're the one who said I needed to leave the streets and stop being a city boy. Now I've put a ring on a lady, and still zero approval from you." Timon playfully jabbed Chikezie on the shoulder. "You're hard to please, man."

Chikezie shook his head at Timon. "Don't try to guilt trip me, T. You know I am happy for you, but I am also your conscience, remember? When it comes to matters of both business and the heart."

Timon sighed. "Yeah, I know, Kez."

"I've married Cynthia for three years, and we have a beautiful daughter. And a big part of why I married her was because I knew she would be a great mother, and she justifies my decision everyday, bro. When I was casually dating girls for fun, as I used to with you back in my wild bachelor days, I never really looked into the soul of those women because I was not going to spend my life with them the way I knew I would with Cynthia. But have you looked into Orisa's soul to determine if she's worthy of being a wife, or are you marrying her because she's something for you to show off? Another trophy. Also, she just turned 23, and you've just turned 30. That's quite the age gap. Is she even emotionally mature enough to be a wife?"

Timon wanted to laugh at Chikezie's commentary but stopped himself. "Firstly, did you just ask if I had 'looked into her soul'? Relax, Nigerian Shakespeare. Besides, I genuinely love her for who she is, not because she's a social media influencer. And, as the late and great Aaliyah once said, age ain't nothing but a number. Besides, I am getting married to a woman in her early twenties. You're going on like she took her A-levels yesterday."

"Yeah, fine, but a gen Z influencer wife? Really?"

"Sure, why not? Don't be so ageist, Kez. And being a social media influencer is a respectable career nowadays."

The two of them went silent momentarily, staring into the blinking night until Chikezie spoke again. "Alright, changing the subject. I know you don't want to talk shop tonight, but I got an email from our irritating business partner, Russell, thirty minutes ago. We're having a Skype call tomorrow morning with Musa at 9:15 am. He'll be calling us from Nairobi."

Timon nodded. "That's good. We have plenty to update him on regarding the portfolio of crypto investments we are managing for him."

Chikezie hummed disapprovingly. "You know I still have reservations about us having Musa as a client."

"Come on, Kez, not tonight, bro," Timon said. He turned away from the view to face the glass windows of the terrace to see inside his penthouse's dining room. Many guests, mainly the women, were still crowded around Orisa, admiring her engagement ring. "And please be nice to Russell."

Chikezie kissed his teeth. "That privileged white boy just gets on my last nerves. Ever since he went to Jamaica last summer, he keeps saying 'wagwan' whenever he meets us and talking about how he needs jerk seasoning on his Caesar salad. Just because he listens to Vybz Kartel now doesn't erase the fact that his ancestors enslaved people."

At this, Timon chuckled. "I know Russell can be a bit much at times, acting like he's all about the culture when he knows two black people, which is you and me," he said, putting a hand on Chikezie's shoulder, "but let's be honest, many of these rich white men in our hedge fund wouldn't trust us to manage their money if Russell weren't vouching hard for us. We need his connections and his face for credibility. We wouldn't be as wealthy as we are now without him."

Chikezie conceded with a sigh. "I know you're right, but that doesn't change the fact he's a twat, though."

* * *

By midnight, all the guests had vacated the penthouse.

In the large master bedroom, with its ensuite bathroom, Persian rug, and 32-inch smart television fitted into the accent wall, Timon and Orisa were cuddled together on the emperor bed. A silky, Egyptian cotton sateen bedsheet half covered them.

"The video of our proposal has been posted on all the social blog pages. Thousands of views on TikTok already. I am even getting hundreds of DMs," Orisa said, scrolling through Instagram on her iPhone. "I need to speak to my agent tomorrow to see what brand deals I can leverage from this." Orisa managed to peel her eyes away from her smartphone and look at Timon. He was lying silently beside her, naked except for the white Tommy Hilfiger boxers he wore. "Look at me, going on about work, and I haven't even given my future husband any attention." Orisa placed her iPhone by the bedside drawer. "I can't wait to be your wife. Mrs Bakare."

"And I can't wait to be your husband. And start a family."

Orisa nodded, her eyes looking into Timon's. "Yeah, kids would be nice later on, I guess. Maybe. But I want to travel with you worldwide and eat at fancy places. We still need to visit the Bahamas, maybe for our honeymoon. I've heard the Bahamas is great for honeymoons, and I can create a lot of content there. I'll ask Betty; she went with her boyfriend to the Bahamas recently."

But Timon was no longer listening to his fiancée. A burning lust had gripped him, and he pulled Orisa towards his chest. *God, she is irresistible*, Timon thought as his eyes danced across Orisa's impeccable body built by her five-times-a-week-in-the-gym routine and weekly pilates classes. Tonight, Orisa wore a see-through nightgown made of soft materials with delicate lace and mesh. Timon stroked her right thigh as he began to play with the brown nipple on her left breast. "I love you, Orissy," he purred as she straddled him.

For the next thirty minutes, in the silence of their bedroom, Timon and Orisa made love. It was a sensual session punctuated by pleasurable moans. Orisa held onto the bed's headboard, eyes closed, as Timon spread over her, hands gripping the bedsheets. The tightness and warmth between her legs made his head spin as he thrust deeper and deeper into her tight body. Orisa, in turn, wrapped her legs around him, whispering soft commands into his ear for him to stretch her out as much as he could.

After they had both passionately climaxed, Timon had gone to the kitchen to make himself a drink. Orisa was laid out on the bed, lying on her stomach, completely knocked out as she snored quietly. Timon poured himself a Hennessy on the rocks in a whisky glass and went outside to the terrace.

It was 2 am, and even now, London's skyline, with its sparkling skyscrapers, provided an arresting view. Timon took a short sip of the honey-coloured cognac, enjoying its sweet texture with an oaky aftertaste. He leaned against the metal terrace and reflected.

I have come far. Timon had achieved an uncommon level of success in the UK for someone of his ethnicity raised solely by a black single mother. At just thirty years old, Timon had a net worth in the lower millions, owned a successful hedge fund business, and would soon marry one of the UK's most attractive black women.

So what was this emptiness that crept up on him occasionally? There were times when, as he drove through London in his Porsche 911 Carrera or had meetings with wealthy clients whose money he managed, he felt like all this success was meaningless. His life had no genuine richness despite the very long digits in his bank account. Of course, he enjoyed being wealthy, but was this all there was to it? If his mother was not so sick, would she approve of how he lived his life, successful as he was?

Timon took a big swig of his Hennessy, letting the cognac

wash satisfactorily down his throat. Tomorrow afternoon, after some client meetings, he would visit his mother at the private care home where she was being looked after. He would also take Orisa with him. Hopefully, his mother would remember her this time.

Feeling the alcohol reach his head, making him feel slightly lightheaded, Timon walked back into the penthouse to join his sleeping fiancée in their king-sized bed.

A few miles from Timon's apartment complex, the boats at the Chelsea Harbour ebbed and flowed on the River Thames. But little did Timon realise that an unforeseeable but dangerous current would soon rock his own life. For in precisely seven days, Timon's seemingly perfect world would spectacularly and violently implode.

10

LEVEL 39, the co-working office space based on the 39th floor in the One Canada Square skyscraper in Canary Wharf and the location of Timon's crypto hedge fund, Secure The Coin Capital, was quiet when Timon and Chikezie exited the elevator at 9 am on a brisk Monday morning.

After ordering their coffee of choice, a double shot with semi-skimmed milk and caramel for Timon and a black coffee with a teaspoon of sugar for Chikezie, the two men made their way to one of the main conference rooms.

Russell Collins, dressed casually for today's meeting in blue chinos and a white Ralph Lauren polo shirt, had just connected his MacBook to the large television screen attached to the front wall when Timon and Chikezie entered the glass conference room. Upon seeing his two colleagues, Russell stood from his chair with a wide grin across his square-jaw, blue-eyed face.

"My boys, *wagwan*," Russell said in his private school British voice as he stretched out his fist. Timon indulged him and bashed his knuckles against Russell's fist, but Chikezie gave him a death stare.

"Come on, Kez. You're gonna leave your boy hanging?"

"Yep, gonna leave you hanging like an oversized white shirt on a clothing line," Chikezie said, sitting in one of the swivel chairs. He placed his coffee on the conference table, opened his backpack and retrieved his MacBook.

After placing his coffee down, Timon sat at the far end of the conference table to face the television screen, and Russell sat near the front.

"It's 11.15 am in Nairobi, so Musa is dialling from his condo. As soon I've done all the pleasantries, I'll give the floor to you boys to do your *thang*."

Chikezie loudly kissed his teeth as he gave Russell a side-eye. Timon nodded stiffly at him with an embarrassed smile and opened his MacBook.

Bearing a strong resemblance to a young Hugh Grant, Russell had been an Economics undergraduate at Cambridge with Timon and Chikezie. When Timon started organising parties, he befriended Russell, a popular student on campus. He was also one of the few at Cambridge who did not look down on Timon's working-class background. Leveraging his popularity and connections, Russell drove a lot of revellers to Timon's illegal raves, which had become infamously notorious and memorable. After establishing their friendship by organising campus parties, Timon quickly learned that Russell came from upper-class English mobility. His great, great grandfather had been a Leader of the House of Lords in 1908, his uncle was the Earl of Wilmslow and sat in Parliament, his father owned one of the oldest breweries in the country, and his mother sat on the board of one of the UK's most prominent fashion houses.

When Timon had quit his lucrative job as a Senior Investment Analyst at Werner Schmitt Bank five years ago to launch a crypto hedge fund, Timon knew he would have to bring Russell on board. Russell was his only way of accessing high-net-worth individuals from old money. Nearly all of the investors who had their money tied up in Timon's fifty million pound hedge fund were Russell's contacts. So yes, Russell's cultural appropriation and stereotyping of black culture could grate after a while, but it was a small price to pay to get access to very wealthy people's money.

"Ok, I am dialling Musa on Microsoft Teams now," Russell said, dragging his left hand on the MacBook's touchpad.

After a few seconds, Musa Jirongo's face appeared on the television screen. The toothpick dangling from his lips was not even the most unexpected part of his appearance today. Musa was utterly topless, so his dark-skinned and muscular upper body was on full display. He wore big, square spectacles over his peanut-shaped head. Despite being fifty years old, Musa did not look his age, with a completely hairless face and a full head of black hair twisted into Bantu knots. From his outward appearance, Musa resembled a comedian and had the flamboyancy to go with it. However, if you gazed into his dark, piercing eyes long enough, you would find a genuinely menacing man.

"Mr London Money! How are you doing today, my brother?" Musa said in his high-pitched and thick Kenyan accent. 'Mr London Money' was the nickname Musa had given Timon, and it would be a lie if Timon said he hadn't taken to it.

A gigantic grin now stretched across Musa's face. Behind him was a resplendent fountain in what appeared to be a large courtyard. A man in army gear, holding a long rifle, walked behind Musa.

"'I am doing fine, Musa," Timon said, forcing a smile on his face. Out of all the investors who had their money tied up in the hedge fund, Musa was the most outlandish. "It must be scorching in Nairobi this morning."

Musa shifted the toothpick from side to side with his tongue. "I am in Africa, brother. Every day is fucking hot."

Russell let out an awkward chuckle. "Mr Jirongo, good to see you in jovial spirits," he said, his lips forming into an uncomfortable smile as if he was eating something nasty but needed to pretend it was delicious to appease the chef. "The purpose of today's short call is to run through the investor report we sent last week detailing your portfolio with us and the dividends you can expect this quarter. I'll now pass it on to my colleagues."

"Thank you, Harry Styles," Musa said with a haughty laugh as Russell sat down. His face had gone bright red as if he had just chewed on a raw pepper.

Timon cleared his throat. "No worries if you haven't had a chance to read over the investor report, but I will say that you can expect solid returns on your money this quarter. With the five million you invested with us six months ago, we have created a diversified portfolio that includes high-performing crypto assets from series A crypto startups, unicorns, and established companies powered by Nexthereum. This powerful blockchain platform is rivalling the big players in the space. Chikezie will elaborate further."

"Hello, Mr Jirongo; I will give you an overview of the types of blockchain companies we've invested your money into," Chikezie said, his eyes on the spreadsheet on his MacBook screen. "Firstly, there is Sentry, a blockchain analytics company that has received backing from some well-established VCs. There's EdgeGalaxy, which is a massive online game that is big with the kids. We've also invested in Greenface Technologies, which uses the Nexthereum blockchain to create an advanced medical record system for private hospitals. Finally, there's Unicorn, a Nexthereum-powered mobile payment app with over three million downloads in Europe."

"This all sounds good, my brothers," Musa said, leaning against his swivel chair, his toothpick hanging from his mouth. "But I did not understand a single word of what you've said. You're the crypto gurus; I am just a Kenyan businessman with a lot of money who wants to double that money. So how about you give me the big figure, boys. How much have you made me?"

As unorthodox and intimidating as Musa was, Timon did appreciate the man's directness. He nodded at Musa. "We originally promised returns of 30%, but I am pleased to report that, due to our diversified investment strategy, you can expect returns of nearly 50% this quarter on the original five million you invested into our hedge fund. This is wonderful news, of course."

Musa swung around on the swivel chair like a grown man-child, and then he jabbed his finger at Timon, Chikezie and Russell. "You are the money guys, man!" he said, almost springing from his seat. "Nothing gives me more of an orgasm than making more money on top of the money I already have. Good sex comes close but not quite." Musa beat his chest with his right arm and then waggled his finger at Timon. "Show me a rich African man who is content with what he has, and I will show you a liar. To be wealthy is to be healthy. Am I right, my brothers?"

Timon nodded and chuckled. "I can't say being rich is an illness that needs a cure." He cleared his throat. "As an investor and partner in our hedge fund, and as stated in our contract, we can pay you your quarterly dividends next week, or you can choose not to redeem your shares yet and wait. We give all our investors, partners and trustees this choice."

The toothpick in Musa's mouth rolled across his lips as he sat quietly in deep contemplation at Timon's proposal. After half a minute of silence, Musa finally responded. "You know, Mr London Money, you know your shit about all these crypto companies and this blockchain technology. So, my question to you is, if I leave my money in your hedge fund, do you think you can make me even greater returns?"

Timon caught Chikezie surreptitiously shaking his head from the corner of his eye, but he ignored him. "The crypto landscape is currently enjoying a healthy bull market, and more people and institutions are buying crypto stocks and tokens," Timon said, speaking directly to Musa, who nodded. "In my professional opinion, if you play a longer game, then yes, we can make even greater returns on the shares you have in our hedge fund."

Musa nodded, stroking his chin. "I trust you, Mr London Money. I always get a good vibe about you. It is settled, then. I'll forgo my dividend payment this quarter and wait for the next quarter. I'll expect big profits on my crypto investments, my brother."

Timon smiled broadly at Musa. "Your money is in good hands."

The call concluded after Russell explained to Musa when he could expect the following investor report and the payment of dividends owed. Timon closed his laptop. He was in buoyant spirits. It had been a good client and always entertaining, especially in Musa's case.

As expected, Chikezie was quick to voice his disapproval. "You two are aware that we're managing the finances of an illegal arms trader, right? He has soldiers with rifles in his condo, for God's sake. You both can't tell me you didn't see that?"

"Come on, mate," Russell said, leaning against his swivel chair. "That's all Western media propaganda. Musa Jirongo is a legitimate Kenyan businessman who was introduced to me by an uncle who is well regarded. There's absolutely nothing dodgy about him. Not all rich African businessmen are corrupt."

"Yeah, because you know so much about Africa, don't you, Harry Styles?" Chikezie said, narrowing his eyes at Russell, who had now gone red again. "I am not painting all rich African entrepreneurs and CEOs with the brush of corruption, but we are still unsure how Musa makes his money. Even the Kenyan president has publicly cut ties with him. We should liquidate his shares in our hedge fund and stop working with him immediately."

"We're not doing that, Kez," Timon said bluntly, turning on the swivel chair so he could look his best friend in the eye. "Musa trusts us with his money. So the longer he keeps his shares in our hedge fund and the bigger returns we make for him, the bigger our management and performance fees will be. We can make a lot more money for ourselves. It's like Musa said, 'To be wealthy is to be healthy'."

Chikezie shook his head. "You do understand that if it comes to light that we've been investing illicit funds into crypto companies, then all of us will potentially be prose-cuted for money laundering. Just because we've got money doesn't mean we are insulated from the law, bro."

"Look, it doesn't matter where the money comes from, so long as we're making more money on top of that money," Russell said, a smug smile on his face. He turned away from Chikezie and looked at Timon. "Am I right, bro?"

Timon nodded. "That's right, Russell. Money is money, and the bag is the bag. That's the motto."

Chikezie resigned with a sigh. "Whatever you say, T. I just hope you know what you're doing."

11

"So sorry, boo; I won't be able to make it," Orisa said down the line, three minutes into the phone conversation.

It was now 4 p.m. Timon had finished a long day in the office reviewing the hedge fund's current positions, speaking with crypto prime brokers about new orders to place for the day, and evaluating potentially lucrative new trading positions. Now, he sat in his black Porsche 911 Carrera parked in the One Canada Square carpark and spoke to Orisa on the phone.

"You haven't seen my mum in a while, babe," Timon said, shifting in the leather driver's seat. "I wanted you to be there this afternoon when I share the good news that we're engaged."

"I know, and I am sorry," Orisa said in that overly girly, almost child-like tone she used when she wanted to mollify you.

"Can't you get out of the studio a little earlier?"

"No can do, boo. I am interviewing that prominent drill rapper I was telling you about today for an exclusive interview for my podcast. But his management messed up his schedule. He's just arrived in the studio now. Knowing him, this is the only chance I'll get to have this interview."

So that was that. Feeling annoyed that Orisa had decided to interview a drill rapper rather than visit her future mother-in-law, Timon drove himself to his mother's care home.

* * *

Loveday Abbey Road, located in London's affluent Maida Vale district in west London, was a private specialist care home for those with dementia or age-related illnesses. With its macaroon cream painted façade, the elegant Victorian townhouse overlooked the famous Abbey Road. It was also a few minutes walk from Regent's Park. Timon's 60-year-old mother, Iyenemi Bakare, lived out her senior years in this exquisite residence. Timon would be lying if he said having his mother stay at Loveday Abbey Road did not cause a noticeable dent in his bank statements. The private suites started at a wallet-busting £3000 weekly fee, but he never gave it much thought. All the success Timon had achieved in life so far, academically and financially, was down to his mother's love, her grit, and just being a badass, all-round single mother. As his mother's only child, Timon owed her the world and then some.

"She's just right this way in the garden, Mr Bakare," said Valarie, the twenty-something female care worker. Timon followed Valarie into the verdant garden with vivid trees and various plants, so he felt like he had entered one of those fancy Chelsea flower shows.

Iyenemi knelt by the courtyard's edge with a metal watering can in her left hand. She was watering a bush of lavender plants. Wearing a dark green, African lace Kaftan dress embroidered with rhinestones, Timon's mother looked more like a woman in her mid-forties than her 63 years. She had a glowing aura around her among the garden's lush foliage.

"Iye, your son is here to see you," Valarie said in a relaxed voice as she stopped behind Timon's mother. Timon stood beside the carer.

Iyenemi stopped watering the plants, stood straight, and regarded Timon and the female carer. For almost a minute, there was a complete blankness on his mother's face as if she had no clue who Timon or the carer were or where she was. But once the moment passed, Iyenemi's face brightened, her dark brownish lips widened into a big smile, and her hooded eyes lit up with happiness. "Timon, I did not know you were coming," she said, immediately throwing her arms him. "If I knew you were visiting, I would have made jollof rice."

"Mum, it's ok," Timon said, hugging her back and trying not to dwell on the fact that he had called her yesterday afternoon and this morning to remind her of his impending visit.

"Thank you, Valarie," Iyenemi said, stepping back from Timon and now sizing him up with her eyes.

"My pleasure, Iye," said Valaire. "If you need anything, I will be in the main parlour." Valarie turned on her heels and sauntered away, leaving mother and son to catch up on life.

"My son, you are looking very skinny, and I hope you have been going to church," Iyenemi said in her watered-down Nigerian accent as she shook her head at Timon. "And have you been eating enough? I always say you need a wife because you cannot cook. A busy man needs a homecooked dinner."

Timon chuckled, feeling less drained now that he was with his mum. "I go to church when I can," he said, although Timon had stopped attending church seriously after he had graduated from university. "And I have been eating, Mum, but I am looking leaner because I am on a keto diet recommended by my personal trainer."

At this, Iyenemi kissed her teeth and resumed watering

the plants. "My beautiful son, you don't need some expensive personal trainer telling you what to eat. You need a good wife. I have been praying every day that you find one."

Timon put his hands in his pockets and looked at his mum as she bent down to douse the leaves. "Well, you'll be happy to know God has answered your prayers. I am getting married." He grinned. "So I'll have a wife who will fatten me up." It quickly occurred to Timon that Orisa had never actually cooked a meal for him since they had been dating. When they wanted to eat, they either went to an expensive restaurant or ordered takeaway. Did she even know how to cook? Why had Timon never asked her?

As if she heard a siren, Iyenemi stood up in surprise and stared at her son with a startled look. Timon could not quite read his mother's expression or reaction as her mouth hung open and her eyes were motionless. It was probably another short episode of her dementia. Slowly, as her mind appeared to reboot itself, Iyenemi's perplexed face morphed into one of joy. "This is wonderful news, my son," she said. She embraced Timon and kissed him on the left cheek. "You are finally marrying Eniola. I always liked her."

Timon raised his eyebrow at his mother but then remembered her condition. He let out a heavy sigh. "No, Mum, not Eniola. She was my girlfriend at university, and we only dated for a year." I am engaged to Orisa. Do you remember her? She came to visit you about three months ago."

Iyenemi shook her head. She then closed her eyes, rummaging through her brain. "Orisa...Orisa..." she said, sounding out the name slowly. She opened her eyes wide with a flash of recognition. "Oh yes, I remember her now. The very pretty Igbo girl." Iyenemi then considered her son, staring into his eyes. "She looked very, very young."

Timon shook his head. "Mum, she's 23, not 18. We have been dating for a year and a half, and I am sure she is the one. I love her. She wanted to be here but got caught up at work."

Iyenemi nodded and then went quiet for a moment. Again, Timon was unsure of what to make of her silence. Was she thinking about the news of his marriage, or was it her Alzheimer's? After saying nothing for a minute, Iyenemi smiled at him. "If you love her, I will be happy for you, my beautiful son." Iyenemi extended her arm and placed her right hand tenderly on Timon's left cheek. Timon caressed her fingers, which felt warm on his face. "I want you to feel fulfilled, Timon. And to start a beautiful family. To this day, I wish I could have given you that. I wish you had a father growing up in your life."

Timon patted his mother's fingers playfully as he warmly smiled at her. "You gave me a family, Mum. Me and you were enough. I don't think about my father. Any man who could leave an actual living goddess like you is a fool who isn't worth my time."

Iyenemi let out a high-pitched laughter, one lifted by a deep joy. She slapped her son playfully on the shoulder. "You and your charming tongue," she said. "You are a Yoruba boy, for sure." She turned away from Timon and continued watering the English lavender plants.

"As soon as you get married I am expecting some grand-children immediately. I have been praying for grandchildren daily, and you have kept your mother waiting long enough."

* * *

A few hours later, in the living room at his penthouse apartment in Lombard Wharf, Timon sat on the ivory sofa with its stylised curves and comfortable cushions. Orisa was beside him, resting her head on his left shoulder. Her dark brown European weave, which Timon had paid over £1000 for her to get done, ran down her neck like a silky waterfall. They were watching Orisa's favourite reality dating television show which had made her initially famous, Single's Paradise.

"I honestly don't know what she sees in Danny, you know," Orisa said, more to herself than to Timon, who looked passively at the television as a scantily clad blonde girl strutted past a swimming pool where two topless boys had just dived into. "Clarissa is too good for that Danny, who looks like a jacked-up toad, but he acts like he's doing her a favour. It's giving toxic and delusional."

"I wish you had come to see my mum today, babe," Timon said, completely ignoring her malarkey about some fatuous television couple. "I didn't like telling my mum I was getting married and you were not by my side. You know how close my mum is to me, but you don't see her enough or even ask how she is."

Orisa lifted her head from Timon's shoulder and regarded him. She had the look of a sad puppy plastered over her face. "I know, boo. I am genuinely sorry about that. Don't stay mad at me, please." Her voice had retaken that childish tone.

"I am not mad, baby," Timon sighed. "I just want you to make more effort with my mum."

"I know, and I will try," Orisa said, smiling half-heartedly. "It's just…it can be hard when she forgets stuff sometimes."

Timon shot her a glare, which Orisa had utterly over-looked. "Yeah, she's forgetful because she has mild Alzheimer's, babe." She had also failed to pick up on Timon's blunt tone.

"I know, and I get that," Orisa said in a dismissive tone that clearly showed she did not get it. "But it can be challenging to get a conversation going. But I promise to pay her a visit before our engagement party, which we must discuss."

"Yeah, yeah, of course," Timon said, rolling his eyes. The last thing he wanted to discuss was how much he would need to fork out for an engagement party designed for social media.

"I know one way I can make it up to you," Orisa said with a devilish grin.

"Really?" Timon said, looking at her. "Maybe we can cook something together?"

"Cook?" Orisa said, her head leaning back in complete disbelief as if Timon had just asked to take an exam on modern macroeconomic theory. "Boo, you know I don't know my way around a kitchen. I was thinking of something a lot more exciting than that."

Timon already knew where this was going. "What's that?"

Orisa slipped her dark blue stretch jeans down to her knees. The sight of her naked, caramel-coloured, toned legs and her perfectly curvy thighs immediately increased Timon's heart rate. But it was her pink, crotchless thong which ultimately sent him over the edge.

"You can fuck me on this sofa right now," Orisa purred, biting her lips and never taking her eyes off him.

Like a brainless fish, Timon immediately took the bait, and he had his tongue down Orisa's throat as he began to strip her naked. Even as he made love to her on his £10,000 sofa, Timon could hear his mind whispering growing doubts.

Maybe she really is too young.

12

Timon's life would implode on a Sunday afternoon during a routine gym session with his personal trainer.

And it began with a phone call.

Timon lay on the bench, panting heavily after completing ten reps of a 40kg bench press. As his pectoral muscles burned from the strenuous workout, he felt his Samsung Galaxy vibrating inside the left pocket of his grey Gymshark joggers. Timon sat up straight and retrieved his smartphone. Chikezie's name was flashing on the screen. *Why is he calling me on a Sunday afternoon?*

Timon turned his body around on the bench to look at his Spanish personal trainer, Fernando, who had been spotting him.

"I am just going to take this call, bro," Timon said, nodding at Fernando.

"No worries, my friend," Fernando said, grinning. He wore a tight Gymshark t-shirt, emphasising his round shoulders and bulging biceps. "A busy man is busy all the time."

Timon grinned at Fernando and answered Chikezie's call.

"Are you at home? Please tell me you've seen the news,"

Chikezie said down the line, dispensing with any pleasantries. There was a noticeable panic in his voice.

"Nah, Kez. I am at the BXR member's gym in Canary Wharf. Are you alright, bro? You sound worried?"

"Go watch BBC News now, and then call me back in ten minutes. I have spoken to Russell as well. We need to be in the office tomorrow at 6 am sharp and think of a plan of action because this is a real shit show."

Timon did not even get to ask Chikezie what he was babbling on about because his business partner immediately hung up. A discomfort crept across Timon's spine as he looked around the busy high-end gym. If Chikezie sounded that worried, Timon knew he should probably start feeling concerned. *A real shit show.* What had Chikezie meant by that?

Excusing himself from Fernando, Timon headed to the gym's reception. Hanging from one of the walls was a widescreen television, which usually streamed live news from the BBC. Today was no different. Timon stood nervously before the television screen with two hands on his hips. He watched the Indian female BBC news presenter report about a crypto hack in that authoritative and official-sounding English voice used by news anchors.

"Analysts and insiders are already calling it one of the biggest crypto heists of the year; just under half a billion dollars worth of USD and ether was stolen from Nexthereum, the biggest Ethereum-linked blockchain in the crypto space. According to a statement released by a Nexthereum spokesperson, hackers were able to hack the blockchain's nodes, which are the computers that process network transactions on the blockchain. The hack has severely impacted several big-name crypto companies powered by Nexthereum. Investigators are currently trying to ascertain who the hackers are."

As Timon continued to watch the breaking news report about the Nexthereum hack, he could feel his heart thumping hard in his chest as panic began to rise through his body. He swallowed a gulp of saliva. Now, he fully understood what Chikezie had meant. This was an absolute *shit show.*

On an epic scale.

✳ ✳ ✳

The next day, at 6 am, as per Chikezie's call, Timon was at the Level 39 office. Russell and Chikezie were also present. Together, all three of them huddled on one of the round work-tables in the main work area of the shared working space. With their MacBooks opened, their eyes were glued to the screen as they frantically monitored the rapidly falling value of some of the stocks and tokens of the Nexthereum-powered companies they had invested much of their clients' money into.

Any self-respecting hedge fund manager - and Timon considered himself firmly in that category - used investors' capital judiciously and understood their investment positions on both a macro and micro level by doing their due diligence and never getting caught up in the hype of the next big thing. It was all about the facts.

Four years ago, when there had been an almost cult-like frenzy surrounding Nexthereum, which was considered the next evolution of the Ethereum blockchain promising faster transactions, more robust security and more accessible devel-opment toolkits, Timon had remained cautious, sticking to safer investments in crypto companies built on already estab-lished blockchains such as Bitcoin, Solana and Ethereum. However, as he began to gather more information about Nexthereum from online chat groups on Discord, internet forums like Reddit and by reading a plethora of articles and attending dozens of industry events, the more Timon became convinced that it was worth buying and holding stock in well-funded crypto companies built on Nexthereum which had solid fundamentals.

Until now, Timon's gamble had paid off. The stocks he owned in several Nexthereum-powered crypto companies had consistently produced healthy returns for himself and sweet dividends for his clients over the past three years. But somehow, the inconceivable had happened, and Nexthereum suffered an unexpected major hack that wiped off almost forty per cent of the total value of Timon's hedge fund. Overnight, Timon's company had gone from rolling in lush green to burning in fiery red.

Timon, Chikezie and Russell slept in the Level 39 office for the rest of the week. Now that they were in serious damage control mode, they would need to pull all-nighters, fuelled by pizza, coffee and cans of Red Bull – a return to their days as Economics undergrads at Cambridge.

Chikezie, the leading analyst, spent most of his time shorting Nexthereum stocks and tokens that had practically become worthless since many Nexthereum companies had entirely collapsed due to the hack. Timon and Russell spent their time calling clients and having awkward conversations where you tell millionaires that you have lost a sizable amount and, in some cases, practically all the money they had put into the hedge fund.

The one client they had been unable to reach was Musa Jirongo. Russell had tried calling him, sending him several emails, and even asking the family member who had introduced him to Musa to get in touch with him, asking him to respond to Russell's communications urgently, but to no avail. There was complete radio silence.

The five million pounds Musa entrusted to Timon for profitable crypto investments vanished during the Nexthereum crypto hack.

This unfortunate event would set the stage for a violent confrontation on Friday night.

13

"THE AUTHORITIES ARE SAYING the group who hacked the Nexthereum blockchain network are Nigeria-based," Russell said as he laid back on the swivel chair in the conference room late Friday evening. Timon and Chikezie were also present. Russell's shirt was partially unbuttoned, and he stuffed a slice of pepperoni pizza in his mouth. "Since when could hackers from Nigeria get the kind of funding to carry out such an attack on this scale?" he continued, his voice muffled as he ate. "I was expecting the Chinese or the Russians. Nigeria is a third-world country." Russell then looked at Timon and Chikezie. "No offence, boys. So these Nigerian hackers would received some serious backing to pull this hack off."

Timon, who had also unbuttoned the top half of his shirt, looked up from his MacBook screen. His eyes were bloodshot red, itchy with tiredness, and he was already on his third Red Bull.

"Who knows, and does it even matter who was behind it?" Timon said. He massaged his forehead. It had been a long week. "We need to think about how we will return our investors' money as quickly as possible because many want to pull out of the hedge fund entirely and liquidate whatever they have tied with us that wasn't stolen in the hack. To spread out risk, we must start looking at alternate investments, such as real estate."

Chikezie, who had been tapping away on his MacBook, surrounded by five cans of empty Red Bulls, looked away from the screen and nodded at Timon. "Crypto was always our USP, T, but I hear you. Because of this hack, the crypto market has been dragged, kicking and screaming, into a bear market. Investors are getting itchy feet about putting their money into crypto companies now, even ones built on established blockchains. Diversifying our portfolio into more stable assets is probably the next best step. Still, we'll need to hire other analysts quickly and contact other brokers."

Before Timon could respond to Chikezie, he heard footsteps in the corridor. When Timon last checked, only himself, Chikezie, and Russell remained on this floor. It was almost 11.30 pm, and it was unusual to find anyone else, apart from the three of them, at Level 39.

Timon did not even get to stand up from the swivel chair to see who it was. The answer came into the room. Timon's eyes widened in surprise, and he was temporarily immobilised by shock when Musa Jirongo entered the conference room flanked by two six-foot, broad-shouldered and big-armed black men in black suits. For the first time since Timon had started doing business with him, Musa wore a dark green pinstripe suit, a red tie, and brown leather monk-strap shoes.

Timon quickly buttoned his shirt, stood up and walked around the conference table towards his client. "Musa, what a welcome surprise to see you here," Timon said, extending his right hand as he approached Musa. "I hope you had a pleasant flight. We've been trying to contact you all week about…"

One of the big, burly men standing on Musa's left side grabbed Timon by the collar of his shirt and dragged him across the room with the strength of a WWE wrestler, to the abject horror of both Chikezie and Russell, whose jaws dropped. The man slammed Timon against the wall next to the television screen. Musa, whose expression remained passive throughout the physical altercation, sighed regretfully.

"Mr London Money," Musa began, shaking his head as he regarded Timon, now pinned against the wall like a fridge magnet. "I thought you were a good vibe, man. But it turns out you're a bad vibe like everyone else." Musa sauntered past Timon, whose heart was beating rapidly now, and droplets of sweat had started to trickle down his forehead. Musa approached Timon's vacated seat and looked at Chikezie and Russell. Both of them looked terrified. "Is it ok if I sit here?" Musa spoke in such a casual tone that it was all the more unsettling. Russell weakly nodded, and Musa sat on the swivel chair. "Can I smoke here, or will it set off some fire alarm? And if you lie, I will eat your tongue."

"You…you…can smoke," Russell stuttered, his eyes darting from Timon pinned against the wall and then to Musa sitting at the conference table.

"Wonderful. I need a fucking cigar. As you all know, it's been a miserable week." Leaning back against the swivel chair, with his feet crossed-legged and now stretched out on the conference table, Musa retrieved a hand-rolled Cuban cigar from the inner pocket in his blazer. "Tito, lighter."

The other tall, well-built thug stepped away from the door and approached Musa. Using a small chrome lighter he fished out of his pocket, Tito lit Musa's cigar and even placed it in his mouth. Once Musa took a drag of the cigar, Tito walked back to guard the door. The smoky and sweet tang from the cigar quickly filled the room.

"Do you want to know how shit my week has been?" Musa said rhetorically. "Well, first, that bastard president of Kenya, Ruto, publicly accuses me of supplying and selling weapons to al-Shabab militants in Somalia, of funding terrorism and betraying the Kenyan government and its people. He then uses these accusations as justification to execute a raid on my fucking condo in Runda. Luckily, I caught wind of the bastard's plan and managed to escape to Lamu Country before Ruto's government-hired thugs could catch me. Calling in some favours, I managed to sneak into Somalia, but now I am exiled from Kenya, my homeland. I mean, that's pretty shit, right?"

Musa looked around the room. The brute, who had Timon restrained against the wall, nodded in agreement. At that moment, Timon felt the thug's grip loosen, but Timon decided that even if he used his strength to break free, it might put him in even more danger. He recalled seeing the armed guards at Musa's condo during their last conference call. Musa's henchmen could be armed.

"Now that I am a fucking exiled war criminal and terrorist, I need to think about how I am going to survive." Musa took another drag on his smouldering cigar. "And you can't survive without money, especially in Somalia. You might as well lower yourself to that of a rat eating from the dustbins if you don't have money in that part of East Africa. So I speak to my accountant to determine how much money I have, what my assets are, etcetera, etcetera. And then my accountant tells me he has received correspondence from you three," Musa jabbed his right finger at Timon, Chikezie and Rusell, "that the five million I gave you to invest in crypto was all gone." Musa chuckled. "How do you lose five million pounds? Naturally curious, I made a few calls and flew to London from Somalia to find out how you boys lost all the money I gave you to invest. So can someone please explain?"

"Look, Musa, let me start by saying, please accept my apologies for the stressful week you've had," Timon began quickly, trying to stop his nerves from cracking his voice despite being pinned to a wall by a man twice his size. "We did not know about the Kenyan government raiding your house and your subsequent exile from the country. We haven't been watching international news."

The brute, whose right arm did not seem to tire, tightened his grip on Timon's shirt, but Timon looked past the man's huge, block-shaped head to look at Musa, who continued smoking his cigar. Not once did Musa look at Timon as he spoke. "The loss of your investment, and you understandably have every right to be upset, was not down to any of our investment decisions. There was a significant hack in one of the major crypto blockchains, the underlying technology for many of the crypto companies in our portfolio, which wiped the value of many of the companies we had invested your money into. To be completely transparent and fair, we warned you, and it is written in the terms and conditions of our signed contract with you, that there is always a level of risk when it comes to crypto investments."

"Risk?" Musa uttered the word as if he found it to be deeply offensive. He removed his feet from the table and stood from the swivel chair. Still chomping on his cigar, Musa ambled towards Timon. "Let go of him, Mahmood."

The brute restraining Timon uncurled his grip from Timon's shirt and stepped aside.

Musa now stood directly in front of Timon. The Kenyan's dark, beady eyes teased violence. "I am on the run from the Kenyan government, exiled from my own country, and I've secretly flown into London on false identification. And you want to talk to me about risk?"

The droplets of sweat felt hot as they slid down Timon's face like condensation on glass after a warm shower. "Look, Musa. I meant no offence. What I am trying to say is…"

"I know what you are trying to say." Musa's tone bubbled with an increasingly heated anger. He removed his cigar from his mouth.

Timon was caught off guard when Musa swiped his right

leg, tripping him over. Timon tumbled backwards, landed hard on his back, and moaned in pain while sprawled on the floor.

With a surprising degree of agility, Musa leapt on Timon and kneed him in the crouch. Timon yelped as he rolled onto his side.

"In my younger days, I used to be a soldier in the Kenyan Defence Forces," Musa said, looking down on Timon as he bent over him like a leopard underneath its wounded prey. "I then became a mercenary for hire for a few years when I left the army. In both roles, I learnt a couple of tricks about torturing people. Do you want me to show you one of them?" There was a primal glee in his voice as if torturing people gave him sexual gratification.

Musa grabbed Timon's throat and pressed the hot, smouldering butt of the cigar onto Timon's flesh as if he was trying to burrow into Timon's neck by burning a hole through it. Timon howled in excruciating pain as he felt the burning butt of the cigar peel the skin from his neck like wallpaper peeling off in a blaze.

"Come on, enough of this!" Chikezie shouted, lunging from his chair. Grim-faced and in shock, Russell could only stare a Chikezie in frozen despair.

Grinning, Musa removed the cigar from Timon's neck and got to his feet. Panting heavily and sweating so profusely his shirt was drenched, Timon slowly rose to his own feet, using the edge of the conference table as support. Failing to hold back the tears now forming on the edges of his eyes, Timon pressed his left hand against the right part of his neck where Musa had burnt him. He winced in pain as he felt the tender wound. It would leave a scab when it healed.

Musa turned away from Timon and faced Chikezie, who had not returned to his seat. He looked at Musa defiantly, but Musa was unfazed. "You three bastards will return the five million you've squandered. Do you understand? You have two months."

"What if we can't do it in that time frame?" Timon said, still pressing his right hand against the wound on his neck. He dried his eyes with his left forearm. "We might need more time to get that kind of money together."

Musa snickered. He turned away from Chikezie to face Timon again who flinched.

"Let me tell you something, Mr London Money. Before I work with people, especially those looking after my money, I do a lot of homework on such individuals. You see, I know about your beautiful Instagram fianceé with her bullshit podcast. I even watched your live-stream proposal. It's very cringe, by the way. I also know about your brain-dead mother who lives in that expensive care home." Musa's lips twisted into a sadistic smile when he noticed Timon contort his face in rage at the mention of his mother.

Not done instilling fear, Musa turned away from Timon to address Chikezie and Russell. "And you," Musa pointed at Chikezie, "you have a beautiful wife and an adorable five-year-old daughter, all living in your nice house with the big garden in Essex." Ignoring Chikezie's glare, Musa smiled glee-fully at Russell, clearly relishing how he could unsettle them with these revelations. "And you, Harry Styles, I know about your divorced mother living in Brighton with her new boyfriend. And your father's frequent trips on his private boat in Southend or your two sisters living in Chelsea. As you now understand, I am aware of all of your families. I know where they live. Where they work, even where they shit, and we can all agree it would be such a tragedy if I put a bullet into every one of them."

"You aren't going to bring any fucking harm to our fami-lies," Timon said, his fists clenched and his tone making no effort to hide his seething anger. Timon did not care about

Musa or whether his two thugs were armed. Nobody threatened his mother, his fianceé and his friends.

Musa turned to face Timon and held his gaze. "Don't test me. Then again, as you seem to know so much about risk, why don't you take that risk and find out what happens."

Even though Timon glared at Musa with impudence, deep within the Kenyan man's eyes was the glimmer of undeniable conviction. Musa would indeed put a bullet in his mother's and Orisa's skulls. This realisation made Timon freeze in despair, knowing he had unwittingly put his loved ones in harm's way.

"Two months," Musa said, raising two fingers on his left hand. "And I wouldn't go to the police. I am sure laundering money for a terrorist financier like myself is illegal and would no doubt land your asses in jail. Should that happen, then no one would protect your loved ones from a bullet to their heads. Besides, between you boys, there are three Cambridge degrees. Making five million in two months should not be difficult with brains like yours, right?"

Timon looked at Chikezie, who turned his head away from him. Russell merely sat in the swivel chair, motionless like a Greek statue and just as white. Musa nodded at his two bodyguards, who followed him as he began to exit the conference room.

Before leaving, Musa addressed Timon, Chikezie, and Russell as he stood in the doorway. "I'll be monitoring all three of you. And please don't let all this unpleasantness ruin your evening. Enjoy the rest of your pizza and it was good seeing you all in person for the first time."

Musa released a high-pitched cackle and left the room, his two thugs following closely.

14

THIRTY MINUTES after the violent confrontation with Musa, Timon was leaning against the bonnet of his Porsche 911 Carrera. He winced in pain as Chikezie stuck the waterproof plaster - which Chikezie had retrieved from the medical kit in his car in case his daughter had a medical emergency - over the fleshy, pinkish scar on Timon's neck.

It was 1 a.m. Timon, Chikezie, and Russell were inside Canada Square car park. Russell was pacing around in circles like a man under severe distress. He was pulling on a cigarette—his fifteenth in the space of an hour.

"Fuck, fuck, fuck!" Russell said, dragging his left hand through his mop of dark brown hair. "We're really in the shit, man. I am talking about that late-night-curry-from-Brick Lane type of shit you do in the toilets."

Chikezie stepped away from Timon and shot Russell a contemptuous look. "Oh, you got jokes," he said, veins popping on both sides of his forehead. "You introduced us to that madman and convinced us to take him on as an investor." He turned to look at Timon, judgment burning in his eyes. "And I warned you, T, that we shouldn't touch his money. I knew it was dirty. Now look at the bloody mess we're in. We can't even go to the authorities because we'd be implicating ourselves for laundering money for a terrorist arms dealer who is now on the run from his government!" Chikezie threw his arms in the air and shook his head. Timon bowed his head.

"Couldn't we just take five million from our hedge fund and pay Musa back that way?" Russell said, looking at both Timon and Chikezie.

"It was that white privilege which got you into Cambridge because it certainly wasn't your intelligence," Chikezie said, scathing in his tone. "Not only is what you've suggested illegal, by abusing the position of trust our investors have in us, but you think our remaining clients wouldn't notice we've extracted some of their money from the fund? Their confidence in us is already at an all-time low because of the money we've lost from the Nexthereum hack. And now you're suggesting we steal from them too?"

Russell opened his mouth to launch a counterargument, but when he looked at Chikezie, who had the face of a man ready to punch anyone, he sealed his mouth shut.

Timon exhaled a sigh of exhaustion and looked at Russell. "Bro, couldn't you ask your family to lend us the five million?"

"No way, T," Russell said, shaking his head. "My family is asset-rich, not cash-rich. My parents are swimming in debt, mate."

"Ok, fine, but can't you at least speak to that family member who initially put you in touch with Musa? You said they had been in business before? Could he talk some sense into Musa? Tell him to be reasonable."

Russell shook his head again. "It won't make a world of difference, T. You saw how batshit crazy Musa is. He won't listen to my uncle."

"Who is this uncle of yours anyway?" Chikezie said, eyeing Russell. "You've never told us."

"It's irrelevant information," Russell said.

"No, I think it's quite relevant given the circumstances."

"Well, I disagree, Kez. I don't think it is." Russell's now sounded irritated.

"Boys, let's not start fighting among ourselves, yeah," Timon said. He removed himself from the Porsche's bonnet. "We're obviously not taking money from the hedge fund to pay back Musa. That's out of the question. We must consider another way to raise five million dollars in two months. Let's look at our savings, what we can sell off and any favours we can call."

"Five million dollars is not chicken change," Chikezie said, looking at Timon. "We aren't just going to raise that amount of money in two months."

"Well, we'll have to try if we don't want the people we love to find themselves in a shallow grave."

Timon felt his Samsung Galaxy make a ping sound. Someone had sent him a text message. Timon extracted the phone from his pocket and looked at the screen. It was a message from Orisa.

It's already past midnight, boo. And you haven't called? I am worried. Please txt me back when u read this msg. Hope u are ok. xxx

"I am going to head home, and I suggest you all do the same," Timon said, pocketing his smartphone. "It's been one of the shittiest days of our professional careers, but right now, we all need some shut-eye. We'll reconvene tomorrow, alright."

* * *

An hour later, Timon walked into the stillness of his penthouse. No sooner had he closed the door and made his way to the kitchen than Orisa's squeaky voice broke the silence of the peaceful tranquillity.

LEKE APENA

"Boo, you're home!"

"Yeah, it's me," Timon said with a weak tone as he took a rocks glass from one of the glass-front kitchen cabinets.

Dressed in a pink, satin babydoll nightdress, Orisa practically ran into the kitchen, threw her arms around Timon, and hugged him tightly. To Timon's surprise and even annoyance, the presence of his fianceé did not calm his anxiety as it should have. If anything, she seemed to add further weight onto his already stressful existence.

Timon gave Orisa a half-hearted peck on the lips and then dragged himself to the kitchen's American-style fridge. He dispensed blocks of ice into his rocks glass and retrieved the 70cl bottle of Hennessey from the refrigerator. Right now, a stiff drink was what he needed.

"Boo, what happened to your neck?" Orisa said, gently pressing her thumb against the plaster which concealed the cigar burn Musa had inflicted on Timon.

Before answering Orisa, Timon took a swig of Hennessey from the rock glass. "It's just an injury from work. Can you please not touch it."

Timon saw no reason to confide in Orisa about the precarious situation he found himself in with Musa. Orisa loved reality dating shows, trips to Dubai, and posting selfies of the upmarket restaurants she frequented with him. When it came to real-life problems, Timon could not rely on her to help solve them. He realised then that she would only ever be an eye-candy wife.

"Do you remember that you'll be appearing on my podcast next Monday as a guest to talk about our upcoming engagement party?" Orisa said, still eyeing the plaster on his neck. "That plaster is going to be distracting."

"I really don't give a shit about your podcast right now, Orisa." The day's stress had finally corked the lid on Timon's patience.

Orisa stepped back, her lips trembling like a chastised

102

child. Timon put his glass on the kitchen top and sighed heavily. "Sorry, babe. I didn't mean that. I am just...so stressed. It's been a very long week."

Orisa's frown quickly flipped into an understanding smile. She stepped towards Timon, pressed her body against his and leaned her head on his chest. "I am sorry to hear that, boo. I can tell work has been crazy for you this past week because of that big hack thing." Being four inches shorter than Timon, she looked up at his chin. "But I know exactly how to relieve your stress." She slid her right hand inside Timon's trousers until she reached his shaft. Gently, she cradled Timon's scrotum in her right hand, juggling them.

"I am not in the mood tonight," Timon said bluntly, removing her right hand from his trousers. There were a lot of troubling thoughts building in Timon's mind like a traffic jam. Any sexual desires would not get through to his brain today, no matter how effortlessly seductive Orisa could be.

"I need some sleep. I have a lot on my plate at the moment."

* * *

By 10 a.m. the following day, Timon was already awake and working. He sat in the living room by the oval dining table with his MacBook open. Orisa had left the apartment at 9.30 a.m. She had several business meetings across the city with potential new sponsors for her podcast. Timon would be lying if he said he was not grateful for Orisa's absence, as it allowed him to be more productive, which he needed to be, given his dire circumstances.

Timon had spent the better part of two hours going through his main bank accounts and making a list on an Excel spreadsheet of the various assets he owned that he could liquidate to raise the five million. He could quite quickly generate that sum by putting his Battersea apartment on the market. But given the woeful economy, it would take some time to find a buyer and not within two months. Besides, even if a miracle occurred, and he did sell his apartment in two months, where exactly would he live? There was no way in hell that Orisa would accept downsizing so radically.

The thought of selling his Porsche 911 Cerra had also crossed Timon's mind, but he had purchased the luxury sports car for just over £100,000 and had driven it for two years, so it wouldn't even cause a dent. Looking at his cash reserves, Timon had about £650,000 in a Santander isa account and another £158,000 in a Barclays savings account. But that was it. Not even close to the five million pounds he needed. Timon suspected that even if he, Chikezie and Russell emptied all their savings, they still wouldn't have enough. Lastly, asking the bank to borrow five million pounds was laughable, given how tanked the economy was.

Timon leaned back against the mahogany chair he was sitting on, dragging his hands down his face. A strong urge came over him to go and visit his mum. In desperate times like this, she was the only person who could calm him when everything around him seemed to be turning into shit.

As Timon stood from the dining table to retrieve his car keys in the main bedroom, his smartphone beside his laptop began to buzz. Someone was calling him. Timon picked up his phone. It was an unknown number.

"Hello, who is this?" Timon said as soon as he answered the phone.

"Am I speaking to Mr Bakare?" The voice on the other end of the line belonged to an adult female. She had a very noticeable African accent that was not harsh on the ears. Timon quickly realised it was a Nigerian accent.

"Yes, you're speaking to him. How did you get this number?"

"I got your business card from a friend you gave it to at

last year's blockchain conference in Singapore. Can you recall?"

"Oh, yes. I do remember," Timon said. Last year, himself, Chikezie, and Russell travelled to Singapore to attend the first-ever Nexthereum blockchain conference.

"It's great to get hold of you finally, Mr Bakare. I am calling to briefly discuss a very lucrative crypto consultant role you might find interesting. Do you have ten minutes?"

Something about the Nigerian woman's voice on the phone made Timon, against his better judgment, want to find out what this 'lucrative crypto consultant role' could be.

"Sure, I've got ten minutes."

14-year-old Yinka Saraki was hiding in the girl's toilets.

Her tormentors at school were hunting for her as they always did during the fifteen-minute morning break. Sometimes, Yinka would wait inside one of the toilet cubicles to avoid them as she was doing now. She sat on the toilet seat to kill time and read Chinua Achebe's Things Fall Apart. It had been her father's favourite book. He had given it to her a few days before he had died of his illness in Nigeria.

The loud school bell rang in her ears. With sadness, she would need to leave Achebe's gripping story about pre-colonial life in southeast Nigeria. Now, it was back to her reality.

Morning break was over, and every pupil at Kingsford Comprehensive, the dreadful secondary school she attended in east London, would return to their classrooms. Yinka hopped off the toilet seat, removed her small rucksack, unzipped it, and placed the novel inside. Once the rucksack was on her back again, she left the cubicle and went to the toilet's exit.

Before stepping out into the corridor completely, Yinka opened the lavatory's door slightly and poked her head through the gap. The long corridor, each side containing a row of classrooms, was empty.

The coast was clear. Yinka stepped out of the girl's bathroom and calmed her nerves by taking short breaths. She turned on her heels and made her way to the end of the corridor. A fire exit door would take her to a stairwell leading to the school's second floor. From there, she would make her way to her English class.

When Yinka pushed the fire exit door open, her tormentors were already lying in wait for her. She had stepped right into their deadly trap. All she could do was stand by the top of the stairwell as her bullies stood just a few steps below her, looking up at her. There were five of them. Three girls and two boys. The primary aggressor in the group, a black girl called Desola Adeyemi, known as 'DeDe' around the school, had a wicked smirk across her face as she looked up at Yinka.

Yinka only had time to think about sprinting back through the fire exit door before Desola and her friend, another black girl named Yetunde, galloped over the stairs and dragged her down by the straps of her rucksack. Fighting off two 14-year-old black girls proved fruitless for Yinka, whose scrawny frame resembled a branch twig. She was soon pinned against the wall, surrounded by the five people who made it a sport to make her life at school as horrible as possible.

"Oh my god, I can't stand so close to her," Desola said, pinching her nostrils. "She stinks so much. Did you ever bath your-self back in your village in Nigeria?" Her four cohorts, standing behind her, snickered and laughed.

"Why can't you leave me alone?" Yinka said, pressed against the wall. In her mind, she was praying that some miracle would cause the wall to swallow her up. "I am not any trouble to you. I want to go about my day. Please."

The slap from Desola was lightning quick and stung like a tennis racket hitting her face. "Who said you could talk back to me, you freshie?" Desola's voice was full of disgust and hatred.

"Someone take this freshie's bag," said Yetunde, a nasty grin on her round, brown face.

One of the boys stepped forward. He had short black hair, light brown skin and small eyes. "Give me your bag, or I'll just take it from you, innit." The boy spoke in that harsh inner-London accent that Yinka still wasn't used to. She had only lived in the UK for three months.

"You gonna make me take it from you?" The boy's dark eyes stayed on Yinka.

Reluctantly, not wanting to get beaten up again like last week, Yinka removed her rucksack and gave it to the boy. The boy grinned at her and threw her rucksack to Desola. She gave the boy a peck on the lips as he came to stand beside her.

"Thank you, Timon," Desola said. She turned her attention back onto Yinka and wore the sadistic face of someone who immensely enjoyed toying with people. "Let's see if this freshie has packed any jollof rice in her bag."

"Please don't," Yinka said, her voice shrill.

But Yinka's pleas fell on deaf ears. Desola unzipped her rucksack, tipped it over, and emptied its contents on the concrete landing. Yinka's plastic pencil case, two textbooks, the copy of Things Fall Apart, and her packed lunch box her auntie had prepared that morning were scattered across the floor.

"What a pathetic nerd," said Yetunde, stamping on the front cover of Things Fall Apart. "You call yourself Nigerian but cannot even bring jollof rice to school. But it is okay for you to bring the smell with you." At this remark, everyone laughed. Yinka looked down at the floor, holding back the tears that threatened to emerge.

"Let's leave her," came Timon's voice. "We have Maths now. I don't want Mr O'Brian chatting shit about giving me detention, innit."

Having satisfied their daily fix of humiliating her, Yinka watched as her five tormentors brushed past her, making their way down the stairwell. Before going down the steps, Timon looked at her with those dark, small eyes and gave her a wink before grabbing Desola's hand and following her down the stairs.

Once Yinka could no longer hear the footsteps and sniggers of her tormentors, she let the stinging tears fall freely down her cheeks as she crumpled to the floor. She hated all of them, but one day, she would make them all pay for doing this to her. All of them would suffer.

15

WEARING HER FAVOURITE SUNGLASSES, Ray-Ban Clubmasters, and her Gucci mini bag hanging from her left shoulder, Yinka sat at the poseur table at the Radio Rooftop bar in the West End. The table she had booked for herself and Timon was at the far end of the rooftop bar's glass terrace, providing a beautiful, panoramic view of London's skyline on a lush summer day in the capital. From this vantage point, she could see many of London's landmarks: the greyish brutalist architecture of Southbank Centre, the white, glistening Ferris wheel that was the London Eye and even the towering family of skyscrapers that characterised Canary Wharf. Below her, millions of cars and people swept through the city's roads, streets and pavements like electrical currents whizzing to their destination with a relentless force.

Yinka had lived in London from the age of fourteen for nine years. Her relationship with the city had been a slow burn. It had started badly, but the capital had narrowly won her over by the time she was at university.

A young waitress with auburn hair and slightly tanned skin, came to stand beside Yinka at her table. She had the warmest smile and spoke with an unmistakable Italian accent.

"What would you like to drink?" she said, notepad and pen ready.

"Hi, could I please have the Monkey 47 gin with lemonade? No ice. Thank you." Yinka was not a big drinker, but she was partial to gin. She developed a love for it as an undergraduate at the London School of Economics.

After jotting down Yinka's request, the waitress departed to the interior bar. As she waited for her drink, Oge's kidnapping in Berlin aggressively came back to Yinka again, her memories forcing her to relive the traumatic incident. The mental image of her boyfriend thrown violently onto the back of the van and then seeing him tied to a chair in some storage room, covered in a white sheet, flashed in Yinka's mind, cruel and tormenting.

And now, with its penchant for irony, the universe had orchestrated the events of Berlin so that Yinka and the rest of the Robin Hoods would return to the city where they had all met for the first time as undergraduates. Back then, still in their early twenties, they all had ambitious goals for their lives once they graduated, until Oge re-entered Yinka's life and changed the trajectory of their futures. Oge had given them a greater purpose, and he had unlocked Yinka's potential, instilling a confidence she did not know she had buried within her. Yinka and the Robin Hoods were indebted to Oge. But for Yinka, it went more profound than that. She loved Oge and could not imagine a world where he was not with her, and she was not with him.

It was this driving force to save the man she loved that forced Yinka to swallow the bile in her throat when she had heard Timon's voice when she called him two days ago. The last time Yinka had seen Timon, he was a nasty and arrogant 14-year-old boy. So when Yinka explained the potential crypto consultant role to Timon, deliberately making details vague and not revealing her true identity, she had not expected Timon's voice to sound so deep and polished. Gone was the insolent and lippy tone he had as a teenager, replaced by a commanding confidence and the tone of a man educated at one of the most elite institutions in the world.

Still, Yinka's secondary school memories of the unending torment that Timon, along with his wretched girlfriend at the time, Desola, and the others in their group, had put Yinka through had never really left her. For six months of her life, Yinka had been terrified of her school in East London in a way she had never been in Nigeria, even though Nigerian teachers could physically punish you in a way that would get a teacher in a UK classroom arrested. So frightened of Timon and the other bullies, Yinka remembered how she had hidden, like an animal being hunted, in toilets and the library to avoid being physically assaulted and humiliated.

But, in a cruel twist of fate, Yinka had exacted her revenge on them all. After getting Timon and the others permanently expelled, using some incriminating evidence and deception, Yinka had never seen Timon's face again and had even forgotten about his existence. Until now.

Fifteen years since leaving that terrible secondary school , somehow Yinka found herself coerced into recruiting her former school tormentor to save her boyfriend's life. *The universe has a twisted sense of humour.*

The Italian waitress returned. She was carrying a plastic tray with a hi-ball glass filled with clear gin and lemonade. Carefully, she set Yinka's drink on the table. "Would you like anything else?" she said, smiling at Yinka and holding the tray by her lap.

"No, I am fine for now. Thank you."

The waiter nodded curtly and departed.

Yinka took a satisfying sip of her gin cocktail, savouring the tangy and sweet taste on her tongue before letting it rush down her throat. As soon as she set her glass back on the table, she saw Timon standing by the far entrance to the rooftop terrace.

Dressed in brown, cropped chinos, black loafers and a black turtle neck jumper, Timon was much taller than his LinkedIn profile pic and the few images of him on his hedge fund's website suggested. Like Yinka, he was also wearing black Ray-Ban sunglasses. She noticed a plaster on the right side of his neck.

Looking like Vogue model with his hands in his pockets as he casually scanned the terrace, Timon finally spotted her by the far end of the rooftop terrace. She raised her left hand at him and gave him a wave. Timon removed his shades, pocketed them and then began to approach her.

Yinka could feel her heartbeat increase as Timon came closer and closer. *Deep breaths. Don't get emotional. You got this.* As soon as Timon was a mere feet away, she immediately caught a whiff of his strong aftershave and got to her feet. Yinka extended her right arm to shake Timon's hand. Their handshake was friendly. So far, so good.

But as soon as Yinka removed her sunglasses, their meeting quickly turned sour.

16

Timon knew he was taking a gamble.

Walking through the lavish interior bar at Radio Rooftop, Timon reflected on the phone call he had received from the mysterious Nigerian woman two days ago. She had not revealed her name on the call; she had only given Timon broad details of a high-paying crypto consultant role and then told him where they would meet to discuss it further in person. So now Timon found himself at Radio Rooftop on a Monday afternoon, driving from Canary Wharf to meet the nameless Nigerian woman who had called him out of the blue.

The deal presented on the phone sounded almost too good to be true. Timon would work with the Nigerian woman's team of *"specialists"* as she labelled them over the phone for a one-off fee of five million pounds to convince a group of wealth managers to invest in a crypto company called Afchain. Timon had heard murmurings about the crypto company before. According to online discourse on industry chatrooms and forums, it was a top-secret project founded in Nigeria that would revolutionise how Nigerians used money and banks. Some were even calling it the cure for corruption in Nigeria. But Timon had never delved deeper into it. All the same, after the phone call, Timon was intrigued. Given the current life-threatening dilemma with Musa Jirongo, the Nigerian woman's phone call was a lifeline from God.

Timon walked towards the roof terrace and stood at the entrance, surveying the elegant rooftop space. It was busy today, with well-dressed patrons sipping cocktails, stuffing their faces with Spanish tapas, and laughing with friends and business acquaintances.

At the far end of the outdoor terrace, Timon spotted the nameless Nigerian woman sitting by one of the round drinking tables. On the phone, she said she would wear a black maxi dress with a Gucci bag and black Ray-Ban sunglasses. True to her word, that is exactly what she wore as Timon looked in her direction. The Nigerian woman spotted him standing by the entrance and waved to him. Timon nodded and made his way to her.

When Timon finally reached the her table, the Nigerian woman stood up to shake his hand, and he was caught off guard by how stunning she was. Firstly, her perfume - a sweet aroma of fresh oranges - enhanced her dark beauty and effortless sex appeal. Her short-sleeved black dress clung to her shapely figure and curvy hips and her braids, which fell to her shoulders, neatly complimented her heart-shaped face and high cheekbones. But the woman's most alluring physical feature was her smooth, earthly rich complexion which had the same colour as liberica coffee beans.

After their handshake - her hands were soft and smooth, and her pink nails were immaculate - Timon and the still-nameless Nigerian woman sat at the table. Then she removed her sunglasses.

Timon's jaw dropped in complete disbelief. Long-buried memories from his early secondary school days blasted back in his face like a hot furnace. "You!" Timon said, aghast with horror, as he realised who he was speaking to. He felt his heartbeat quickly rise in anger. Although Yinka Saraki had evolved from the stick figure of her teen years, her almond-shaped dark eyes and button nose had been the dead give-away. "It was *you* who called me?"

Yinka smiled at him, but it was not friendly. "God knows I would be telling the biggest lie if I said it was nice to see you again."

It had been sixteen years since Timon had seen Yinka. His last memory of her was of her smirking at him in the play-ground after he, his girlfriend at that time, and their friends were permanently expelled from school. And it was Yinka who had engineered their fates through blackmail and deception.

"This is bullshit," Timon said, shaking his head incredu-lously and chuckling bitterly. "How the hell did you get my number? And don't repeat that damn lie about getting my business card from someone I gave it to."

"Does it really matter?"

"Yeah, it bloody matters because you're a lying *bitch*. Don't think I've forgotten what you did."

"Excuse me, watch your tone and language. Don't you ever speak to me in that way again." Yinka now wore a stern frown, visually making her loathing for Timon as clear as the afternoon sky. On Timon's side, the feeling was entirely mutual.

"There's no way in hell I am having a sit-down discussion with you. Delete my number expeditiously. Understand?" Timon sucked his teeth loudly and stood up from the chair, ready to depart. But then Yinka firmly placed her left hand on Timon's right hand. Despite wanting nothing to do with the person who had ruined a significant part of his teenage life, for some inexplicable reason, Timon did not fling Yinka's hand away and storm off as he should have done.

"Let me make this very clear to you," Yinka said firmly, visibly straining to remain imperturbable. "If you walk away from me right now, consider the job proposal I shared on our phone call off the table. You walk away; you will no longer be considered. Understand?"

Timon took a deep intake of air and exhaled loudly. *Fuck it, let's hear what she has to say.* He sat back down.

"In all fairness, you have the right to know how I obtained your number," Yinka said, her face returning to a neutral expression. "My team could not find your number on your company's website, and we did not want to contact you through your website's contact form as you might take long to respond. So, my team researched various crypto conferences and discovered that you attended one in Singapore last year when your company sponsored the event. Using the process of elimination, we contacted everyone who visited the conference that you would have had contact with, claiming we were a financial authority who needed to speak with you urgently. One of the event planners, understandably rattled to receive such an official-sounding call, was more than happy to give us your number from the business card you gave her."

"Your team did all that?" Timon said, admittedly impressed but also confused as to why they went to such lengths to contact him personally. "Well, you and *your people* sound very dodgy, and the person who gave you my contact details violated data privacy laws." He sneered at Yinka. "But it doesn't surprise me if I am being honest. Someone like you would keep company with unsavoury characters. Probably a bunch of 419ers."

Yinka sighed deeply and robbed her forehead. "Look, you don't like me. Trust me, the sight of your face makes me want to vomit as well. But let's put our secondary school history aside and behave like adults, or will that be too hard for you, Timon?"

"Just hurry up. I don't have much patience for someone like you."

Yinka gnashed her teeth, and Timon could tell she was

using all her willpower not to let his antagonising behaviour get under her skin. He enjoyed seeing her frustration.

"I have told you about this rare business opportunity to work with me and my team as a crypto consultant to help us secure capital for Afchain, one of the biggest African crypto projects, as I am sure you've heard about. Doesn't five million pounds as a fee for your troubles sound attractive?"

"Oh, of course it does. But when that five million is being promised to me by someone like you, well…I have my reservations." Timon leaned back on his chair and narrowed his eyes at Yinka. "Besides, other crypto hedge fund managers and experts are out there. Why have you gone through all this trouble to recruit me specifically? It certainly wasn't because of our fond memories of going to school together." Timon winked at her, and for a moment, it looked like Yinka had had enough and was about to stand up and leave.

"As hard as it is to believe, you're considered one of the country's best crypto hedge fund managers and experts. Your reputation precedes you and my team could use that credibility and your specialist knowledge."

Hearing that he was "considered one of the best crypto hedge fund managers in the country" had admittedly stroked Timon's ego. It was always nice to be recognised and wanted. "Okay, let's say I do potentially take this job offer. What exactly would it entail?"

"It will be an international role with quite a bit of travelling if you're not afraid of flying. Although I can't imagine how a plane could liftoff if it has to carry the weight of your big head."

Timon chuckled. "For someone who needs my help, you're very insulting, you know that?"

"Oh, please," Yinka said, dismissively waving her left hand at him. "You can pretend all you like but I see through it. The fact that you've come here after a brief phone call with me offering you five million for a crypto consultant job tells me that you most likely need this money."

"You don't know shit about me. Got that?" Timon could feel his annoyance rise.

"Look, you have two days to make up your mind," Yinka said, shaking her head at him. She opened her Gucci bag, fished out a card and handed it to Timon, who snatched it from her. "On that card is an address in Shoreditch where my team and I are staying. If you want to be part of this, you will come to that address in two days. If we don't see you after that, then don't bother."

As Timon looked at the address on the white paper card, written in pen, Yinka put her sunglasses back on. She took a long swig of the cocktail drink on the table, finished it and stood up. "Opportunities like these seldom come twice," Yinka said, looking down at Timon as she spoke. "So put your emotions aside and look at the blessing before you."

Timon sneered and looked at Yinka's face, which he kept annoyingly finding attractive. "Well, it could be a curse in disguise if it's a blessing from you."

Yinka stuck her lip up at him. "Two days. Sleep on it."

With those final words, Yinka strolled away from the drinking table, leaving Timon alone. As she walked away, Timon turned his head back to look at her. Tried as he might not cast his eyes down, he couldn't help but survey the satisfying roll of her tantalisingly round derriere filling out her dress. He had to admit, puberty had been very gracious to Yinka, transforming her from the stick skinny black girl he remembered from secondary school into a fully grown black woman with lustrous curves, beautiful skin and a body brimming with fullness and confidence.

Timon shook his head to dispense the thoughts about Yinka's attractiveness and faced forward. *Remember what she did to you, no matter how long ago.* Timon flipped the card Yinka had given him. There was no denying that this crypto consultant role was tempting, but it also invited suspicion. Who exactly were Yinka's team? How could they have five million pounds at their disposal? Why did they need to convince some wealth managers to invest in Afchain? These were important questions that Yinka had provided no answers to yet.

After sitting alone at the table for ten minutes in silent contemplation, Timon decided to regroup with Chikezie and Russell and relay what Yinka had shared with him. Then, he would choose to take up Yinka's offer or not.

Before he left the rooftop bar, Timon ordered Hennessy on the rocks; no chaser. He needed a stiff drink for the road.

17

Taking a swig from his Peroni bottle, Russell leaned back against the sofa as he sat beside Timon. "I am not religious," he said, with a cheeky grin, "but if I was, this is the kind of random job offer I would have prayed for given our very shitty situation."

Timon and Russell were in Chikezie's country-styled living room at his four-bedroom, semi-detached house in Brentwood. After Timon and Russell chatted with Chikezie's adorable five-year-old daughter, Susanna, mostly asking her how school was going, her mother came and whisked her to the park so the men could talk among themselves. Chikezie served Timon and Russell beers, and they immediately got down to serious adult matters. Timon had just finished recounting his meeting with Yinka at the West End rooftop bar two days ago.

"Let's be rational here, T," Chikezie said, ignoring Russell's remark and speaking directly to Timon. "It is very convenient, almost *too* convenient, that this business opportunity has come to you exactly when we need five million pounds. And to be honest, bro, it feels dodgy."

"Kez, I hear what you're saying," Timon said, leaning back on the sofa. He took a slug of his Peroni and let out a sigh. "And I don't even trust the woman who offered the job. Her name's Yinka. She sort of fucked me over in secondary school."

"Secondary school?" Russell said, springing upright on the sofa and staring at Timon with intense curiosity. "You went to school with this woman?"

Timon nodded. "We were in the same secondary school for about a year. When I was in Year 9, she got me and my friends permanently expelled by blackmailing us." He sighed as he thought about one of the most painful memories from his past. "I've never seen my mum so disappointed in me."

"What did you do that she managed to get you kicked out of school?" Chikezie said, looking amused.

Timon shrugged and shook his head. "I was fourteen, just a kid, and I can't be bothered to explain what happened. But I keep asking myself, could she mess with me again?"

"Bro, whatever she did to you, that was sixteen years ago," Russell said. "You're grown adults now. Let bygones be bygones. If she's offering you five million pounds to convince some rich assholes who manage money for other rich assholes to invest in this Nigerian crypto company, I say do it. Let's be real: between us, we aren't going to raise five million in two months to pay Musa back."

Chikezie looked down at his Peroni bottle, heaved a heavy sigh, and then looked at Timon. "The crypto company, Afchain, I've heard people in the crypto industry talk about it. It's got some backing from a very high-net-worth individual, but no one is sure who it is. And it's supposed to be a very top-secret project. No one has seen a prototype of the technology or what it does exactly."

Timon shrugged and took a swig from his bottle. "Well, somehow, Yinka and her team have acquired the Afchain technology. So I'll have all I need to sell it as an investment vehicle to investors."

"I don't like it, T," Chikezie said. He finished his beer and placed the empty Peroni bottle on the coffee table. "But if you take this gamble, ensure you get paid some money upfront. That way, we can give some of the money back to Musa to keep him off our backs for the time being, but also, you'll have the certainty that this Yinka woman is serious about this consultant role and not trying to take you for a mug. Again."

* * *

At a four-bedroom apartment on Club's Row, a boutique street in Shoreditch, a fashionable area in East London, Yinka was sitting by the window ledge and looking through the glass pane. It was just a few minutes past seven, and the sky had turned lavender, and the clouds had become pinkish wisps gliding in the sky.

From this corner of the apartment, Yinka had an excellent view of Shoreditch with its blend of converted offices, Georgian-styled homes, towering, newly built skyscrapers housing modern flats and the imaginative street graffiti sprayed on concrete walls. East London had transformed drastically from when she had lived here as a teenager. Gentrification had given the area a new makeover as a playground for London's creative minds.

Elsewhere in the Shoreditch flat, the rest of the Robin Hoods kept themselves preoccupied as they waited nervously to see if Timon would arrive. The two-day deadline Yinka had given Timon to come to the address would be over in a few hours, and there was still no sign of him. Joshua was sitting on the wooden dinner table in the dining room area with two laptops in front of him. Somehow, he seamlessly went from typing on one to the other. Sitting beside him, Kisi was reading a London magazine called Time Out. She looked disinterested as she flipped through the pages. Montana was watching BBC News on the flat-screen television on the couch to the right of the communal area. Jaali, who was topless, was doing some push-ups behind the sofa. After his twentieth push-up, he got to his feet. Montana looked at him and handed him the plain, white t-shirt he had given her.

"Are you sure this guy is coming?" Jaali said, putting on the T-shirt. "Because this entire operation is already a flop from the start if he decides not to show up."

Yinka looked away from the window and turned her whole body to face Jaali on the other side of the room. "He'll turn up."

"How can you be so sure?" Kisi said, looking up from the magazine. "It's not that I doubt you, Yinks. But any sane person would have a lot of reservations about this job offer."

"Of course they would, but sane people do crazy things when they're desperate," Yinka said, thinking back to the frosty meeting she had with Timon two days ago at the rooftop bar. "He tried to hide it behind all this bravado, but he looked stressed out. He even had a plaster on his neck. Once he realised who I was and he was about to leave, it didn't take much to get him to sit back down. And eventually, he took the card I gave him with our address."

Joshua turned away from his laptop screens and addressed Yinka directly. "And I assume that when you had your parley with him at this rooftop bar, you did not inform him that you have been specifically instructed to recruit him?"

"Come on now, Engineer. I am not careless. I can already see that Timon is the type of man who, if you tickle his ego, you can easily manipulate him to do what you want. In our meeting, I told him I wanted to recruit him because he was considered one of the best crypto specialists in the country. And his eyes lit up. He's pathetic."

"Well, as *pathetic* as he sounds, we need his help," Jaali said. "Oge's kidnappers, who I still believe have been employed by the Bankole family, specifically said we need to recruit him and no one else for this mission."

"Even if these British mercenaries are working for the Bankole family," Kisi said, speaking directly to Jaali, "which I have my doubts about, how would Oge's kidnappers and whoever their employer is know that we have successfully recruited this crypto guy anyway?" Kisi said.

"It's a good question, and we honestly have no idea," Yinka said, folding her arms and leaning back against the window frame. "We don't even know how these British mercenaries managed to intercept me and Oge's taxi back in Berlin. For all we know, they're spying on us right now." Yinka shook her head. "Oge's freedom depends on us recruiting Timon. Trust me, no one regrets that more than me."

"Well, let's hope this guy turns up soon," Jaali said.

"Can we briefly review the plan again for when the crypto guy gets here?" Montana said.

"Sure," Yinka said, smiling at Montana. "When Timon arrives, we'll give him a false backstory about how we came into contact with the Afchain crypto company and use the materials from the package mailed to us by Oge's kidnappers. After that, we'll give him some intel on the three private bankers that we need his help convincing to invest in Afchain. Then we'll see what he says."

As Yinka finished speaking, everyone in the apartment jerked their head towards the door. Someone had rang the doorbell.

Heart racing, Yinka stood from the window and walked to the door where the home security camera had been fitted. She pressed a button on the display console to see who was outside the apartment. On the 3.5-inch LCD colour screen, Yinka could see a clear view of the street. Standing by the doorway was a black man with light brown skin, short black hair, black jeans, and a black leather jacket. Yinka pressed a button on the panel to open the door, and the man stepped inside the building.

Yinka turned to look at the rest of her team. They started back at her expectantly.

"He's here."

18

WHEN YINKA OPENED the apartment door to let him inside, Timon did not expect to be greeted by the faces of four other black people. They all looked about the same age as Yinka.

Timon scanned his surroundings as Yinka closed the front door behind him. It was a medium-sized apartment, with abstract paintings hanging from the white plastered walls and the corner window providing a decent view of Shoreditch. He would have thought Yinka and her team would be operating from an office rather than some chic east London apartment for art students. Already, Timon's *'these people are dodgy'* alarm was going off in his head.

"I'm glad you took my advice and looked beyond your emotions," Yinka said, now standing by the dining table.

A young man with big, square-framed spectacles was seated on the table with two laptops behind him. A dark-skinned black woman, who resembled a punk with her short red hair and nose ring, sat beside the spectacled man. Both of them were narrowing their eyes at Timon with blank faces.

Timon took two steps from the front door and then looked at Yinka. Dressed more casually than their last meeting, Yinka was wearing skinny grey jeans and a white, chequered T-shirt. "Firstly, I don't take advice from you," he said, frowning at Yinka. "Just because I've come here doesn't mean I've agreed to anything yet."

"Well, this one is mouthy, ain't he," said the man with the dreadlocks who was sitting on the sofa next to a plump but pretty brown-skinned woman with a round face and big curly hair. Being a born and bred Londoner, Timon's ears immediately recognised the boy's inner city accent. Timon turned to look at the man on the sofa who stared right back at him, unflinching. "You're from the ends?"

The man with the dreadlocks nodded, sizing up Timon. "Yeah, I am. From Tottenham, innit."

"Might as well get introductions out of the way now," Yinka said. She pointed to the man on the couch with the London accent. "That's Jaali, and woman sitting next to him is Montana." Montana waved at Timon with a cherry demeanour, the only person so far to show him any warmth.

"This is Joshua," Yinka continued, placing her hand on the right shoulder of the young man with the big spectacles.

"And this is Kisi." Yinka gestured at the black girl with the short red hair and nose ring. Kisi lifted her left hand and made a peace sign at Timon. "We mean no harm, bro," she said, in a noticeable African accent, but Timon couldn't place where in Africa. Kisi gave Timon a cheeky grin.

The introductions had only made Timon even more perplexed as to who these people actually were. When Yinka had mentioned her team, he envisioned older people who wore suits, not this eclectic bunch of melanated twenty-somethings staring at him.

"What exactly do you lot do?" Timon said. "Because I am bloody confused."

"I told you before. We've been employed by Afchain independently to help them secure financial backing as the company moves into series A funding," Yinka said. "We're acting like business development consultants. Our objective is to secure three million pounds each from three private bankers of interest."

"Okay, I get that. But what exactly is Afchain?" Timon sat down at the edge of the couch's armrest and put his hands on his lap. "I live and breathe the world of crypto. It's part of my job and how I make my money and no one in the crypto community knows what it actually is."

"But we do," Joshua said. "And I can show you."

Joshua stood from the dining table and took one of the laptops into his hands. Carefully, balancing the laptop on his palms, Joshua walked over to Timon as everyone's eyes in the room trailed him. When he reached Timon, he knelt down on one knee and faced the laptop screen towards Timon. "Afchain is basically going to be west Africa's first crypto currency exchange. As someone with in-depth crypto knowledge, I will assume you know what that means. The platform is being trialled in Nigeria first and it will enable Nigerians to trade and buy crypto coins, purchase goods in crypto and even convert their digital assets into naira and other currencies. It will basically be Africa's version of Binance, giving many Nigerians financial independence. I am sure you understand how significant that is."

"It's definitely ambitious," Timon said, studying the laptop screen in front of him. As far as Timon could see, from the interface on Joshua's laptop screen, he was running a prototype version of the Afchain trading platform. The interface was advanced but clean and it seemed very user intuitive. "And I am guessing what you're showing me is just the beta version of the platform?"

"Exactly," Joshua said. He stood up and closed the laptop. "Afchain has the potential to really bring crypto to Africa in a way no other crypto project has managed to do so far. It should not be too hard for you to sell it as a very profitable future investment."

Timon chuckled. "Well, it depends on who I am trying to

convince. Many still doubt the potential of cryptocurrencies and blockchain technology and think it's all hype and a scam. And this distrust has only increased since the Nexthereum hack." Timon turned away from Joshua, who continued to stand beside Timon, looking unsure of what to do with himself, and spoke to Yinka. "So who are these three private bankers you need my help in convincing to pump their money into this great crypto project?" He coloured every sentence with a splattering of sarcasm.

Yinka nodded at Joshua, who sprung to life again. He re-opened the laptop, knelt down, and began clicking on some files. After a few minutes, he showed Timon the screen. Timon took the laptop from him this time and studied the three folders labelled Silvio Mancini, Emiko Shinoda, and Abdul Kazem Mustafa.

"We actually received physical dossiers on each of the three private bankers, but I decided to digitise the documents," Joshua said, sounding very proud. "It makes it easier to organise all of the information. Would you like the physical files instead?"

"Nah, I am good, thanks," Timon said. He had already started clicking on the folders, which were filled with Word documents detailing each of the three private bankers in depth. There was intel on their lives, online coverage, and other useful trivia.

"I don't understand something," Timon said, looking up from the laptop screen and surveying the faces of everyone in the room. "Why do you need investment specifically from these three private bankers? Why are they so important to Afchain?"

Yinka let out an impatient sigh as she furrowed her brow. "We don't know, ok. For whatever reason, these bankers have been identified as persons of interest that Afchain's board would like to receive investment. Now that you know the details, the real question is, do you accept the job offer?"

Timon chortled hysterically, slapping his hands on his knees in an exaggerated manner while Yinka rolled her eyes and everyone else in the room eyed each other bewilderingly. "How do you lot put up with her?" Timon said, wiping an imaginary tear from his left eye. "Doesn't her voice just annoy you?"

"Hey, watch how you speak about my friend, bro," Jaali said, standing from the couch and facing Timon, glowering at him. "Don't walk in here like you're some top g, crypto boy."

"Calm down, babe," Montana said, tugging at Jaali's wrist. "Sit down, okay."

"Yeah, Jaali, leave him. Timon can be rude all he wants," Yinka said, fixing her eyes on Timon as Jaali sat back on the couch. "But you still haven't answered my question."

After a minute of deliberate silence, Timon let out a sigh. "Alright, I'll admit, this Afchain crypto company shows great potential. I could feasibly convince these private bankers to invest three million of their client's money into the platform. But one condition must be met for me to take this job."

"And what would that be?" Yinka said, folding her arms.

"I want two million paid upfront first into my account by tomorrow morning." Timon winked at Yinka. "Consider it a joining fee for my services. Then you can pay me the remaining three million when I've completed the job."

The room fell silent for a moment and Timon felt like he could hear the gears in everyone's brains turning. Clearly, they had not expected Timon to drop that demand into negotiations. Their response would either confirm or dispel his suspicions that he was being swindled by Yinka and her team.

"Fine," Yinka said finally. "Two million will be paid into your account tomorrow. I'll give you my number before you leave, and you can send over your bank account number and sort code, and we'll deposit that amount into your account."

"Good," Timon said, scowling at Yinka.

"Good," Yinka said, scowling at Timon.

"All good, then. Shall we…talk next steps?" Montana said, looking at both Timon and Yinka whose eyes remained locked like the horns of two clashing bulls.

"I have informed you already that this consultant job would involve a lot of travel. So, you'll be heading to northern Sardinia, where you'll be staying at a resort in Costa Smeralda," Yinka said. "Do you know where Sardinia is?"

"Yes, it's an Italian island in the Mediterranean Sea. I am well travelled, you know," Timon said, huffing at Yinka.

Yinka shrugged her shoulders with a smug smile. "How should I know? With you, I have to check."

"What's in Sardinia?" Timon said, ignoring Yinka's jibe.

It was Joshua who answered. "We have to come to learn that Silvio Mancini, one of the private bankers, is hosting an exclusive party on his superyacht, *The Mangano*, at Perto Cervo, a seaside resort in the Costa Smeralda which is in northern Sardinia. It took quite a lot of research to find the right contacts and quite a sizeable amount of money to grease a few palms, but we've managed to get two of you on the guest list."

"Two of us?" Timon said, raising his eyebrows at Joshua.

"Yes, you and Yinka will be attending the yacht party. We will be here in Shoreditch, providing useful intelligence when you need it."

Timon chuckled. "Oh, this just gets better." He shook his head at Yinka. "I don't see why I need you to come with me."

"I want this whole thing to go very smoothly," Yinka said, raising her top lip at Timon. "So I have decided that I'll be on the ground right there with you. I'll be acting as your business partner. Is that going to be a problem, Timon?"

"Whatever," Timon said, turning his attention back to Joshua. "As you were, mate."

"Oh yes," Joshua said, looking slightly rattled with his train of thought having been cut off by Timon and Yinka bickering. "I have only managed to get you both access to the yacht party. Mr Mancini, I imagine, will be difficult to secure a private audience with, but we'll do our best from here to help you with that. We also have someone on the ground, Kebba, who you might remember, Yinka. Anyway, he is doing us a massive favour and agreed to be your driver when you arrive in Costa Smeralda."

Timon was astounded by the level of planning and execution by Yinka's team. It was clearly bullshit that Yinka and her team were simply independent business consultants hired by Afchain to secure investment from three private bankers. There was a lot more going on here, but Timon decided not to dwell on it for now. As long as he was getting paid the five million, he did not care.

"We'll be flying to Olbia Costa Smeralda Airport on Wednesday afternoon," Yinka said, now looking at Timon with a blank face. "So you should start packing. Oh, and bring some nice suits with you. Since you've made a fortune from crypto, I assume you must have a few."

19

TRUE TO HER WORD, which came as a genuine shock to Timon, Yinka transferred two million pounds into his bank account the next day. Upon receiving the payment, Timon immediately wired it to Musa's bank account. An hour later, Timon received a text message from Musa with a thumbs-up emoji. *Cheeky bastard.*

Since Yinka and her team would not be covering the cost of Timon's flight to Sardinia, he had to dip into his own pockets to fund it. Thankfully, the business class outbound flight on British Airways was cheap. He would fly out from London Heathrow Airport at 3 pm on Wednesday and arrive at Olbia Costa Smeralda Airport two hours and thirty minutes later. Unfortunately, not only would he be on the same flight as Yinka, but the two of them would be seated next to each other.

With the initial payment received from Yinka and the flight to Sardinia booked, Timon's next hurdle was telling Orisa he would be out of the country for as long as a month. Framing it as a business trip, which it technically was, was not the tricky part - it was the fact he would be travelling with a woman. Telling your fiancée, especially if she's Nigerian, that you'll be near another woman overseas for an extended period would not be easy. For any man. Nigerian or otherwise.

"Why do you have to travel with this woman anyway?" Orisa said, two nights before Timon was due to fly out.

Timon lay next to Orisa on the king-sized bed in the penthouse's master bedroom. Tonight, Orisa wore a silk and lace camisole to bed, and Timon wrapped his arms around her waist. They snuggled together in the spooning position.

"She's a consultant for this crypto company I am helping to attract investment for, that's all," Timon said. "We used to go to school together. We didn't like each other then and definitely don't like each other now. I doubt we'll even talk much on this business trip. It's strictly professional, babe. Separate rooms and everything."

Orisa huffed and scrunched her face. "Well I won't pretend I am not annoyed that some other woman gets to be around my sexy future husband. But if you have to do this to earn your money and give us this amazing life, I guess I must be understanding. As your future wife."

Timon sighed in relief, thankful that Orisa had not gone into full-blown hysterics. She turned to face him and now looked like a whimpering puppy. Timon used to find this cute, but now it greatly irritated him.

"But baby boo, I am going to feel so cold in this big bed all by myself," Orisa said. She ran a finger down Timon's bare chest.

"I don't want you to stay in the penthouse alone." Musa's threats tugged at the back of Timon's mind. "Please go and stay with your mum, okay, while I am abroad."

"Okay, boo, boo. If that's what you want," Orisa said. "But promise me, when you're overseas, that you'll text me everyday and face time me at least three times a week."

"You know I will." Although Timon had been sincere and intended to follow through on it, it irked him that the thought of face timing his fiancée seemed like a chore rather than something to look forward to.

After the bedtime talk, for about an hour, Timon and Orisa had their usual rambunctious rounds of sex. Although his physical desire for her had not waned, Timon was now beginning to question if he would still love Orisa if their sex life wasn't so explosive. Could you sustain a whole marriage and build a family on just sex and vibes?

On the Wednesday that Timon was due to fly out, now satisfied that he had packed everything he needed for the trip, he ordered an Uber to Heathrow Airport. He could not be bothered to drive and pay the long-stay parking fees. After switching off all appliances, Timon left his penthouse. When he reached the lobby, dragging his Gucci suitcase behind him, Timon had expected to see the concierge.

Instead, he came face to face with Musa Jirongo. The mad Kenyan arms dealer was standing in the lobby. His two henchmen, who had been present when Musa had turned up unannounced at Timon's Canary Wharf office, were flanking him as he stood blocking the exit out of the apartment complex.

Consistent with his flamboyant dress sense, Musa wore a pink, pinstripe suit with white shoes and matching gloves. He looked like he was attending a fancy dress gala dressed as an American pimp.

"I like this place, Mr London Money," Musa said, looking around the lobby and feigning wonderment. "So this is how the one percent of London live."

Timon sucked his teeth quietly. He used all his willpower to keep his voice even. "Why are you here?"

"I told you my boys would be keeping an eye on you and your two business partners, remember?" Musa said. His voice had a playfulness to it like he enjoyed tormenting Timon. "And guess what? It has been brought to my attention that you've been packing your suitcase. Are you going on holiday when you still owe me three million pounds? How very Nigerian of you."

"I am going abroad for business for a few weeks, alright," Timon said. He checked the time on his silver Rolex watch. It was 12.15am, and he needed to meet Yinka at Heathrow Airport's Terminal 4 in the next hour and a half to catch their flight to Sardinia. "You don't seriously think I am running off?"

"Well, you are a risk taker, aren't you? So I have to make sure you're not taking any stupid risks. You can't always trust what a Nigerian man will do when he owes you money."

"Whatever, you'll get your money, alright," Timon said, his patience with Musa now depleted. "Anyway, I have a flight to catch. I would say it's nice of you to drop by and see me off, but it wasn't. At all."

Musa chuckled and adjusted his glasses. "It's great that you haven't lost your sense of humour despite our recent misunderstandings and altercations."

Timon stared at Musa blankly and decided not to respond. He walked past him and his two goons, dragging his two suitcases as he made his way to the building exit until Musa spoke again from behind him.

"Your fiancée."

Timon stopped just before the lobby's exit. He turned around to face Musa, narrowed his eyes and clenched his teeth. "What about my fiancée?"

Musa flicked his tongue like a python, and his dark eyes narrowed into slits, like that of a snake, from behind his spectacles. "My spies have been sending me some photos of her. She has such a nice ass, my brother. You must just enjoy hitting those perky cheeks every night."

"Fuck you, Musa," Timon said. Consumed by rage, Timon sprang forward, ready to land a satisfying punch on Musa's jaw. And he would have done it without hesitation if Musa had not pulled out the charcoal black Beretta from inside his blazer jacket and pointed the gun at him. Timon immediately stepped back, his heart pounding as fear squeezed his body so tight he could barely move.

"Make sure wherever you're travelling to, you come back with my money. Because if you don't," Musa waved the Beretta at Timon, "I will stick this gun right up your fiancée's beautiful ass and pull the trigger. Then i'll pay your brain dead mother a visit at her care home afterwards." Musa's sinister grin stretched across his thin face. A full display of his sadistic madness. "I wish you a pleasant flight, Mr London Money."

Paralysed by both the shock of seeing the gun and the weight of Musa's threats, Timon could only stand there, immobilised by dread, as Musa and his two bodyguards barged past him and exited the lobby of the apartment complex.

20

Yɪɴᴋᴀ sᴀᴛ on the metal airport chairs at Heathrow Airport's Terminal 4. She wore her Ray Ban sunglasses, light blue tight-waisted shorts, and a matching loose-fitting blouse.

Having arrived at the airport two and a half hours before the flight, Yinka had already checked in her suitcase. The only carry-on luggage she had on her person was her Gucci bag and her brown Mulberry City backpack, where she kept her small MacBook and two books: a novel called 'We Should All Be Feminists by one of her favourite Nigerian authors, Chimamanda Ngozi Adichie who her father would have adored if he was still alive. The other book was a historical and analytical account of Robert Mugabe titled 'Mugabe: Power, Plunder, and the Struggle for Zimbabwe's Future by Martin Meredith.

While she waited for Timon, who was already running late, Yinka had her MacBook propped on her lap and connected to the airport's Wi-Fi. She was having a Microsoft Teams conference call with the rest of the team.

"How are you feeling, babe?" Montana said from the screen. The rest of the team huddled around her.

"I am feeling good, thanks," Yinka said. "I know our

mission, but I must ensure our crypto consultant stays focused."

"Please try not to strangle him to death while you're both in Sardinia, okay," Kisi said. "You two have to get along if you want this to succeed."

"Kisi ain't wrong, Yinks," Jaali said. "You were already at each other's throat at the Shoreditch apartment. Not even Oge gets you worked up like this crypto guy does."

"My focus is on Oge, guys," Yinka said. The image of her boyfriend tied to that chair, held captive, flashed in her mind and hardened her resolve. "We're doing this all for him. That's why we all pulled our money from our bank accounts to give this fool his two million upfront fee. Oge would do the same for any of us."

"No doubt about it," Jaali said, nodding.

"Once you've landed, Kebba will meet you at the airport and take you to the resort you will be staying in at Porto Cervo," Joshua said. "He will also give you the invitations to Silvio Mancini's yacht party. Have you thought about how you plan to get a private audience with him?"

"Not yet, Engineer. But I'll have a proper think about it when we've landed in Sardinia," Yinka said. She looked up to see if Timon had arrived but saw a middle-aged man in Khaki pants holding a young girl's hand, presumably his daughter, with a woman in a sunflower dress walking beside the two of them, presumably the mother and the man's wife—an average family on a regular holiday. Meanwhile, Yinka was travelling to Sardinia to convince an Italian private banker to invest in a crypto startup so she could save her boyfriend's life. *I need a normal life after all this is over.*

"Well, we'll need to devise a plan soon," Joshua continued. "If you don't manage to secure an audience with Mancini, this trip will be an expensive waste of time and resources."

"We understand the enormity of the task at hand, Engineer," Jaali said, patting Joshua on the shoulder. "We'll figure it out."

Yinka looked away from the laptop screen and saw Timon dragging a large Gucci trolley across the airport terminal. He wore brown shorts, a white Ralph Lauren polo shirt with sunglasses tucked in between the collar, and white Ralph Lauren trainers on his feet.

"Okay, team, our crypto boy has arrived," Yinka said. "I'll let you know when I've landed safely as soon as I get a signal."

After saying goodbye to the team, Yinka ended the Microsoft Teams call. She then shut her MacBook and slotted it inside her backpack, which she strapped on. She stood up from the airport chair and walked over to Timon. He was facing away from her and looking up at the electronic notice board for inbound and outbound flights. When she reached Timon and tapped him on the shoulder, he swung around to look at her with such panic that he almost knocked her sunglasses off.

"Bloody hell, you scared me," Timon said, looking startled as if he was caught doing something he shouldn't have been doing. "Can you not sneak up on me like you're Catwoman."

"Oh my gosh, relax," Yinka said sarcastically as she adjusted her sunglasses. She inspected Timon's face, noticed he was sweating profusely, and looked visibly stressed. "Is everything alright with you? You're not actually terrified of flying, are you?"

"Haha," Timon said drily, but Yinka sensed something was troubling him. "I am good, okay. I am here and focused on what we need to do. But are you ready?"

"I've been ready and focused since waiting for your big head to arrive." Her teasing remark made Timon smirk. When he was not insufferable, which was as rare as an honest Nigerian politician, he had quite a nice smile to go with his great teeth.

"Alright, I am going to check in my luggage, and then we can head to security." Timon winked at Yinka, his demeanour now more upbeat. "And before you ask, I did bring my best my best suits."

PART THREE

SEDUCING THE ITALIANS

21

Sixteen hours after leaving his foster brother's lush wedding in Santorini's balmy climate, Intelligence Officer Kojo Owusu-Harrington entered the underground office at Vauxhall Cross with his heavy-built frame and wearing a long grey overcoat. The office belonged to Tiwa Akintola, the recently appointed chief of MI6, the foreign intelligence service for the United Kingdom. Following closely behind Kojo was Ravi Yadav, Tiwa's executive assistant.

Tiwa stood before two flat-screen monitors perched on a black desk. The doughnut-shaped office's interior was sparse, modern, and sleek. Apart from the black leather sofa to the room's right and the silver swivel chair in front of the desk where Tiwa stood, there was no other furniture. Personal artefacts were also scant, save for Tiwa's framed picture on her desk. It was a photo of herself and her late husband on their wedding day in Lagos fifteen years ago.

"Ma'am, he's here," Ravi said, standing next to Kojo with his hands by his lap. The executive assistant was sweating with nerves.

Tiwa waited to acknowledge both Kojo's and Ravi's presence. Her dark eyes remained intently focused on the two monitors before her. When she finally looked up from the screens and regarded the two men's presence, her face displayed a completely neutral expression. "Thank you, Ravi. You're excused."

"Ma'am," Ravi said with a curt nod. He turned to Kojo, gave him a warm smile, then left the office, closing the steel door behind him.

Kojo sauntered to the leather couch, sat down and crossed his legs. Even though Tiwa was Kojo's boss, with a penchant for making her subordinates quite nervous around her with her icy demeanour, he had a very casual working friendship with her. Not only did the two of them have an on-again, off-again intimate relationship in the early 2000s, before she married her late husband, but they were also two of the most senior-ranking black officers at MI6. From that shared connection alone, they always had each other's backs.

"You look stressed," Kojo said, with a solicitous tone, trying to lighten her mood. "I think you could do with some brandy. That always cheers you up."

But Kojo's banter failed to have the desired effect.

Tiwa shook her head in frustration. "It's these bloody newspapers," she said with contempt, not looking at Kojo as she spoke, focused instead on the monitors. "At the Prince of Wales's Intelligence Community Awards yesterday, I decided to wear a kente scarf with my dress, and the Daily Mail uses that to publish a ridiculous fluff piece about how I am bringing some 'tropical' flavour to the UK's intelligence community. It is as if black people are made of coconut and mango and not flesh and blood like everyone else. And then The Sun runs a piece on me. The first thing they write in the first paragraph is 'the widowed and childless new head of MI6' as if I have two of the most unfortunate circumstances ever to befall a woman." Tiwa released an exasperated sigh, closed her eyes and gripped her desk.

At only forty-nine years old, Tiwa had made history by

becoming the first woman and the first person of colour appointed chief of MI6. It was a highly coveted position in the British intelligence community, which she had narrowly won under intense and often nasty British media scrutiny. Many of her loudest critics attacked her appointment as 'a woke hire for diversity's sake.'

"Don't mind what the papers say," Kojo said, waving his left hand dismissively. "The media was always going to behave like this. You expected that. Focus on the job. The Foreign Secretary would not have appointed you if he did not deem you capable of this position."

"Yes, you're right," Tiwa said with a relenting sigh. Finally, she looked at Kojo. A half smile that lit up her light brown face. Today, she had tied her afro hair into a jumbo high bun and worn a white shirt and navy blue suit trousers. "How rude not to ask how my favourite intelligence officer has been."

Kojo chuckled as he stretched his arms out on the couch. "Well, at least you've finally noticed me. I've been ignored for the past five minutes."

Tiwa sighed. "My apologies, Kojo."

Kojo waved his hand dismissively. "I am just making you feel bad on purpose. I am doing all right, for all intents and purposes."

Tiwa took a seat on the swivel chair and crossed her legs. "How was your brother's wedding?"

"Pleasant, for the most part. Santorini is ready-made for postcard weddings. However, it did get a little tiresome with every family member trying to set me up with one of the bridesmaids." Kojo shook his head. "My family believe I am a sorry case because I am in my mid-forties with no wife and no children. The fact that I live with my cat merely under-scores how sad my existence is to them."

Tiwa cackled. "And how do you feel about it?"

Kojo shrugged. "What is there to feel? Life happened. I've

been busy protecting Queen and country from global threats. Never had time to stop and think about a wife or children." His lips curved into a grin. "Not when there are villains out there in the big bad world to defeat."

"You were never the one to commit to a long-term relationship, Kojo. I learnt that the hard way with you. When a new mission presents itself, you're back in the field without hesitation. Any woman with you must always accept that your MI6 job comes before her. Always."

Half a minute of contemplative silence passed between Kojo and Tiwa until she spoke again. "Anyway, apologies for dragging you away from the beautiful cliffside views of Santorini, but this was urgent. I've received a case from the Foreign Secretary, and MI5 is already pissed off that it is now MI6's responsibility."

Interest piqued, Kojo sat upright on the sofa. "MI6 have been handed over a case that originally belonged to MI5? Wow, that must have been a shit show."

"Don't get me started," Tiwa said, standing from her chair. She took the remote control on her desk and pointed it at the wide-screen 4K HD screen built into the curved walls. Immediately, the image of an older white man, around his mid-sixties, with bright blue eyes, a chiselled jawline, and swept-back silver hair, appeared on the screen. He was dressed in a black paisley tuxedo and shaking Prince Charles' hand inside a church hall.

Tiwa turned to look at Kojo. "That man shaking Prince Charles' hand is Sir Richard Dugard. Does that name ring a bell to you?"

Kojo leaned back on the sofa. He stroked his chin as he mentally searched through the cabinets of his memory. "It does...it does. Didn't he once serve as the British High Commissioner to the Federal Republic of Nigeria? I believe he received his knighthood from the Queen in 2011 as well."

"Your memory serves you well," Tiwa said, nodding. "MI5

has been monitoring Dugard's activities for the past year or so. His family have always had strong ties to Nigeria, dating back to the colonial era, and he has several businesses there with links back to Britain. However, there has been some concern that he has been potentially laundering Nigerian criminals' money into Britain, largely through real estate purchases and buying shares in British companies. Quite recently, in Knightsbridge, he met this man."

Tiwa pressed a button on the control again. A new black-and-white photo appeared on the screen, showing what appeared to be Dugard having an alfresco lunch at a fancy cafe in Soho with a dark-skinned man dressed in traditional Nigerian clothing and wearing a fila, a popular type of hat worn in that part of Africa. The Nigerian man had a long face with small eyes and wore spectacles.

"That man Dugard is having lunch with is Mobolagi Bankole. He is considered the Warren Buffet of Nigeria, owning businesses and real estate mainly in Lagos and Abuja. Recently, several members of his family, mostly his children, have been exposed in a series of corruption scandals. His eldest son was caught tied to a bed in a hotel in Berlin last week and stripped down to his boxer shorts after giving a speech at a health tech conference earlier that evening."

"Well, that paints quite an image in my head," Kojo said, concentrating on Mobolaji's face. "But I can't help but feel there's more to this. The Foreign Secretary wouldn't task MI6 to investigate a potentially dodgy relationship between an English aristocrat and a Nigerian business mogul."

Tiwa grinned knowingly at him. "Let me finish, Kojo. AISE, our Italian counterparts, have shared intelligence with us of Dugard travelling to Italy on several occasions to meet this man." Tiwa changed the image on the screen again. It now displayed a low-res photo of Dugard, now in a white t-shirt and shorts, on the upper deck of a yacht, surrounded by scantily clad young women. Another topless white man with a chiselled physique was on the deck. He had white, shoulder-length hair and a face that had gone under the knife one too many times, as it looked almost plastic. He was groping the bum cheeks of one of the young women on the boat.

"The man with the busy hands is Silvio Mancini. Although not proven, Italian intelligence agencies believe he is a private banker for several mafioso families in Milan. He is also a huge film financier, respected by many in Hollywood, although, in some circles, he is considered the Italian Jeffery Epstein."

"So what links all three of these wonderful gentlemen?" Kojo said.

"Now you've asked the million-dollar question," Tiwa said, smirking. She sat on the edge of her desk and pressed a button again on the remote. The faces of Sir Richard Dugard, Mobolagi Bankole and Silvio Mancini appeared in square boxes, side by side. "We believe all three men are part of an international criminal organisation called *The Cable*."

Kojo raised his eyebrows. "*The Cable*?"

"Yes. Although it's all conjecture at this point, given our limited intelligence, several of our analysts believe there is a network of international private bankers who work together to invest their clients' illegal proceeds into various financial instruments in each other's countries. Many of their clients are drug dealers, illegal arms traders, mob bosses and even human traffickers. This criminal enterprise has flooded millions and millions of dirty money into different countries."

"So The Cable is essentially a global investment bank for the world's biggest criminals?" Kojo said, nodding as he digested the information. "So, not too dissimilar to the banks on our high streets, then?" Kojo sniggered and winked at Tiwa.

"I have no comment on that," Tiwa said, chuckling herself. She sat back on the swivel chair and turned to face Kojo. "The mission I am assigning to you is to gather as much intelligence as you can on Dugard so we can prove two things:

firstly, that he has been laundering illicit funds from Nigeria, Italy and other countries into the British economy and secondly, to prove the existence of The Cable. As we're now dealing with foreign actors, it's no longer just a domestic issue, so the case now falls under MI6's jurisdiction." Tiwa heaved a heavy sigh. "This has put a lot of unwanted pressure on me on top of the threats from China and Russia that I still need to get a handle on, as my predecessor failed to extinguish those dumpster fires adequately. But if we can prove Dugard's involvement in an international money laundering operation, substantiate the existence of The Cable, and clarify its scope, it would be a massive win. Not just for me but for MI6." Tiwa smiled warmly at Kojo as she stood up, walked over to him and placed her left hand on his shoulder. "This is why I've chosen you for this mission. There's no one else I trust more at this circus."

"You know I'll do my best. For you."

"I know," Tiwa said, removing her hand from Kojo's shoulder and returning to her desk. "Tomorrow evening, Mancini is hosting a party for wealthy European socialites. Dugard will be in attendance. The party will be taking place on Mancini's superyacht in Costa Smeralda. It's a place in…"

"I know where it is," Kojo said, winking at Tiwa.

"Of course," Tiwa said, returning the wink. "We've managed to get you on the guestlist for the big soiree. You'll be undercover as Steven Hartlett, an HM Treasury consultant seeking new investment opportunities for the UK government."

"That's a pretty unimaginative cover," Kojo said, lifting himself from the sofa and standing before Tiwa's desk. "Couldn't I be Idris Elba's secret brother?"

Tiwa sucked her teeth and gave him a mirthful smile. "A passport with your new identity is waiting for you back at your flat. You will also find a suitcase containing state-of-the-art surveillance equipment to gather intelligence for our analysts. We've also booked accommodation for you at the Grand Hotel in Perto Cervo." Tiwa looked at her gold watch. "Your flight to Sardinia leaves at 9 am tomorrow." Her lips flipped into a smirk. "Aren't you lucky? Flying out to another beautiful European location, all sponsored by taxpayers' money."

"See, being unmarried and childless in middle age could be much worse," Kojo said. He checked his silver Omega watch. It was approaching 6 p.m. in the evening. "I better head home and rest, seeing I have a flight tomorrow. But please drink some brandy. You need it."

Tiwa chuckled. "Don't worry, I will. And good luck with this mission, Kojo. I am putting my faith in you."

22

DURING THEIR FLIGHT TO SARDINIA, Timon and Yinka did not utter a single word to each other. Yinka was engrossed in one of her books. Timon slotted his AirPods into his ears, listening to his favourite 90s R'n'B songs as he studied the documents about Afchain that Joshua had provided. But the peace between them would prove temporary. They were soon bickering once they landed at Olbia Costa Smeralda Airport.

"I don't see why we can't just order an Uber," Timon said. With his Ray Ban sunglasses on, he sat on a marble seat outside the airport's arrival zone. It was currently 5.45 pm in Costa Smeralda. The sky was a cloudless Maya blue, and the sultry temperature was 30 degrees. The heat provided a pleasant warmth that felt great on Timon's skin.

"You need to clean the earwax from your ears because why do I keep repeating myself?" Yinka said, standing by the edge of the pavement looking for a specific car—a turquoise Fiat 600 Multipla minivan. "We already have a contact who will collect us from the airport. So we need to wait for him."

"Yeah, but he's late."

Timon huffed as Yinka ignored him and continued to scan the road.

"Look, I can see his minivan approaching. Now, can you stop giving me a headache with your constant moaning?"

Timon stood from the seat and joined Yinka by her side. Indeed, a turquoise Fiat minivan, which looked like it had time travelled from the sixties, was driving in their direction from the end of the road. As the vehicle got closer, the driver became more visible. He was a black man, no older than his mid-20s, and wore a green Hawaiian shirt and a straw trilby hat. There was a massive smile on his face as he waved at Yinka. Timon figured that Kebba was the driver of the minivan—the contact on the ground.

"We're seriously getting in that?" Timon asked Yinka as they dragged their suitcases towards the minivan now parked a few feet away.

"Oh, I am sorry it's not a Lamborghini," Yinka said, laying the sarcasm very thick. "But feel free to walk. It will only take you around seven hours." Yinka gave Timon a sharp side-eye.

"Sorry, I am late. But, *oh my God*, it's so good to see you again, Yinka!" Kebba squealed with a loud explosion of flamboyancy as he exited the minivan and practically threw himself onto Yinka for a hug. Timon instantly suspected that Kebba was either gay or extremely metrosexual.

"And you look absolutely stunning babe, I must say," Kebba said. He pressed his lips together and looked Yinka up and down as if he were tailoring a dress for her. "You've certainly put on weight since we last met, but in a good way. Fills you out. Must be all that jollof rice and pounded yam."

"Oh, I have missed you too much, Kebba," Yinka said, broadly smiling as she held onto Kebba's waist. "How's your mother?"

"She's fine and recovering from her tumour surgery back in my village in Gambia." Kebba now looked like he was close to tears. "I can't thank you and your team enough for paying the medical bills for her operation in the States. If not for what you did, she would have died."

Although Timon did not say anything when Kebba said this, he noted it mentally. *Paying for medical bills?* The more information that came to light about what Yinka's team did, the more Timon was convinced that they were more than just business consultants. What else was Yinka concealing from him?

"And this is Timon," Yinka said, looking at him as she introduced him to Kebba. "He's acting as a crypto consultant for my team."

"Damn, you look like Will Smith. But the Men In Black era of Will Smith. Not the Oscar slap era of Will Smith," Kebba said, shaking Timon's hand.

Timon chuckled. He had to admit that Kebba was a like-able character already. "I'll take that as a long-winded compli-ment. Nice to meet you, man."

Five minutes later, Timon and Yinka had hurled their luggage into the minivan's boot and headed to their accom-modation. Yinka sat in the minivan's passenger seat, while Timon sat in the back.

As Kebba drove through the Sardinian highway, speaking about how he had left Gambia a year ago to become a leading chef at a restaurant in Porto Cervo to support his family back home, Timon admired the lush, rocky canyons, the golden beaches and the sparkling blue bays which stretched into the sparkling ocean. Although he was here for a job, Timon couldn't help but feel like he was on holiday. His focus on the beautiful views was interrupted when Kebba asked Yinka a question that surprised him.

"So, how's your boyfriend? You are still dating Oge, right?"

"Yeah… we're still together," Yinka said, sounding oddly sheepish.

"You didn't tell me you had a boyfriend?" Timon said, looking at Yinka with an amusing smirk.

"Oh yeah, they've been dating for a long time," Kebba said, oblivious to Yinka's disapproving shake of her head. "They were childhood sweethearts who grew up in Nigeria together but rekindled their love as adults. Gosh, it's so help-lessly romantic. They are the melanin, Bonnie and Clyde."

"Excuse me, that's enough about my personal life, Kebba," Yinka said, who now seemed flustered. "And Oge is doing fine. He's back in Nigeria." She turned around to look back at Timon. There was a scowl on her face. "And I don't need to tell you about my personal life. I haven't asked you about your fiancée."

"You know about her?"

"How could I not? A member of my team showed me your eye-rolling wedding proposal, which was shared all over social media, when we were trying to contact you." Yinka sniggered. "Your fiancée looks like a small girl, but it's no surprise you like them young and dumb."

The snarky tone in Yinka's voice and the disrespectful manner in which she had just spoken about his future wife deeply angered Timon. She was lucky Kebba had spoken before Timon could call her out on it.

"It's a shame Oge isn't here. Porto Cervo is a beautiful getaway for couples, especially at this time of the year when all the rich types dock their big, expensive boats and bring all the glamour and glitz. I once served Geroge Clooney at the restaurant."

After forty minutes of driving, Kebba finally arrived at the Cervo Hotel. As Timon stepped out of the minivan, his first thought was that Porto Cervo was a magnificently gorgeous Italian seaside resort. Around him, he saw sun-washed stucco buildings with red terracotta tiled roofs and Spanish-style archi-tecture. The beautiful columns and arches gave the rural village a strong Mediterranean aura. From where he stood, Timon could also see the harbour on the horizon, with its glistening, clear waters and small boats anchored to the marina—even the air smelt of fresh water. Timon sighed longingly. If only he were visiting this Italian paradise with his wife-to-be rather than sharing a hotel suite with the insufferable Yinka Saraki.

Once Timon and Yinka had removed their luggage from the minivan, Kebba handed them their paper invitations to Silvio Mancini's yacht party tomorrow evening. After giving them both big hugs, Kebba bid them farewell for now. He would return tomorrow to drive them to Waterfront Costa Smeralda, where Mancini's superyacht was moored.

Two Italian hotel porters took their luggage as Timon and Yinka reached the reception to check themselves into the deluxe suite Joshua had booked.

"Vorremmo fares il check-in, per favore," Yinka said in fluent Italian to the female receptionist at the quaint, white-plastered reception.

Timon jerked his head back and stared at Yinka in shock. "You can speak Italian?" He was grudgingly impressed.

Yinka smiled wryly at Timon. "I speak several European languages. What can I say? I am not just a woman from Nigeria. I am a woman of the world." She winked at him.

As the receptionist handed Timon and Yinka the card keys to access their hotel suite, Timon stood back and watched Yinka saunter ahead of him. *Just who is this woman, really?* His eyes trailed Yinka briefly before he left the reception desk and followed her to the elevator.

The double suite where Timon and Yinka were staying was exquisite as it was instantly homely. The white adobe living room went well with the maritime white furniture, the cream-coloured curtains and the dark brown tiled flooring. There was a wooden square table with a fruit bowl and a widescreen television perched on top of an in-built alcove cabinet facing the cream sofa. An outdoor terrace provided a scenic view of the hotel's outdoor pools, footbridges and marina. The hotel parlours had already delivered Timon and Yinka's luggage, which stood in the middle of the living room.

"The king room is mine. Called it first," Yinka said as she gripped the handle of her suitcase. "I am going to take a nice, warm shower, read and then sleep. Please try not to play any loud music."

"You don't need to speak to me as if I am a child," Timon said aggressively, furrowing his brow. "I am a 30-year-old man who has done very well in life. I am not some small boy to you. Also, watch how you speak about my fiancée. You were very rude earlier. Now that we're business partners, you should treat me with some respect, Yinka. Is that understood?"

It looked as though Yinka was about to fire her retort but decided against it at the last second. Instead, she pierced her eyes at Timon. "I'll see you in the morning," she said coldly. Without saying anything else, Yinka wheeled her suitcase into the king-sized room and slammed the door shut.

Timon let out an irritable sigh. "This trip is going to be a lot of fun, I can just tell," he grumbled as he marched over to his suitcase to it room.

* * *

The following morning, after Timon had a one hour Skype call with Orisa in his room, he joined Yinka on their shared balcony. The beautiful weather washed their opulent surroundings in a tropical filter, and the slight breeze was a satisfying counterbalance to the blazing sun.

Yinka, dressed in a brown tiger-striped mini-cover-up dress and straw sun hat, sat by the round marble table on one of the wooden chairs. With sunglasses on, she was, as usual, reading a book. As he walked past her, Timon remembered her being a bookworm, even at school.

"Good morning," Yinka said without looking up from her book as Timon sat opposite her. "I ordered us some breakfast. Help yourself."

Timon looked at the white tray on the round table. There were plates of toast, pineapple slices, pastries, tea bags, a box of Lavazza ground coffee, a jug of milk, and a metal kettle with hot water. Not feeling too hungry at the moment and deciding he would have a big lunch at one of the fancy restaurants in the resort, Timon opted for a simple croissant and a slice of pineapple.

As Timon bit into the fresh and juicy fruit, he heard Yinka sigh loudly from across the table.

"I am sorry about what I said about your fiancée yesterday," Yinka said in a flat voice and without peeling her eyes away from her book. "I don't know her, so I shouldn't have made those remarks."

Feeling a little smug now, Timon swallowed the chunk of pineapple he was chewing before he responded. "I accept your apology."

"I saw a red suit on the sofa," Yinka continued, swiftly changing the subject and still not looking up from her book. "Is that what you plan to wear to Mancini's yacht party tonight?"

"Yes, that's what I am wearing. Do you have a problem with that?"

Yinka did not answer but continued to concentrate on her book.

"So, what are you reading?" Timon asked after wolfing down a croissant, one of the most delicious croissants he had ever eaten.

"A book."

Timon shook his head hopelessly. "Bloody hell, you're so difficult. We're business partners on this trip. And guess what? Business partners engage in casual convo. It's necessary for a productive and harmonic working relationship, didn't you know?"

Yinka let out an impatient sigh, closed her book and placed it on the table. Finally, she looked at Timon. "I am reading a book which explores and examines Robert Mugabe's life as Zimbabwe's ruler for 37 years."

"Interesting. Any reason in particular as to why you're so interested in Mugabe's life?"

"There's no particular reason. I like to understand the minds of powerful men." Yinka grinned at Timon, removed her sunglasses and placed them on the table. She then took a white teacup from the breakfast tray, put a tea bag inside it, and poured hot water from the kettle. "Can I now ask you a question, *business partner*?" She pressed her dark lips against the base of the teacup and sipped her brew.

"Of course you can. So long as you're not rude when you ask it."

"OK, so to prepare for this business trip, I have been doing my homework on crypto. I've read various online articles about blockchain and watched YouTube videos explaining NFTs, tokens and airdrops. I am not an expert like you are, but I understand the basics of crypto now. But I want to understand something about you. Why did you quit a lucrative career at a big investment firm to become a crypto investor?"

Timon flashed Yinka a grin. "Because crypto is the future of money. I made a calculated gamble in my early twenties and invested in bitcoin very early when I heard much online excitement about it. All this was well before crypto went mainstream. It paid off, and I made big financial gains quite quickly. So I quit my job as an investment analyst and started by own crypto-focused hedge fund. And now I am a rich black man." Timon smirked at Yinka. "A modern day fairytale."

Yinka chuckled lightly at Timon's joke and he found her laugher cute. She then leaned forward, her face serious. "Do you think crypto is the future of money? Care to elaborate?"

Timon leaned back on his wooden chair, smirking at Yinka.

"*Please,* could you elaborate," Yinka said, rolling her eyes.

Satisfied, Timon nodded. "OK, hear me out," he said, craning forward as he spoke, excited to impart his knowledge to a keen audience. "The financial system we have now is rigged. Always has been. Cryptocurrencies, powered by blockchain technology, as you know, give the power and freedom of money back to the people. Back to us." Timon took a bite out of another sliced pineapple on his plate before he continued to speak.

"All these banks that manage our money, they are eating out of us with these bullshit interest rates, these sneaky money transfer fees, and just printing money whenever the economy needs a booster shot. But cryptocurrencies cuts out all of that crap. They are finite, unlike paper money, so they have real value. It's also decentralised, so people can trade with other people without needing banks. No middlemen means no paying additional fees for someone to handle our own money or control our money. Your crypto coins are yours alone, as they live on the blockchain and can't ever be altered. And the value of a true cryptocurrency is determined by the people who use it and the services who accept it. It's unregulated and based on trust. That's how money is supposed to work."

Yinka nodded but was stroking her chin now. "But if we have an unregulated financial system, then these cryptocurrencies, which live on this blockchain, can be used for criminal purposes," she said, looking at Timon. "Think about it. Corrupt people can hide their illegal money through crypto because no regulatory body oversees it. Like this Afchain technology we're making a strong investment case for, it could all be a front to help criminals launder their money."

Timon nodded. "That's very true, but that's why safeguards are in place—identification and all that. Blockchain and crypto are not perfect yet, but what new technology is?"

"Well, let's hope you can convince these private bankers that crypto is the future of money in Africa."

Timon chuckled. "I am a Nigerian man, aren't I? Being very convincing is my superpower."

Timon managed to force a smile out of Yinka for the first time on this trip, brightening her face. She was an unquestionably attractive woman when she was not overly snarky and supercilious.

"I am going for a walk around the town to think about how we're going to get a private audience with Silvio Mancini tonight to pitch Afchain," Yinka said as she stood from her chair. "We'll have a call later this evening with my team to discuss logistics at the yacht party." Yinka picked up her book on Mugabe and her sunglasses and walked away from the table. Before she stepped into the hotel suite parlour, she looked back at Timon. Now she was doing that grating thing again where she looked at you as if you were an imbecile. "And I strongly suggest you rethink your attire for tonight. We're not going to a Michael Jackson-themed fancy dress party."

Timon glared at Yinka, rattled by her disparaging remark. But before he could launch a passionate defence for his choice of evening ware, Yinka stepped out of the terrace and left their hotel suite.

23

Many Nigerian women Yinka knew in Lagos, who lived in their wealthy father's gated mansions in Ikoyi or drove their expensive sports cars through Lekki, would have fallen in love with Porto Cervo. The piazza had a boutique brand on every corner, from Valentino to Gucci to Louis Vuitton. But Yinka, being an unconventional and bookish Nigerian woman, was utterly disinterested in these emporiums of luxury. While Yinka herself owned a Gucci bag and other expensive accessories, paid for by the corrupt African men she had beguiled and then blackmailed - and she would be lying if she said it did not feel nice to have these possessions - wealth in and of itself had never really meant much to her, not in the way it practically defined many Nigerian women's sense of self.

So it was with boredom that Yinka strolled through Porto Cervo's town centre, which was quieter than expected. She had visited Italy before when she and Oge had travelled to Venice for a romantic sojourn two years ago, so she was hoping to fall in love with Porto Cervo similarly. But in this particular part of Italy, the majestic and beautiful grandiosity that enchanted Venice was oddly absent. Porto Cervo had a surface-level and synthetic beauty. It was all about the money and the glamour here.

After strolling around the piazza for ten minutes, watching wealthy Italians walk into boutique shops or eat at the swanky cafes and restaurants, Yinka decided to venture into another part of the town. She walked another ten minutes to the old port to see the docked floating mansions. Fortunately, the port had more of the scenic vibe that Yinka preferred. Walking along the promenade, she discovered a nice outdoor bar and restaurant, Nikki Beach, where young holidaymakers were sunbathing in swimsuits, frolicking in the clear waters or eating fresh seafood.

In her heavily accented Italian, surprising the bartender, Yinka ordered a gin and tonic at the outdoor bar. Preferring to stand and enjoy her pricey cocktail, which cost almost 25 euros, Yinka took in the views. She was mesmerised by the white sand and the shimmering, practically crystallised surface of the coast. If only she were here with Oge and not that big-headed Timon Bakare.

Yinka took a sip of her beverage and sighed deeply. The significance of tonight's party weighed on her mind, heavy as the anchors holding these superyachts on the port. It had taken a lot of phone calls, emails, favours and money wire transfers, in the thousands of Euros, to gain access to Mancini's super exclusive gathering of wealthy socialites. If Yinka and the rest of the Robin Hoods could not find a way for her and Timon to have a private conference with Mancini for at least ten minutes at the party, then it would have been a wasted trip, one they could not afford to squander. Oge's life hung in the balance.

An older caucasian man who looked to be in his late fifties strolled towards the outdoor bar. Wearing a pink, long-sleeved linen shirt, brown cargo pants and Gucci sandals, he came over the counter and stood next to Yinka. She turned to look at the man. He had silver, gelled-back hair, deep blue eyes, like sapphires, and a chiselled jawline with a boxed beard in the same greyish colour as his hair. Despite the man's age, he had broad shoulders, a good posture and the disposition of someone used to being an important man in a room full of important people.

"I am tempted to order what you're drinking," the man said, turning to Yinka and flashing his snow-white, straight teeth. He had an easy smile and spoke with an accent befitting a British politician.

Yinka gave him a wink. "It's only a gin and tonic with lemon and ice. A simple cocktail."

"A simple cocktail, perhaps, but not necessarily a lesser one for it," he said, returning Yinka's wink with his own. Yinka instantly found the older gentleman charming with his upper-class English temperament. He was channelling strong Colin Firth vibes with a sprinkle of that Daniel Craig edge.

"Take your dress, for example. One could say it's simple but no less elegant, which you pull off with aplomb."

"Well, you've made a good first impression of yourself," Yinka said with a faint chuckle.

"Fortunately, for both of us, you met me on fine form today," the man said as he stretched out his hand for Yinka to shake. He had a shrewd smile across his face. "My government name is Sir Richard Dugard, but we can both agree that's far too posh and pretentious, so I'll shorten it to Richard or Dugard. For simplicity. And yourself?"

"Yinka Saraki," Yinka said, shaking Dugard's hand.

There was a glint of recognition in Dugard's eyes when Yinka gave her name. "Saraki. Ah, so you are Yoruba?"

Yinka raised her eyebrows, completely blindsided. "Yes, I am. Now that's impressive. I did not expect you to know Saraki is a Yoruba name."

Dugard called the bartender over and ordered his gin and tonic. "Do you want another drink?" he asked, looking at Yinka with a pleased-with-himself grin.

"I am OK for now. But thank you."

"I have a very strong connection to Nigeria, "Dugard said. He shuffled closer to Yinka as he held the whiskey glass with the gin and tonic he had ordered. "Both personally and professionally."

"Is that so?" Yinka took a long sip of her cocktail.

"Yes, my great grandfather, Sir Rupert Dugard, had been the Governor of Lagos from 1825-1829, during the British colonial era. My grandfather and then my father had capitalised on their ties to Nigeria, becoming successful businessmen in Lagos, Abuja and some northern states. Before his passing, my father had cultivated strong friendships with Aguiyi-ironsi, Gowon, Murtala and Obasanjo. And as for me, a few years ago now, I was the High Commissioner to Nigeria for the British government. I held the position for five years."

It was an impressive resume, Yinka thought to herself. "Wow, you would have strong grounds to call yourself a Nigerian, seeing as you're so connected to my homeland."

"Funny you should say that. At the time, the Yoruba chiefs used to refer to my great-grandfather as *Oba Dugard*. Perhaps I should resurrect that title. What do you think?"

Yinka chuckled. "Well, I am not the daughter of any Yoruba chief. You certainly don't need my blessing."

"Well, you, my dear, resemble Yoruba royalty."

"You may have the face of an English gentleman, but you have the smooth tongue of a Yoruba man," Yinka said, giving Dugard a Duchenne smile. She was enjoying this entertaining dance of benign flirtation.

"I am going to finish this cocktail before I decide if that's a good thing," Dugard said with a knowing smirk. "So, if I may be so inquisitive, what brings you to the emerald coasts of northern Sardinia?"

"I am here with my business partner to promote a blockchain company. We're seeking investment."

"Ah, I see," Dugard said, levelling his eyes on Yinka as he

sipped his cocktail. "I am a qualified private banker for a few wealthy people, shall we say. Many of my clients have spoken to me about crypto. I understand the gist of it, but I would love to hear more about this blockchain company of yours. What is it called?"

For the next ten minutes, drawing as best she could from her rudimentary understanding of cryptocurrencies, blockchain, and decentralised finance, Yinka gave Dugard an overview of Afchain.

"It sounds like a truly disruptive technology," Dugard said after Yinka had finished her short pitch. "Cryptocurrencies have yet to penetrate West African markets at scale, but this new platform you've described could open up the world of digital currencies and decentralised finance to millions of Nigerians and beyond. I see the potential in it. It's a shame I can't invest right now, but I know a few people who could."

"Oh? Well, it must be fate that brought you to me then," Yinka said, smiling at Dugard. She finished her cocktail with a final sip through her straw and placed the whiskey glass on the bar.

"Perhaps you're right. I am attending a party tonight on one of these behemoth yachts called The Mangano. The gathering is hosted by a good friend and fellow banker, Silvio Mancini. He is the owner of the yacht. As your luck would have it, he has recently spoken about getting into the crypto space somehow."

Yinka felt like her heart had done several somersaults. "Well, I think our paths were meant to cross today. I have an invitation to that very same yacht party tonight."

"Looks like I was right to follow my gut feeling and come and speak to you," Dugard said, flashing those pearly whites alongside his confident smile. "When you arrive at the yacht, come to the upper deck, and I will come and find you. I'll introduce you to Silvio. He would love to hear about Afchain. Better yet, why don't you take my contact details."

Feeling in much better spirits now that the universe had dropped a solution to her Mancini problem, Yinka cheerfully added Dugard's number to her iPhone.

"It should be quite the party tonight," Dugard said, looking at the young women who had thrown themselves into the sea. "Silvio seems to know everyone who is rich and lives in Europe, from Hollywood stars to Russian oligarchs. Expect a lavish affair where everyone dresses to the nines."

Yinka smiled at Dugard. "Speaking of well-dressed people, do you know where I could find a nice shop for men's suits? It's for my business partner; he forgot to pack a suitable suit for tonight. I did see an Armani shop on my way here, but maybe you know a tailor?"

"Honestly, dear, where would you be if you did not meet me this fine morning?" Dugard said, shaking his head amusingly at Yinka. "As luck would have it, I know a tailor not too far from here. A skilled man with impeccable craftsmanship. If you know the measurements, he can tailor a suit with a same-day turnaround. Of course, he'd charged a hefty premium, but it would just take a few hours."

"Money is not an issue for me, and I know the measurements. Please take me to your tailor."

24

"THIS IS EXCELLENT NEWS, YINKA," Joshua said from the screen on Yinka's MacBook. "This development is what we needed."

Timon stood behind Yinka, who sat on one of the wooden chairs on the balcony with her MacBook placed on the marble table. It was late afternoon, and the sky had begun to fade to dusk. Timon and Yinka were having their conference call with the rest of Yinka's team back in Shoreditch. Yinka had just updated them about this posh English gentleman she had met in town, Sir Richard Dugard, who had agreed with Yinka to arrange a private audience with Silvio Mancini at his yacht party tonight.

"We've sent you both a WhatsApp message with all the details of nearly everyone invited to tonight's party, including photos," Montana said, standing next to Joshua. "Familiarise yourself with them so it's easier to start a conversation. Try not to get too crazy over any celebrities."

"And word of caution," Kisi said, squeezing into the frame. "Be wary of this Mancini guy, Yinka. I've read some stories about him online. He's a predator apparently and has a taste for young women."

Yinka shrugged. "Powerful, rich men with busy hands is nothing I haven't handled before."

Hearing this, Timon furrowed his brow in confusion but said nothing. It was just another piece of evidence he filed in his brain.

"Good luck, alright," Jaali said somewhere offscreen. "Ya'll got this."

Yinka ended the call. She stood from her chair and faced Timon. "I will start getting ready, as I need to wash my hair and do my makeup. I am also taking out my braids, which takes a while. Please do some homework on Mancini. It makes sense to understand the man you'll be convincing to part with three million pounds."

"Don't worry about what I have to do. Just watch me in action tonight as I work my magic."

Yinka rolled her eyes and walked into the living room, her MacBook by her side. "Oh, by the way, you've got a surprise coming."

Timon raised his eyebrows at her. "What'd you mean I have a surprise?"

As if on cue, there was a knock on the front door.

"You should go get that," Yinka said aloud, walking into her bedroom.

Intrigued, Timon left the terrace, bopped into the living room, and went to the front door. When he opened it, to his bemusement, one of the hotel porters was standing in front of him. In his right hand, he was holding a suit carrier.

"I have a suit here for Mr. Baka...ka," the hotel porter began, scrunching his face as he struggled to pronounce Timon's surname from the card he was reading from his other hand.

"Yeah, don't give yourself a haemorrhage, mate; it's for me," Timon said, taking the suit carrier from the hotel porter's hand. "Cheers."

Timon slammed the door shut before the hotel porter

could say, "My pleasure," and walked into the living room. He placed the suit carrier on the cream-coloured sofa and unzipped it. Inside was a complete tuxedo set: a u-neck waist-coat, a black dinner jacket, a white marcella-bib evening shirt, a black bow tie, and pleated front trousers.

Fuming, Timon whipped his head in the direction of Yinka's room. "Why would you order me a tux?" he shouted. "You know I already have a suit for tonight."

Yinka appeared at the doorway of her room, wearing a white bathroom robe and a white towel wrapped around her forehead. "Look, Timon, you won't embarrass me tonight by wearing that ketchup-coloured monstrosity you call a suit. We'll be rubbing shoulders and eating caviar with some of the richest people in Europe. So I need you to look like a man who deserves to be among such prestigious indi-viduals."

Timon's mouth hung open in utter disbelief at her audac-ity. *Who does she think she is*? "Firstly, that 'ketchup-coloured red suit' cost me just under a grand. And it's from Saville Row, just so you know," Timon said, grinding his teeth as he glowered at Yinka. "Secondly, I am trying to make a statement tonight. Be bold. Make an entrance. That way, those rich people on that yacht will take notice of an accomplished black man."

Yinka let out an exasperated sigh. "Why do so many black men who have money always feel the need to make a show of it? Be the loudest in the room? You can communicate your status and wealth without turning yourself into an exhibition. There is sophistication in keeping it simple."

"Whatever," Timon said, shaking his head and not caring for a single word she had said. "And besides, this suit you've ordered for me is tailored."

"Yes, I know that. I've sized you up. You're basically the same height and width as my boyfriend." Yinka sighed. "Look, at least try it on. If you hate it, I'll give it to my boyfriend as a gift, and you can wear your Heinz ketchup suit. Deal?"

Timon snorted loudly. In a huff, he took the suit carrier from the sofa and went to his room. As deeply offended as he was by Yinka's actions, he was admittedly intrigued to see how he looked in the tuxedo.

And Yinka was right. He looked damn good.

In the shared bathroom, Timon inspected himself in the full-length mirror. The tuxedo fit was impeccable, and the dinner jacket and trousers wrapped nicely around his athletic figure, making him look taller and leaner. When he completed the attire with the bow tie, Timon knew he couldn't deny the truth in the mirror's reflection. The look was the chief's kiss. The tuxedo was much better than his red suit, he had to acknowledge grudgingly, and he would be keeping it – and wearing it tonight.

Yinka had come to watch him try on the tuxedo. She stood at the bathroom doorway as Timon inspected himself in the mirror, adjusting his bow tie. From the mirror, he saw her beam at him admiringly. To Timon's surprise, Yinka's approval made him like the tuxedo even more.

"Look how dapper you look," Yinka said, arms folded across her bathroom robe. "Very handsome."

Timon turned his whole body around to face her, feigning shock. "Do my ears deceive me? Did you call me handsome?" he said with a mischievous smile. "So you've finally noticed."

"Simmer down," Yinka said, waving her right hand at him playfully with a grin. "It's just a compliment. I didn't say you were the Nigerian Chris Brown."

An hour later, after showering and putting on his Tom Ford aftershave, Timon went to the resort's front car park, where Kebba was waiting to drive them to the Waterfront Costa Smeralda marina. Yinka had spent almost two hours taking out her braids, but now she needed to complete the complex ritual of applying makeup and foundation to her face, so Timon left her to it.

When Timon walked out of the hotel to meet with Kabba, the Gambian chef thankfully had the good sense not to have driven in that shabby minivan. Instead, he was leaning on the bonnet of a BMW i7. The electric vehicle had a sleek carbon black metallic finish that would make James Bond blush.

"Come on, *fresh prince,* you didn't seriously expect me to pull up to a yacht party in that ancient relic," Kebba said after he had hugged Timon. "I would never subject Yinka, you or even myself to such embarrassment. Shame is not free here."

Timon stood beside Kebba as he pulled on a cigarette. They were both standing by the car's bonnet. Now that they were both alone, waiting for Yinka, Timon sought answers to his lingering questions.

"Can I ask a question? A few, actually?" Timon said, looking at Kebba.

Kebba blew a whisp of smoke into the evening air as he dangled his cigarette between two fingers. "Ask away, my fellow, melanated brother."

"When you picked Yinka and me up from the airport yesterday, you said she and her team helped you pay your mother's medical bills. How exactly?"

"Oh, they embezzled money from a corrupt government politician in Gambia who was pocketing taxes and used some of it to pay for my mother's medical costs in the States." Kebba's mouth curved into a thoughtful smile. "That's what the Robin Hoods do. Steal from the rich assholes and give to the poor souls."

"The Robin Hoods?" Timon raised his eyebrows.

"Yep, that's what Yinka and her team are informally known as in many parts of West Africa where they've oper-ated. They've helped many downtrodden Africans who have been victims of corruption, forgotten by those in power meant to serve them."

"And the leader of the Robin Hoods is Yinka's boyfriend, Oge, right?

Kebba took another pull on his cigarette and nodded. "Yep, that's right. He's a mixed-race man. I believe he's half Nigerian and half English and resembles that Jidenna singer quite a lot. But Oge has a nasty scar on his face. But he's a good man. Very handsome, even with that scar, but very intense, though."

Timon pursed his lips, digesting this information. So his suspicions were correct—Yinka and the others back in Shoreditch were not business consultants but some Robin Hood-inspired blackmailers and extortionists. That being the case, why did they need Timon's help securing investment for Afchain? And why wasn't Yinka's boyfriend with them? These questions, floating in Timon's mind like clouds, were dissolved when Kebba asked him a question.

"So, how did you get entangled with Yinka and her merry crew of good-natured thieves?"

"I wouldn't say I am entangled with them. I am just a consultant for them on this one occasion. It's more of a 'I'll-scratch-your-back-if you-scratch-mine' sort of arrangement."

Kebba nodded. "Ah, one of those. But do you and Yinka have some history? It's obvious you two had something going on in the past. I could feel the energy between you two heating up around me in my minivan."

Timon chuckled. "It's not like that. I knew her briefly when we went to the same secondary school back in the UK, but I didn't like her at all, and she didn't like me. But in the end, she got the last laugh."

"What'd you mean by that?"

Just as Timon parted his lips to answer Kebba's question, his focus was snatched away by the sight of Yinka walking out of the hotel lobby and towards them, holding a silver clutch bag by her waist. For a good few seconds, Timon's jaw remained slack, as if he were on drugs.

Sporting a long, flowing and high-quality black wig instead of braids, Yinka looked enchanting. Sashaying effortlessly on black stilettos, she wore a sleeveless, off-shoulder, bodycon sequin black dress, which her figure poured into. Silver tassels hung from the neckline and dangled down Yinka's shoulders like she was a Moulin Rouge showgirl. The shiny, disk-shaped ornaments that decorated her dress twinkled like stars against the backdrop of a moonlight canvas, and Yinka's dark complexion gave off an ethereal glow.

"You look…you look beautiful," Timon said, the words stumbling out of his mouth as Yinka stopped before him and Kebba.

"Thank you. You can pick your jaw up from the floor now." Yinka smirked playfully.

Timon shook his head, snapping out of the mental haze triggered by Yinka's disarming beauty. "It's just a compliment," he said as nonchalantly as possible, trying to sound unbothered but unsure if he had succeeded.

Kebba, who had placed his left knuckle in his mouth once he saw Yinka, removed his hand from his mouth. "Yinka, babe, if I had an ass and hips like yours, I'd slay in your dress. Listen, you put a beautiful black woman in a dress like that; she's going to make a lot of husbands drool and a lot of wives pissed. Gurl, you should come with a warning sign."

"Kebba, please don't make me die of laughter this evening," Yinka said, smacking Kebba playfully on the shoulder. She looked at Timon. "Shall we?"

Timon nodded. "I am ready when you are, *business partner*."

Yinka flashed him a grin.

Timon helped Yinka into the backseat of the car, holding her hand and then closing the door once they sat inside.

Kebba gave them a warning when he stuck the key into the ignition.

"Don't scratch the seats. I am pretending to be a valet, and I think this car belongs to a Russian guy, and I don't want my head caved in by one of Putin's thugs. So please be extra careful."

With that, Kebba started the powerful electric car and drove towards the waterfront, where the coast was shrouded in darkness, and a lavish yacht party was raging on its shores.

25

Over the years, Timon had been invited to his fair share of yacht parties by his super-minted clients. But those cruise ships paled in comparison to The Mangano.

At 140 feet, The Mangano was an engineering marvel with four decks, a sleek exterior coated in the elegant whiteness of a swan, glazed windows, and an aerodynamic shape—a mansion on the sea. It was clear to Timon that Silvio Mancini was an obscenely wealthy man. If you wanted to swig your rich balls around in everyone's faces, having a big boat like this was the way to do it. \

After handing their invitations to the smartly dressed security guards and being thoroughly frisked, cabin crew members escorted Timon and Yinka to the sun deck.

About twenty eloquently dressed guests were schmoozing, many with a wine glass in their hands. Men wore their finest suits, and Timon spotted a few Rolex, Patek Phillipe and Richard Mille timepieces. Women had expensive evening gowns and jewellery, with more than a few clutching Birkin, Hermes and Louis Vuitton bags. Barely dressed female fire breathers were providing pyrotechnic entertainment, blowing balls of intensely bright flaming balls into the night sky, much to the delight and awe of the distinguished guests.

As Timon expected, having seen the guest list, most attendees were white and European. However, he spotted a dark-skinned woman with a slender frame and a long neck talking with an older white gentleman in a bowler hat. Timon recognised her as a world-famous model.

While standing by the polished, stainless steel guardrails, with Yinka by his side, Timon noticed another black person by the open bar a few feet away, a man. He was tall, more than six foot, maybe in his late forties, with a clean-shaven head, a square jawline, upturned eyes, and a rugby player's physique. Despite his muscular build, Timon knew this mysterious black man was not security as he was dressed too fashionably in an Italian style navy blue suit with a black tie.

The man's eyes met Timon's for a second, but there was no acknowledgement between them. The man turned away from Timon to look at the jacuzzi in the middle of the deck. Three young women had decided to strip themselves down to their bras and underwear. They jumped into the jacuzzi, eliciting the older guests' judgemental frowns and disapproving head shakes.

"Who do you think that guy is?" Timon said, leaning towards Yinka and nodding towards the muscular, well-dressed black man by the bar. "I don't remember seeing him on the guest list your team sent us."

Yinka looked at the man at the bar for a second and turned away, unbothered. "Does it really matter?" she said. "Focus, alright. Dugard is walking to us now."

"How utterly delightful to see you again, Yinka," Dugard said as he took Yinka's left hand and planted a kiss on the front of her palm.

Dugard, who looked like your quintessential English gentleman in a black double-breasted suit with matching trousers and a bowler hat, turned his attention onto Timon.

"And you must be Timon Bakare, Yinka's business partner. It is a pleasure to meet you. My name is Sir Richard Dugard. But feel free to call me Richard or Dugard. I am not precious about titles." He flicked a smile at Timon.

"A pleasure to meet you, sir," Timon said, shaking Dugard's hand and code-switching to sound more eloquent. Dugard reminded Timon of his hedge fund clients and many of the people he had gone to Cambridge with - white, rich and from old money. Over the years, Timon had learnt how to adapt himself around these denizens of upper-class society who came from a different world to the one he had inhabited in his formative years – a gritty council flat in east London.

"Shall we head down to the master stateroom?" Dugard said, checking his silver Patek Philippe watch. "I'm conscious of time, and I don't want us to miss the small opportunity we have for an audience with Signor Mancini."

Timon and Yinka followed Dugard through the yacht's bridge deck as he led them to Mancini's quarters. Dugard then led them through the spacious, elegant sky longue on the second deck, where other guests congregated and danced to the DJ spinning techno music. After another security guard patted them down, Dugard led Timon and Yinka to Silvio's master suite bedroom on The Mangano's lower deck.

When Dugard turned the bedroom door handle and stepped through, Timon and Yinka were greeted by what looked like Mancini's personal harem. About eight young women were dallying around in tight, skimpy dresses inside the vast, spacious room, the size of Timon's entire living room in his penthouse. There were buckets of champagne on the polished marble tables and some lines of questionable white powder on the smooth tabletops. Grinning at the excessive display of spoilt rich behaviour, Timon, with Yinka by his side, followed Dugard further into the vast master room with its wool carpeting and Persian rug.

Silvio Mancini was sitting on a beige sofa, arms spread

vertically on the backrests. Two young girls in skin-hugging bodycon dresses and wearing heavy mascara sat on either side of him. The first thought that came to Timon's mind when he saw Mancini was that he reminded him of a much older Leonardo DiCaprio, only with long, shoulder-length hair and a face that had gone through one too many rounds of Botox. He was dressed in a white suit jacket, matching trousers, and a slightly unbuttoned black shirt so you could see the white hairs on his chest, like thin whiskers and had brown leather brogues on his feet. On Mancini's right finger, Timon noticed a golden wedding band. *This man is married and lives like this?* Timon thought.

Mancini's eyes glossed over Timon as if he was merely part of the cabin crew; they rested briefly on Dugard but then shifted and stayed on Yinka.

"Is now a good time, Silvio?" Dugard said, standing slightly forward from Timon and Yinka. "These are the two consultants I talked to you about from that crypto company, Afchain, as we discussed earlier. I will give them the grace of introducing themselves." Mancini remained silent, eyes leering on Yinka.

"Ho degli affari da discustere, ragazze mie," Mancini finally said, in a deep Italian accent. When his mouth moved, the rest of his facial features remained stiff like a wax model. "Time to leave, ladies."

Without saying a word, the two young girls, with glazed eyes, looking high or drunk, Timon couldn't tell, stood from the sofa and tottered past Timon, Yinka and Dugard. Timon followed the two young girls with his eyes as they giggled. They looked no older than maybe eighteen or nineteen.

"My friend here," Mancini began, waving his left hand at Dugard as he regarded Timon and Yinka, "says you are seeking investment for a crypto company based in Nigeria." Mancini's thin lips curved into a conceited smirk. "Please convince me as to why I should give a shit?"

Timon cleared his throat, a little unsettled by Mancini's unexpected coarseness. "I will answer your question, Signor Mancini. But firstly, my name is Timon Bakare. I am a crypto hedge manager with years of experience investing in high-yield crypto companies." Timon gestured to Yinka standing beside him. "This is my business partner, Yinka Saraki. Thank you for sparing us some of your time, Signor Mancini. To answer your question, this isn't just any investment." Timon stepped forward and smiled confidently at Mancini. "I don't know how much Dugard has told you, but this is an investment in the future of finance in West Africa, which will only enrich you for years to come. Nigeria alone has over 200 million people, and Afchain's technology will change how Nigerians use money to buy and sell food and services. Just imagine you get a piece of every transaction that Afchain processes. With 200 million people, that will be a lot of transactions. And a lot of money."

"*Interessante*," Mancini said, rubbing his stomach. He leaned back into the sofa's cushions. It was hard for Timon to read Mancini's expression when his face looked like an aged Barbie Ken action figure. "I am familiar with Nigeria's volatile economy. Still, I have invested some money into companies in that part of West Africa, which have proven profitable over time, mostly exporting but no technology business, not yet." Mancini shifted his gaze onto Yinka again, and Timon noticed something flicker in the Italian man's eyes. A leering desire. "Where are you from, signora?"

"I am from Nigeria, signor," Yinka replied.

"*Bellissima*," Mancini said softly, almost purring. He clapped his hands together, appearing fascinated by Yinka. "Your accent is as beautiful as the richness of your skin. Do you think this technology can revolutionise finance in Nigeria or is your business partner sprouting bullshit?"

Timon did his best to stifle his irritation at Mancini's disrespectful dismissal of him.

"Yes, I deeply believe this technology will disrupt the finance industry in Nigeria and other West African countries," Yinka said, meeting Mancini's gaze. "Afchain's technology will remedy several economic challenges facing Nigerian's population by promoting financial inclusion for the poor and providing greater access to capital for businesses and entrepreneurs. The highly user-intuitive platform will be easy to access for millions of Nigerians, unlocking the nation's potential. I do not exaggerate when I say this investment is a once-in-a-lifetime opportunity, Signor Mancini. You don't want to be the man who missed out on what will be Africa's answer to Bitcoin."

Timon turned to look at Yinka, highly impressed by her response. Unfazed by Mancini's vulgarity, she had delivered a calm and collected speech. Considering she was not even a crypto expert, Yinka had spoken about the subject matter with convincing credibility.

Mancini regarded both Timon and Yinka before speaking again. "You are looking for a three million investment, correct?"

Timon nodded. "That's right."

"Well, provide me an investor report on Afchain, including details on who is building it, its core features, and how much I stand to make in three years should I invest." Mancini licked his lips, and Timon saw that amorous tint in his eyes again. He unashamedly examined Yinka's figure. "Then I will give it more thought. As you said, I don't want to be the man who missed out on Africa's bitcoin."

"So, how well do you think that went?" Timon said to Yinka.

Ten minutes ago, the meeting with Silvio Mancini concluded. Yinka and Timon were now in the sky longue, which had turned into a fully-fledged party. Both of them had a cocktail in their hands. Yinka had gone for her usual gin and tonic on the rocks, and Timon had gone for a Hennessy and Coke with ice.

Dugard had left Yinka and Timon about five minutes ago. The three young girls he had brought with him were his nieces and goddaughters. They had taken one too many trips to the open bar and needed to be escorted home. Before he left, he told Timon and Yinka he would be in touch.

"He seems interested, but it's hard to tell with a face made from the same silicon they use on BBLs," Yinka said. She took a sip of her ice-cold cocktail. "But we'll need to present that report to Mancini if we want him to put ink to paper. How long will it take to get an investor report to him?"

"I can mock one up, with both qualitative and quantitative analysis, in three hours," Timon said, swirling his cocktail. "You just text your friend, Joshua, to send screenshots of the Afchain platform that I can include in the report. Mancini will want to see what it looks like."

"Agreed. I'll text Joshua first thing in the morning."

Timon took a sip of his cocktail and looked at Yinka. "Did you see how young those girls looked? The ones sitting beside Mancini before they left? He's a piece of work. And you must have noticed the way he kept dressing you down with his eyes."

Yinka shrugged and took a short sip of her drink. "He's just behaving the way most old rich men behave." She sensed Timon wanted to respond to what she had said but remained silent.

"It's not a bad party," Yinka said, changing the direction of the conversation. "Music could be better, but I doubt the DJ will play any Burna Boy songs."

Timon chuckled. "Yeah, but you can still find a rhythm to it. We should dance."

Yinka looked at Timon incredulously, to which he responded with a chesty laugh. "Don't give me that look," he said, his tone light-hearted. "A dance is not a relationship. I am practically a married man, and you have a boyfriend. But we might as well have some innocent fun at the most exclusive party in Europe."

Yinka sucked her teeth and shook her head. "Would you have asked me for a dance when we were at school together? I remember you and your friends calling me 'freshie', 'darkie', and 'ugly', but now I am *pretty* enough for you to dance with? What's changed, *Timon*?"

Timon looked startled. Yinka took satisfaction knowing she had caught him on the chin with that verbal haymaker.

"Come on, that was years ago. We were kids. Besides, it's not like you didn't get me back. You lied and got me expelled from school. Ruined my life for a year."

"No, *you* ruined *your* own life for a year. You shouldn't have broken the school rules. You and your friends got what you deserved." Yinka raised her lips into a snarky smile. "I don't regret what I did."

Yinka's biting words had extinguished Timon's playful mood. He glared at her. "What's your problem? I am just trying to lighten the mood between us."

"Excuse me? Lighten the mood? I think you must be confused. We're on this Italian island with a clear objective. You don't need to lighten any mood, OK. Just because we're working together now doesn't mean I have forgotten how you and your friends treated me at school, destroying my confidence and mental health when I was just a young girl. I don't want any friendship with you. Understand? Our temporary partnership is strictly business."

Timon nodded stiffly and looked straight ahead at the dance floor with a cold stare. "If that's how you want it between us, then it's cool with me. Anyway, I am going to mingle with some famous people. You're a bit of a vibe killer." Timon left her side and strode onto the dancefloor before going up the metal stairs towards the sun deck.

Yinka took a long swig of her cocktail, finishing it in one

long gulp and slammed the empty rock glass on the bar top with more force than was necessary. She chuckled bitterly and in disbelief at Timon's nerve, asking her for a friendly dance when he had mistreated her so wrongly in the past. And it did not matter how long ago it was; Timon and his friends' campaign of bullying still triggered her. *Typical Nigerian man. No emotional intelligence.*

Timon had so riled her up, it took a second for Yinka to realise Mancini was standing before her. His celluloid face had a tight grin, causing diagonal lines to appear on each side of his nose and under the bridge, making his face look stretched.

"*Balla con me,*" Mancini said in his deep Italian accent and stretched out his hand. He had not asked Yinka to dance with him. He had commanded it.

It did not matter what part of the world you were from. Most old, grey-haired men who possessed great wealth and status were always attracted to one thing—a beautiful young woman who presented a challenge. Yinka knew how to be that woman.

With a faint smile, Yinka took Mancini's hand and let him lead her to the dance floor. Yinka could feel the other guests' eyes on them as Mancini placed his bulky hands on her hips, moving in rhythm with her as the dancehall-influenced and fast-paced reggaeton music blasted from the speakers.

"I see you understand Italian," Mancini said, his lips brushing Yinka's right ear lobe as he glided on the dance floor. Yinka followed him as his right knee slid between her legs. "But I like your Nigerian accent better when you speak English. I love the rhythm of it."

"That's a very nice compliment, Signor Mancini." Yinka smiled at him, but a small one. She could not show too much interest when playing this game. She teased but remained just out of reach.

"This crypto company of yours, Afchain, I see the potential," Mancini said, his hands steadily sliding further down Yinka's back. "But I need more persuasion. Could you personally talk me through the numbers when the report is ready? I prefer doing business with smart women as opposed to men. I tend to find women pay more attention to detail and are much more... hands-on."

Yinka felt Mancini gently squeeze her right buttock and then leave his hand there. In any other circumstances, Yinka would have given him a Nigerian woman's slap that would have sent him spinning like a tipple top, but she was playing a game now, a game she was adept at.

"Let me know the time and place, Signor Mancini."

"11 am tomorrow morning on my yacht. We will go over the finer details in my master room." As he said this, Mancini stared into Yinka's eyes, and she held his gaze. It was all too easy.

"I should go and find my wife," Mancini finally said after dancing with Yinka for five more minutes. He removed his left hand from Yinka's ass.

Yinka nodded courteously. "Of course, Signor Mancini."

"Enjoy the rest of the party, Signorina Saraki."

"*Buona notte*," Yinka said, flashing him a seductive smile, playing into his desires. "I look forward to our meeting tomorrow."

26

At FIRST, Kojo did not give much thought to the stylishly dressed black woman and black man, who looked to be in their late twenties, as they climbed onto the sun deck together.

Standing by the open bar on the yacht's upper deck and dressed in a £300 navy blue Italian suit - courtesy of MI6's generous purse strings - Kojo had a good view of the two black people who had joined the party. They stood a few feet from where he stood at the bar, looking like a very aesthetically compatible couple as they engaged in a private conversation by the steel guardrails. The young black man, in his tailored tuxedo, reminded Kojo of a less muscular and slightly less taller Anthony Joshua, with the same light brown complexion and pretty boy looks. As for the young black woman, she wore a dazzling black dress that twinkled, and she had the envious facial anatomy of a young Naomi Campbell but with a slightly darker complexion.

Kojo and the Anthony Joshua lookalike met each other's eyes across the deck for a split second but said nothing to each other. But quite quickly, Kojo lost interest in the two of them. They weren't important. Or so he thought.

No sooner had Kojo turned away to chuckle at the three young women who had jumped into a pool on the deck in their underwear than he saw Sir Richard Dugard, his primary target for this undercover intelligence mission. Kojo curiously watched as Dugard conversed with the black man and woman. He then gave the woman a gracious kiss on her left hand.

A microscopic camera was built into the dial of Kojo's golden Rolex watch – a costly intelligence collection technology developed by MI6's tech division. It enabled the wearer to capture high-res photos with better quality than the latest smartphones. Kojo took a quick succession of pictures by gently clicking the watch's crown. Now, he had images of Dugard speaking to and then escorting the black man and black woman to the second deck of the yacht.

Making sure he was a few feet behind so they wouldn't notice him, Kojo followed Dugard as the black man and woman walked behind the British aristocrat.

On the main deck of the sprawling yacht, a glass door led to the cabins, the guest hall, and the master room. Two body-guards flanked the door. After patting them down, they let Dugard pass through the door with the black man and the woman.

Kojo hung back in the main deck lobby. He knew he would not have access to the lower decks where Mancini's private room was. But it did not bother him too much. Now that he had these pictures, Kojo would send them to the MI6's intelligence analysts, who would use their advanced facial recognition technology to identify the nameless black man and black woman by crunching through the MI6's expansive database of British citizens. If they weren't British, they were likely Dugard's business associates from Nigeria, given Dugard's close relationship with the country. Either way, given their proximity to Dugard, the black man and black woman had become potential persons of interest to Kojo.

Seeing as he could not do much else now that Dugard was out of sight, Kojo resolved to socialise with the affluent and the wealthy guests. It would be a lie if he said it was not mildly fun schmoozing with celebrities, artists and politicians. Kojo had spoken to a famous black model, who was much more interesting in person than her television interviews suggested. He then spent fifteen minutes debating the ramifications of Brexit with a well-known Italian politician with a strong accent who spoke moderate English. But after thirty minutes, Kojo found all the palavering exhausting - he could pretend to be a social extrovert for only so long. Before midnight, he excused himself from the other guests.

Kojo took a solo superyacht tour, walking along the aft deck. He soon spotted a lady leaning against the yacht's fold-out balcony. She was looking out into the sea. As Kojo approached her, he realised she was an older woman, probably in her early forties, and she immediately commanded his attention. Like the most expensive wine, the woman's beauty was graceful and sophisticated. She wore a champagne-coloured, mermaid hem sequin dress with long split sleeves, a high waistline, and a V-neck headline, which showcased her ample bust. Her long, flowing hair was as black as ink and her skin tone was a light gold brown like the shell of fresh onions. The woman's venetian red lipstick, sexually inviting, drew Kojo to her as if she were a siren of the sea, casting an amorous spell on him.

"It does get boring, doesn't it?" Kojo said as he came beside the woman. He leaned on the metal balcony with his right elbow. "Navigating the egos and pretentiousness of the rich and the privileged. You need a break from the pomposity of it all to appreciate the silent beauty of the sea."

The woman turned her gaze towards him. Her eyes were an emerald green and contained within them the depth, wisdom and sadness of a wealthy woman who had lived a life of both luxury and loneliness.

A short smile formed on the woman's face as she curiously regarded Kojo. "How very poetic, but you're only half right," she said, her accent smothered in an unmistakable Italian cadence that sounded like musical notes to Kojo's ears. "I am also hiding from my insufferable husband. He is frolicking with his young playthings in his private quarters and I have no intention of humouring him tonight. So yes, I have come here to appreciate the tranquillity of the sea and for a brief respite from my marriage." The woman then narrowed her eyes at Kojo, reading him. "What is your name?"

"Steven Hartlett," Kojo said without any hesitancy as he stretched out his left hand for the woman to shake. "I work for the British treasury, so I am here for business just as much as pleasure." Kojo held her gaze.

"Federica Mancini," the woman said, shaking Kojo's hand with her soft fingers before releasing them. "So you are British. When you first approached me, I thought you were African American with your muscular physique."

Kojo chuckled. "Easy mistake to make. People often confuse me with Dwayne Johnson all the time."

Federica chuckled lightly. Her laughter was endearing to Kojo.

"I am sure they do."

"I presume you're the wife of Silvio Mancini?" Kojo noted that Federica was not wearing a wedding ring.

"Please, do not remind me I am married to *that man* tonight," Federica said, a bitter undercurrent in her voice. "I am doing everything in my power to feel like a single woman in her forties who wants to be swept off her feet by an exciting lover, temporarily escaping the loveless marriage to a *pezzo di merda*."

"And how is that going for you?"

Federica blinked slowly, her long eyelashes seeming to suggest something. She gave Kojo a coy smile. "*Vedremo*. The night is still young, but it is improving."

191

"Well, this night would have much more potential to surprise us both if we left this big boat and shared a bottle of expensive Italian wine at my hotel. You know, sweep you off your feet." Kojo let his eyes linger on her lips. He wanted her to notice his attraction to her.

"You certainly don't waste time, do you, Steven?" Federica said, her lips curved into a grin, her eyes on Kojo. "But you've stroked my curiosity, I admit, which is not an easy accomplishment for many men. So, how far is your hotel from here exactly?"

"I am staying at the Grand Hotel. It is about a ten-minute."

There was a moment of silence as Federica stared silently into Kojo's eyes. He knew she was assessing him, feeling him out mentally to determine if tonight would be worth it and, more importantly, safe for her.

Finally, she acquiesced. "Let us get a taxi, but we must be discreet so my husband and tonight's guests do not notice us leaving together." She clasped her fingers around Kojo's left hand. "You better sweep me off my feet tonight, British man."

With the moonlight pouring through the balcony window, Kojo made love to Federica on the soft, king-sized bed in his hotel room.

Being someone who had a sporadic dating life - sex was not a regular occurrence for Kojo - when he had a free night, he would visit bars in Clapham and Soho, his favourite spots for going out in London. Should the night favour him, he would, after much talking and drinking with a pretty lady, who was almost always a mature professional woman, order a taxi back to his flat and have consensual sex. These trysts were always nothing more than one-night stands, but it meant that when he did have a night of passion with a stranger, it was always messy, sloppy and in a haze of drunken stupor. He could barely recall most of the sexual encounters with these women. None of them called him back.

But with Federica Mancini, it was different from the start. The sex had been like slowly undoing a bow on a box of expensive chocolates.

Without saying a word, they undressed each other while occasionally finding and enjoying each other's lips, pulling and sucking. Once they were both naked, Federica gently pushed Kojo onto the mattress, slid down the bed and expertly performed oral fellatio on him. Kojo held onto her forehead, feeling her long, soft hair between his fingers as he enjoyed the sensation of her warm mouth wrapping around his penis. As he felt the rising tension in his shaft, Kojo quietly whispered for her to stop so he could return the favour. In less than a minute, they had switched places and Kojo was gently sucking on her clitoris and the outer lips of her vulva, eliciting quiet, pleasurable gasps from her in the stillness of the room.

Once Kojo had pleasured Federica orally, to the point that she was clutching the bedsheets, he crawled on top of her, and she enthusiastically pushed him deep inside of her. Kojo's thrusts had been slow and steady, as opposed to quick and rushed as they had been with other women, as he wanted to enjoy the warmth and heat of her body. By the time they both climaxed, Kojo was pinning Federica's hands above her head.

After sex, both of them wordlessly cleaned themselves up in the ensuite bathroom. They retired to the bed, where they immediately fell asleep.

The high-pitched sound of Federica's shrieking woke Kojo early the following day. Felix, Kojo's white ragdoll pet cat, had leapt onto the mattress and stretched beside Federica's head before strolling over to Kojo's lap and curling up into a ball, nose to tail. Kojo sat upright and stroked Felix's white fur.

"This is your cat?" Federica said, sitting upright on the bed and lying against the bed's headrest. She was naked with the bedsheet covering her lower torso, but her fulsome, bell-shaped breasts were impressively on display and were even more alluring in the morning light.

"Yes, his name is Felix," Kojo said, smiling down at his pet cat. "He's probably the closest thing I have to a close friend."

Federica chuckled. "I wouldn't have considered you a cat person, let alone someone without many friends. No room for such things in your life?"

"Too busy."

Federica looked at him, regarding him silently, before speaking again. "Is it ok if I smoke?"

Kojo chuckled. "Be my guest but people still smoke? Aren't vapes in fashion?"

Federica's pink lips curved into a grin as her eyes met Kojo's. "Following fashion is boring. Besides, there's something about smoking a cigarette that feels timeless."

Kojo watched as Federica bent down at the edge of the bed to pick up her YSL handbag. She fished into her bag and pulled out a packet of Lucky Strike Original Red and a rose gold Cartier lighter. She lit the cigarette slotted between her lips, took a deep draw, and then exhaled, letting the thin smoke glide from her mouth. Kojo grinned at her.

"Do you want to hear something funny about me?" Federica turned to look at Kojo. The corners of her mouth had bent into a smirk, but one that seemed cynical.

"Well, so long as you find your self-deprecation funny," Kojo said with a wink.

Federica swallowed a laugh. "I don't expect you to recognise me," she said, pulling on her cigarette. "But I am an actress in Italy. I have starred in many independent Italian films financed by my husband. He loves Italian cinema, so he named his yacht The Mangano after his favourite Italian actress, Silvana Mangano. Anyway, do you know what he would demand from movie directors whose films I starred in that he had financed? I was never to have any sex scenes with a *muliganan.* An Italian-American slur for a black man." Federica rolled back her head in maniacal laughter. "If he knew I slept with you last night, *dio mio!* He would, as Americans say, lose his shit."

"So, I am the first black man you've slept with?"

"Yes," Federica said, nodding as she blew wisps of smoke from her lips. "I turned forty last month and this is the first time I have gone to bed with a black man." She gave Kojo a playful smirk. "I should have done it sooner."

"Well, I am honoured to have been your first." Kojo winked at her, and Federica laughed. Even her laugh sounded glamorous, as if only an actress could laugh that way.

After smoking her cigarette and killing it on the ashtray on the bedside table, Federica stretched out her arms, rolled out of the bed, and got to her feet. Kojo, still lying naked on the bed but covered by the bedsheets and stroking Felix, watched as Federica dressed herself.

"I am going to head back now before my wretched husband begins to notice my absence," Federica said, who was now fully clothed and putting on her stiletto heels as she sat at the edge of the bed. Once her heels were on, she stood up from the mattress again and turned to face Kojo. She had a sombre expression. "Thank you for last night, signor Hartlett," she said, biting her lip playfully. "It is a shame we did not get a chance to enjoy the wine."

Kojo chuckled. "We were so eager for each other but I have no regrets." He gave her a cheeky grin. "Did I sweep you off your feet?"

At this, Federica laughed, putting her right hand on her chest. "Well, at one point, my feet were in the air. So, I think that answers your question." Then, a flash of sadness washed over Federica's face. "I'll order my taxi." *Ciao* signor Hartlett. You take care."

Federica turned on her heel and left the bedroom. Kojo leapt out of the bed, Felix jumping from his lap onto the floor, landing perfectly on all fours. He put on his boxer shorts and chased after Federica, calling out to her when he reached the parlour. "Could we stay in touch? I would like to if you want to?"

Federica, whose right hand was already on the front door's doorknob, turned to look at him, bemused. "I was under the impression that last night's romp was simply a one-off episode in our lives. Signor Hartlett, I am married to a very powerful man. To begin an affair would be unwise."

"A married woman who does not wear her wedding ring and refers to her powerful husband as a piece of shit. It does not sound like matrimony bliss to me."

Federica glared at him, her emerald eyes blazing. "We slept together last night, but it does not mean you suddenly understand my life. Just because you've unstripped me doesn't justify you to judge me." Her tone was sharp.

"I did not mean to offend," Kojo said, raising his hands in surrender to show he came in the name of love, not war. "Please accept my apologies. Truthfully, I enjoyed your company last night and would love to be blessed with another opportunity to enjoy it again."

Federica pressed her lips together and regarded Kojo. She was in deep thought for almost half a minute. Finally, she released a sigh. "Give me your number, but I cannot promise I'll call you. You may never hear from me or see me again."

"A man can always hang on to hope. Nothing wrong with that."

Federica smiled at Kojo as he gave her his number which she entered into her phone as she stood before him. Once she had saved his number, she pocketed her phone in her handbag. There was no goodbye kiss; instead, Federica gave him a warm smile before twisting the door handle and leaving his hotel suite. Felix strolled into the parlour and came to rest by Kojo's left ankle.

As much as Kojo had enjoyed Federica last night, it was not the only reason he wanted to see her again. She was Silvio Mancini's wife, so she could prove an important asset on his mission. If Kojo could get closer to Federica, he could use her to extract information about her husband's dealings with Dugard. But did he genuinely like her? She was certainly a beautiful Italian actress with a depth that intrigued him, but Kojo was an MI6 agent on a mission. His objective took precedence over any sentimentality. Federica Mancini was a means to an end. Hopefully, her resentment towards her husband would convince her heart to give Kojo a call.

23-year-old Yinka stood on the terrace of an expensive apartment in Banana Island, Nigeria's version of California's Palm Beach—a haven for the country's one percent.

From where she stood, Yinka had a panoramic view of Lagos Lagoon. She could see the Makoko and Ìlàje fishermen on the far horizon in their wooden canoes. They were casting their nets in the tortilla-brown coastal waters, hoping to catch fish they could later sell to feed their families. Surrounding the lagoon were the floating slums, constructed from makeshift stilts, some metal, some wooden, but all decaying. These were the homes of the Makoko and Ìlàje waterfront communities, some of the poorest in Lagos.

The white, sleeveless Prada mini dress Yinka currently wore could feed the average Lagos fisherman's entire family for a month.

Behind her, Yinka could hear footsteps approaching. She turned from the balcony to see her boyfriend, Oge, walking towards her. He wore a white vest, showing off his toned biceps with its curling veins, black shorts and brown sandals.

For the past two months, Oge had been undercover as a head houseboy for Oluwasegun Ikeji, a prominent Nigerian senator who owned the apartment. From what Oge had unearthed in his investigations, Ikeji had been embezzling public funds throughout his time in office. This afternoon, Yinka was going to seduce and then drug Mr Ikeji. Once he was unconscious, Oge and the rest of the team would safely enter the apartment after Oge had disabled the security cameras and break into the safe where Mr Ikeji kept 500 million naira of stolen money in cash. Using bin bags to load the cash into, they would relieve Mr Ikeji of this stolen haul. It was Yinka's first time partaking in such an operation. Anxiety crawled all over her dark skin like invisible, tiny ants.

Oge gave Yinka a full kiss on her lips, and she wrapped her hands around his waist. She wished she could abandon this mission and just make love to Oge on the leather settee in the living room. But she couldn't let the team down on their first mission. She could not disappoint Oge.

"He is going to be arriving here in five minutes," Oge said, placing his sandy-coloured hands on Yinka's shoulder as he looked her up and down. "You look irresistible, Coffee Bean. You're exactly his type, which is to say you are every rich and corrupt Nigerian politician's type. I definitely selected the perfect outfit for you."

Yinka chuckled nervously. "Do you think he will like me? Am I not too skinny? Is my bum big enough?"

Oge bit his lip, chuckling, and rubbed Yinka's shoulders. "You are perfect. Just remember what I've taught you about seducing powerful men. Play to their ego, make them feel important, and never show your intelligence, but don't be taciturn. Touch his knees and thighs, not too much, but just enough to excite him. Always be teasing your body. And most importantly, when you look at him, act as if you're in the presence of a God. Make him believe he is the one seducing your heart when, in fact, you're wrapping your fingers around his."

"And I don't have to actually…" Yinka grimaced, which made Oge smirk, "sleep with him?"

"Come on, Coffee Bean, of course not," Oge said. "I would never make you do that. You don't need to have sex with a man to have his heart in your hands. You just need to make him feel like he's George Clooney."

Yinka chuckled, poking Oge on his chest. As always, Oge's way with words managed to shove away some of her anxiety.

The sound of the doorbell ringing made both Yinka and Oge jolt.

"The man of the hour is here," Oge said with a self-satisfying grin. "Looks like the show is about to begin. Let's get this bag, baby."

27

SITTING on the white sofa in the shared living room of the hotel suite, Yinka skimmed through the investor report for Mancini that Timon had spent all morning preparing, head down on his MacBook as he sat on the balcony. After he finished the report, Yinka printed it using the hotel reception printer.

Considering how quickly Timon had put it all together, Yinka was very impressed. She was not a hedge fund manager, so a lot of the figures, analytics and investment jargon in the report might as well have been Latin to her, but it all looked solid from a glance and seemed like it could stand up to scrutiny if Mancini probed into it further. Although she would keep it to herself - Timon's asteroid-sized ego did not need further massaging - Yinka had to admit that Timon was a brilliant man with a sharp mind. Now she understood why he had graduated from Cambridge.

"So you're one hundred per cent certain that your forecast on Mancini's quarterly returns, should he invest in Afchain, are solid? Irrefutable?" Yinka looked up from the report to face Timon. He sat opposite her in the living room, wearing a white Ralph Lauren polo shirt, shorts and Gucci sandals.

"If the technology behind Afchain actually works, then yeah, those projections I've put into the report are as accurate as possible," Timon said. "If Mancini cares about making money as much as he cares about pumping Botox into his plastic face, he'll invest that three million into Afchain after reading my report."

A chuckle escaped Yinka's mouth. She stood from the sofa with the investor report by her side. Even without looking at him, she could feel Timon silently scrutinising what she was wearing to the meeting – a white crop cami top, displaying her toned midriff and a jade-coloured front wrap skirt that exposed most of her left leg.

"How can you dress like this to your private meeting with Mancini on his yacht?" Timon said, shaking his head at her. "Which, let me remind you, is meant to be a business meeting, and I didn't even get the invite. Just you." Timon huffed with more aggression than Yinka expected. *Was he seriously jealous?*

"You saw how he was looking at you last night with those rapey eyes. Yet you're visiting him alone dressed like a belly dancer?"

"If we want to increase our chances of him investing in Afchain, this is how I've got to dress. Trust me."

Timon waved his left hand dismissively. "Really? So you mean to tell me you have to dress in a sexually provocative manner to do business with a man? Is this how you and your team, the *Robin Hoods*, do it?" Timon smirked when he noticed Yinka widen her eyes in surprise. "You steal money from rich guys by seducing them. That's right, Kebba told me all about you and what your people *really* do."

Yinka narrowed her eyes at him, her irritation steadily rising. Timon really knew how to sprinkle pepper on her mood. "I don't care what Kebba has told you; besides, it changes nothing."

"Well, it does, actually, because you lied to me. You're not business consultants; you're thieves. Criminals."

Yinka sighed impatiently. "Okay, so what? Now you know. Do you still want the remaining three million for this consultancy job or not?"

Timon's mouth parted to say something, but he sucked his teeth instead and shook his head.

"I thought so. Also, you're the last person who can judge me on how I use my body to move through this world as a woman. God armed me with breasts, hips and an ass. These are my greatest arsenal in a world run by greedy, corrupt and powerful men."

Timon sniggered, shaking his head as he put both hands on his hips. "I would have thought since you read all these feminist books, that you would be way too smart of a woman to think that your body is the only power you have to get by in this world. How can your boyfriend be comfortable with you doing this?"

In a way Yinka had not expected, Timon's words pierced her —like darts hitting a bullseye. Nobody had ever said this to her, and she was taken aback by the surprising truth in Timon's blunt words. Yinka clenched her teeth, seething.

"You think you know who I am, but let me tell you now, you don't," she said, putting in a concerted effort to control her now heavy breathing as she teemed with triggered rage. "I am not that skinny Nigerian girl you used to terrorise at school anymore. So stay in your lane, Timon. Like I told you last night, we are here with a clear objective. You do want us to secure the bag, right?"

Timon stared at her, blinking. Finally, he let out a sigh of defeat. "Just be careful. Please."

The surprisingly touching tone in Timon's voice took

Yinka by surprise. It made her uncomfortable. He was the last person she wanted kindness from.

Yinka turned away from Timon, picked up her Gucci mini bag and flung it over her right shoulder. She walked to the front door, still clutching the investor report. As she placed her hand on the doorknob, she turned back to look at Timon, unsmiling. "And I am not going to open my legs for Mancini. I use my body to get what I want from men, but that doesn't mean I sleep with them. I am not a prostitute."

"What are you then?"

"A dangerous woman."

And with that, Yinka opened the door and left their hotel suite.

28

FEDERICA MANCINI WAS SUNBATHING on The Mangano's sundeck. Dressed in a black one-piece swimsuit and red Prada sunglasses glinting in the sunshine, she clutched her iPhone in her left hand as she lay on the bamboo sunbed. Her AirPods were plugged into her ears, and she was listening to Beyonce's 'Break My Soul'.

Since her romp with the British civil servant, Steven Hartlett, last night, Federica was in the best mood she had been in for some time. It had been a while since she had laid down with another man who passionately tended to the desires of her body. Being in a marriage where your husband was more interested in women who could be his daughters, Federica had reconciled her sex life to unsatisfying liaisons with young Italian men, mostly indie actors, who she taught in her acting classes in Milan. But the rabbit-like enthusiasm of young men in bed rarely compensated for their lack of passion or technique. But Steven, by contrast, had traversed her body with such a confident and refined hand that she still remembers her skin becoming heated with pleasure. He had re-energised her interest in quality sex again. Equally surprising but also alluring was that it was an older black man from the UK, of all places, who had given her the first orgasm of the year. Perhaps she could do with a few more.

"Get up, woman."

Speaking in Italian and snapping Federica out of her thoughts, Silvio, her pig of a husband, towered over her, blocking the sun.

"Did you not hear me the first time, whore?"

Silvio aggressively pulled Federica's left AirPod from her ear. Beyonce's voice was instantly gone, and Federica's escapism was over, thrust back to the reality of being married to what must be the most abusive and vilest man on God's good Earth.

"Why can't you leave me in peace?" Federica said in her southern Italian accent, with its closed vowels, compared to her husband's northern accent. She stood from the sunbed and squared up to Mancini. He glared at her with that rubbery, hideous mask he called a face. He was dressed in his ridiculous, silky red robe, completely barefoot.

Silvio grabbed Federica's wrist and held tight. She was always surprised by her husband's ferocious strength as he did not have the stature of someone physically strong or even imposing. But like everything in their marriage, nothing was as it seemed.

"Where the hell did you go last night?" Silvio said, teeth clenched and his eyes flaring with rage. "You bitch. Who did you leave with?

"I went home with Amelia Durant," Federica said, using all her will to stop herself from spitting in her husband's face. After leaving Steven's hotel this morning, she had already called Amelia, a French film director and a close friend. Amelia was more than happy to support her alibi. "You were preoccupied entertaining your little girls, so I saw no reason to stay for the whole party."

Silvio's backhand was swift and without warning. It connected against Federica's right cheek. Pain exploded

LEKE APENA

across her face as if a hot frying pan had whacked her. With a shriek, Federica stumbled back onto the sunbed.

"Keep biting the hand that feeds you, and that hand is going to take away the food you enjoy, and I will smile as you starve," Silvio said, his lips curved into a snarl as he looked down at Federica.

Rubbing her right cheek, Federica shut her eyes, holding her tears back. She would not give Silvio the satisfaction of seeing her cry.

"Don't think I won't give you the same treatment I gave our rotten daughter. I will cut the golden straw you drink from."

"Okay, Silvio," Federica said with a deep and relenting sigh. Although her cheek still stung and she tasted blood inside her bottom lip, she summoned all her willpower to open her eyes and look up at her husband. "What do you want from me today? What can I do for you?" Her voice was passive. Tired.

"I have received an invitation from Emiko Shinoda to her cousin's birthday celebrations in Tokyo," Silvio said. He produced a cigar from the pocket of his silky red trousers, lit it with a golden chromed lighter and pulled on the cigar. "The family is very conservative, so it is in my best interest to attend the party with my wife by my side." As Silvio said this, he looked at Federica as if she were an old suit he needed to wear to a party because he could not find a replacement in time. "You'll be travelling to Tokyo tomorrow but won't stay with me at my hotel."

Federica shrugged. "Naturally."

"But you will attend the party by my side. I'll pay for you to stay at a separate hotel. You remember how to play the dutiful wife?" Silvio snickered as he flicked ashes from his cigar at her. The flecks of burnt nicotine landed on her hair.

"I'll give an Oscar-winning performance," Federica said through clenched teeth. She turned away from Silvio to look into the gleaming, crystal-clear waters. The waves of the sea were gentle. If only she could be lost in its tranquillity all afternoon.

Silvio bent down and attempted to kiss Federica on the lips, but she stood from the sunbed and walked over to the metal safety rail at the front of the yacht. She would rather slit her wrists with a hunting knife than let her husband taste her lips.

"Hate me all you want, but you're still my wife, and I am the only reason you still have access to this world of luxury and wealth you've become so accustomed to. Never forget." Silvio was standing a few feet behind her. "And make sure you wear your wedding ring when we're in Tokyo. Don't embarrass me like you did last night."

Just when Federica hoped she could breathe a sigh of relief that her ears would be temporarily free of her husband's despicable voice, he had one last thing to say.

"I am also expecting a visitor shortly with whom I will discuss business in my master bedroom. Do not disturb me or my security. In fact, I would appreciate it if you could make yourself scarce."

Federica did not look back as Silvio left the sun deck. She heard him walk down the metal steps to the lower decks.

Enough was enough now. Federica had cemented her decision. She would run away from her husband. In Tokyo, Federica would play the role of a respectable wife one final time. Then, she would execute her escape plan.

With a satisfying smile, she envisaged a bright future without her bastard husband. Federica returned to the sunbed and picked up her phone. She would spend the rest of the day at Amelia's villa, but first, she had someone to call. Federica scrolled through her contact list to find the number of the man who had swept her off her feet.

29

FIFTEEN MINUTES after leaving her hotel, Yinka was escorted by two bodyguards to Mancini's main suite on his super yacht.

The Italian banker was standing outside on the balcony in his private quarters. He was leaning against the guard rails with a smouldering cigar in his left hand. When the body-guard led Yinka to him, Mancini turned around to look at her. A wide smile instantly stretched across his sculptured, hard face. He was dressed in a silky red nightwear and was bare-foot. Already, his eyes were lingering on Yinka's exposed leg through her front wrap skirt. Timon hadn't been wrong. Mancini did have rapey eyes.

"*Ciao bella,*" Mancini said, kissing Yinka lightly on both cheeks as she stepped into the balcony. He placed both his hands on her shoulders and examined her. "*Dio Mio!* How do you look even more beautiful than last night?"

Yinka gave him a demure smile and fluttered her eyelashes, feigning modesty to exude her feminine energy. Despite his undisciplined male gaze, Yinka might have found Mancini a little charming if his face did not look like it was ripped from a mannequin.

After excusing his security and putting his cigar in an ashtray on one of the balcony tables, Mancini led Yinka back into the master suite. Once they were inside, Yinka handed him the investor report.

"That is the report you requested. It details the quarterly and annual returns you can expect should you decide to invest in Afchain," Yinka said, watching Mancini's eyes hover over the report he had opened. "I am in no doubt that you will find this is a very safe investment promising very high dividends. Profitable with a capital P."

Mancini continued to silently flip through the pages of the report as Yinka stood a few feet away from him by the king-sized bed, hands by her lap. After about five minutes of examining the report, Mancini looked up and smiled at Yinka.

"Well, I am very impressed. It is a detailed report and gives me confidence that my three million will be invested well in a profitable and thriving technology company." Mancini then placed the report on the chest of drawers beside him. He rested his eyes just below Yinka's neckline. "May I call you Yinka?"

"Of course you can, Signor Mancini."

Mancini raised his left hand. "Please, call me Silvio. No need for us to be so formal if we're about to go into business."

"You have made up your mind then?" Yinka said, beaming at Mancini but hoping she did not sound too eager.

Mancini did not answer Yinka immediately. Instead, he pushed himself up from where he was leaning and walked to the kitchen. Perched on the silver metallic countertop was a square-shaped glass decanter filled with a dark orange liquid. Beside the glass container were two lowball glasses. Mancini opened the glass decanter and poured the liquid into the two lowball glasses. He then picked up the two glasses and turned to face Yinka, flashing his white teeth with a smile.

"In answer to your question, I would love to invest. But if

we are going into business, we must celebrate with a drink. It is how us Italians seal the deal."

Yinka laughed lightly, putting her hand on her chest. "What better way is there to celebrate getting richer than with a toast?" she said, taking the lowball glass from Mancini when he walked over to her and handed it to her.

As she held her glass, Yinka inspected its contents. Mancini had poured her a shot of whiskey. She looked at him to find he was already raising his glass.

"Saluti."

Yinka nodded in agreement and clinked her glass against Silvio's. "Saluti."

Closing her eyes, Yinka knocked back the shot of whiskey. Its bitter taste felt like a fireball surging down her throat, and she winced. She would never be fond of whiskey.

Mancini placed his glass on top of the chest of draws. "If you would excuse me for a moment, Yinka. I need to use the bathroom."

When Mancini excused himself to the ensuite lavatory, in surprisingly hurried steps, Yinka sat on the beige leather sofa.

At first, Yinka felt completely fine as she examined the modern and sleek interior of the master room. But then she began to feel light-headed, and she experienced the alarming sensation of not being able to move, as if her muscles had decided to collapse into mush. Her vision began to blur as if someone had sprayed water in her eyes, and an extreme wave of tiredness engulfed her.

The last image Yinka remembered seeing was Mancini walking out of the bathroom, his lips stretched into a slimy smile across his plastic face.

Then Yinka completely blacked out.

30

YINKA SHOT up from the bed, startled and disoriented. "Where am I? Oge, is that you!?"

"No, it's me," Timon's calm and reassuring voice said. "You're alright, don't panic. You're back at our hotel."

Yinka pulled herself upright so her back was against the headboard. She took in her surroundings, trying to gain hold of the confusion galloping around her senses like a wild horse. Gradually, the concepts of time and space began to solidify. The white adobe walls in her king-sized room became familiar again, as did the pineapple-coloured curtains and the sliding glass door which led to the balcony. Even Timon's face was a welcoming sight to see. His genuinely concerned expression tugged at the strings of her heart against her will.

"What happened to me?" Yinka said, massaging her throbbing forehead as she closed her eyes.

"What do you remember?" Timon said, in a low voice.

"I was at Mancini's master suite on his yacht," Yinka started, shaking her head as she tried to extract crumbles of memory from her business meeting with Mancini. "I gave him the investor report, which he read, and then he said he'd invest in Afchain ." Yinka put both hands on her face and felt Timon put a hand on her right shoulder. "Then he gave me a drink which I drank and then…nothing. I can't remember anything after that."

"I became concerned when I didn't see or hear from you after three hours and when I called you, you didn't answer your phone," Timon said. "I then managed to get hold of Kebba's number and asked him to try calling you, and that's when Mancini picked up your phone. From what Mancini told Kebba, you collapsed in his room, and he called his medical team on the yacht. They checked your pulse and temperature and said you appeared fine, so you didn't need to be taken to the hospital. Kebba then drove over to Mancini's yacht, and he and Mancini carried you to his minivan when you were still unconscious. Kebba drove you back here, and we carried you back to your hotel room."

Yinka groaned and knocked her head back against the headboard as she closed her eyes again. "How long have I been out for?"

"About five hours. It's almost 6 pm."

Yinka's eyes shot open as she stared at Timon, horrified. "Five hours!"

Timon removed his hand from Yinka's shoulder and looked into her eyes. "Is there anything else you remember? Do you usually faint like that?"

Yinka's lips began to tremble, but she fought off the tears that threatened to emerge. Instead, she shook her head at Timon, gripped by disbelief. "I think I was drugged, Timon. I think…I think Mancini put something in my drink."

There was a knock on the front door before Yinka could fully let the implications of her admission sink in. Even Timon appeared shocked, judging by his hanging jaw. There was a delayed reaction from both of them until there was a second knock on the front door. It was Timon who spoke.

"Who is it?"

"It is Richard. Richard Dugard," came the English aristo-crat's voice from outside the door. "May I come in? I come bearing gifts like one of the three wise men."

Timon gave Yinka a reassuring smile, which did little to make her feel better, but she oddly appreciated it. Then he stood from the bed to go and get the front door.

To Yinka's surprise, when Timon returned to her room, it wasn't only with Dugard. The bodyguard who had escorted Yinka to Mancini's master suite earlier had also walked in. He appeared to be clutching a silver metal briefcase.

"Mancini told me what happened when you came to visit him," Dugard said, looking crestfallen like a father visiting his sick daughter at a hospital. He sat at the edge of the bed beside Yinka. "What happened, and how are you feeling now?"

Yinka flicked her eyes at Timon. He was now standing at the front of the bed beside Mancini's bodyguard. Timon gave her a sorrowful nod and then began to speak. "We think Mancini might have---"

"I am fine now," Yinka said, swiftly interrupting Timon as she looked at Dugard and gave him a big smile. "I didn't drink much water today, and it's been quite hot, so I guess I was just very dehydrated." Even as Yinka told this lie, she could feel the weight of Timon's eyes on her as she deliber-ately avoided looking at him.

"Well, please keep a bottle of water with you at all times, my dear," Dugard said, smiling warmly. "I may not look it, but I am much too old to have a panic like I did when Mancini informed me that you had collapsed on his yacht."

"Thank you, Richard. I appreciate your concern."

"Fantastic. Very well then," Dugard said, suddenly in chirper spirits as he clapped his hands. "Now that I have peace of mind knowing you're fine, I can reveal the second reason I am here." Dugard stood from the edge of the bed and turned to look at Mancini's bodyguard. "Apologies if you're both aware, but Mancini has agreed to invest three million pounds into Afchain. He's a hard man to convince, you can believe me on that, so congratulations are most certainly in order. Now, as I am one of Mancini's closest associates, he has asked me to oversee the transfer of the funds for the investment."

"So...the money is in that suitcase?" Timon said, pointing at the silver, metal briefcase that Mancini's bodyguard was holding.

"My dear friend, Mancini is not going to carry around three million pounds of cash in a suitcase," Dugard said, chuckling. "No, inside that suitcase is a wire transfer console enabling Mancini to wire you the funds immediately to a designated bank account. He's graciously allowed you a day to prepare all the paperwork, but he has no issue transferring the money immediately. He trusts your integrity, which is very unlike him." Dugard turned to Yinka, smiling. "You and Timon have made quite the impression on our Italian banker."

Yinka coughed and shifted uncomfortably on the bed. She did not want to think about Mancini and what he had done to her. *Focus on the objective.* "That's wonderful news, Richard," Yinka said, forcing herself to sound escalated. "I am happy to provide the account details, and Timon will prepare all the contractual documents."

Dugard nodded at Yinka. "Certainly. Lorenzo, if you will."

Lorenzo, Mancini's bodyguard, walked to Yinka's side of the bed with his hulking frame. He placed the suitcase on her lap and lifted it open. Inside the suitcase were numbered keypads and a monitor displaying the figure of three million. Underneath was the icon of a loading bar.

"Could you please pass me my handbag, Timon," Yinka said.

Timon narrowed his eyes at her, and she could tell he silently questioned her actions. Still, he did as she asked and handed her the Gucci mini bag on the dressing table.

Yinka extracted her iPhone from her mini bag and scrolled down to a secure, encrypted app where she saved sensitive information.

When Oge's kidnappers had delivered the thick dossier about Afchain and the three private bankers, it also included the details for the account where Yinka would transfer the investment money to. Yinka had saved the bank details in this secure app, which she accessed with her password. Once inside the app, the bank details were in front of her on the phone screen, and she keyed them into the tiny computer inside the silver briefcase. With the details accurately entered and showing up on the screen, Yinka pressed the ENTER button. Immediately, the loading bar quickly filled up and the word SUCCESSFUL flashed on the screen.

"That's done," Yinka said. She slotted her phone back into her Gucci mini bag.

"Brilliant," Dugard said, clapping his hands again as his mouth curved into a wide grin. "The money should be in the account within the hour."

Lorenzo closed the suitcase and removed it from Yinka's lap. He nodded stiffly at Dugard, left the room and exited the hotel room completely, closing the front door quietly as he went.

Dugard looked at both Yinka and Timon. His whole demeanour seemed overly jubilant. "Now, there's also a third reason why I have come by here," he said. "You have shown exceptional sales acumen to convince Mancini to invest in Afchain, so it would be my pleasure to introduce you to two other business associates of mine. They are also private bankers."

"Who are they?" Timon said, hands in the pockets of his shorts as he leaned against the wall facing Yinka's bed.

"Emiko Shinoda, who comes from a powerful Japanese family, and Abdul Kazeem Mustafa, a sheikh well-respected among Dubai's elite circles. Both of them are good friends of mine, and the opportunity to invest in Afchain would interest them.

"Your business associates, did you say?" Yinka said, raising her eyebrows at Dugard. Initially, she had considered her chance encounter with Dugard and the fact he did business with Mancini as a mere stroke of luck. Yet now, Dugard wanted to introduce Yinka and Timon to the two remaining private bankers she and her team were targeting for investment. It could not be a mere coincidence. Could it?

"Yes, that is correct," Dugard said. He still had that overly satisfied smile on his face. "I have worked for many global businesses as an accountant and private banker, so I've made many international friends. As my late father would always tell me: your net worth increases as your network increases."

"Well, we'd loved to be introduced to them both," Yinka said, directing her eyes at Timon and silently beckoning him to agree.

"Yes, of course," Timon said, nodding, although he looked at Yinka with a weary stare. "The more high net worth investors we can bring onboard, the better."

"Right you are, my friend," Dugard said, nodding. He began to stroll around the room with his left arm behind his back, thinking about something. After a minute, he addressed Timon and Yinka again. "Jin Shinoda, the head of the powerful Shinoda family and Emiko's cousin, is hosting a big party for his 30th birthday in Tokyo. Emiko has invited me, Mancini and Mustafa, as we have all done business with her family over the years. I would like to extend that invitation to you both so I can introduce you to Emiko and Mustafa at the party."

Timon chuckled. "So you want us to travel to Tokyo for a birthday party?"

"It will be much more than a mere birthday party, I assure you. You will be in the same room as some of Tokyo's biggest movers and shakers."

"And you said Mancini will be there?" Yinka said, meeting Dugard's eyes and hoping she was not projecting her discomfort.

"Yes, he will be present."

Yinka caught Timon sending her another probing look. He was waiting for her response.

"Thank you for the invitation, Richard," Yinka said, making sure her voice did not carry any of the trepidation she felt about coming into contact with Mancini again. "And we graciously accept."

"Wonderful," Dugard said, clapping his hands once more. "I have a private jet waiting for me at Olbia airport, which is leaving for Tokyo tomorrow morning. You are both welcome on board, of course. And I am happy to sort out last-minute hotel accommodation for you both."

Timon chuckled. "I see why you're a popular man, Richard. Thank you for that."

"Oh, it's my pleasure, but I suggest you pack your luggage tonight. My private jet leaves for Tokyo at 8 am. It's an eight-hour flight to Japan."

Dugard stopped circling the room and beamed at both Yinka and Timon. "If this is your first time in Tokyo, you'll fall in love, I promise. It is one of the most interesting cities in the world."

31

KOJO SAT by the circle wooden table on the balcony of his hotel suite. His white, short-sleeved Hawaiian shirt was unbuttoned in the sweltering heat. In front of him was an MI6-issued Lenovo Laptop ThinkPad, an unimpressive tech considering all the advanced gadgets MI6 gifted him. He was having an encrypted Microsoft Teams call with Tiwa.

"The sun's cooked you over there, hasn't it?" Tiwa said from MI6 headquarters as she sat on the silver swivel chair in her office. "You're starting to resemble a cookie in the oven too long."

Kojo chuckled as he crossed his legs on the bamboo garden chair he was sitting on. "You know, I can't say I ever liked your sense of humour," he said, smirking. "Thank God the Foreign Secretary hired you to head up MI6, so you never started a career as a comedian. It would have been tragic."

"Many people find me to be quite funny, actually.

"Your mother doesn't count as 'many people'."

"Okay, okay, no need to get personal, *officer*," Tiwa said, throwing a grin at Kojo. She let out a sigh and put on a serious face. "Alright, let's talk shop, shall we? Excellent work taking those photos of our friend Dugard at Mancini's yacht party last night, but I am afraid it did not give us much to go on."

"I know, it's frustrating," Kojo said, looking over the balcony when he heard a big splash of water. A man with considerable body weight had cannonballed into the leisure pool below. "Mancini had a lot of security at the yacht party, and he did not leave his master room on the lower deck. Dugard left the party rather early as well."

"So Mancini stayed in his private room throughout the whole duration of his party?"

"I didn't stay for the whole party, so I can't confirm that."

Tiwa raised his eyebrows at him. "Why? Where did you go?"

"I engaged Mancini's wife, Federica. She could prove a useful asset. If I can get close to the wife of one of the alleged members of The Cable, then I can extract potentially useful intelligence."

"I can't argue with the logic," Tiwa said, nodding. "But I am curious as to how you *engaged* Mrs Mancini?"

Kojo cleared his throat of some imaginary phlegm. "We simply met at the yacht party, returned to my hotel after a friendly chat and…got to know each other better." Even as he finished his sentence, Kojo could tell Tiwa was repressing a laugh.

"I won't request further details as I've just finished my footlong Subway sandwich," Tiwa said, the side of her mouth curving to a smirk. "But if you can use her to get closer to her husband and Dugard, she will be a very effective asset. But you'll need to do this as quickly as possible, Kojo. We can spend only so much time and resources on this operation."

"Of course," Kojo said, scratching his clean-shaven face. "Also, in the photos I took, there were two people that Dugard was engaging with. A black man and a black woman. Late twenties or early thirties and smartly dressed. They both followed Dugard to Mancini's private room. I requested that our analysts do a facial recognition background check on them. Did anything come up in our databases?"

"Well, for the young man, nothing unordinary came up in our records, but the young woman did raise a few eyebrows."

"Well, don't keep me in suspense now. What do we have?"

"Okay, I'll start with the man. His name is Timon Bakare. Thirty years old, born in Britain in 1992 at Newham General Hospital in East London. There is no record of his father on our files, but his mother is a Nigerian woman, Iyenemi Bakare, who left Lagos in 1992, settled in Canning Town, gave birth to her son and raised him alone. She founded a successful hair salon business but developed mild Alzheimer's about three years ago. She now resides at an exclusive care home near Maida Vale."

"Who's paying for that?"

"He is. Mr Bakare is quite the overachiever, considering his working-class background. He studied Economics at Cambridge, graduated first-class, and then had a lucrative and successful career as a senior analyst at Werner Schmitt Bank before quitting and starting his crypto hedge fund four years ago, which has done very well. He's a wealthy man now."

Kojo snorted with a bit of envy. "He's probably earning quadruple my salary. That crypto stuff is all the craze now, and these young cats are getting rich from it overnight. Anyway, I digress. What about the young woman?"

"Like I mentioned before, she raises many questions and red flags. From the little we have on her in our database, we know her name is Yinka Saraki. She was born in Abeokuta, which is the capital of Ogun state in the southern part of Nigeria. At around 14, she was sent to London to live with her late father's cousin, Grace Audu, who had a property in Canning Town. Miss Audu became Miss Saraki's legal guardian but has since returned to Nigeria. Interestingly, for a brief period, a whole school year, Miss Saraki attended the same secondary school as Mr Bakare."

"Okay, so there's some history between them."

Tiwa nodded. "There is, but that is not even the most interesting part about Miss Saraki. She went to a college in Essex and then attended the London School of Economics to study Social Anthropology. She's an overachiever too, achieving a First Class."

"And what else?"

Tiwa shrugged her shoulders. "That's all we have on her in our database. It's like after she graduated, Miss Saraki completely vanished. No history of employment. Or paying taxes. Absolutely nothing. We can't even find a trace of her on any social media or the wider web. Digitally, she's non-existent. It's like she's dead. So the question is, what has Miss Saraki been doing for nine years since she graduated?"

Kojo stroked his chin. How does someone have no employment history and no online presence, especially in these times when almost everyone leaves behind a digital footprint of some kind? It was not a stretch to assume Dugard had taken an interest in crypto investing, being a private banker, so having a crypto hedge fund manager like Mr Bakare as an acquaintance made sense, but what was Miss Saraki's involvement? The fact she had also followed Dugard to Mancini's master room meant Miss Saraki was involved in whatever dealings Mr Bakare had with Dugard.

"I am going to have to cut our meeting short, Kojo," Tiwa said. "But in the meantime, continue to find other ways to gather new intelligence on Dugard and Mancini. Establishing a relationship with Mancini's wife is a good idea. Should you need other methods to gather intelligence, we have the resources if you need them."

"Thanks, ma'am."

No sooner had Tiwa ended the Microsoft Teams meeting than Kojo received a call on his Samsung Galaxy from an unknown number. When he answered it, he recognised the female Italian accent from last night. It brought a smile to his face quicker than he intended.

"*Buon pomeriggio, signor Hartlett,*" Federica said from the other end of the line. Her voice seemed electrified with a kind of forbidden excitement.

"Good afternoon. So it seems God has answered my prayers."

Federica chuckled. "Well, I wouldn't give thanks to God just yet. Whether I see you again depends on how you respond to my request. You can say yes or no, but if you say no, we'll never see each other again."

Kojo laughed, already knowing what his answer would be whatever she asked. "Sounds like you're emotionally manipulating me. It's kind of sexy. Well, what is your request, Federica?"

"Would you like to spend a few days with me in Tokyo?"

PART FOUR

THE TOKYO AFFAIR

東 京 の エ ピ ソ ー ド

32

ALTHOUGH HE COULD AFFORD IT, Timon had never flown on a private jet. Experiencing what that would be like had been on his bucket list since he was fifteen, when he watched his favourite rappers from the nineties flaunt their envious lifestyles.

Dugard's large business jet matched Timon's fantasy with its white and blue body paint and eagle-shaped fuselage. The aircraft was ultra-modern, with all the luxury amenities one would expect. Instead of a row of seats, as you would find on regular planes, when Timon boarded Dugard's private jet with Yinka, he entered a sleek lounge area with reclining, white leather seats which retracted into beds. There was a fully functioning kitchen where Dugard's chefs prepared dishes for the flight. Every aspect of the aircraft's lounge was built with the most high-end technology, with a wide-screen LED television providing in-flight entertainment, free Wi-Fi, ambient lighting, Blu-ray players and even the newest gaming consoles to enjoy.

But Timon's enjoyment of flying like a pampered celebrity was tempered by his growing concern for Yinka's mental wellbeing.

As Dugard talked passionately about why he loved Tokyo throughout the flight, Yinka had been listening but looked oddly disinterested. Timon had been in her presence long enough to understand that Yinka was already quite a cooly detached person anyway. Still, she seemed more emotionally disengaged than usual as she nodded silently as Dugard spoke. Timon knew she was feeling this way because of the Mancini incident, which would massively impact any woman, but he was unsure how to approach the topic. Yinka was still quite antagonistic towards him, and even Timon was surprised by how much he was starting to care for her wellbeing, given their history.

By the time they had landed at Haneda Airport, passed customs and security and collected their luggage, Timon had begun to feel tired from the journey. When he had boarded the black Rolls-Royce Phantom with Yinka and Dugard, with his luggage put in the boot of the vehicle by the short Japanese driver wearing a face mask, he immediately knocked out in the backseat. Thirty minutes later, Timon was awoken by Dugard when they arrived at Shinjuku Park Tower located in Nishi-Shinjuku.

According to Dugard, Nishi-Shinjuku was known as Tokyo's high-rise district. As Timon stepped out of the Rolls-Royce, he immediately understood why. Everywhere his eyes turned, enormous skyscrapers sprouted from the ground like metallic trees and bore down on him like the steel gods of capitalism. Nishi Shinjuku made London's Canary Wharf feel like a small village.

The five-star hotel Dugard had booked for himself, Timon, and Yinka was the Park Hyatt Tokyo at the top of the Shinjuku Park Tower, which Timon was now looking up at in awe, feeling like an ant.

After checking in at the lobby, which had a sleek and exquisite interior, Dugard bid Timon and Yinka a temporary farewell as he had booked a presidential suite.

Similar to their setup back in Sardinia, Timon and Yinka stayed in a double suite with two separate rooms. When they entered the suite's spacious luxury guestroom, they admired its understated elegance: plain cream walls, white carpet and curtains, black leather furniture, a wooden bookshelf stacked with Japanese literature, and even a grand piano.

Yinka saw her luggage by the black leather sofa and went to it. She opened her backpack, took out her laptop and placed it on the black, circular glass dining table. Ten minutes later, Timon and Yinka were having a Microsoft Teams conference call with the rest of Yinka's team back in Shoreditch.

"If I knew there was a possibility I'd get fly on a private jet and stay in a luxury hotel in Tokyo for free, I would have followed you guys on this work trip," Montana said from the screen. She was in the living room of the flat, Joshua sitting beside her left and Jaali on her right. In the background, Timon could see pizza boxes on the floor, unwashed dishes in the sink and the black girl with the short, red dyed hair, whose name Timon had forgotten, walking around the living room, reading a magazine. They lived like a bunch of first-year university students.

"I did not expect I'd be flown around like Beyonce," Yinka said, managing a small smile as Timon stood beside her. It was the first time in twenty-four hours that Timon had seen Yinka's spirits lift slightly. "Anyway, what have you managed to find on our good friend, Sir Richard Dugard?"

Jaali nodded, his long dreads swishing from side to side. "Since you asked yesterday, we have been doing some research on him, and to be honest, Yinks, he just looks like your typical rich English geezer swimming in old money."

"I would have used different vernacular, but Jaali is correct in his assessment," Joshua said, adjusting his spectacles. "I carried out an extensive analysis of Dugard's profile from sources I could find online. As he told you, his great-grandfather was the Governor of Lagos during the colonial era. He's

Oxford-educated, naturally, has been married three times and has been an investment banker for almost four decades. He's also worked as an accountant, private banker and business development consultant for several Nigerian companies. So nothing appears suspicious given his background and credentials."

Yinka leaned back against the chair. She narrowed her eyes and pressed her dark lips together. Timon could tell she was in deep thought. "It seems like too much of a coincidence that he knows every private banker we've been tasked to gain investment from for Afchain, and he's even gone through all the trouble of flying Timon and me to Tokyo to introduce us to them. I am just curious why he is helping us so much."

"It's a fair point," Montana said, nodding. "But we can't find anything on him that makes him seem untrustworthy. From our information on Afchain, Dugard is not one of the original investors."

"Having said all that, I would still advise you to keep a watchful eye on Dugard," Joshua said. "The fact he has close relationships with all the investors we are targeting and he is actively introducing you to them does seem more than a stroke of luck."

Yinka nodded. "My thoughts exactly. And don't worry, I will be watching him."

Montana tilted her head and looked at Yinka with the kind of caring eyes a concerned mother would give to their sickly child. "Hey, Yinks, babe, are you alright? You look exhausted. I hope Mr Crypto Guy isn't stressing you out too much."

"You do know I am standing right here, and I can hear you," Timon said, frowning. He sucked his teeth.

Yinka shook her head and let out a muffled laugh. "Don't worry; he's become less annoying over time. But I am fine, Monty. Thanks for asking. Anyway, I'll speak to you guys soon when I have more to update. Miss ya'll."

Yinka closed her laptop and sighed heavily. Timon could hear the exhaustion in her body. She then stood up from the chair and turned to face him. "My team is right. We should keep our eyes on Dugard. As charming as he is, something in my chest tells me he knows more than he's letting on."

"As long as Dugard introduces us to the right people we need to meet, why does anything else about him even matter? I don't understand your concern."

"My team and I have our reasons."

Once again, it was clear to Timon that Yinka was still keeping some secrets from him, but he decided not to press the issue as he was more bothered about something else.

"Why didn't you tell them?"

Timon could tell Yinka had deliberately avoided looking at him as she turned away from him to pick up her laptop from the table. "What didn't I tell them?" she said, placing her laptop underneath her right arm, her back to him.

"You know what I am talking about. Why didn't you mention Mancini spiking your drink? It's terrible what he did to you, Yinka. You can't just brush that off."

Yinka let out a long sigh and then turned around to face Timon. Her eyes were defiant, but Timon could see the mist of pain and vulnerability that clouded them. "If I had told them about the incident, they would have started worrying about me. I need them to focus entirely on this mission. We managed to get the investment from Mancini. Nothing else matters."

"Okay, I hear that," Timon said, keeping his voice even toned. He knew Yinka was sensitive about the Mancini incident, contrary to her words. "But are you okay, though? Do you…do you want to talk about what happened?" The words had tiptoed on eggshells out of Timon's mouth.

Yinka's eyes widened in surprise, and then her expression softened to Timon's surprise. "I appreciate your concern, Timon. Really, I do. But I am fine, okay. I don't believe Mancini..." Yinka's voice broke off, and she appeared to swallow a lump in her throat before she continued, "I don't believe he raped me. I don't have any bruises or cuts, and nothing was unusual on my clothes when I gained consciousness, nor did I feel I had been...penetrated." Yinka shut her eyes and robbed her forehead with her right hand. "Look, please, I don't want to talk about Mancini and what happened anymore. Can you respect that?"

Despite her stubbornness, Timon could see the pain leaking out of her like streams of water pouring from the gaps in a pile of stones. But if Yinka did not want to discuss the Mancini incident further, he would respect her wishes.

Timon nodded. "Okay then. I won't bring it up anymore."

"Thanks," Yinka said, giving him a soft but pained smile.

A shadow seemed to descend over Yinka's dark brown face, and she now looked severely tired and gloomy, as if she were carrying a considerable burden that Timon knew she would never reveal to him.

"I am going to shower, and then I am going to bed," Yinka said in a laboured voice. "It was a long flight, and I am exhausted. I'll see you in the morning, Timon."

33

DRESSED in black high-stretch skinny jeans, white Air Force One trainers and a white turtle neck tank top, Yinka sat on one of the chairs around the dining table in the parlour of the hotel suite. She was currently enjoying a slice of delicious strawberry pistachio tart she had ordered from the hotel's pastry boutique. Timon was sitting opposite her, going for a casual look today in a black Ralph Lauren polo shirt, white cargo shorts and black Yeezy trainers. He was sipping on Japanese green tea from a black mug.

It was 11 am the following morning after arriving in Tokyo. Two hours earlier, Dugard visited Yinka and Timon to share the news from Emiko Shinoda that her cousin's party had been moved to tomorrow due to some issues with the venue. So now, Timon and Yinka had the whole day to do whatever they wanted. Dugard, whose hospitality seemed unlimited, had even offered to provide a private chauffeur to drive them around Tokyo if they wished to.

"You want to go sightseeing today?" Yinka said, her legs crossed as she looked at Timon. "I don't know how I feel about that. Maybe I'll stay in and catch up on some reading.

My team sent us some articles on Emiko Shinoda and her cousin, Jin, which we still need to read."

Timon shook his head at her, eyebrows raised. "I know you love your reading time, but come on, we're in Tokyo. When Dugard told us the party was postponed, I went on my phone and checked out all the tourist spots. Do you know there's a samurai museum? We can even go to one of the big shopping malls or national parks. We have to explore this city."

Yinka sighed but had to admit that discovering the delights of Tokyo sounded more fun than reading right now. Plus, Timon's enthusiasm for sightseeing around Japan's capital city was infectious. When he got excited about something, Timon was cute, in a boyish way, as his dark eyes lit up on his chiselled brown face. Yinka quickly swatted her thoughts about Timon's handsomeness away as if it were an irritating mosquito.

"And you're not going to annoy me?"

"Oh my God, are you serious?" Timon said, shaking his head. He then leaned forward towards her and put one hand on her left shoulder. "Look, I know you'll make me climb a mountain if I want you ever to see me as a friend. And I don't blame you. But will you at least give me a chance to climb? You've been through a lot, Yinka. Let me cheer you up."

Yinka looked at Timon, who was now staring at her with pleading eyes and an exaggerated wobbling of his lower lip, like a boy begging his mother to let him go to the park with his friends. She had to restrain the laugh, which almost escaped her throat when Timon put his palms together as if praying. She had to admit that his goofy side was amusing.

"Okay, fine," Yinka said, relenting. "Just stop making that offputting face at me."

Timon punched the air. "Great! And I promise we'll have a fun time today. But I'll be real; we'll probably stand out in this part of the world. Like, this isn't London or Lagos. Not every day you see two incredibly stylish black people just casually strolling around Tokyo."

Yinka gave Timon a side eye with a smirk to go with it. "I would have thought your big head would have liked all the attention?"

"I do, and now I get to share all the attention with you." Timon winked at her. "Let's get some breakfast and then leave in an hour."

* * *

Against her better judgment, Yinka let Timon convince her that exploring the Shinjuku ward of Tokyo on foot was better than being chauffeured around. After buying two disposable facemasks from the hotel's lobby, Yinka and Timon ventured out into Shinjuku's sprawling and dense streets.

Walking alongside Timon, who had set a route on Google Maps on his iPhone to Shinjuku Station, Yinka took in her surroundings. It was clear that Shinjuku was a central commercial hub of the city with its endless stream of people crossing the wide roads, many dressed smartly in formal suites and others more casually in jeans and jackets.

Yinka saw boutique retail shops, restaurants, and cafes with large Japanese letters in neon lights everywhere. Even the digital billboards, looming over them as they hung from the towering skyscrapers and multi-storey buildings, seemed to come alive with their bright colours of animated cartoon characters, some of which looked like depictions of humans with exaggerated proportions. Other billboards displayed fantastical dragons, beasts, and animated, impressive 3D renderings of cute cats. Yinka's eyes were constantly flooded with digitalised visual renderings that, at times, she felt she had been teleported into a video game. Yet even with all the towering buildings and neon billboards, there was still plenty of greenery as ginkgo trees lined the pavements and sidewalks.

Having spent much of her time in Lagos and London, Yinka was used to being surrounded by throngs of people, cars and endless noise in a dizzying vortex of human existence. Yet Tokyo did not have any of the franticness and hard hustle of Lagos or London's cold and uncaring air. Japanese people constantly moved in this part of Tokyo, yet they were relaxed. While Yinka noticed some curious stares from pedestrians as they noted Yinka's and Timon's rare presence, people in Tokyo were unbothered by them and always very polite. Yinka began to feel a newfound appreciation for Japanese culture. People here were at ease with life and each other.

Once Timon and Yinka reached Shinjuku Station, which was so grand and sprawling that it felt more like an airport, they found themselves lost within minutes. Fortunately, two American women studying in Tokyo gave them directions to Hanazono Shrine, the first tourist sight on the list Timon had compiled this morning.

Five minutes after leaving Shinjuku Station, they found Hanazono Shrine. Almost instantly, Yinka fell in love with this quiet, calming part of the city, surrounded by lush greenery and bubblegum pink cherry blossoms.

"You can't tell me that this isn't beautiful," Timon said, standing next to Yinka at the bottom of the stone steps leading to the shrine.

"I can't even disagree with you," Yinka said, admiring the elegant beauty of the shrine. Its red and white façade, decorated with golden East Asian designs on its walls, gave the shrine a spiritual quintessence. Yinka felt her heartache, and she let out a quiet sigh. If only she were experiencing this wonderful moment with Oge.

"You want me to take a picture of you standing in front of the shrine?" Timon said, who had now moved closer to Yinka.

"I know the perfect caption on Instagram to go with the pic as well: 'The sophisticated Nigerian woman doing up Tokyo'."

"Firstly, I don't use social media," Yinka said, turning to face Timon, who looked at her with an amused grin. "And secondly, that's not a bad caption if I did have Instagram. At least you didn't describe me as a 'Bad B' or something as equally cringe."

Timon chuckled. "Describe you as 'Bad B'? I wouldn't dare. You're way too sophisticated a woman for that kind of description. You're definitely stubborn, however. Stubborn sophistication. That's it, Miss Stubbornly Sophisticated. That should be my nickname for you."

Yinka sucked her teeth and smacked Timon playfully on his left shoulder.

"You are not to call me by any nickname. Under any circumstances."

Timon nodded but still wore that stupid but admittedly cute and charming grin.

Yinka took her phone from her Gucci bag on her right shoulder and passed it to Timon. "Okay, please take a photo of me standing before the shrine. And please make it a nice one."

"Don't worry, I know how to take great photos. My fiancée makes me take at least fifty photos of her every time we go out."

After spending another twenty minutes exploring the shrine and treating themselves to soft-serve ice cream, Yinka and Timon continued the rest of their sightseeing. The Samurai Museum, which they visited after Hanazono Shrine, was a lot more fascinating than Yinka thought it would be. Seeing Japan's famous warriors' ancient relics had been quite an enriching experience. Yinka even surprised herself with how fun it was to witness the little kid within Timon emerge as his face lit up with glee when he held a replica of a Samurai sword known as a wakizashi.

Afterwards, Yinka and Timon visited the Meiji Jingu stadium for an hour. Then, they treated themselves to some delicious ramen for lunch at a restaurant in a neighbourhood called Kagurazaka. Yinka could tell it was quite a fashionable part of Shinjuku with its boutique shops and French-inspired cafes.

For the remainder of the afternoon, Yinka and Timon strolled through the narrow alleyways and passageways of the Golden Gai district, visiting some of the quaint ramshackle bars plastered with American pop culture posters. After drinking bubble tea at one of the bars, Yinka and Timon shopped at a vast underground mall called the Shinjuku SUBNADE. Yinka bought a few souvenirs for her team, and Timon purchased a necklace for his fiancée.

By 6 pm, Yinka convinced Timon that they should return to the hotel and visit one of the restaurants for a fancy dinner. It had been a lovely day out in Tokyo, and, against all odds, Timon had managed not to get on her nerves. Spending time with him today had proven a welcome distraction from what happened on Mancini's yacht, the stress of this whole mission and Oge's situation. Now, she was grateful that Timon had convinced her to leave their hotel this morning to explore Tokyo. She had needed this more than she realised.

34

HAVING SPENT the best part of the last decade as an MI6 intelligence officer, Kojo's profession saw him travel to some of the most breathtaking places on Earth. He had conducted secret operations on mountainside favelas overlooking Rio De Janeiro to stop a group of traffickers smuggling young women and children into the UK. Not too long ago, he had pursued illegal poachers through the dense jungles of the KwaZulu-Natal park in South Africa to break up an unlawful ivory tracking operation originating from the UK.

But as Kojo sat on the bench in Shinjuku Gyoen National Park, a sprawling and splendid celebration of nature against the all-consuming modernity of Shinjuku city in Tokyo, he realised none of the places he had visited on his missions had given him the sense of serenity he was experiencing at this moment. The park was the most beautiful garden he had visited. Surrounded by lush greenery, Kojo took in the sounds of tweeting birds, admired the blooming cherry blossoms in all shades of pink and took in the serene view of the lake with a Taiwan pavilion overlooking the olive-tinted water.

It was Kojo's first time in Japan. While he felt like pinching himself that he was here, he knew he must remain professional and not forget why he was in Tokyo. Now that Kojo had established a relationship with the wife of one of the alleged members of The Cable, he was in an advantageous position.

Dressed in a black, light trench coat, a navy blue crewneck sweater, black trousers and brown desert boots, Kojo had opted to look casual for his meeting with Federica at the park this afternoon. When he landed in Tokyo late yesterday evening and checked into his hotel, The Knot Tokyo, he called Federica to let her know he was there. Federica, who was staying at the Shinjuku Washington Hotel, curiously without her husband, had said she would meet him at the Shinjuku Gyoen National Park as it was the most accessible location for them to meet. Although she had not outright said it, Federica had heavily implied that Kojo would be spending the night with her.

In Kojo's brain, the section where logic resided, he framed his interactions with Federica as nothing more than 'utilising an asset'. However, in his heart, he knew he was excited to see her again and anticipated making love to her tonight. It had been a very long time since Kojo had felt this way about any woman. Federica had somehow unearthed a part of him he thought was lost.

As if sensing her approach, Kojo looked to his left to see Federica striding towards him with her phone out. His heart spun on itself as he admired Federica's understated and confident beauty. The way she walked, head held high and with an assured gait, showed a woman utterly comfortable in her skin and age, even though a sense of sadness still lingered around her aura. Today, she wore a white, floral corset mini dress with white pearls across her exposed collar bone and her long dark hair, resembling the texture of silk, flowing down to her neck. On her left shoulder hung a black YSL bag. Kojo immediately noticed she was also wearing her wedding ring.

"I look at you and immediately understand why only

Milan can match Paris when it comes to fashion," Kojo said, standing from the bench as Federica drew closer. They embraced each other, but it was not a tight hug. Instead, there was a noticeable reservation between them, veering on awkwardness, as the sexual tension stood between them like a third wheel on a date. They had only had sex with each other once and very recently. They were not yet comfortable lovers.

"Thank you for the compliment, Steven," Federica said, her lips curved into a faint smile. "Although I live in Milan with my husband, I am not from Milan. I was not born into wealth. I grew up poor in a small but beautiful village in Sicily called Savoca. They filmed some of The Godfather in my town, which inspired me to pursue acting."

"Interesting. Well, you've certainly come far from small beginnings. Now you're an actress who sips cocktails on big yachts surrounded by Europe's wealthiest assholes."

Federica chuckled, but Kojo caught the cynicism underneath it. "Sometimes I wish I stayed in my little commune." She cast her eyes towards the lake. "Have you ever felt like an imposter? Like you don't naturally belong somewhere, and everyone around you secretly knows that? I used to feel this when surrounded by people who have always had money. Sometimes, I still feel like I don't belong in those privileged circles. Even now."

"I do know what it feels like to be an outsider. I was a black child adopted by a white family, and I went to boarding school in England, where there were only two other kids who looked like me. But you are where you are for a reason. Or you else wouldn't be there. So you own it."

Federica's lips curved into a small smile. After a brief silence, during which she seemed to be contemplating something, she looked at Kojo, her demeanour now lighter. "You said this is your first time in Tokyo, so I wanted to take you to one of the most beautiful places in this part of the city: the greenhouse. You're not allergic to plants, are you?"

Kojo shook his head and smiled at Federica. "If I were, I wouldn't be able to stand next to a beautiful flower like yourself. Poetry is my hidden forte, as you can tell."

"Obviously," Federica said, stifling a laugh. "Come, follow me, Romeo."

The Shinjuku Gyoen Greenhouse was a manufactured glass oasis and a botanical paradise. Walking beside Federica, Kojo observed the manifold types of plants, flowers, and other exotic flora housed in the greenhouse.

"I love coming here because it reminds me of my town where I grew up," Federica said, brushing her left hand against a bright green leaf protruding from a long bark. "Earlier in my marriage, when my husband still cared to show me affection, he would take me here during his business trips to Tokyo. I quickly fell in love with this sanctuary of flowers and plants."

"I noticed you are wearing your wedding ring this time," Kojo said, his eyes glancing at her golden wedding band. "Has something changed between you and him?"

Again, that cynical chuckle limped from Federica's mouth. "Oh no, I still hate my husband," Federica said, turning slightly to flash Kojo a cheeky smile. "But as I told you on the phone, he is here on business, so I must play the dutiful wife. What is that saying? Oh yes, I am keeping up appearances."

"Why don't you leave your marriage if you're so unhappy? Why allow yourself to suffer?" Kojo said, standing behind Federica. She had stopped to inspect a collection of plants with ripe orange fruits hanging from the branches. "I looked into your career online. You have had leading roles in some successful films, so you must have the financial means to divorce your husband."

Federica did not look at Kojo but continued inspecting the leaves of the orange trees. "How do you think a young girl from a small village managed to become an actress living a life of luxury in Milian? Nineteen years ago, I met Silvio when I was 21 and he was 43. Even back then, he was already a respected private banker and a well-known film financier in Milan. We came across each other when I was a waitress at an event he was hosting for his friends in the filmmaking business. He instantly fancied me, and I thought he was handsome, rich, and well-connected enough to give him at least a chance to court my heart. We married shortly after we started dating, and he used his connections and influence to land me leading roles in the Italian films he financed. Through him, I manifested my dreams of becoming an actress, but dreams seldom become reality without paying a heavy price."

"Which was?"

Federica shook her head and chuckled bitterly. "He owned me completely. My earnings from the films I starred in were paid into his accounts. Every penny I made as an actress belonged to him. I had signed my life to him when I signed those film contracts. Later, he would use his influence in the industry to restrict me if I tried to get an agent or work on other films without his involvement. After our daughter was born, he exerted even greater control over my life and eventually our daughter's. By the time she was eighteen, he had pushed our daughter away. Even from me." Federica let out a deep sigh as her chest rose and fell. "Throughout most of my marriage, I have had no autonomy. I have been a blank canvas, and my husband has painted my whole life with a golden brush of shit." Federica snorted, and her mouth took on a twisted grimace. "That is the type of man Silvio Mancini is. He relishes control over the women in his orbit, dependent on him like the Earth is to the Sun."

Federica wiped her left eye. "Many times, I have thought about going to the authorities to report his abuse, but he is so well-known that even if he were arrested, it would just draw too much attention. I do not want my acting career to become overshadowed by domestic abuse, which tends to happen with women in my line of work. We become defined by our relationship to a powerful man instead of our talent."

Kojo put his hands on Federica's shoulders, which felt tense. "I am sorry for what you've been through, Federica."

"Well, at least I have you here, Steven," Federica said. She raised her left hand across her chest and placed it on Kojo's left hand, holding her shoulder. "You are my temporary escape."

"Only temporary?"

Federica turned around to face Kojo. Her lips parted, and she held his gaze. "Maybe not. But let us see where this will lead us down."

Offering no resistance, Kojo closed his eyes and savoured the taste of Federica's lips.

* * *

Several hours later, in the luminescence of the Tokyo night, Kojo found himself lying next to Federica back at her hotel. As he sat upwards, leaning against the king-sized bed's head-rest, Federica, who was naked, positioned herself into the foetal position and rested her head on Kojo's partially hairy chest. Kojo stroked her long dark hair as she slept; it felt like expensive velvet between his fingers, and he sighed regret-fully. If only he could stay in this blissful moment with her, exploring Tokyo, dining on fine cuisine and making love. But that was a fantasy. He had an assignment. A mission. With the nature of his profession, there was no space for love.

Reconciling himself with the truth, Kojo shifted his mind to focus on what he needed to do. When Federica had called him back in Sardinia and invited him to Tokyo, she explained that she was travelling to the city to attend a party with her husband to celebrate the birthday of a Japanese business magnate named Jin Shinoda. However, Kojo was interested when Federica mentioned that her husband's other business associates would be present. Kojo's instinct told him Dugard would be an attendee at Jin Shinoda's party. It would be the perfect opportunity to gather further intelligence. Fortunately, Kojo's reasoning had been convincing enough for MI6 to send him to Tokyo. All expenses paid.

Delicately, so he did not wake up Federica, Kojo slipped from the bed. He picked up his boxers from the floor, slipped them on, and walked over to a wooden chair where his trousers hung from the top rail. Kojo retrieved a small black box from the left pocket. He glanced at Federica, still sleeping peacefully, and opened the box.

One of the world's tiniest and most expensive video cameras was placed on top of a white cushion inside the box. Developed by MI6's technology division, which had re-engineered microscopic cameras used by surgeons to carry out complex surgeries, the camera, dubbed 'The spec', was the size of a grain of rice. The micro camera looked like a tiny dot to the untrained eye but had a 50MP sensor with a 12MP ultrawide and 48MP 5x optical zoom. The video quality rivalled the best smartphones. It was the most impressive espionage technology in the world, costing millions to produce.

Kojo carefully took a metal toothpick with a magnate at its tip from inside the box and lifted the tiny camera from its cushion. Holding the toothpick with the microscopic camera now attached to the lower point, Kojo walked over to the bedside chest of draws where Federica had placed her YSL handbag. Like a watchmaker delicately fitting the pieces of a watch together, Kojo carefully placed the microscopic camera on the left face of the designer handbag. Underneath the microscopic camera was a synthetic mesh that enabled the device to stick to almost any surface.

Satisfied that he had securely attached the camera onto Federica's handbag, Kojo returned to bed. Tomorrow, he would activate the camera from his laptop back in his hotel so he could watch the party unfold in real-time, all from the vantage point of Federica's handbag. Once he had the footage, Kojo would convert it to a video file so he could analyse it on the computer. With today's surveillance technology, you could have the eyes of an omnipotent God.

Federica stirred and half-opened her eyes. "Are you okay, Steven?" she said, her words slow and faint.

"I am fine," Kojo said, snuggling closer to Federica so her forehead was touching his. She closed her eyes, smiling, and placed her arms around his torso. "I just went to drink a glass of water."

"Before you leave tomorrow, we must make love again in the morning. How I wish it were you by my side at that party tomorrow instead of that sickening man I have to call a husband."

–

At last, she finally had it.

14-year-old Yinka had the evidence she needed to destroy her tormentors. Those kids who said she smelt of dog shit. Or teased her that her Nigerian accent made her sound like she was an illegal immigrant who swam here. Or the most painful insult, that her skin was so black because she was so dirty not even a shower could cleanse her.

But now Yinka would have her revenge. All it had taken was an accidental eavesdrop between Desola and her big-headed boyfriend, Timon. Once she knew what they were planning to do, Yinka went to the classroom, where it happened on a Friday evening after school. Using her phone, she recorded Desola, Timon, and the rest of their idiot friends. It had been that easy. Now, she could not wait to see the look on their faces when she showed them the footage.

As usual, during lunchtime, Desola and her batch of miscreants sat on the green metal bench in the main playground reserved for the popular students. Although her hands were shaking, Yinka approached the bench, head raised high.

Desola was sitting on Timon's lap and feeding him some Walker crisps while two black girls, Bolu and Elizabeth, were talking to two other black boys, Kunle and Michael, who sat on the bench. They all seemed so full of themselves, but Yinka was about to ruin their day completely.

When Yinka stopped before the bench, Desola and her gang immediately stopped chatting and they all turned to her. Timon raised his eyebrows, confused about why she was intruding in their exclusive space. Desola flung Yinka a filthy look.

"What does this freshie girl want?" Desola said, her top lip curved upwards into a sneer as her gang laughed around her. "Don't start begging us for money with your burnt lips." Desola then pinched her nostrils. "Do you have your bath in mud or something? We are not in your village in Nigeria, freshie. You do know they sell soap over here in the UK, right? Ever heard of Dove?"

Desola's admirers laughed and hooted. Timon looked at Yinka and shook his head at her, smirking. Soon, she would wipe that smugness from his face—from all their faces.

Yinka narrowed her eyes at Desola. "I have something to show you."

The group on the bench now gave Yinka a bemused look as she dipped into the left pocket of her black school trousers and pulled out her Blackberry phone. She opened the video she wanted to play to the group from one of the files on her phone. She pressed play on the MP4 video and held the Blackberry frontwards towards Desola and her gang.

Although the footage was low resolution, you could see Desola, Timon and four others smoking cigarettes, drinking cheap Vodka from a bottle and snogging each other in a classroom as a Lil Wayne song played from a CD player on one of the desk tables.

Yinka felt an immense swell of joy as she watched Desola's self-important smile fade away, and her eyes widened with abject horror.

"You sneaky little bitch," Desola said, standing up from Timon's lap. She marched towards Yinka and smacked the phone from her hand. The Blackberry fell onto the concrete ground. Desola stomped on it hard with her right foot.

"You don't have any evidence now, freshie," Desola said, her arrogant smile returning.

Yinka sniggered and shook her head. "Do you think I am so stupid? I have made so many copies of that footage."

Desola stepped back, her mouth wide open and trembling. Now, she was looking at Yinka as if she were staring at the face of a demon that had spawned from hell. It satisfied Yinka to see her tormentor now become tormented.

"You know if I show this video to the headteacher, you're all going to get expelled for sneaking alcohol and cigarettes into school and breaking into a classroom in the evening. What will your parents think? I am sure you'll all be sent back to Nigeria." Yinka smirked. "And then you'll smell just like me."

"Okay. So what do you want, innit?" Timon said, glaring at Yinka as Desola sat back on his lap, visibly distressed.

"You will not call me names anymore, chase me around or ambush me on my way to class. And for all the bad things you've said to me, you'll each have to give me five pounds every week till the end of the year."

"Fuck off, you little witch. I am not doing that," Desola spat, glaring at Yinka.

Yinka threw daggers at Desola with her eyes. "If you don't, I am heading to the headmaster's office with the footage. You've been warned. Every lunch break meet me here to give me your money."

Seeing as she had made her threat clear, Yinka turned away from Desola, Timon and the rest of the pathetic gang. She picked up her cracked Blackberry from the ground, still working fine despite the cracked screen, and walked away from the bench.

Today had been the best day at school. Yinka smiled to herself, feeling powerful. Even when she collected the money from Desola and the rest of her gang, Yinka planned to share the footage with the headteacher anyway. But first, she would have a little fun with the power she now had.

35

TIMON AND YINKA sat at an upscale restaurant, the New York Grill, on the 52nd floor of the Park Hyatt Tokyo Hotel. In the evening, the panoramic views of Tokyo's skyline were breathtaking. Yinka felt like she was staring into an electric neon city of the future.

The New York Grill had a swanky vibe that characterised the restaurant's décor with its open kitchen and a wine cellar boasting over 1,800 bottles. Yinka felt like she had stepped into the eloquent world of The Great Gatsby, one of her late father's favourite books. The restaurant tables had dim lamp nights, the smell of fried stake lingered in the air, Japanese waiters, some wearing face masks, were dressed in tuxedo jackets, and a live jazz band serenaded the diners at the front of the restaurant. A beautiful Japanese lady wearing an embroidered emerald sequin maxi dress sang a stunning rendition of Shola's Ama's 'You Might Need Somebody.'

Once the female waiter had brought Yinka and Timon's food over—Yinka had ordered the Kagawa olive-fed beef sirloin with fries, and Timon had gone for the Gunma Toriyama Akagi ribeye also with fries—they immediately dug into their pricey but very well-cooked meal. On their table was a bottle of exceedingly expensive red wine they had both agreed to share.

The Japanese waiter filled both of their glasses. "Enjoy your meal."

Yinka began to eat her food and drank some red wine, which went down smoothly. It was one of the best red wines she ever tasted; its sweet and dark flavour sliding satisfyingly down her throat. The wine also made her tongue a little loose, and an urge soon arose to strike up a casual conversation with Timon.

"I want to know something, "Yinka started, cutting off a piece of beef sirloin, "whatever happened to your girlfriend when we were at school together? I couldn't stand her. She was an Igbo girl."

Timon, still chewing, began to cough as if he were choking. He squinted his eyes, hit his chest with a clenched fist, and raised his finger at Yinka, indicating that she should wait for his response. After taking a swig of his wine to wash down what appeared to be a challenging piece of steak, Timon looked at Yinka.

"You're talking about Desola? Or DeDe as everyone knew her by," Timon said, having regained composure. He propped his elbows on the table.

"Yes, that was her name. You two were always eating each other's lips at school. It was very embarrassing."

Timon chuckled. "I was only fourteen; give me a break, please. Anyway, after you got me..." He sighed deeply, and Yinka saw a flash of regret or discomfort across his face. "After me, her and the rest of our friends got expelled from school; I did not see her again until my mid-twenties. Her father was a proper, no-nonsense Igbo man and sent her on the first plane back to Nigeria. The last time I saw her was randomly at a club in Soho when I was still a Junior Analyst. She was with some rich uncle at a party I was invited to. He was old enough to be her father, but she didn't mind being all over him. We caught up on life for a bit; she was living in New York, working in fashion or something like that, and that was it. Never saw her again after that night."

Yinka nodded and hummed as she considered what Timon had divulged about her former school tormentor. "And she never mentioned me when you two caught up?"

Timon laughed so loudly that Yinka could feel the other diners looking in their direction. "Why would she ask about you? We all hated you for what you did to us. Remember you lied to us and got us permanently expelled from school?"

Yinka popped the piece of beef sirloin into her mouth and chewed the tender meat for a minute before swallowing it. She looked at Timon and shrugged her shoulders. "And you don't think you deserved it? You and your friends broke the school rules, or did you forget?"

"Yeah, we did. But I also remember we gave you our pocket money for a month so you wouldn't show that footage to the headteacher. Like you promised. Yet you still did it anyway. You didn't have to play us like that, you know."

"And you and your friends didn't have to make it a game to bully and torment me every day at school." Yinka narrowed her eyes at Timon, and she could feel the goodwill toward him she had started to build begin to leak out of her body. "Anyway, in retrospect, I did you a favour; let's be honest. Would you have graduated from Cambridge if you stayed in that rubbish school with those types of friends you had?"

Yinka watched as Timon silently considered what she had said. He shook his head, now looking irritated. "Ok, probably not, but that's not the point, is it. You still lied."

"If you want an apology, you won't get one, Timon." Yinka took a swig of the wine and gave Timon a hard stare. Thankfully, he was smart enough to read the room.

"Look, what happened at school is a touchy subject for both of us," Timon said, leaning back on his chair. He gulped down some red wine. "Let's not talk about those days. I want to ask you something else."

Yinka narrowed her eyes curiously at Timon and took a sip of wine. "Okay, ask me."

"Who do you want to become in the future?"

Yinka raised her eyebrows at him. That was not the line of inquiry she was expecting Timon to go down. And she wasn't even sure how to respond to such a question. "What do you mean by that?"

Timon put his hands together in a ball and looked deeply at Yinka as if he were her psychologist. "I have to be honest; you confuse me. You're a smart woman. You speak fluent Italian."

"German, Spanish and French," Yinka said with a wink.

Timon chuckled. "See what I mean. You must have gone to university, right?"

"Yes, I did. I went to the London School of Economics and studied Social Anthropology with Languages." Yinka gave Timon a slight grin. "Not quite Cambridge."

"It's not a competition," Timon said, smiling at her. "Black excellence is black excellence, and we both got it like that. We're Nigerians, so we're naturally brainy. But what I don't understand is why you've chosen to use your talents just to steal money from rich African men. I know you use some of the money to help the less fortunate, but is this really what you want to do? You could be more than just a do-gooder fraudster and a thief, Yinka." Timon then raised both his hands. "And I am not judging you. So don't bite my head off, please. Just saying."

Much to Yinka's surprise, Timon's words did not rile her up as she expected. No one, not even Oge, had ever directly asked her what she wanted to do. What she wanted never really mattered. Whatever Oge needed her to be, she would be.

"I have my reasons for doing what I do," Yinka said finally

after a moment's silence. "But…my long-term goal, I guess, is to build an all-girls school in my father's village in Nigeria. It's a place called Abeokuta. I was born there and spent much of my childhood there before coming to London. My late father was a journalist in Nigeria. He always wanted to build a school in my village to teach Nigerian children about the world outside their own. That is why I studied Social Anthropology and Languages at university. Like my father, I am fascinated by the world."

"That's a beautiful dream, you know, to build a school," Timon said, his eyes on Yinka. "And it sounds like you were very close to your father. I am sorry he passed away."

Yinka felt warmth in her chest, as always, when she thought about her late father. Then she suddenly felt very exposed in front of Timon. She couldn't look him in the eyes and stared down at her plate. She realised that Oge knew only about her ambition to build an all-girls school in Nigeria. Now, she had shared such a personal detail about herself with Timon.

"Hey, are you okay?"

Yinka looked up at Timon and gave him a short smile. "I am fine. It's just…nothing. Yes, I was close to my father. I loved him dearly."

"Well, I hope you build that school one day and make him proud," Timon said, smiling warmly at her. "You would be a great headteacher. Probably a little too strict sometimes, and you'd need to work on your sense of humour, but I can see it." Timon stretched out his hands as if he was making a banner. "Yinka's school for gifted girls. You know, it has a ring to it."

Yinka sucked her teeth but chuckled. "That wine has gone to your head, crypto boy. So, what about you and your father? Did you get your black excellence from him?" Yinka sipped some wine and smirked at Timon.

The grimace that scrunched Timon's facial features told Yinka all she needed to know about Timon's relationship with his father. "I get all my black excellence from my mum," he said, defiant and proud. "She raised me all by herself while running her successful salon business. I think I saw my father once my whole life when he visited me on my graduation day. I didn't feel any connection to that man." Timon snorted. "He's a big deal in Nigeria. Too important for my mum. Or me."

The pain, the kind which belonged to a hurt child, tinged Timon's voice. To her surprise, Yinka didn't want to see Timon dispirited after seeing the childlike side of him. She gave him a kind smile. "Well, your mum raised a black man who graduated from Cambridge. Seems like she is all you ever needed."

Timon nodded, but Yinka detected a painful sadness in his smile.

"Yeah, she's amazing."

* * *

By the time Yinka and Timon finished their meal, it was 9 pm. With the red wine spinning in her head, Yinka felt very drunk. Fortunately, Timon helped her to their shared hotel suite, holding her by her shoulders as they walked along the corridor.

"I didn't know you were such a lightweight," Timon said, with a muffled laugh as he opened the door of their hotel suite so Yinka could stumble through.

"I don't drink red wine," Yinka said as she swayed into the parlour. Unsteady on her feet, she moaned and rubbed her forehead.

Timon went over to the sink, poured her a jug of water and then walked over to hand it to her.

"Thanks." Yinka took long and loud gulps of water, emptying the whole jug. She let out a loud burp, causing

Timon to giggle, and placed the jug on the dining table. "I am going to bed. Like right now."

Timon nodded with a grin. "I think that's best. I'll see you in the morning."

Yinka gave him a thumbs up, and Timon shook his head, amused by all this. *How embarrassing to get in this state in front of Timon of all people,* Yinka thought as she swayed towards her room.

Despite the occasional awkwardness during their dinner, it had not tainted what had been a pleasant time with Timon. Now, a growing part of her felt guilty that she was keeping certain truths from him and had slightly manipulated him into joining this mission. But he was still getting paid five million pounds to help her.

"Hey, Timon," Yinka said. She had opened the door to her room but stood in the doorway.

Timon, who had already walked halfway into his room, stepped back out and looked at her. "What's up? You want more water?"

Yinka lifted her right hand in the air and shook her head. "No, I am fine. I just wanted to say thank you for today. When you're not behaving like a stereotypically egotistical Nigerian man who has money…"

Timon chuckled. "That's not a totally accurate view of me."

"…You're actually a decent guy." Yinka cast her eyes to the floor. "You know, I will never understand why you and your friends put me through all that abuse when we were in secondary school. Things might have been different between us. We could have been friends. Maybe."

Yinka looked up and saw Timon staring back at her silently and looking puzzled. His lips parted, but he said nothing.

"Anyway, goodnight." Yinka stepped inside her bedroom and closed it, leaving Timon dumbfounded in front of his room door.

36

"THERE WILL BE a lot of important guests at tonight's birthday gala for Mr Shinoda," Dugard said, talking to both Yinka and Timon as the three of them sat at the back of the Rolls Royce Phantom cruising through Tokyo's evening roads. "Please stay close to me as I introduce you to a few people. Also, I have spoken briefly to Emiko and her cousin, Jin, about your proposition. Because Signor Mancini has already invested in Afchain, it bodes well for your chances with the Shinoda family." Dugard smiled, seemingly pleased with himself. "As for our sheikh, Mustafa, I am not entirely sure if he is in Japan or Dubai, but I guess we'll find out tonight."

"Sounds good," Timon said, nodding at Dugard. "And thank you again for all your hospitality. You've been too generous."

Yinka wasn't sure if Timon had caught it, but a flash of something dark coloured Dugard's features. It lasted for a split second as he smiled at Timon.

"No need to thank me, Timon. The pleasure is all mine, believe me."

At precisely 10 p.m., the Rolls Royce pulled up at the Tokyo Metropolitan Government building, the venue for Jin

Shinoda's 30th birthday gala, as light rain drizzled outside. To host a party in such a politically significant building was a testament to the Shinoda family's influence.

When the Japanese driver, wearing a face mask and holding a large umbrella, opened the back compartment doors, Dugard was the first to step out, dressed in a grey slim-fit two-piece tuxedo. Timon, who had gone for a cream-coloured two-piece suit with a white shirt and an unbuttoned collar for a smart casual look for tonight's bash, was about to follow Dugard's lead but sat back down. He turned to look at Yinka instead. This evening, she had chosen a classy and understated attire, rocking an all-black batwing sleeve coat and one-shoulder ruched dress.

"That Botox-faced bastard is going to be at this party," Timon said, a faint hint of malice in his tone. "If he comes up to you or makes you uncomfortable, you can give me a secret sign."

Touched by Timon's protectiveness, Yinka was also slightly amused by how it came out.

"What secret sign should that be? Say something to you in Yoruba?"

Timon chuckled with a grin. "Don't cuss me out but I can't speak much Yoruba. I know a few words and phrases only. My mother didn't really teach me."

Yinka sniggered and patted Timon playfully on the shoulder. "You're too much of a British boy. But, in all seriousness, thank you for your concern, Timon. But I'll be fine. I am focused only on what we came here to do."

Timon nodded in response and did not push further, which Yinka greatly appreciated. He exited the car, stood by the door, and stretched out his left hand. Yinka held onto his outstretched hand as she carefully manoeuvred out of the Rolls Royce, careful to maintain balance on her stiletto heels against the wet pavement. She was clutching her Gucci bag. Dugard and the driver and approached them, and they huddled underneath the umbrella the driver held up.

Timon gave Yinka a wink as she let go of his hand and straightened her evening dress.

"Let's go secure this bag, business partner."

* * *

On the observatory deck on the top floor of the Tokyo Metropolitan Government building, Jin Shinoda's birthday gala provided a magnificent, panoramic view of Tokyo's neon-washed metropolis. So high was the observatory deck that Yinka could even make out the silhouette of Mount Fuji, the tallest mountain in Japan, among the pitch blackness of the evening.

The gala's theme was a mixture of high-end European fashion infused with Japanese cultural sensibilities. Yinka saw a wide range of designer handbags, from Fendi to Birkin, hanging from the shoulders of Japanese and non-Japanese women in long evening dresses, wearing pearls and diamonds that twinkled like tiny stars. Most of the men were in suits, and all wore watches that instantly communicated their status and wealth. Even Timon's Rolex felt prosaic among some of the impressive timepieces.

Gliding between the guests, holding trays with delicately prepared canapes, were Japanese women in heavy makeup, their faces as white as baby powder, and wearing kimono dresses. When she was at university, Yinka had read about these kimono dresses, which had once been very popular among Japanese women with their bold colours and arrest-ing, intricately drawn imagery and patterns. Although a kimono was very different in its tailoring compared to the traditional dresses worn by Nigerian women, in a way, both served a similar purpose - to emphasise and enhance the beauty of a women.

A band played music on a makeshift steel stage at the front of the observatory. The music reminded Yinka of disco music from the 80s her father had sometimes listened to. A Japanese woman, wearing a fiercely orange and yellow kimono with a drawing of a long, black dragon twisting vertically across the dress, held a microphone to her mouth. She was singing a catchy and soulful melody in Japanese.

Dugard had yet to formally introduce Yinka and Timon to any of the guests before Yinka felt her chest clench tight as she saw Mancini making a beeline towards them with a woman hooked onto his left arm. The Italian bastard was wearing a dark navy dinner jacket, with a white shirt and white loafers. Around his neck hung a crimson, silk paisley scarf. Everything about his attire communicated loudly that he was a rich asshole.

"Dugard, my favourite English man," Mancini said, with a tight smile on his stiff face. The woman he was with let go of his arm as she embraced Dugard.

After hugging Dugard, Mancini stepped back from him and turned his attention onto Yinka and Timon. When she had first met Mancini, he had acted like an excited dog wagging its tail when food appeared before it. But the way his eyes pierced into her in this moment, now shining with a hideous and newly acquired intimacy about her body, made Yinka want to throw up. She felt her heartbeat increase and her skin tingle with anxiousness. It was Timon squeezing her wrist gently that calmed her nerves.

"Yinka, you look astonishing as always," Mancini said. He licked his lips and briefly levelled his eyes at Timon. "And Signor Bakare, nice to see you again. So you're aware, I have seen the contract you have sent over regarding my investment into Afchain. My lawyers have looked at it and I will sign it shortly. I look forward to seeing what comes of this crypto company you've convinced me to put my money into. I hope it will make me an even richer man."

Yinka could feel Timon's anger manifest from the heat radiating from his body as she stood beside him.

"I specialise in making rich people even richer," Timon said, his tone stretching like a rubber band as he tried to remain polite. "Even the one who are *pricks*. Not saying you're in that category, of course, Signor Mancini."

If Mancini had caught Timon's backhanded insult, and he would have as Timon had thrown it at his face like a pie, he seemed unbothered by it. Instead, he gestured to the woman standing beside him the whole time, clutching her black YSL bag in silence.

"I would like to introduce you both to my wife, Federica. She's a talented actress."

Yinka was the first to shake Federica's right hand and the woman gave her a tight smile. Mancini's wife looked in her early forties with a light brown complexion, so she appeared tanned, black, long flowing hair and the poise of a golden age Hollywood actress. Perhaps it was because she was a woman, but Yinka could feel the deep unhappiness that tightened around Federica like a strait jacket. She could not imagine how it must feel like to be married to piece of shit like Silvio Mancini.

"I hope you are enjoying Shinjuku. It is my favourite part of Tokyo,"Federica said, her voice rich with her Italian accent. "Are you all staying in the same hotel?"

"We are," Dugard said, flashing his white teeth as he smiled. "We're at the Park Hyatt Tokyo. Such value for money and with a splendid view of the city."

"Sorry, can you all excuse me for a moment?" Yinka said. "I am just going to get a drink. I am feeling thirsty."

As Yinka walked away from Timon and the others, she was beside herself. She could no longer bare Mancini any longer as those cold eyes continued to glance at her, each time relishing whatever secrets about her body it contained. The urge to strangle him became too overbearing.

Yinka fount the makeshift bar in the corner of the observatory. She did not know a word of Japanese, beyond *kon'nichiwa,* but thankfully the drinks menu was in English and Japanese. She ordered her usual cocktail of choice, gin and tonic on the rocks, and took a satisfying sip from the highball glass. She would wait a few minutes by the bar before returning to Timon and Dugard. Hopefully, Mancini had fucked off somewhere else.

But much to her despair, Yinka saw Mancini coming alone towards her, his thin lips bent into a twisted smile on that artificial old face. Yinka's first thought was to leave the bar, but she decided against it. No man was going to intimidate her, certainly not a white man.

"A glass of whiskey sour," Mancini said to the Japanese bartender as he stood next to Yinka who did not immediately pay him any mind. After making his order, he turned to Yinka. "Just ordering a drink for my wife. What do you think of her?"

Yinka took a swig of her gin and tonic and did not look at Mancini as she spoke, her voice cold and sharp like glaciers. "She must wake up to a living hell everyday."

Mancini chuckled. "I am sensing some curious hatred towards me. Have I done something wrong?

"You put something in my drink when I was on your yacht. I passed out immediately after I drank the drink you offered me. I've never fainted in my life till then. I grew up in and spend a lot my time in Nigeria. I don't faint because of the heat."

"That is a bold accusation against me, Yinka," Mancini said. Yinka caught Mancini's mouth curve from the side of her eye into a wicked and knowing grin. "You should be more careful with what you say to the man who has just invested three million into your little African tech company."

Yinka wanted to turn around and throw her cocktail in Mancini's face and it took all her willpower to stop herself. As much as she detested Mancini, she still needed his investment. Her boyfriend's life depended on it.

Mancini had not finished toying with her. "Besides, even if I did lace your drink with something, you should be grateful I didn't do more to you when you were in that debilitated state. Maybe all I did was get a sneak peek at what was underneath your delightfully tight skirt."

It was enough to make Yinka's sense of control snap like a twig. If Timon had not entered her vicinity just as she was about to turn around and raise her hand, Mancini would have been on the receiving end of a Nigerian's woman hot slap.

"Is everything ok?" Timon said, his voice stern as he stood beside Yinka. He glared at Mancini.

"I was just thanking your beautiful business partner for making me see the potential in Afchain. She knows how to be a very *persuasive* woman." Mancini took the cocktail he had ordered as the bartender handed it to him. "I must return to my wife. She sometimes gets very intimidated by these social gatherings. It was a pleasure seeing you two again. Enjoy the party." Mancini gave Yinka and Timon a curt nod before walking off.

"You looked like you was about to smash your glass over his head," Timon said, looking at Yinka, concerned. "What did he say to you?"

"He confirmed that he spiked my drink, Timon," Yinka said, through gritted teeth as she gripped her cocktail glass. "I hope his face swells up one day and explodes into a mess of Botox and pasta. He is a vile and wicked man. *òpònú*.

"What does that mean?"

Yinka looked at Timon and grinned. "It means bastard in Yoruba."

"You do need to teach me Yoruba. Especially all the curse words."

A light chuckle bounced from Yinka's mouth and lightened her mood. Before she could respond to Timon, a commotion diverted her attention.

A Japanese man, in his early 30s, with a dark curly hair fade and a boyish face, ran onto the makeshift stage. He wore a white suit but nothing underneath the jacket so his toned bare chest was on display. Two burly security guards rushed onto the stage but the Japanese man gave them the middle finger. Much to Yinka's surprise, the bodyguards rolled their eyes and walked off the stage, shaking their heads in embarrassment. The Japanese man, drunk from how he swung on the mic podium like a deranged rockstar, started to speak into the microphone in Japanese. Whatever he was saying held the guests' attention who began to laugh and raise their glasses to him. The Japanese man broke into song, singingly drunkenly into the mic, his voice crooning. It sounded like a man crying in pain.

"Please excuse my cousin," came a Japanese female voice from behind.

Both Yinka and Timon turned around to find a beautiful Japanese woman, who looked around Yinka's age, standing behind them. She had dark eyes and shoulder length hair in wavy curls dyed red orange. On her left ear was a golden helix piercing and she had applied coral coloured lipstick on her thin lips which complimented her hair colour. Unlike the other women at the gala, she was not in a formal evening gown. Instead, she wore a grey, unbuttoned cotton blazer with nothing but a sports bra underneath and grey waist belted trousers with a wide leg. She completed her chic look with white heels and a silver pendent around her neck. Immediately, Yinka liked her style. Rebellious yet sophisticated.

The snazzily dressed Japanese woman stretched out her right hand, and Yinka and Timon gave her a handshake. "Emiko Shinoda."

"Wow, it's a pleasure to meet you, Miss Shinoda," Yinka said, smiling.

"So I assume the man on the stage singing his heart out is your cousin?" Timon said.

"Unfortunately, for my family, yes," Emiko said, shaking her head as she glanced at Jin who was still belting his lungs out on the front stage. "He likes to live up to his party boy image and has gone all out on his special day, consuming one tomany glasses of Shōchū."

"Shoshew?" Timon said, not quite nailing the Japanese pronunciation. "What's that?"

"It's a popular beverage in Japan," Emiko said, in a casual tone. "I want to say it is similar to Vodka in the west but I would be disingenuous. It's uniquely Japanese. I would recommend the beverage. They are serving it at the bar. Although,I must warn you, it is strong."

"All the more reason to try it," Timon said, with a cheeky grin.

Emiko's smile stretched as she regarded Yinka and Timon with her dark, almond-shaped eyes. There was an air of nonchalance and easy confidence about her. "Dugard and Mancini have spoken highly about this African-based crypto finance platform you seek investment for. Both men have been my family's trusted investors and advisors for several years. I discuss with them often about how I should invest my family's money as I mainly oversee the management of the Shinoda fund."

Yinka gave Emiko a smirk. "Makes sense. If you want to ensure your money is in good hands, let a woman keep hold of it."

Emiko chuckled briskly. "I can't say I disagree." She put both hands behind her back. "Given my cousin's...inebriated state, tonight is not the best time to discuss business. If you are free two days from now, I would like to invite you to my family's estate. You can properly pitch to me and other important stakeholders in my family's fund on why we should invest in your company."

"Yes, let's do that," Yinka said.

"Perfect," Emiko said, with a nod. "Apologies I can't stay with you and talk longer, I have other matters to attend to, least of all making sure my cousin does not break his neck falling from that stage. But it has been a pleasure to meet you both."

"Likewise," Timon said.

Emiko gave them another nod and seemed ready to turn on her heels and leave Yinka and Timon's company before turning back to address them.

"Oh, if you drink some Shōchū tonight and enjoy it, let me know. I can have it served at our meeting." With that, Emiko walked away into the crowd of guests, leaving quite an impression in her wake.

37

Wearing his long, black trench coat, Kojo stood outside Shinjuku Park Tower by the corner of the towering building with his hands in his pockets. A patchy drizzle of rain ran down his face. He was waiting for a man named Hiroshi Watanabe, a 23-year-old clerk at the Park Hyatt Tokyo, for whom Kojo had paid 180,000 yen yesterday evening—just under a grand if converted to pound sterling—to access Dugard's hotel suite along with that of his two associates, Timon and Yinka.

Kojo had watched the footage of Jin Shinoda's birthday gala two nights ago from the microscopic camera he had covertly placed on Federica's designer handbag. The footage had given him so much useful intelligence. More than he dared hope for. Not only had his hypotheses that Dugard was in Tokyo with Mancini proved true, but, to his surprise, so were Timon and Yinka. The most interesting information Kojo had learned from the footage was that Mancini had invested in a crypto company called Afchain, which Timon and Yinka seemed to be involved in, but what did that have to do with Dugard? Crucially, Kojo also now knew that Dugard, Timon, and Yinka were all staying at the Park Hyatt Tokyo. So he had decided he would bug their hotel rooms.

Hiroshi Watanabe was now walking towards Kojo, coming from around the corner. The skinny, young Japanese man had a long, thin neck, round spectacles, and shifted bangs. He kept looking back as he walked as if someone was following him.

"We have to go in from a back door, okay?" Hiroshi said as soon as he reached Kojo. He spoke good English but had a squeaky voice, breathed heavily and his eyes kept darting from left to right. "The cameras don't work there. No one will see us enter."

Kojo nodded and followed the skittish hotel clerk around the building until they stopped in front of an aluminium door. Hiroshi looked over his shoulder, which Kojo found very amusing as it was clear no one had followed him, then retrieved a keycard from his wallet and swiped it against the card reader attached to the door. The door opened with a clicking sound, and Hiroshi stepped in with Kojo following him.

After walking down an empty corridor, Kojo and Hiroshi took a lift to the 52nd floor of the building.

"You're certain all three of them are not in their rooms right now?" Kojo said, standing behind Hiroshi in the elevator. The hotel clerk kept fidgeting on the spot as if he had a bug crawling around in his underwear.

"Yes," Hiroshi said in a low voice. "I saw the three guests you described leave about an hour ago in a black Rolls-Royce."

"Good, because this is very important."

Hiroshi slightly turned his neck and gave Kojo a side-eye. "Are you a terrorist? You told me you wanted to plant a device in their rooms. Is it a bomb? I don't want to be involved in any murder."

Kojo had to suffocate his laugh, not wanting to make

Hiroshi more on edge than he already was. "No, Hiroshi, I am not a terrorist."

"So why do you want access to these three people's rooms? What are you planning to do?

A part of Kojo wanted to ignore the question, pretend he hadn't heard it. But he thought it better to soothe the young, terribly scared Japanese man. The last thing Kojo wanted was for the hotel clerk to change his mind at the last minute and return Kojo's monetary bribe.

"I work for the British government, Hiroshi," Kojo said casually. "These three individuals may potentially pose a national and global threat to Britain and even Japan. I am simply gathering information on them by placing recording devices in their rooms."

"So you're a spy?"

"Yes, I suppose you could say that. But I am on the side of the good guys."

Thankfully, Kojo's explanation seemed to have massaged Hiroshi's nerves as he did not ask Kojo further questions. Once they exited the elevator on the 52nd floor, Kojo followed Hiroshi down the sleek and sparse corridor, with Japanese artwork hanging from wooden frames, until they stopped at room 5012.

Hiroshi again made his 'looking-over-the-shoulder' gesture before producing the keycard from his left trouser pocket. He swiped against the electronic keylock attached to the black door's handle. There was a click sound, and Hiroshi squeezed the handle and pushed the door open. Kojo followed him inside.

"This is the presidential suite for Mr Dugard," Hiroshi said.

Standing next to Hiroshi, Kojo inspected the place. Like the rest of the hotel, the suite had the same consistent theme of elegant quaintness with its cream-coloured walls, a black dining table, a grand piano, oak shelves stacked with

Japanese literature, and Akari lamps around the room. There were no bells and whistles, but maximum comfort none-theless.

However, Kojo had not come here to inspect the standards of the hotel. He dipped his right hand into the inner left breast pocket of his trench coat and retrieved a black plastic case the size of the palm of his hand. He opened it to find six thin poles, the size and length of small white candy sticks, lined horizontally inside. These were mini voice recorders, another intelligence-gathering equipment from the tech wizards at MI6. The mini voice recorder had a continuous recording time of 200 hours and a powerful battery, so it did not need to charge for days. The best part was that Kojo could activate the devices from miles away.

"Get out your phone and record where I am placing the devices," Kojo said, turning to look at Hiroshi, who was standing in the middle of the room with a tense face. "When the guests have checked out from the hotel, you are to retrieve these devices from their rooms, bring them to me at an address I will send you, and then delete the video recordings from your phone. This is very important. Do you understand, Hiroshi?"

Hiroshi gave a stiff nod.

After planting three mini voice recorders in Dugard's suite, Hiroshi led Kojo to Timon and Yinka's shared suite. Kojo planted three further devices there, one in the parlour and one in each room. Hiroshi had silently recorded where Kojo had planted the devices.

"You have my number, so call me as soon as they've checked out," Kojo said to Hiroshi. They were outside the Shinjuku Park Tower complex in the back corner. "Once you've retrieved all six recording devices, I will pay you an additional 180,000 yen."

Hiroshi nodded quickly, and without saying a word, he

briskly walked away from Kojo. He turned a corner until he disappeared from view.

With the rooms now bugged, Kojo simply had to sit and wait. Hopefully, the secret recordings would reveal the nature of Dugard's and Mancini's business dealings and expose the existence of The Cable. Kojo also hoped he would finally learn what Timon and Yinka were doing flying around the world with two potentially corrupt private bankers.

Kojo looked up at the Shinjuku Park Tower one final time, put his hands in his coat pockets, and then walked towards the main road as the rain poured down on a drab and wet Tokyo afternoon.

38

THE RAIN HAD STOPPED when Yinka stepped out of the Rolls-Royce and gazed at the sprawling three-storey residential building located in Den-en-chōfu, an exclusive neighbourhood in southern Tokyo. The stunning property, nestled on a quiet leafy street lined with blossom trees, was elegant in its architectural design. It had an onyx-coloured façade made from reinforced concrete, a black metal gate ring-fenced around the building, and a garage where a black Ferrari and a white Mercedes G-wagon were parked. This was the Shinoda estate.

Timon and Dugard had now exited the Rolls-Royce, both dressed in their tailored suits and came to join Yinka, who was wearing a white polyester blouse, black high-waisted trousers and black slingback heels.

Being invited by Emiko to her wealthy's family home was a rare opportunity. The Shinoda family, from what Yinka had learned about them in the dossier sent by her team, were fiercely private. Yinka was determined to make sure she walked out of there with an investment deal. She may not get another chance.

"The Shinoda family are extremely particular about which

businesses they invest their family's fund into," Dugard said, looking at Timon and Yinka as they all stood a few feet away from the estate's metal gates. "Despite the investment you've already secured from Mancini and a glowing endorsement from me, you two will still need to do much more convincing. It is far from a done deal."

"We've got this," Timon said. He turned to look at Yinka and grinned. "You're looking at a power team right here. We could enter Dragon's Den and walk out with a million in investment in five minutes."

Yinka chuckled, although she would be lying if she said she wasn't feeling slightly nervous. Having briefly met Emiko, Yinka had quickly discerned that she was a sharp woman.

"This meeting is going to be more gruelling than Dragon's Den," Yinka said, looking at Timon. "But we've been practising our pitch for two days. We're as ready as we'll ever be."

Two Japanese security guards in black suits, with ear pieces and wearing dark shades, stood guard at the at the sliding gate which led into the compound. As Yinka approached the gate with Timon and Dugard, she was not surprised by the intense level of security, recalling what she knew about the Shinoda family.

For almost three decades, the Shinoda family had been one the biggest Yakuza families, with a sizable stronghold in Shinjuku. Kiyoshi Shinoda, Emiko's father and Jin's uncle had been equally revered and feared as one of the most violent and fiercest Yakuza bosses, involved in everything from extortion to racketeering. Eventually, Kiyoshi's criminal activity caught up with him, and the Yakuza patriarch was arrested almost ten years ago following the Japanese government's severe crackdown on Yakuza gangs. Kiyoshi was sentenced to twenty years in prison. Since then, the Shinoda family has made a concerted effort to overhaul their image to become recognised as a family dynasty that owned several companies and real estate in Tokyo. Yet many still believe that the family's Yakuza empire never really ended, and many of their legitimate companies were merely fronts for criminal enterprises.

After the two security guards checked Yinka, Timon, and Dugard's passports and thoroughly frisked them, one of the guards radioed a message in Japanese through his earpiece. The sliding gates slid open, and Yinka, Dugard, and Timon were escorted into the compound.

Yinka and the others followed the security guard through an expansive formal garden with tall hedges, neat trees, several water fountains and evergreen shrubs. They walked across the whole yard until the security guard finally came to a halt in front of another part of the enormous estate with bifold aluminium doors. Through the door windows, Yinka could see several Japanese men in black suits and ties sitting around a conference table in a room made of what looked like white marble. Sitting at the end of the table was Emiko, and Jin was at the other end.

The security guard squeezed the handle of the bi-fold aluminium door and pushed it open, holding it for Yinka, Timon and Dugard to walk through,

As soon as Yinka stepped into the room, she immediately felt all eyes turn on her, Timon and Dugard. There were ten seated Japanese men, dressed in suits and in their late sixties with dull faces and dark eyes who looked at Yinka with a curious stare. Emiko, dressed in a fire-orange single-button orange blazer with matching trousers, gave Yinka a smile and a nod. At the other end of the table, Jin was dressed bizarrely in a white tank top and high-waisted slacks. He was eating an apple while scrolling through his phone and had barely lifted his head when Yinka and the others entered the room.

Dugard gave a short bow before greeting the room. "Thank you, Miss Shinoda, for inviting us into your home for this special meeting. We are very grateful for this opportunity."

Following Dugard's lead, Timon and Yinka bowed as well, following the rituals of politeness in Japanese culture.

"It is a pleasure to have you here," Emiko said with an easy and relaxed voice. "Please be seated, and we can begin the meeting. We have also brought light refreshments: green tea and biscuits." Emiko addressed Yinka and Timon directly. She winked. "I know I said I would offer Shōchū at the meeting, but I was advised that it would not be appropriate."

Yinka heard Jin snigger at his cousin's remark as he continued looking at his phone.

"No worries. Green tea is fine, "Yinka said, curtsying to Emiko. "Thank you."

Once Yinka and the others had taken their seats and completed all the introductions, she and Timon began their business pitch. Dugard remained silent but watched and listened intently. As they effortlessly took turns discussing the merits of Afchain and why it was a worthwhile investment, Timon doing most of the heavy lifting as he was the crypto expert, Yinka would scan the faces of the Japanese men. Their facial expressions remained blank, giving nothing away. Emiko nodded her head during moments of their pitch but said nothing, and not once did her face lit up in visible intrigue. As for Jin, he kept scrolling through his phone, seemingly disinterested. Dugard was right. Getting investment from the Shinoda family would not be as easy as it was with Mancini.

"For the past 50 years, Japan has been one of the most steadfast purveyors of innovation in Africa," Timon said, confidence sailing through his voice. "Japan has invested in the continent's infrastructure, from railways to schools, greatly improving the standard of living for generations to come. By investing in Afchain, you will continue Japan's legacy of innovation within Africa by having a hand in a technology that promises to transform the utility and power of money and potentially bring millions and millions of people out of poverty."

If Timon was expecting a round of applause after concluding the pitch, it would not come from anyone in the room. The formally dressed Japanese men, some of whom had been taking notes, looked at each other and gave silent nods. Emiko reclined on her swivel chair, her hands in a ball as she stared at Yinka, but it was hard to discern what she was thinking.

After spending the entirety of the meeting on his iPhone, Jin finally looked up from his screen and acknowledged the guests in his room. "You know, I invested a lot of my money into NFTs when there was all this hype around it," he said, in a voice that was deeper than Yinka was expecting, considering the last time she had seen him, he had been singing drunkenly on a stage. "And I lost all of my money in the end when these NFTs amounted to nothing. Crypto is a scam. And my family don't invest in scams."

"NFTs are nothing more than overhyped digital pictures of cartoon monkeys endorsed by clueless celebrities, and I am sorry, Mr Shinoda, that you lost money investing in them," Timon said, addressing Jin directly, who was now giving Timon his undivided attention. "But Afchain isn't some fad. It is the future of e-commerce in West Africa. We're talking about an advanced digital platform enabling all Africans to buy and trade in a new currency that will generate wealth for them and, I guarantee you, for your family as well. For generations to come."

Jin nodded, looking quite impressed by Timon's response. "Well, that does sound promising," he said, now reclining on his chair. He then placed his two feet on the table, drawing disapproving head shakes and glares from the older Japanese men in the room. "What'd you say, Emz? Should we help continue Japan's legacy of innovation in Africa?"

Emiko did not acknowledge her cousin, and instead, she turned to look at Yinka and Timon. Her lips curved into a small smile, and she gave them a curt nod. "Thank you for your pitch. It was very interesting, but of course, we cannot decide today. I must discuss it with the other shareholders of the Shinoda fund sitting around this table. But it won't take long for us to make a decision. I hope you understand."

"Certainly, Miss Shinoda," Yinka said, making sure she did not sound impatient or defeatist but grateful despite knowing she had a specific deadline to obtain all the investment. "Take as much time as required to come to your decision."

"Wonderful," Emiko said, with a wide smile. "Now that the meeting has concluded, I would like to invite you all to some light lunch and refreshments in the garden served by our chefs."

Ten minutes after the meeting ended, everyone at the meeting was now in the luxuriant garden, engaging in discussions. Yinka was standing by Timon who was having quite an animated conversation with Jin about NFTs and the best crypto coins to invest in while Dugard was talking to some of the Japanese men in another part of the garden. Yinka was only half listening to Timon's and Jin's exchange as she nibbled on a deliciously well-cooked chicken skewer called *yakitori*. She gave her now empty skewer stick to a passing waiter holding a tray.

"How do you find the food?" came Emiko's voice behind Yinka.

Yinka turned around to see Emiko standing behind her with her hands behind her back. She looked effortlessly debonair today. Yinka desperately wanted to ask her where she shopped. "The food is very nice. Thank you for the hospitality, Miss Shinoda."

"You can call me Emiko. May I call you Yinka?"

"Of course you may."

Emiko smiled at Yinka and then glanced at Timon and Jin,

who were still engaged in their intense conversation. "Yinka, please walk with me. I would like to speak with you privately."

Yinka was taken aback by Emiko's request but did not inquire further. She nodded and followed Emiko as they quietly walked away from the group of men.

"It is always a pleasure to meet another confident and competent woman in business," Emiko said, giving Yinka a friendly smile as they walked side by side at a casual pace. "You're certainly very convincing, and you and your business partner make a very good team. You complement each other."

"Thank you," Yinka said, surprised by Emiko's assessment. When Yinka thought about it, she had, against all odds, developed an easy and even playful partnership with Timon now. No longer did she despise his very existence, he was definitely tolerable now, even nice company, but she had not forgiven him completely for how he had mistreated her at school. Of course, she had put that all aside for what was at stake.

"Be thankful you have a business partner who is competent, unlike my cousin," Emiko said, rolling her eyes. "When my father was incarcerated and my mother passed away, my cousin was automatically put in charge of the family business as my father had no sons. I am his only child. In Japanese culture, the woman cannot lead the family, no matter how qualified she may be to do so." There was a sense of anger lingering underneath Emiko's voice.

"Forgive me if I sound rude, but your cousin doesn't strike me as the leader type."

Emiko chortled. "There's nothing to forgive as you're not wrong. While he is officially the head of the Shinoda family, it is just for appearance's sake. To keep tradition. When it comes to matters concerning my family's business affairs and maintaining the legacy my father built, it is me who makes the executive decisions behind closed doors." Emiko grinned at

Yinka. "Every powerful family has a powerful woman behind it to maintain its position of strength. My late mother was a great preserver of my family's power after my father's downfall."

"She sounds like she was a formidable woman. I am sorry to hear of her passing."

Emiko raised her right hand and shook her head. "It is ok; she passed away a few years ago." Emiko came to a halt in front of a stone fountain with a statue of a galloping horse. She turned to face Yinka who had stopped behind her. There was now a gloomy expression on Emiko's face as she narrowed her eyes at Yinka. "I am going to invest the three million you are asking for into Afchain."

Yinka felt her chest swell in relief and had to restrain herself from embracing Emiko in a hug. But when she looked at Emiko, ready to shake her hand and thank her, Emiko was grim-faced as if she had just delivered the most terrible news.

"But the decision to invest has not come from me personally. I have been forced to do it."

Yinka raised her eyebrows at this startling revelation. "Forced? By whom?"

"Sorry, Yinka, I cannot divulge that. I would be compromising my position. But I feel obliged to warn you, as a woman to another woman, that you're entering a very dangerous world and you may not realise it yet." Emiko turned to her left and stared out into the garden's expanse, her eyes resting where Dugard was still talking with three of the Japanese men from the meeting.

"A word of caution. Be careful of the company you keep close, Yinka. For they may not have your best interest at heart."

The words sunk into Yinka right down to her stomach. Why was Emiko saying this to her? "Are you in trouble, Emiko?"

At this, Emiko gave Yinka a sarcastic smile. "I was born

into a Yakuza family. My life was in trouble the day I emerged from my mother's womb, but I accept my destiny and whatever comes with it." Then to Yinka's shock, Emiko held onto Yinka's right hand.

"I like you, Yinka, despite knowing very little about you, and you remind me of myself. That's why I am telling you all this. Some powerful men playing a game of chess, and you and your business partner are merely pawns on the board."

39

"YOU THINK Emiko was referring to Dugard?" Joshua said, adjusting his spectacles as he spoke to Yinka from the screen of her MacBook. She was providing her usual updates to the team on a Microsoft Teams call. Timon was in the other room having a phone call with his fiancée.

It was a warm evening in Tokyo. Yinka was dressed in dark green lapel silk pyjamas and sat cross-legged on her bed in the hotel room. On her screen, Kisi and Jaali sat on each side of Joshua. In the background, Yinka saw Montanna taking a pizza from the fridge.

"It has to be him, but she refused to confirm it," Yinka said. "Our whole conversation was odd. She told me someone had forced her to invest in Afchain, but she wouldn't tell me who. In her own words, 'It compromised her position,' whatever that means. My gut feeling tells me Dugard has something to do with all this."

"This whole Afchain business we've been coerced into has been dodgy from the start," Kisi said, chewing gum. "First, we had to deal with some British mercenaries abducting Oge in Germany and then us being tasked to specifically recruit a crypto expert by Oge's kidnappers so he can help us get investment for this obscure crypto company in Nigeria. And now there's this rich English guy just randomly helping us out. None of this has made a pinch of sense. Now to add to all this *wahala*, you've just been warned by one of the private bankers we were tasked with getting investment from that you should be careful of the company you keep. Honestly, what sort of conspiracy have we been dragged into?"

"Have you told crypto boy what Emiko told to you?" Jaali said.

Yinka shook her head. "Nope, I haven't spoken to Timon about it. And I don't intend to. It doesn't concern him."

"My advice to you, Yinks, is that we proceed with the mission but with caution," Jaali said, his face stern. "This whole ordeal is all fucked up, as Kisi has pointed out, but our main objective is to get the full investment for Afchain, so Oge will be freed. That's still the deal as far we know."

Yinka could not argue with Jaali's sound logic. She nodded in agreement. "You're not wrong."

There was a knock on her room door, followed by Timon's voice. "Hey, Dugard is here to see us. He has some news to share."

"I'll call you guys later once I've gotten further updates. Miss ya'll."

"Stay safe, Yinks," Kisi said.

After ending the video call and closing her laptop, Yinka rolled out of bed and walked to her room door. She opened it to find Timon in white shorts and a black vest, showcasing his surprisingly toned arms, standing at the doorway. Behind him, in the parlour, stood Dugard.

"You good?" Timon asked.

"I am fine, thanks," Yinka said, stepping out of her room and entering the parlour.

"Seeing you always makes me smile," Dugard said. When Yinka walked up to him, he threw his arms around her. He stepped back and beamed at her and Timon, who had come to stand beside her.

"You two are quite the formidable duo. You've secured another investment for Afchain and so quickly from the Shinoda family. I knew there was something special about Afchain and you two. It's why I am risking my reputation introducing you to my closest business associates. I believe in it, and I believe in both of you."

"We appreciate that," Timon said, nodding at Yinka and smiling at Dugard.

"Emiko said she would transfer the money to the necessary account as soon as she receives your investor report, Timon. As I did with Mancini, I am happy to act as a middleman in this process. I can share the details of where to send the necessary admin."

"Thanks for your help, Richard. You said you had other news to share?" Timon said.

"Ah yes, of course," Dugard said, noding. "Unfortunately, Mustafa could not travel to Tokyo to meet you both and discuss Afchan. But, the great news is that he is keen to hear your investment proposal. So much so that he has sent a personal video invitation."

Yinka raised her eyebrows. "A personal video invitation?"

Dugard gave Yinka a knowing smirk. "Mustafa is...quite the showman, shall we say. I'll play you the invitation."

Yinka and Timon looked at each other, bemused, as Dugard dipped his left hand inside his burgundy blazer. He pulled out his iPhone, fiddled with it for a few seconds and then held up the screen for Yinka and Timon to see.

The video on Dugard's iPhone showed an older Arab man Yinka immediately recognised as Mustafa. In the video, Mustafa, who looked to be approaching his late sixties, was wearing a traditional white headdress, which Yinka knew was called a *keffiyeh* and dressed in a white kaftan robe with a golden collar and golden designs sewn into the fabric. The wealthy Arab sheikh had heavy bags underneath his eyes and a zappa style beard. Shimmering in the distance stood a towering skyscraper of architectural ingenuity and wonder. Although Yinka had never been to Dubai, she recognised the structure. It was the Burj Khalifa—the world's tallest building.

"Hello. My name is Abdul Kazeem Mustafa, but most people just call me Mustafa," the sheikh said in a strong, glottal Arab accent. "Please accept my apologies for not being able to come and see you in Tokyo. I was looking forward to hearing about your crypto company, Afchain. My business partners have spoken highly about this investment opportunity."

Mustafa adjusted his robes and began to walk across a wide town square with date palm trees rooted in the ground and luxurious, modern buildings surrounding him. "I will not be in Dubai for another week as I am currently preoccupied with tedious business meetings abroad." Mustafa let out a loud sigh. "A man with a lot of money will always be a man with many demands on his time. Having said that, if you're willing, I would like to invite you both, Miss Saraki and Mr Bakare, to Dubai, where you have the pleasure of staying in one of the many apartments I own in the Burj Khalifa. Once I am back in Dubai, we can talk properly about your investment opportunity. I hope you accept my gracious offer." Mustafa looked directly at the screen and gave a wide, toothy smile. The video ended.

Dugard placed his phone back inside his blazer jacket and clapped his hands. He was smiling broadly. "So what do you say to Mustafa's offer?"

"I am not about to say no to an invitation to stay at the Burj Khalifa," Timon said, not even attempting to hide the excitement in his voice. "I've been to Dubai a few times now. It's one of my favourite parts of the world and practically invented for people who love to enjoy their money."

Yinka was not surprised that Timon was already jumping

at the prospect of flying to Dubai, but after Emiko's warning, she was less overjoyed at the invite. She felt apprehensive about everything now. When she stared at Dugard, he still had that big smile.

"Why are you helping us, Richard? You're not getting any commission for all your troubles," Yinka said, levelling her eyes at him.

"I believe in the potential of Afchain, Yinka," Dugard said, his smile and charm never wavering. "West Africa, particularly Nigeria, is part of my family's legacy, as I've told you. I am invested in the future of the entire continent, and what you're seeking investment in is the future of Africa. Is there a greater purpose?"

Dugard had a way with words; Yinka had to give him that. He had charmed her effortlessly when he introduced himself at the beach bar in Costa Smeralda. Yet Yinka was no fool. She knew Dugard had ulterior motives, and Emiko's warning had confirmed that. But as Jaali had said in the video call earlier, she had no choice but to proceed with this mission if she wanted to save Oge.

Yinka nodded at Dugard, giving him an insincere smile. Then she looked at Timon, who gave her a wink and a grin. If you had told her a week ago that she would have to spending a week in Dubai with her former school tormentor, she would have torn out her hair extensions in frustration. But now, she did not mind. It might even be fun.

Yinka smiled at Timon. "Well I've never been to Dubai before."

40

IT HAD BEEN ALMOST 24 hours since Kojo received the six mini voice recording devices he had secretly planted in Dugard's, Timon's, and Yinka's hotel rooms.

Now, as he lay next to a naked Federica in her king-sized bed at her hotel - she was smoking a cigarette as she relaxed beside him after another round of mutually pleasurable sex - he thought deeply about the contents of those recordings which he had thoroughly listened to. Multiple times.

The nature of Timon and Yinka's dealings with Dugard had felt like scattered pieces to a puzzle. But with the recordings, he could now partly put the puzzle together only with a few missing pieces to give a complete picture. He now understood that Timon and Yinka were working with Dugard to raise investment for a Nigerian-based crypto company called Afchain. Earlier today, before coming to spend the night with Federica, Kojo had conducted online research into Afchain. According to chat groups on Reddit and Discord, Afchain was a top secret Nigerian-based crypto trading platform, developed by some of the smartest software developers in Africa, that would enable Nigerians to buy products, pay for services and trade in digital currencies with ease.

Yet none of this explained why Dugard had helped Timon and Yinka gain investment for Afchain from Silvio Mancini and, as of two days ago, Emiko Shinoda. And now Dugard, Timon and Yinka had travelled to Dubai yesterday to potentially secure investment from Abdul Kazeem Mustafa, a wealthy sheikh. But what Kojo could not decipher was Dugard's stake in all this.

Yinka was an even more curious character. The recording device he had planted in her room had revealed to Kojo that she appeared to be seeking investment for Afchain to save a kidnapped person named Oge but this person's significance was unclear to Kojo. In the recordings, it sounded like Yinka was speaking to some people from a video call, telling them that Emiko - Kojo assumed this was Emiko Shinoda - was coerced into investing into Afchain by external forces. It sounded like Emiko refused to divulge why she was forced to invest and had warned Yinka to keep a watchful eye on the company she kept. Yinka had felt Emiko's warning was referring to Dugard. So it sounded to Kojo that Yinka did not trust Dugard. Kojo also now understood that Timon was specifically recruited by Yinka and the people she was video calling to help them secure investment for Afchain. This new intelligence was intriguing but made little sense to Kojo without the full context.

Ultimately, the secret recordings gave Kojo as many answers as they presented new questions and intrigues. But one thing was certain—he would take a plane to Dubai tomorrow to continue spying on Dugard. The truth about Dugard's business dealings and the existence of The Cable were within Kojo's reach but he just needed to gather a little more intelligence.

Federica pulled Kojo from the depths of his thoughts with her sultry, Italian accent. "I spoke to that filthy husband of mine earlier today," she said. "He is flying to Dubai in the morning to meet with some business associates later in the week." She looked at Kojo, her long dark hair ruffled over her face. Her messy look accentuated her unexacting sex appeal. She took a drag on her cigarette.

Upon hearing what Federica had said, Kojo immediately pulled himself up from the mattress and leaned against the bed's headrest. "Business associates in Dubai?"

"Yes, my husband has been invited to a private meeting with a wealthy sheikh named Abdul Kazeem Mustafa and this very rich Nigerian businessman, Mobolagi Bankole." Federica pulled on her cigarette and blew faint whips of smoke from her bow shaped lips. "My husband has worked with them on various investment opportunities for years and I have even entertained them as guests at our home in Milan before. But what kind of investments my husband has with the Nigerians, the Arabs and even the Japanese confuses me as it intrigues me. But I've never asked about the nature of these business dealings. Not that he would confide such things to me anyway."

It took a moment for Kojo to let this new and astounding piece of intel to sink in. The implications of what Federica had so casually revealed were far reaching and substantial to Kojo's mission. Could it be that Emiko Shinoda and Adbul Kazeem Mustafa were in fact part of The Cable alongside Dugard, Mancini and Bankole? Why else would Mancini be flying to Dubai, the same time as Dugard, Timon and Yinka, to all meet Mustafa? And who had organised the meeting between Bankole, Mancini and Mustafa in Dubai and why was Dugard absent from it?

"My husband wants me to travel with him to Dubai and stay at a rented apartment with him but I am not going." Federica scrunched her face in defiance. "Steven, I am finally running away from him and deserting our awful marriage."

Kojo's eyes widened at Federica's second big reveal of the evening. She took another long pull from her cigarette and her green eyes were steely.

"I have spent too much of my life being under my husband's abusive control but after many years, I can finally free myself of him."

"How?" Kojo asked, watching Federica as he anticipated what she would say next.

'While my husband has been busy conducting his businesses and largely ignoring me, I have, for quite a long time now, been running my own acting school in Milan which he knows nothing about. And finally, I have saved enough money from my business to divorce him and restart my life."

Kojo was still staring at Federica, shocked by all of this. "And where will you go?"

"To Monaco. My eighteen year old daughter, Isabella, lives and studies in Monte Carlo with her boyfriend, and I will go to live with them for some time." Federica now looked close to tears. "For so long, *too long*, I stood by helplessly and watched my vile husband emotionally and, even physically, abuse our daughter. Isabella ran away at sixteen, and wanted nothing to do with me. But recently, she got in touch and we've since reconciled." Now tears trickled down her cheeks. "I have my daughter back and my financial independence back too. I will never be Mancini's wife again."

Kojo sighed deeply as he took in what Federica had just told him. He knew what he was about to tell her would shatter the emotional connection they had built. But he was on an important mission. It had to come before his heart.

"You are a brave and beautiful woman, Federica," Kojo began, staring at her as she looked at him with her teary eyes brimming with joy. "But I need you to go to Dubai with your husband and plant a mini camera on him."

Federica let the cigarette between her fingers drop to the floor. She frowned in utter confusion as if Kojo had demanded her to jump in front of a speeding train. "What are you talking about, Steven?"

"Forgive me, Federica, but I have not been completely

honest with you. My name is not Steven Hartlett. It is Kojo Owusu-Harrington. And while my occupation as an employee of the British government is true, it is not in the treasury department. I am an intelligence officer for Her Majesty's Secret Service, MI6."

Federica shook her head, eyes wide with incredulity and her lips now trembling. "So you've been a spy this whole time?"

The pain in Federica's voice stabbed at Kojo. He nodded stiffly. "Correct. My assignment is to uncover the existence of a complex international money laundering organisation called The Cable. The group cleans money for drug dealers and human traffickers around the world through all types of investment instruments within their respective nations, from real estate to company stocks. MI6 believes your husband and two of his close business associates, Sir Richard Dugard and Mobolagi Bankole, head up this organisation."

Federica laughed. It was shrill and bitter. She stood from the bed, letting the duvet fall from her. She picked up her still smouldering cigarette she had dropped on the floor and then went to stand by the large window, her naked and slender body turned away from Kojo. "So you've been using me to get close to my husband?" Her voice had a kind of painful anger in its cadence. She took a long drag on her cigarette and blew wisps of smoke into the air. Kojo knew his deception had wounded her emotionally, and it surprised him how much he hated himself now for making her feel this way.

"I have been using you, yes. I planted a small camera on your handbag when you went to the Shinoda gala so I could spy on your husband and Dugard. I am sorry, Federica."

"So none of… *this*…whatever we have… is real, then? Have I just been a game to you?"

"My feelings for you are real, Federica," Kojo said, softening his voice. "Please look at me." But Federica did not turn around. Kojo sighed. "When I saw you on your husband's yacht that evening on the coast of Sardinia, you caught my attention and captivated me within seconds of me setting eyes on you before I even knew your relationship to Mancini."

Federica cackled, a dry and spiteful laugh, as she shook her head, still not facing Kojo. "You say all this *poetry*, and yet you are asking me to spy on my husband after spinning a web of lies. I am not a foolish young girl, *Kojo* if that is your real name. A man's passionate words do not so easily sway my heart. Be upfront with me right now, or I will kick you out of my hotel room tonight."

Kojo sighed. "I need your help to take down this corrupt organisation, and spying on your husband will help me accomplish that. But I genuinely care for you, Federica. More than any other woman I have cared for in a long time. But I need you to do this for me. Your husband deserves to have everything taken away from him just like he took everything away from you. Tell me I am wrong?"

Federica sighed heavily. She turned away from the window to face Kojo. Even now, he couldn't help but admire her naked and toned figure. But he felt wrong lusting for her at that moment. After a few seconds of contemplative silence between them, she responded coldly, a flame burning in her emerald green eyes. "It would bring me joy to witness my husband's empire collapse."

"So then help me do that, Federica. Help me destroy the man who has brought so much pain and misery to your life."

293

PART FIVE

SEVEN NIGHTS IN DUBAI

41

IF MONEY HAD A UNIVERSAL SCENT, it would smell like Dubai.

Timon would always say this jokingly to himself whenever he visited the most popular city in the UAE. Sometimes, he travelled here for business and to network at extravagant crypto conferences and events. Other times, it was for pleasure when he flew here with Orisa for a vacation.

But travelling to Dubai with Yinka felt like he was coming here for the first time again—in a good way.

When they arrived in Dubai, Timon felt like something was preoccupying Yinka's mind. Sometimes, he wondered what was running through her head, considering the duplicitous life she led. Yet as soon as they had left Dubai International Airport and entered their luxury two-bedroom apartment in the Burj Khalifa, designed by Giorgio Armani himself and located on the 63rd floor, Yinka's demeanour instantly flipped into one of awestruck and wonder. Her eyes widened in amazement as she stood before the apartment's panoramic windows and gazed at the grandiloquent display of Dubai's breathtaking excess of Arab wealth, power and ingenuity. Dozens of glimmering skyscrapers, in all sizes and shapes and built with an imagination that only money could manifest, stretched out before Yinka's eyes. Below, she was treated to an incredible bird's-eye view of the curvaceous and expansive Burji Khalfi Lake with its vivid turquoise waters and state-of-the-art fountain curving around the whole Burja Khalfi complex.

"I feel like I am staying at a grand palace," Yinka said in awe.

Timon came next to Yinka. He looked at her and smiled. "Welcome to Dubai. Pleasure, luxury, and sophistication await. We're going to have a good time."

* * *

For the first three days in Dubai, Timon showed Yinka the delights of the emirate. But she did not want to do the typical exploits tourists often do when they come to Dubai, like go shopping or take endless selfies in front of Dubai's many Instagram-worthy landmarks—the kind of activities Orisa would do. No, Yinka wanted culture and exploration.

On the first day, Timon and Yinka ventured into the histor-ical neighbourhood of Al Fahidi, exploring its traditional buildings crafted from stone, palm wood, and gypsum, a world away from modern Dubai's glass and steel towers. Rather than be bored by the trip, he wasn't particularly inter-ested in history like Yinka was; Timon had surprisingly enjoyed the heritage tour. It was something different. Plus, something about seeing Yinka's eyes lit up with wonder as she listened to the history of Dubai from the tour guide made Timon's chest expand with a rush of something warm. Seeing her smile now felt like he was witnessing a beautiful sunset every time, and Timon could not understand why he experi-enced such joy seeing her happy.

On their second day in Dubai, Timon and Yinka, dressed in matching white kaftan robes purchased earlier in the day, visited the majestic Sheikh Zayed Grand Mosque. Timon had always wanted to visit here during his past trips to Dubai but never had the opportunity, and Orisa was never interested.

As he walked through the resplendent courtyard with Yinka, surrounded by the glistening white and gold Islamic architecture, he listened to her speak passionately about the mosque's history, which she had read about at university. Yinka's passion and knowledge of other cultures and customs were infectious, and Timon realised he could easily listen to her talk for hours.

During their third day in Dubai, Timon and Yinka enjoyed a tranquil boat ride across Dubai Creek, watching the sun collapse in a fiery glow that turned the sky into the colour of volcanic lava. After that, they visited the Al Shindagha Museum, where they learnt about the history of Arabic perfumes. Later in the evening, they visited the Meena Bazaar, where they ate delicious street food at a delightful Punjabi chicken tikka spot.

Timon noticed that Yinka had not taken a pretentious selfie once, something Orisa would do. She just lived in the moment and absorbed all she saw with a mesmerising wonder. For Timon, it felt so refreshing being around someone who was more interested in enjoying the beauty and mysteries of the physical world around her than constantly posting on social media on her phone.

"I'll admit, I had my doubts when you said you could make jollof rice that would make my tongue dance," Timon said, placing his metal fork back on his plate as he sat by the glass dinner table in the Burj Khalifa apartment on their fourth day in Dubai.

A plate of orange-tinted jollof rice, correctly cooked with long-grain rice by Yinka, was in front of Timon. A glass filled with red wine was beside him as he shared a bottle with

Yinka. "But this is top-tier jollof rice," Timon said, licking his lips. "Good thing we found the ingredients in that market. It's nice to have a freshly cooked meal for once."

Yinka sat opposite Timon. She wore an elegant, figure-hugging yellow and green Kente print bodycon dress. Her hair was now in braids that she had plaited at the saloon in the afternoon. She also had a plate of the jollof rice she had cooked and had filled her glass with a conservative amount of red wine. She playfully rolled her eyes at Timon's remark.

"Firstly, I am glad you're enjoying my food," she said. "I only cook for my friends and my boyfriend, so count yourself privileged." She chuckled as Timon playfully bowed to her from across the dining table. "And secondly, you had your doubts about a Nigerian woman cooking jollof rice? Look, I don't know what type of Nigerian women you have back in London, but we Nigerian women from Lagos can cook jollof rice with our eyes closed. Doesn't your fiancée cook?"

Timon let out a howl of laughter. "Orisa? She's Nigerian but born and raised in the UK. On the rare occasions when she makes me a sandwich, she considers that the equivalent of cooking a roast dinner." Timon let out a sigh. "If we're not ordering takeaways from Just Eat, then we're eating at some fancy restaurant in Mayfair or Knightsbridge."

"Well, you're a wealthy man. You should have no problem taking your fiancée to fancy restaurants every week." Yinka smirked. "If you lived in Lagos, you would be most Nigerian women's dream husband. You're who they pray for at church."

"Ah, so you've finally discovered the humour bone in your body," Timon said, chuckling.

"I can be quite funny if I feel like the person I am talking to is worthy of my witty banter."

Timon shook his head and smiled as he scooped some jollof rice onto his fork and ate it - savouring the warm and spicy sweetness – before letting it slide satisfactorily down his throat. "When it comes to cooking, my mother was chief's kiss. Growing up, she made everything from jollof rice and pounded yam to pasta and even sushi. She could cook just as well as she could do women's braids at her salon."

Yinka's eyes softened as she looked at Timon. "You speak about your mum as if she's passed away. Did she?"

"Oh no, she's alive," Timon said, scratching his head. "It's just...she developed Alzheimer's. It's a very debilitating illness, and my mother is unable to do many of the things she could effortlessly do before, like be a great cook or run her salon." Timon's eyes fell to his plate, and he ate more of his jollof rice silently. Thinking about his mother's condition always lessened his mood.

"I am sorry to hear about your mother," Yinka said, still staring at him with her eyes generous with sympathy. "I know how it feels to see a parent slowly succumb to an illness. When I turned twelve and was still living in Nigeria, my father was diagnosed with lung cancer. For a year and a half, I saw my father go from the strongest man I knew to an almost skeletal frame, shrivelled and barely able to lift a finger. When he died, I was so deeply heartbroken, not just because I knew I would never hug him again or listen to him read me one of his books or read me the articles he wrote for the newspaper, but that my future children would never know what an amazing man their grandfather was."

"Is that why you came to the UK? Because of your father's passing?"

Yinka nodded. "Yeah. I had no immediate family in Nigeria, so I went to live with my father's older sister in London after he passed away. My auntie was very caring and supportive, but adapting to a new life in east London while still reeling from my father's death was difficult for me. And, as you know, my school life in London wasn't exactly great for me at the start. But let's not revisit that."

Timon could feel his heart become heavy with deep shame

when he realised, in retrospect, that he had participated in a bullying campaign against Yinka in their youth when she was just a young girl processing the death of her father. He owed her a huge apology, but now wasn't the right time. Timon wanted to steer their conversation back into more light-hearted ground.

"Before, you mentioned future children. So you want to be a mother one day?"

Yinka nodded as she swallowed some of her rice. "Yes, I do. Pretty soon, hopefully. As far as I can tell, I am 29 years old and not ageing backwards. Also, I don't want to be spending my whole life stealing from rich criminals. As fun as it's been." Yinka's eyes then seemed to brim with wonder, as if she were imagining a fulfilling life raising her children. "Being a mother one day is very important to me. My mother died when I was young, and I never got to know her properly. But I want to be the kind of mother my father and auntie always told me she was. Kind, attentive and loving."

"It's beautiful that you want to be a mother but kind, attentive and loving? You? Miss Stubbornly Sophisticated?" Timon gave her a playful smirk, and Yinka sucked her teeth at him in jest.

"What did I say about nicknames"? Yinka said, her tone jovial rather than defensive. "And just because I don't show it all the time doesn't mean I don't have a very soft and feminine side." Yinka flicked one strand of her braids, falling to the left side of her face, and sighed with a sense of hopelessness. "But...I don't know...I am not sure if my boyfriend wants children."

"If having children is important to you, you should have that conversation with your boyfriend. Am I wrong?"

Yinka snickered, yet to Timon's surprise and intrigue, her tone had an underlying irritation, even resentment. "It's not like I haven't tried." Yinka shook her head, and Timon could tell she did not want to dwell on this topic. "What about you?

A wealthy Nigerian man who is a big-time hedge fund manager in London, you must want many children. You can afford it."

Timon chuckled. "I do want a big family. Five children. Three boys and two girls."

"Wow, that's very specific," Yinka said, grinning. "Your fiancée is going to be a busy woman."

"Well, I am unsure if she wants kids herself."

"So you're getting married to a woman and unsure if she wants kids, but you do? Isn't that a conversation you should be having with your future wife? Am I wrong?" Yinka winked at Timon.

Timon chuckled, enjoying this tête-à-tête with Yinka. "Touché. Sounds like we both need to have important conversations with our significant others."

Before their discussion could continue, Timon and Yinka heard the doorbell ring.

"Don't worry, I'll get it," Timon said, already standing from his chair.

Timon opened the door to find Dugard standing in front of him. As always, he wore a sharp suit, which he seemed to have an endless supply of. Timon welcomed him into the apartment, and as he walked into the parlour, Timon noticed Dugard was holding two gold-coloured paper slips.

"Apologies for disturbing you on this warm evening," Dugard said, standing in the parlour as Timon and Yinka regarded him. "Firstly, I must say that is a sublime dress, Yinka. I know you deny being Nigerian royalty, but I must be frank and say you are wrong."

Yinka shook her head, smiled and waved her hand dismissively at Dugard. "You're going to suffocate me with compliments at this point, Richard."

Dugard chuckled lightly and then cleared his throat. "As part of his continued generosity and hospitality, as you wait for his arrival, Mustafa has secured you both invitations to the annual Dubai Fashion Week Show tomorrow evening at the Jumeirah Beach Hotel." Dugard waved the golden slips he was holding at Timon and Yinka. "It promises to be quite the extravagant show, so please doll up and look glamorous. But from what I've seen, that will not be a problem for either of you."

42

THE DUBAI FASHION WEEK SHOW, which took place at the Janat Al Bahar outdoor event space, was one of the most outlandish and outrageous fashion displays Timon had experienced.

Sat next to Yinka and a dozen other eloquently dressed guests around a glass table populated with expensive champagne, Timon was soaking in the atmosphere. A kaleidoscope of neon colours from dozens of LED lights lining the runway coloured the evening sky like the northern lights.

Timon watched models with sculpted cheekbones, long legs, and tall heels sashay across the narrow runway with refined allure. A female model emerged on the runway wearing a dress made from a flamingo's feathers. Another model wore a bodysuit that changed into different colours as she strutted down the stage.

Despite all the eye-popping fashion and slender models, Timon's eyes kept gliding to Yinka. Tonight, she had surpassed the look of royalty and ascended to the level of an African goddess. Dressed in a spectacular silver, one-shoulder embellished maxi dress she had purchased from the Dubai Mall earlier this afternoon, Yinka might as well have been on the runway herself. When they had walked into the venue, Timon saw every man and woman in attendance gape at Yinka, absorbed by the visual splendour of her Nigerian beauty. Her dark braids rested on her shoulders, and her diamond pear-shaped halo earrings twinkled like shooting stars against her coffee-dark brown skin.

"You do look good in that tuxedo I brought for you," Yinka said to Timon as she held a glass of gin and tonic in her right hand. "But I could also see you pulling off that flamingo dress we saw on the catwalk."

Sitting beside Yinka at the bar, Timon grinned and turned to face her. "I could probably pull it off. Nigerian men look good in anything we wear. Our natural sauce leaks onto everything."

Yinka giggled, shaking her head at Timon. "Spoken like a true, big-headed Yoruba man."

The Dubai Fashion Week show had ended fifteen minutes ago. Timon and Yinka had left their seats when it was over, went to the bar to order two tequila shots, necked quickly, and then ordered their preferred cocktails. Now, they stood by the hotel's expansive outdoor pool, which looked like millions of electric eels were charging it. In the far distance, looming tall in the gloom of the evening, Timon could make out the silhouette of the soaring, fin-shaped Burj Al Arab luxury hotel.

"You could have been on that runway tonight," Timon said, the words sliding out of his mouth, encouraged by the tequila shots.

Yinka sucked her teeth dismissively, but Timon caught her smiling. "Are you trying to one-up Dugard with the compliments tonight?"

Before Timon could tell Yinka that he was completely

sincere, he heard a female voice from the past call out his name — a voice from a history both he and Yinka shared.

"No way, is that you, Timon?"

Timon and Yinka turned away from the pool to face the female voice behind them. Timon's first reaction when he saw Desola 'DeDe' Adeyemi standing right before him was to widen his eyes in perplexity and uselessly blurt out: "DeDe?"

Desola wore an elegant, tribal-print blue maxi dress that complimented her caramel-shaded skin. Her hair, with its red extensions, was tied into a braided topknot bun. Despite looking visibly older than the last time Timon had seen her, she was still an unquestionably attractive Nigerian woman.

"I haven't been called that nickname in years," Desola said, the smile on her full lips extending. "Oh my god, I haven't seen you since...that time at that club in Soho, right? That was ages ago."

"Yeah, that was the last time we bumped into each other," Timon said, rubbing the back of his neck while holding his Hennessey and coke with his free hand. Desola had not yet recognised Yinka, but Timon felt the awkwardness collapsing on them. The approaching confrontation was inevitable, so getting it out of the way now was better. "You remember Yinka, right? From school?"

Desola slowly rotated her head as she turned her attention to Yinka. Timon looked at Yinka. She had narrowed her eyes at Desola so they now resembled the slits of a venomous snake. Her lips were unsmiling.

Desola squinted as she studied Yinka, then after several seconds, her head jerked back as if a firework had just gone off in her face. "No way. Skinny Yinka from school?" she said, her two hands raised to her mouth. "It's really you?"

"Oh, it's definitely me," Yinka said. Timon could hear Yinka's contempt for Desola spice every word from her mouth. "And I am not so skinny anymore."

Timon gulped, unsure how this entire exchange would

play out. The atmosphere between them grew tense as if they were in a three-way standoff.

"Wow," Desola said, chuckling, her sarcasm loud, "you've certainly glowed up from…well, whatever was going on with you at school."

"And you're still…well, whatever you were at school. It's ok, though. Not everyone glows up."

Desola huffed. "I never needed to glow up, babe. I was always glowing, you lying and two-faced freshie."

"What did you just call me?" Yinka had taken a step forward, her head raised at Desola, her fierce eyes burning as she glared at her.

"Come on, let's not do this, ladies," Timon said, resting a hand on Yinka's shoulder. "We're adults now. All of that is history."

Desola chuckled and shook her head. "Don't tell me you two are…a couple?"

"We're here on business. So why don't you mind yours." Yinka's breathing was noticeably heavier as her chest rose and fell.

"Business?" Desola said, her lips now shaped into a smug grin. "Wow, life really is stranger than fiction sometimes. I am on holiday with a few friends, and we're staying at this hotel. You know what, I better find my people. It was nice seeing you again, Timon."

"Yeah, same," Timon said, hearing how strained he sounded, entangled in this uncomfortable confrontation.

Desola shifted her dark eyes on Yinka. "No hard feelings?"

Yinka shook her head and sucked her teeth. "I am going to get another drink."

Timon called after her. "Yinka, wait."

But Yinka had already marched off.

· · ·

Ten minutes after the encounter with Desola, Yinka stood alone at the Janat Al Bahar outdoor field underneath the moonlight in the humid evening. She faced the beach, staring into the calm sea shrouded in a veil of darkness, and held an old-fashioned glass in her left hand with her second top-up of gin and tonic on the rocks. It was a strong double.

"Hey, are you alright?" came Timon's voice from behind her.

Yinka pivoted slightly on the spot to look at Timon, who was walking towards her. He looked worried. "I know what happened back there was…uncomfortable," he said.

How could I get triggered by her even after all these years? Yinka thought, taking a swig of her drink. She let out a long sigh. "I overreacted, to be honest. I am a grown woman. I didn't need to make such a drama from seeing her again. But wow, even after all these years, she's still so spiteful. Seeing her just brought back a lot of unpleasant memories." Yinka looked at Timon, who now stood so close to her that their shoulders were touching. "Sorry if I made it even more weird for you."

"You don't have anything to apologise for, Yinka," Timon said.

Yinka turned to look at Timon. Although she tried not to, throughout the fashion show, she found herself stealing glances at him, her body getting hotter with each look. This evening, his trimmed hair and well-groomed beard gave him major Micheal B Jordan vibes. Yinka had to mentally remind herself that she had a kidnapped boyfriend whose life she was currently trying to save.

"Thanks, Timon."

"Can I tell you something?"

Yinka raised her eyebrows but nodded. "Sure."

"When I got accepted into Cambridge, that was the first time I experienced what it was like to be an outsider. Growing up in Canning Town, I was surrounded by people who looked like me and grew up in similar ways. It was easy to find other black people I could relate to."

"But in Cambridge, I was treated like I didn't belong there from day one. I had severe imposter syndrome in my first year. Everyone was smarter than me, and I felt like I was only there to fulfil some diversity quota. And those posh Cambridge lot made me feel like an outsider with their snide remarks about how I spoke, how I dressed, what I liked and the fact I did not come from wealth like them. If I hadn't met my best friend, Chikezie, I would have probably dropped out."

"It's not nice being bullied because you're different from everyone else, right?" Yinka said, her eyes searching Timon's face. He was now staring out into the pitch-black sea.

"No, it's not. But you know what? That was my karma."

"Karma?" Yinka said, staring intensely at Timon, latching onto his words.

"Yeah, Karma, for how I treated you at school, Yinka." Timon now turned his head to look at her. There was a softness in his dark monolid eyes and a magnetic pull that kept Yinka rooted on the spot, her eyes unable to look away from him. She felt her heart rate increase and her skin heat like a radiator.

"To be honest, the reasons why Desola, myself and our friends back then bullied you was down to our self-hate and ignorance. At school, in those days, being Nigerian, or just being African generally, was ridiculed by everyone. Because of that, some of us at school were already embarrassed to be African, and so when you arrived, with your thick Nigerian accent and your dark skin, you just reminded us of who we truly were and all the mockery we suffered from other kids. And we hated that, so we took that out on you." Timon shrugged his shoulders. "I mean, of course, we were kids back then, but as an adult now, I can be honest about the shame I felt about my own...ethnic heritage. Which is funny because it's all cool to be proudly African now." Timon sniggered. "We owe a lot to Afrobeats."

Yinka chuckled. "So it took Afrobeats becoming a global success for you to be proud to be Nigerian?"

"I know it sounds stupid, but growing up in England as a first-generation British Nigerian was weird when I was young. To be an African was to be an outsider back then," Timon said. "But I say all that to say I should never have mistreated you the way I did, regardless of how I felt about my identity. You were mourning your late father, and I was harassing you every day. You didn't deserve that. And I am truly sorry."

Timon went silent, and his expression became more thoughtful before he spoke again. "Having spent time with you, Yinka, you're easily the smartest and most impressive woman I've ever been around. Stubborn, of course. I can't leave that out."

Yinka laughed, but it was almost like a snort and sounded girlish. Only Oge had made her laugh that way. "Being stubborn is a trait all Nigerian women have. Especially us Yoruba women."

"Yeah, but your brand of stubbornness is entertaining. Well, sometimes."

"You and your strange style of compliments, Timon."

Timon now fully turned his whole body to look at Yinka, and she did the same, looking up at him now, being four inches shorter than him. Under the evening sky, Yinka could feel the pace of her heartbeat thump like drums doing overtime at a concert. As she stood so close to Timon, she could feel his breath on her skin, the bitter-sweet chocolate aroma of his cologne tingling her nose, and the warmth of his whole body pressing against her. Was it the alcohol that made her want to be this close to him?

"Yinka, I apologise for everything I did to you at school. I was a stupid boy. *Oponu*, is that how you say stupid in Yoruba?"

Yinka sniggered. "Pronunciation could use some work, but you're in range."

"I'll work on that," Timon said, chuckling. "Can you forgive me, Yinka?"

As soon as Yinka heard Timon's full apology, everything about him burst into a bright and radiant glow: his angular cheeks, those light pink and deliciously curved lips, and his white teeth. The more she looked at his handsome face, the more she could feel herself, voluntarily or by some other invisible force, leaning towards him, yearning intensely to feel his lips pressed against hers. In a calm voice, one Yinka did not recognise as her own; she said: "I forgive you, Timon."

The whizzing sound of fireworks launching into the air and loud bangs as the evening sky lit up woke Yinka from her trance-like state. She shook her head and took a step back from Timon. Now, she felt lightheaded, and Oge immediately occupied her thoughts. Then, overcome with a swarm of emotions, Yinka felt warm tears involuntarily trickle from her eyes and down her cheeks.

"You're crying," Timon said, his voice distant even though he was right in front of her. "Are you alright?"

"I am just overwhelmed with a lot," Yinka said, wiping her wet eyes with the palms of her hands. "Can we order an Uber and go back to the apartment, please? It's been a long evening, and I just want my bed now."

43

Federica had been waiting for the right moment.

In the Downtown Views One luxury apartment in a high-rise building in the historic Dubai district, Bur Dubai, Federica lay on her side on the black leather sofa in the parlour. She was dressed in an apricot off-shoulder dress with a butterfly embroidery mesh and reading Cosmopolitan.

Silvio came and stood at the doorway. She lifted her head from her magazine and regarded her pig shit of a husband. He wore a crimson overcoat with a black shirt, grey trousers and black lace-up boots and had combed back his white silver mane of hair so he resembled Robert De Niro, only with more plastic injections in his face. Her husband looked down at her with naked contempt.

"I am going to a business presentation with Mr Bankole and Mr Mustafa. They both arrived in Dubai earlier this morning," Silvio said, fixing the cufflinks on the folded cuffs of his shirt. "Then afterwards, I'll return here with them to have a private meeting in my room. Do not disturb us, and do not make a sound." His lips curved into a smile, but his face remained stiff like cement. "Play dead for all I care."

"Being silent is all you've expected from me over the last

ten years of our marriage, Silvio. I am more of a statue now than an actual wife. And guess what? Statues don't talk." Federica threw him a loathsome grin.

Silvio sniggered smugly. "Fucking bitch." He then left the doorway.

Federica heard Silvio open the apartment's front door and then shut it as he left. As soon as she heard the door close, Federica sat up. She could feel the nerves come over as her heartbeat grew faster. Now was the moment.

A few steps before her stood a rectangular, glass dining table. On top of it was her YSL handbag. Federica lifted herself from the sofa, walked towards the dining table, opened her bag and began to rummage through it. Seconds later, she took out a black box, slightly smaller than the palm of her hand.

When Kojo revealed his duplicity to her and his job as an intelligence officer for MI6, Federica was initially livid. At her age now, and after she endured and suffered so much as a wife and a mother, she had no desire to start a relationship with men who kept secrets from her. Yet her initial anger at Kojo's deception was quickly replaced by excitement akin to the exhilaration she experienced when playing a new character in one of her films. Being asked by Kojo to help him bring down her husband gave her a sense of empowerment. It was a chance to illicit some revenge on the man who had tormented her for so long. The fact Silvio would never know it was her who engineered his downfall made it all the more gratifying.

Federica opened the box to find a small metal button inside. Hours before, at Kojo's rented studio apartment in Downtown Dubai, he had told her that this tiny, circular object was a state-of-the-art microscopic camera and recording device. It was surreal to Federica that a camera could be so small. The technology of the modern age was as astounding as it was terrifying.

Beside the tiny camera was a thin metal stick the size of a toothpick. As Kojo had explained earlier, she was to use the toothpick to pick up the camera and put it somewhere strategically so the device could film her husband and capture his interactions. Whatever Silvio would be discussing with Mr Mustafa and Mr Bankole today, especially behind closed doors, would surely provide Kojo with crucial intelligence to implicate her husband in whatever unscrupulous and corrupt business arrangements he was involved in. So Federica had decided she would bug her husband's room.

Holding the black box in her left hand, Federica entered her husband's spacious double bed room. Almost identical to the adjacent double room she slept in by herself, Silvio's room was elegant with spotless white walls, a flat-screen television perched on a metal stand in front of the king-sized bed, and a large, fixed window providing a majestic view of Dubai.

Federica looked around the room, considering where to place the microscopic spy camera covertly. Kojo had advised her to set the tiny camera in a position that would enable the device to capture a clear view of her husband and make it easier to record the conversations for more precise playback. Also, Federica had to return the camera to Kojo so he could analyse its contents, so she had to position the camera somewhere she could easily retrieve it.

After scanning the room for a minute, Federica decided the television frame was the most advantageous place, but it was an educated guess. After all, she was an actress, not a seasoned spy.

Carefully removing the miniature camera from the box with the metal toothpick, Federica planted the tiny device on the side panel of the flat-screen television. As Kojo had said, the camera was built from a synthetic material to stick to almost any surface—a marvel of modern technology.

The sound of the front door opening and then closing jolted Federica. Surprised, she dropped the empty box on the floor. Now, she could hear loud and heavy footsteps heading to the room. They could only belong to her husband. What was he doing back so early?

Panicking, Federica bent down and picked up the box. But as soon as she stood up, she came face to face with Silvio standing in the room's doorway.

"I left my phone but what are you doing in my room, Federica?" Silvio's voice was deep, low and immediately threatening.

As her husband took two steps into the room, Federica put her left hand behind her back, where she was holding the box. "I walked into the wrong room, Silvio. Sorry." She looked directly into her husband's face as he slowly advanced towards her, his narrowed eyes digging into her, never leaving her face.

"I am not going to ask you again, woman." Silvio's threat filled Federica with dread.

"I just gave you the answer to your question."

Federica was flung onto the bed by the ferocity of Silvio's arms. Despite being in his sixties, her husband possessed a surprising strength. As she fell on the mattress, landing on her back with a slight bounce, the box fell from her hand. But Silvio had not noticed, so caught up in his rage, his eyes widened in a crazed mania as he leapt onto the bed and loomed over her.

Just by looking into Silvio's enraged face, Federica knew she was facing a man who possessed enough hatred towards her that there was a real possibility he would finally kill her today.

"You filthy and lying piece of shit," he spat as he pinned her against the mattress despite her struggle to free herself from his grip. "I'll teach you a lesson."

"Get off me, Silvio!"

Silvio's right clamped around Federica's whole face like a

headpiece for prisoners, and he pushed her down on the bed as she thrashed her body, desperately trying to escape.

"We haven't fucked in a long time, have we?"

Federica felt Silvio lift her dress. His cold, dry fingers scraped across her right leg, his nails like a garden rake. When she felt his right hand grip her underwear and begin to pull them down, Federica knew at that moment that she would rather die fighting her husband than allow him to rape her.

Harnessing her feral instinct to survive, Federica raised her right leg and kneed Silvio hard in his groin. Silvio howled in pain, loosening his grip on her face. Seizing the opportunity while her husband was momentarily incapacitated, Federica shot up from the bed, slapped Silvo hard across the face and then pushed him off her. He tumbled backwards, falling off the mattress.

Federica stood up from the bed, panting heavily. Silvio had torn the top right half of her dress, exposing the left cup of her pink bra. He was now getting to his feet, rubbing his left cheek and his murderous eyes set on her.

Heart racing with fear and adrenaline, Federica ran out of the room, into the parlour, and headed straight for the open-plan kitchen. Hearing Silvio's heavy footsteps behind her, Federica reached for the drawers with the cooking knives.

"Bitch!" Silvio screamed, entering the parlour.

Frederica turned around, gripping a chef's knife she had taken from the draw, and faced her husband. Dishevelled and sweating, he stood in the middle of the parlour. His shoulders and chest rose and fell in sync as he breathed through his nostrils like a dragon.

Federica raised the chef's knife towards him. "You take one more step towards me, Silvio, and I will plunge this knife into you. I will fucking do it!"

Despite the heavy Botox on his face, Mancini managed to

contort his features into a vile grimace. "So the statue has finally found her voice, and now she threatens the man responsible for everything she has."

"I don't fucking need anything from you anymore," Federica said. Silvio took one step towards her. Federica slashed at the air with the chef's knife. "I am warning you. Don't come next to me."

He did not take another step. Instead, Silvio straightened his shirt collar and rubbed the sleeves of his long overcoat. "You better be out of this apartment by tomorrow morning. Our marriage is over. We are getting a divorce."

Federica snarled, still pointing the knife at him. "Our marriage was over a long time ago. And don't worry, I already have the divorce papers ready, Silvio."

"You won't enjoy any of the luxuries of this world without any of the credit cards I give you; the many perks you benefited from because you were my wife will be gone, and you will no longer be able to access the circles of influence I belong to. The acting career I built for you will be over. Do you understand that? You will never act in another film again so long as I fucking breathe."

"I don't need your money or your contacts anymore. And I'll do just fine, Silvio. Believe me. I'll do just fine."

Silvio sniggered and huffed. He then spat at her. "*Sporca puttana*." He turned his back towards Federica and walked out of the parlour. The front door slammed shut.

In the stillness and silence of the apartment, Federica stood on the spot, still clutching the chef's knife and the adrenaline charging through her body. Then she let her hand drop to the side and released the knife from her grip. It fell to the floor with a clang.

All the emotions came at Frederica simultaneously, like violent waves crashing against a beach. She stumbled against the kitchen island and sank onto the floor. Tears were now streaming down her eyes. Yet she was not crying because her husband almost raped her. No, she was crying because she was finally free of him.

44

A DAY after the Dubai Fashion Show, Dugard informed Timon and Yinka that Sheikh Abdul Kazeem Mustafa would return to Dubai in the next two days.

He had requested that instead of a private meeting with him, Timon and Yinka should put together an investor presentation pitching Afchain. Mustafa would invite around fifty people, including members of his highly esteemed family and other business associates, to watch the presentation and judge the merits of Afchain as an investment opportunity.

With such a mammoth task thrust upon them on such short notice, Timon and Yinka had spent the last two days holed up in their Burj Khalifa apartment, preparing a fancy presentation that would convincingly sell Afchain as the best crypto investment in Africa. With the help of Yinka's team back in Shoreditch, they had created a presentation with animated infographics, flashy images of the Afchain platform in action and visualisations which illustrated the very profitable quarterly returns an investor could expect if they put their money behind the crypto tech company.

With their working partnership now on solid ground, Timon and Yinka had spent hours perfecting their sales pitch while listening to Burna Boy or Tems, their favourite Afrobeats artists. On one occasion, they even shared a bottle of red wine. During the preparation, they had agreed that Yinka, who had proven she was an excellent speaker, would explain the concept behind Afchain and Timon, given the fact he runs a crypto hedge fund, would break down the numbers around quarterly dividends and annualised returns for investors. Timon was impressed by how quickly Yinka had gotten to grips with some of the more technical aspects of crypto.

When Mustafa finally arrived on their sixth day in Dubai, Timon and Yinka walked with Dugard through the futuristic interior of the Dubai Opera Theatre which embodied Dubai's extravagance with its dome-shaped architecture, metallic pillars and the mesmerising Symphony chandelier hanging from the ceiling.

Mustafa and his party had already arrived at the theatre and were congregating at the state-of-the-art studio where Timon and Yinka would be presenting. Dugard was escorting them to the studio.

For the presentation, Timon wore his most expensive Armani suit, which consisted of a navy blue suit jacket, waist-coat, and trousers, all matching for a harmonious look with black polished Dior Oxford shoes. Yinka also wore formal clothing for the presentation, effortless effusing sophistication in a black wrap-over neckline suit jacket, matching straight-leg trousers, and black leather court heels. Together, they looked like Barack and Michelle 2.0, ready to conquer the world.

"I must say, you two certainly effuse confidence and charm," Dugard said, who was walking slightly ahead of Timon and Yinka as they made their way to the studio. "And believe me, you'll need plenty of both today as you'll be pitching to some of the wealthiest entrepreneurs in Dubai. I want to say no pressure, but I'd be disingenuous."

"Yinka and I have already secured six million in investments from a rich Italian mogul and from a woman residing over one of Tokyo's richest families," Timon said, holding his closed MacBook by his side where he had saved the presentation. "So you should know by now, Richard, that we thrive and kick ass in the face of pressure." Timon winked at Yinka, who shook her head at him and gave him a big smile.

Dugard stopped in front of a closed double door. "Well, this is the grand finale. Let's stick the landing." He pushed open the studio door to reveal a packed and busy room. The studio's interior had smooth wooden walls, laminated flooring, and LED ceiling lights. Inside, around two dozen people were mingling and engaging in animated chatter. Many men wore traditional white or black thawb robes with the ghutra headscarf. A few women wore abaya dresses, some even wearing the hijab headdress, but others came in formal suits.

Observing the room, Timon noticed around fifteen rows of fold-up chairs facing a large screen. In front of the screen was a metal stage and two wooden podiums.

A theatre staff member approached Timon and took his iMac from him to set up the presentation so he could display it on the large screen. After the theatre staff member had hurried away with Timon's MacBook in his grasp, Timon was going to ask Dugard where Mustafa was so he and Yinka could formally introduce themselves. But Timon did not need to ask as the wealthy sheikh was already making a beeline towards them. Mustafa wore an ostentatious gold Emirati kandora and a matching ghutra headscarf. Not only did he carry the aura of a sultan, but the sheikh was much taller than Timon expected, at least 6" 5.

So distracted by the sheikh's height, Timon had not immediately noticed Mancini, dressed in a dark red overcoat, walking beside Mustafa on the right or the much older black man dressed in a dark green, traditional Yoruba agbada. The finely dressed Nigerian man was wearing a green cap, called a fila, that Timon had seen many older Nigerian uncles wear at some of the Nigerian parties he occasionally attended back in London. Curiously, the Nigerian man limped as he walked but steadied himself with a black and gold walking crane with a lion head. As Mustafa, Mancini, and the older Nigerian man came within their vicinity, Timon now noticed that the Nigerian man had golden rings on each of his fingers; each ring contained a dark, circular gem. *Where have I seen those rings before?*

When Mustafa stopped in front of Timon, Yinka, and Dugard, flanked by Mancini and the Nigerian man, Timon felt a shock jolt his body. Timon's mouth parted in bewilderment when he looked at the Nigerian man's face.

"So it really is you, my son," Mobolagi Bankole said, his dark and small eyes, almost identical in shape to Timon's, widening in surprise. "You have grown a bit of a beard since we last met."

"Why did you not tell us you were in the company of one of Mobolaji's children, Richard?" Mustafa said, narrowing his eyes at Dugard. "This is quite the plot twist. You've stunned Mobolagi. And that rarely happens."

"It's a pleasure to meet you, Mustafa," Yinka said, extending her hand and hastily shaking the sheikh's hand. "Excuse me for a second; I must go to the lavatory."

Timon noticed the shakiness in Yinka's voice, as if she had just seen a ghost. This was similar to how Timon felt in the current moment, as he stood, face to face, with the father he had not seen in a decade. When Yinka walked briskly from the group, Timon had not even looked at her. His brain had frozen, like a computer with an overloaded processor, as he stared at his father's dark brown complexion, perplexed and completely thrown off balance.

"Mobolagi and Silvio," Dugard said, sounding unconfident for the first time since Timon had met him, "this is quite...the surprise. You did not make me aware you two would be in Dubai and attending this presentation."

Mobolagi peeled his eyes away from Timon and regarded Dugard. Timon noticed his father grimace as he frowned at Dugard as if looking at an irritating insect. "Richard, neither myself nor Mancini are required to make you aware of our travel plans if they don't concern you. Never address me in such a manner again. Understand?" He spoke in a thick, heavy Nigerian accent, immediately commanding and authoritative. The sound of his father's voice made Timon clench his fists.

Again, for the first time, Dugard's veneer of charm cracked. He glared at Mobolagi and seemed to swallow his words as he coughed. "Apologies, Mobolagi. I meant no disrespect, of course." Every syllable Dugard uttered strained friendliness.

"It's a pleasure to see you again, Timon," Mancini said, extending his right hand. Timon shook his hand, but it was an involuntary gesture. He had not heard Mancini's greeting, as he was still trying to comprehend how he was standing before his father—all the way in Dubai.

"Timon, I am so happy to see you again," Mobolagi said, his attention now back on Timon as he rested his eyes on him. "It has been too long, but we can catch up after your presentation, which I look forward to. Silvio and Emiko have told me so much about Afchain and how it can usher in an age of crypto in Nigeria and West Africa. I can't wait to learn more, my son."

"And as you're one of Mobolaji's children, I have even higher expectations now," Mustafa said with a hearty laugh, both hands on his slightly round and protruding stomach. He seemed to enjoy that Timon and Dugard had been caught off guard by Mobolaji's and Mancini's presence. "If the apple doesn't fall far from the tree, you should be quite the convincing talker."

"Mustafa, please, you play too much," Mobolagi said, patting Mustafa on the shoulder like an old friend.

Timon wanted to say something to his father, but his brain was still completely overwhelmed by the shock of seeing him, rendering his mouth frozen.

Mobolagi nodded at Timon, giving him a quick smile, and then turned away with Mancini following suit. Neither of them had even bothered to acknowledge Dugard as they departed from Timon and Dugard's presence to speak to the other guests in the studio. Suddenly, Timon felt a shortness of breath. He needed to get out of here.

"Timon, where are you going?" Dugard said.

But Timon did not bother responding to Dugard as he hurried away to find the nearest toilet where he could hide and possibly not come out.

45

MOBOLAGI BANKOLE WAS Timon's father? But how? Why?
Yinka had left the studio and was now in the theatre's lobby. She leaned against one of the metal handle railings as she gathered herself. Seeing Mobolagi had wholly thrown her off, but the fact that he was Timon's father was a complete mindfuck. For the past year and a half, Yinka and The Robin Hoods, under Oge's leadership, had systematically been targeting every member of Mobolaji's corrupt family, with the latest victim being Mobolaji's eldest son whom Yinka had successfully seduced and blackmailed in Berlin, which felt like a lifetime ago. Yet, she had been unknowingly working with one of Mobolaji's sons all this time. Not only that, Mobolagi seemed to be an associate of Mancini, Mustafa and Emiko, the three investment bankers that Oge's kidnappers had coerced Yinka and her team to target for investment into Afchain. Even Dugard was linked to Mobolagi. *Just what the bloody hell is going on*? Yinka thought back to what Emiko had told her in Tokyo:

"Some powerful men playing a game of chess, and you and your business partner are merely pawns on the board."

Yinka closed her eyes, took a deep breath and exhaled

loudly. She needed to relax and think logically. Yes, Mobolaji's sudden and unexpected appearance, connection to the three bankers she had been targeting all this time, and the fact that he was Timon's father raised a truckload of questions. But those answers were not important right now. At this moment, the objective was to secure Mustafa's final investment for Afchain. Once achieved, Yinka and her team would then seek out answers to everything else.

Feeling like she had regained control of the situation, Yinka decided to return to the studio. She lifted herself from the railing and walked through the theatre lobby. As she moved through the lobby, her pace brisk, she caught sight of Timon a few feet away. She saw him enter the men's bathroom in a hurry. There was something about his face; it looked like he was in a state of shock that immediately troubled Yinka. She changed her direction and headed towards the men's lavatory.

"Timon, are you ok?" Yinka said, knocking on the bathroom door. "We have to present this sales pitch shortly."

"I don't know if I can do this," came Timon's loud response from inside the lavatory. His tone was heavy with anxiety. Never would Yinka have imagined that Timon, who behaved like his blood cells naturally produced greatness, would be experiencing what sounded like fear. With less than ten minutes to deliver the most important sales pitch in this joint enterprise they had embarked on since leaving London, now was not the time for Timon's crisis of confidence.

"I am coming in."

Even though Yinka knew she could get into severe trouble if caught entering the man's lavatories in a strictly Islamic place like Dubai, this was an emergency. She pushed open the men's lavatory door and walked in.

Inside the spacious and pristine marble lavatory, Yinka found Timon leaning against one of the golden wash basins. When Timon noticed Yinka had entered the toilet, he turned his head to look at her and wore a dour expression. His whole body was in a slumped posture. All of his natural self-confidence seemed to have vanished.

"I still remember the last memory I have of my father," Timon said without any prompt from Yinka, the sound of his voice soft yet thick with a painful and noticeable grief. "When he came to my graduation day. My mother, whom my father had abandoned when I wasn't even born yet, had not wanted him there, but my father had insisted. It's funny because it's not like he bothered to see me as a child. I received the occasional call from him when he was in Nigeria, sometimes a birthday card and a little money here and there. But now, he only wanted to see me in person because I was graduating from one of the top universities in the world. He probably just wanted to boast to all his friends back in Nigeria." Timon snarled. "So pathetic."

As Timon spoke, looking at the toilet urinals and not at Yinka, she did not say a word. She knew Timon needed to share these emotions, which he had bottled up for a long time, so she would give him space to do that.

"He hugged me for the first time that day, and we took photos while he waxed lyrical to the Dean and my lecturers about how he had been such a great father and nurtured me." Timon lifted the edge of his lip as he shook his head and scowled, his face contorted in bitterness. "After the ceremony, behind one of the university's faculties, we had engaged in a tense exchange of words which blew up into a full-blown fight. I ended up decking my father in the face, sending the bastard stumbling to the ground, and walked away from him. This happened nine years ago, and we haven't spoken to each other since then."

"I hated how he had taken all the credit for my educational achievements and upset my mother on what was supposed to be one of the proudest days of our lives." Timon's chest expanded as a deep and heavy sigh left his body. "And now he is here, in Dubai, to watch me give a presentation. I have to face that audience in there, Yinka, and see him in that crowd as I deliver this sales pitch. The face of a man I hate. How do I do that?"

Now Timon turned to face Yinka, and she saw a burning rage in his eyes, but within those flames was a raw vulnerability she would never have expected from him. Having been with Oge for many years, Yinka knew that when a man was vulnerable to a woman, it was a brave risk he was taking. It was not something a woman should take lightly if she genuinely cared for that man. Whatever Yinka said next to Timon, she had to be sympathetic and kind.

"I am definitely in shock that one of the most powerful men in Nigeria is your father," Yinka said, walking towards Timon. She came to stand next to him and leaned on the wash basin. They were so close now that their fingers touched.

Timon chuckled cynically. "Yeah, he might be a big man in Nigeria, but he is a small man when it comes to being a father."

"You have every right to feel the way you do about him, Timon," Yinka said, looking at him as she spoke, searching his deep black eyes as he stared blankly ahead. "I had a lovely and supportive father, so I won't pretend I can relate. But what I will say Timon, is that you are a brilliant man. You graduated from Cambridge and accomplished that as a black man who grew up in a council house in east London and raised by a single mother. You have had much success with your crypto hedge fund for someone your age. You spotted the massive opportunity that crypto was before many other people did. Plus, you're also about to marry a beautiful woman."

"Remember, you accomplished all of this without your father's help or guidance. It was just your determination and your mother's love and support." Yinka lifted her left hand and placed it on top of Timon's. This gesture, small in its movement but massive in its tenderness, caused Timon to turn his head and look at her finally. His eyes seem to shine as if Yinka were a magnificent light. To her surprise, she felt a kind of warmth inside her when he looked at her this way.

"I know your father being in that audience will be uncomfortable for you, but don't let that man make you forget who you are and what you're capable of, Timon. I have seen first hand you talk about crypto and investment dividends, and you know your shit. Remember, we're Nigerians and as stubborn as we are smart. We are not easily intimidated. Not us."

Timon's demeanour had now changed. He sat upright and straightened his shoulders. "You're speaking nothing but real facts," he said, smiling. "I need to tap into my inner Yinka and live in my stubborn energy. I will not fumble the bag when we've come this far."

Yinka laughed. "Your inner Yinka? That's a good one."

Timon lifted himself from the wash basin and stretched out his arms. It looked like his natural confidence had come surging back. "Thanks for the pep talk, business partner. I needed to that."

A big smile stretched across Yinka's face, and she felt relief. "No problem. I got you." Yinka then observed her surroundings. "But can we please get out of the men's lavatory before a man comes in here and I am thrown into a Dubai prison for the next ten years."

Timon nodded and chuckled. "Yeah, let's go secure this bag. Like we always do."

46

IT HAD BEEN ALMOST twenty-four hours since Timon and Yinka had delivered their investor presentation for Afchain to Mustafa and his associates to a standing ovation.

Now, Timon was lying on the king-sized bed back at the Burj Khalifa apartment, hands behind his head as he stared at the spotless white ceiling. After Timon and Yinka had undoubtedly hit it out of the park with their sales pitch, Timon drawing from Yinka's confident energy to get through it, his father confronted him afterwards. It was this meeting, between estranged father and son, that Timon had been reflecting on for most of the day.

"That was an outstanding presentation, my son," Mobolagi told Timon as they stood in the corner of the studio at the Dubai Opera Theatre. Yinka had gone to talk to some guests who wanted to ask further questions about Afchain. Unsurprisingly, Timon saw her deliberately avoid Mancini, but curiously, she also seemed to steer clear of Mobolagi.

"Son? That word sounds foreign to me coming from you," Timon had said, frowning at his father—the earlier, paralysing shock of seeing his father had evaporated now, replaced by cold indifference.

Mobolagi sighed. "I was not expecting a warm greeting from you, and of course, given our last...interaction...it would be foolish of me to expect one." He raised his right hand and placed it on Timon's right shoulder.

"But I am proud of what you've made of yourself, Timon. Unlike your half-siblings, you did it all without any of my resources. A true self-made man. Like his father."

Timon gave his father a mirthless smile and shoved his hand from his shoulder. "I may be your son, which is unfortunate, but I am nothing like you. *Dad*."

Mobolagi huffed, and his lips bent into a calm smile. "We got off on the wrong foot, as the English love to say. I want to build a relationship with you, Timon. You are my son, and I love you; that is the truth. I will ask Dugard to give you my number. If you want to talk to me or visit Nigeria and find yourself in Lagos, call me, son. I will welcome you with open arms."

After his father had left, Timon went to Dugard an hour later and, against his better judgment, asked for his father's number. But why had he done so? Did he want to form any relationship with his father? A part of Timon, like any son naturally, slightly longed to understand the man behind his existence, but would it do any good for him in the long term? As Yinka had told him yesterday, during his mini breakdown, he had accomplished so much in his life without ever having a relationship with his Dad. Why start now?

The apartment doorbell ringing popped Timon's thoughts like air bubbles. He raised himself from the mattress to sit upright at the tail of the bed. After stretching his arms, he walked to his bedroom door, dressed casually in a white Ralph Lauren polo shirt, black denim shorts and Gucci sandals, and opened his room door. Yinka was already by the apartment's front door, looking effortlessly chic in a beige, loosely fit, short-sleeved t-shirt dress and brown sandals. When she opened the apartment's front door, Dugard was the first to enter the apartment. But what happened next was unexpected.

Eight Arab men, all wearing white kaftan robes, entered the apartment in a uniform line like soldiers in an army. All were gripping silver suitcases. Timon looked across the room to Yinka, who shrugged her shoulders at him as they both witnessed the bewildering spectacle before them. Dugard had a broad smile on his face. The Arab men placed the suitcases on the floor, opened them and then turned them around so Timon, Yinka and Dugard could see the contents. In each suitcase were dozens upon dozens of neatly stacked 100 pound notes.

Timon blinked at the suitcases, scratched his head, and turned to look at Dugard. The English aristocrat was smiling like a Cheshire cat. "Richard, what exactly is happening right now?"

Dugard clapped his hands and began to laugh. "I told you Mustafa has a taste for the theatrical," he said, shaking his head. "In these suitcases is the three million investment you wanted for Afchain. Congratulations, Timon and Yinka. My word, you two have done it."

Timon felt his heart somersault in his chest as he walked over to the leather couch and dropped onto it. He looked at Yinka, who was still staring at the suitcases of cash. Her two hands were over her mouth, and her eyes were swelling with such happiness that it looked like she wanted to cry.

"Thank you, Richard, for everything," Yinka said, clearly holding back tears, her voice sounding like it could crack. "You've helped us so much; we could not have done this without you."

Dugard waved his right hand dismissively. "Nonsense. All I did was introduce you two to the important people with the big pockets." He gave Yinka a big and toothy smile. "It was you who did all the magic." Dugard then turned his attention to Timon. "Mustafa will expect the investment contract and a detailed report on expected returns and his quarterly dividends. I will send you the details of where to forward that to." He then looked at Yinka. "I'll also need the bank details again for Mustafa to deposit the money into."

Yinka nodded. "Of course, I'll retrieve them for you now."

"You must celebrate this momentous achievement and make the most of your last night in Dubai," Dugard said, looking at Timon, his face brimming with joy. "You have both certainly earned it."

A few hours later, in her bedroom, Yinka was carefully and gently applying dark brown eyeshadow to the top of her left eye as she sat in front of a dressing table. She had perched her MacBook on the chair she had dragged close to her legs as she was having a Skype call with her team. For the last hour, she provided them with a lengthy and detailed update about the events that had transpired in the previous twenty-four hours.

"Well, the good news is that we have the full investment now to guarantee Oge's release," Jaali said from the laptop screen.

"And the bad news is that this whole ordeal has just become even more shady," Montana added, finishing her fiancé's sentence. Yinka briefly looked at the screen and saw Montana sitting next to Jaali. Joshua and Kisi were also present beside them.

"Someone or some people are messing with us," Kisi said. "How is it that Mobolagi Bankole has been an associate of every single one of the private bankers we were targeting for this investment all this time? And then it turns out Crypto Boy is his son as well. We've spent the better part of almost two years blackmailing and stealing from Mobolaji's family, but we've been working with one of his children all this time. And remember, Crypto Boy was pre-selected for this whole mission by Oge's kidnappers." Kisi turned to Joshua. "Come on, Engineer. You're the main brains. You can't tell me this doesn't feel like a set-up."

Yinka heard Joshua sigh heavily. He adjusted his glasses and stroked his chin. "From the moment Oge was kidnapped, and we were tasked with this mission by his kidnappers, nothing has made sense. It is hard for me to piece together the machinations behind all this."

"Yes, everything about this whole mission doesn't make sense. But what matters now is that we have the money, so we need to know how Oge will be released back to us," Yinka said. She placed the eyeshadow brush on the dressing table. She was currently wearing her evening attire for tonight—an ivory floor-length dress with a plunge cowl. The dress wrapped around her curves and her bum like clingfilm. "Any status on that?"

"Currently, we don't have a clue," Joshua said. "If you recall, Oge's captor said that as soon as the full investment for Afchain is confirmed, they would contact us about Oge's release. At this point, all we can do is wait to hear from them."

Yinka nodded. Now that she, along with Timon and her team, had secured the total investment for Afchain, Oge's freedom was in sight. Soon, very soon, she hoped, she would be reunited with her boyfriend, the love of her heart. Until then, Yinka would patiently wait, but already, she felt much lighter, knowing Oge would soon be back with her.

"Yinks, babe; where exactly are you going tonight anyway?" Montana said, her tone heavy with playfulness. "And you're seriously wearing *that dress* when going out with Crypto Boy?"

"Monty, his name is Timon. Let's be respectful. If not for him, we couldn't have secured Oge's freedom," Yinka said. She picked up her Chanel lip balm, a dark brown shade —her favourite as it perfectly complimented her skin tone—and applied it carefully over her lips. "And Timon and I are going to BLU Sky Lounge nightclub to celebrate, as it's our last night in Dubai."

"We get that," Jaali said in a teasing tone. "We're just surprised you're wearing *that dress* out tonight. Isn't that the dress Oge, you know, *your boyfriend*, whose freedom you've just secured, bought for you?"

Yinka sighed impatiently. "You guys are reading too much into nothing. I like this dress, so I want to wear it tonight. Is that okay with you, Mum and Dad?" Yinka turned to the screen and stuck her tongue out playfully.

"Just getting on your nerves, Yinks," Jaali said, smiling at her from the screen.

"We've missed you, so you know we're going to tease," Montana said, making a mock sad face.

"They're right. You need to get your ass back here. I need to give my fellow bad bitch a hug," Kisi said, grinning.

Her team's words genuinely touched Yinka, and she could not wait to return to London and be reunited with them. The Robin Hoods had become like a surrogate family to her.

"I miss you guys too. I will start heading out now, but as soon as you hear anything about Oge, please let me know."

* * *

Ten minutes after the Skype call, Yinka stood outside the towering Burj Khalifa landmark on a sultry evening. It was just coming to 11 pm, and Dubai's skyscrapers were brimming with neon light against the pitch black sky. The Burj Khalifa was lit up by a spectacular array of LED lights, giving it the effect of a sparkling fortress which bathed the Burja Khalifa lake and the Dubai fountain in a fluorescent glow. As manufactured as it all was, Yinka had to admit that Dubai sometimes felt almost magical.

Currently, she was waiting for Timon to come and pick her up. He had left their apartment two hours ago but had not disclosed where he was going, only that he would collect her later. Just what he was up to, Yinka had no idea but felt giddy with excitement, like she was going to a school prom. Who would believe she was looking forward to having a good time tonight with Timon? It would be their last night in Dubai and most likely the last time they would see each other. The thought of that surprisingly made Yinka's heart drop. After everything they had been through, she had admittedly grown close to him - closer than she fully wanted to admit.

Yinka was snapped out of her thoughts by the screeching sound of what sounded like a car careering from the corner. Seconds later, Yinka watched from her left as Timon drove a sleek Porshe convertible - with a jet black metallic exterior and its iconic shield logo glistening on the bonnet - down the road, speeding towards her direction. The sports car's powerful engines engulfed Yinka's ear drums as Timon brought the Porshe to a grinding halt a few feet from her.

With a wide grin stretching across his face, Timon exited the convertible and waved at her, dangling the car keys. "I present to you the Porsche 911 S Cabriolet," he announced with exaggerated pomp. "I rented it for tonight. We're hitting the town in style, baby. You like it?"

Yinka shook her head and chuckled as she walked towards him. "Please don't say *'baby'* like that; it makes you sound like a cringe-worthy American guy, and yes, it's a very nice car."

Tonight, Timon wore his red suit with a black sweater underneath the suit jacket, well-polished black leather shoes, and a black and gold Gucci belt across his waist. When Yinka had first laid eyes on the red suit during their stay in Sardinia, she had thought it was singlehandedly the worst suit she had ever seen. But tonight, perhaps because Dubai itself was extravagance personified, the flamboyancy of the red suit suited the environment. Also, she had to admit that Timon wore the suit quite well, and its colour complemented his light brown complexion. Not for the first time, Yinka was reminded of how handsome he was, and he most certainly took after his mother's side of the family because he certainly had not inherited his chiselled jawline from his father.

"Admit it; you were wrong about the red suit," Timon said, those nice lips of his curved into a cheeky and boyish smile, one that could get an unassuming girl in trouble.

"It's only acceptable because we're in Dubai," Yinka said, shaking her head at him but grinning as she walked to the Porsche's passenger door. "Anywhere else, I still think it would be a terrible miscalculation of fashion."

Timon chuckled. "Just look at us. You are in that stunning dress, me in this red suit, and this Porsche we're cruising around in. Name a Nigerian male and female duo who can pull off style like we do?"

Yinka burst into laughter and shook her head at Timon. *Oh, tonight would be fun.* With the success of the mission and Oge's freedom assured, Yinka wanted to enjoy herself on this dazzling Dubai evening and let loose. It had been a long time since she had gone partying. "Okay, black James Bond, can we get in your fancy car now and leave? I am ready for some cocktails and dancing. Hopefully, they play some Afrobeats and R'n'B at this club."

Timon opened the passenger door for Yinka, who carefully entered, ensuring she did not trip on her crystal-embellished Gucci heels.

"Ah, so the lady is ready to shake a leg tonight?" Timon said once he sat in the leather driver's seat. "But can Miss Stubbornly Sophisticated dance, though? That's the question I want answered tonight."

Yinka turned to face Timon. She had to admit, she did like the nickname he had given her. "Let's get to the club, and you'll get your answer."

Timon gave her a devilish grin, tipping into being an

openly flirtatious one, as he twisted the key in the ignition. Yinka put on her seatbelt, heart racing with excitement.

The Porsche convertible roared into life as its engine growled. Then Timon released the handbrake and pressed his feet against the gas pedal, and they shot off into the night with a loud screech, ready to enjoy Dubai's nightlife.

47

OVERLOOKING the Dubai Greek and Persian Gulf, the BLU sky lounge offered some of the most arresting views in the emirate. A grill restaurant by day but transformed into a nightclub in the evening, the establishment was everything one would expect from a nightclub in Dubai. Yinka had been to high-end nightclubs before: as an undergraduate in London when she could occasionally afford it and, more recently, whenever she was in Lagos. Yet BLU sky longue was on another scale.

Tonight, the place was heaving with revellers as booming sound speakers rumbled in Yinka's eardrums as the DJ spun loud music from African American rappers. Glowing lanterns hung from the roof, spreading golden light over the smooth surfaces and the cylinder-shaped exquisite décor made of polished marble and glass. Some young men of various nationalities sat around curved tables with buckets of cham-pagne and gorgeous women around them as they smoked on long shisha pipes.

Yinka wasn't the biggest partygoer; she preferred evenings lost in a good book or watching a fascinating documentary with Oge, but when the mood to party caught her, she liked to do it in style. Tonight, it seemed that would be the case.

"Gin and tonic on the rocks for the beautiful lady," Timon said, handing her the rock glass with the cocktail drink he had bought. He had ordered a Hennessy and coke, which Yinka realised was his favourite cocktail.

"Thank you for getting me a drink," Yinka said. She took a sip of her cocktail. It was pitch perfect—bitter with enough tonic water to temper it with sweetness.

"So, what'd you think of the venue?" Timon said, standing close to her.

"I like it." Yinka looked at Timon and sent him a mischievous grin. "After we finish these cocktails, let's get three tequila shots and then get on the dance floor."

"I do love this wild side to you," Timon said, smirking. "Book nerd and a temptress of men by day, party animal by night."

"I wouldn't call myself a party animal," Yinka said, chuckling. "But we worked well together. We secured the bag, so we deserve to celebrate in style."

Timon nodded. "Yep, that we did. So let's toast. To a great partnership and securing the bag."

Yinka raised her highball glass and clinked it against Timon's. Just then, the sound of an annoyingly familiar voice entered Yinka's space.

"Dubai can feel so small sometimes, am I right?"

Much to Yinka's revulsion, Desola had come to stand in front of her and Timon. She wore an all-black, skinny jumpsuit with solid mesh stitching, displaying her admittedly toned midriff and curvy shape.

"Nice to see you again, Desola," Timon said. Yinka detected the insincerity in Timon's voice.

"And it's even nicer to see you, Timon. I don't think you realise how dangerously good you look in red," Desola said, her eyes entirely on Timon as she acted as if Yinka was invisible. "I told the girls I was with who saw you come in here that we had a little thing when we were kids. One of my girls was eyeing you up."

Timon raised his eyebrows. "Really?"

"Yep," Desola said. She bit her lip.

Yinka had to use all her willpower not to throw her cocktail all over Desola's face.

"Why don't you come and say hi."

Timon chuckled mockingly, to Yinka's surprise and Desola's, judging by the stern frown now on her face. "At your big age, you're still behaving like some bratty schoolgirl. We're not fourteen anymore. Please grow up. Besides, I am with Yinka tonight, as you can see. So I don't need to speak to any of your *friends*."

Desola stood there, looking dumbfounded. Her mouth opened, but no words materialised. For Yinka, this was pure gratification. She never expected to see the day Desola would be humbled by Timon. If only she could frame a picture of Desola's face in this moment.

"You can leave now. No need to keep standing in front of us looking like a sad frog," Yinka said with a delightful smirk.

It looked like Desola wanted to raise her hand towards Yinka but decided against it. A smart decision. Instead, she sucked her teeth loudly and stormed away from them in a fit, embarrassment trailing her like a long shadow.

Timon turned to look at Yinka and chuckled. "A sad frog, yeah? I am stealing that insult. It's brilliant."

Yinka smiled and took a long sip of her gin and tonic before addressing Timon. "Let's order those tequila shots and get dancing."

After finishing their cocktails and consuming three tequila shots each in quick succession, Timon and Yinka made their way to the grand dance floor on the venue's top floor. A broad and long stage stretched across the room's length, and beautiful female dancers in sequin dresses paraded on the stage and swung from poles, putting on quite a spectacle.

Timon and Yinka joined the hundred or so revellers around the dance floor. While the DJ had been blasting out rap music before, he must have somehow read Yinka's mind because now he had changed the mood by switching to Afrobeats. Not only that, but the DJ was playing Tems' *'Free Mind.'* It was Yinka's favourite song by the Nigerian singer.

As the flashing blue and red rays of light from the LED roof lights flooded the dancefloor and washed Yinka and Timon in a vivid kaleidoscope of colours, she found herself standing in front of Timon, now so close to each other that their chests were touching. Lost in herself to Tems' soulful vocals and freed of any inhibitions by the alcohol she had consumed, Yinka swayed her hips from side to side. At the same time, Timon followed her rhythm with a simple but smooth two-step dance, his eyes trailing her every move.

"Looks like you have some rhythm in those hips," Timon told Yinka. She felt the heat of his breath on her skin and the smell of his tantalising and masculine cologne tingling her nose.

"Oh, this is just a tease."

Timon grinned wickedly at Yinka as he put his arms around her waist. And Yinka should have stopped it there. She should have gently removed his hands, but she did no such thing. No, instead, she wrapped her arms around his torso and pulled him into her body for a tight embrace. Then she moved her arms upward and curved them around Timon's neck. Now she was looking up at him, admiring those dark eyes and then his lips, weighty and fleshy pink. Her heart was racing because Yinka could feel she was utterly allowing her lust, and maybe even loneliness, to drive her actions at this moment. When her lips had fount Timon's, it was too late to pull away. Nor did she want to.

The kiss with Timon exploded across her body like

someone setting off hundreds of dynamite charges filled with pleasure. The feeling of his mouth pressed against hers reverberated through her skin, and the texture of Timon's lips, soft and wet, made her knees weak as she poured more of herself into him. Timon, who seemed just as possessed by lust as her, held the back of her head with two hands behind her braids and took her into himself. Yinka could feel herself sinking deeper and deeper into the moment; eyes closed as her lips and tongue tangled with Timon's as if it were the most satisfying feeling in the world. Then Oge appeared before her as if he were an apparition, with his light complexion, dark brown braids, and the scar on the left side of his face.

Yinka pushed Timon away from her and stepped back in shock as if someone had shot her. Her breathing was as heavy as the beating of her heart. Timon looked equally stunned, his mouth agape as he stared wide-eyed at her.

"Yinka...I...I am...sorry," Timon said, his words stumbling out.

"I need some fresh air," Yinka said, placing her left hand on her throbbing forehead. "And I need to be alone right now."

Timon nodded. "Sure."

Five minutes later, Yinka was on the balcony. Not only could she still hear, albeit faintly, the sound of music booming from inside the club, but there was also the sound of speeding cars racing across the highway below.

Tears fell from her eyes. *How could she do that to Oge*? She felt deeply ashamed that she had kissed Timon. But it wasn't just kissing Timon but the fact that, although she tried to deny it, she had enjoyed it. Immensely. Even now, she could feel the residue of Timon's lips on hers, as if he'd left an imprint on her. Yinka knew she needed to be reunited with Oge as soon as possible. She was missing him too much, and the whole ordeal behind his kidnapping had caused her to behave erratically and engage in a rare moment of madness and lust.

It was the only explanation Yinka could tell herself to contextualise and give sense to her betrayal. But did she believe it? Yinka could not allow herself to entertain the possibility that tonight's kiss with Timon had meant something more profound.

48

THE FOLLOWING MORNING, back at the Burj Khalfi apartment, the space between and around Yinka and Timon had become incredibly awkward and tense.

Last night, after Yinka had returned to the club, located Timon and asked to leave, the drive back to their apartment had been wordless, with only the loud humming of the rented Porsche's engine filling the strained silence in the car. They had not even dared to look at each other, and Yinka could tell Timon was feeling just as embarrassed and confused about the kiss as she was.

When they arrived back at the apartment, they went to their rooms without saying a word to each other. Neither of them was ready to address what Yinka now called her in the head, '*that kiss.*'

At 11 am the next morning, Yinka had finished packing her suitcase. A day ago, she and Timon had booked their afternoon flights back to London on the Emirates airline. Her team back in Shoreditch had told her that London was a little chilly, so Yinka was wearing a white, ribbed knit long-sleeve body suit, a black leather jacket and high-waisted flared jeans with white Nike Air Force One trainers. Grabbing the handle of her suitcase and her backpack secured over her shoulders, Yinka walked towards her bedroom door.

As soon as Yinka swung the door open, she came face to face with Timon standing in the parlour with his Gucci trolley beside him. He had returned from the car dealership where he had rented the Porshe. Today, Timon had worn beige trousers and a dark brown crewneck jumper that nicely hugged his athletic frame with his white Ralph Lauren trainers. In her head, Yinka cursed herself for eyeing him like he was a delicious roast. It had been a long time - too long from the way she was behaving around Timon - since she had sex with Oge. The prolonged absence of intimacy with her boyfriend was starting to mess with her hormones. But she needed to get a firm grip on herself.

"Hey," Timon said, his eyes seeming to struggle to look at her as he spoke in an uncharacteristically shy voice, which Yinka found, against her better judgment, so cute and endearing that it added another layer to his attractiveness. "How are you feeling? Hope you're not too hungover?"

"I am actually pretty good, thanks. I got a good amount of sleep." Yinka then smiled at Timon, and she could feel it was awkward. Timon responded with an uneasy smile of his own. At this point, Yinka knew they could not go on like this. *We're adults, for God's sake.* They would be in the same Uber, taking them to Dubai International Airport and flying on the same plane. 'That kiss' needed to be addressed now.

"Look, Timon, about that…what happened at the club last night," Yinka began, and Timon shot his eyes at her, suddenly alert. "I just got caught up in the moment with everything that's happened. I shouldn't have kissed you, but it didn't mean anything. And I am sorry I did that."

Although he tried to conceal it, Yinka saw the discomfort in Timon's face as she spoke with such frankness, but he quickly recovered and composed himself. "Oh yeah, of course," he said, adding a forced chuckle. "I feel the same way."

"Exactly," Yinka said, nodding. "We're both in very serious relationships, so we owe it to our partners and ourselves to be faithful to them. That kiss between us was just a brief bout of overexcitement from both of us. " Even Yinka could tell she was doing too much to convince herself of this.

"I agree," Timon said, also nodding. He then let out a short laugh, levelled his eyes at Yinka and gave her a small smile. "It was a nice kiss, though. Meaningless as it was."

Against her better judgment, Yinka found herself chuckling. She gave Timon a warm smile. "It was a nice kiss. But yes, absolutely and completely meaningless."

There was a knock on the apartment door. Timon went over to the door and opened it. Dugard stepped into the parlour with a cheerful demeanour, dressed in an all-black suit. Yinka wondered if Dugard had anything else in his wardrobe apart from expensive suits.

"I had to compose myself before I came to see you both and say our farewells," Dugard said, looking at both Yinka and Timon. "Alas, all journeys must come to an end. *Omnes iter mut finem,* as they say in Latin." Dugard, who was clearly in a highly buoyant mood this morning, laughed heartily. "Apologies, that's my privileged education rearing its head. I don't mean to show off."

Although Yinka still had reservations about Dugard and his true motives, he had helped them immensely on this mission, so she owed him her gratitude. "You're quite a character, Richard," Yinka said, stretching her left hand for Dugard to shake. "But thank you for all you've done for us. Without access to your network, we wouldn't have secured the total investment needed for Afchain."

Dugard shook Yinka's hand, lifted it to his lips, and planted a soft peck. "It has been a pleasure meeting you, Yinka. You are as beautiful as you are intelligent. Nigeria has a bright future if it produces exceptional women like yourself."

Yinka shook her head at Dugard, grinning at him. "You'll make my head swell and explode if you keep singing my praises."

"Sorry, I can't help myself," Dugard said, winking at Yinka. "And you, Timon, my good man," Dugard said, now turning his attention to Timon. He stretched out his right hand, and Timon shook it firmly. "Although I was quite surprised to learn you are the son of my dear friend, Mobolagi, it does make a lot of sense. You are a sharp man like your father, and I wish you all the best in your future endeavours."

"I appreciate that, Richard. Thank you," Timon said, who looked more uncomfortable than grateful being compared to his estranged father.

Dugard turned his attention to Yinka again and gave her a suspiciously knowing smile. "I can't wait to see how Afchain develops, and I am certain we will see each other again."

Something in Dugard's tone troubled Yinka, but Timon spoke before she could ask Dugard why he was so sure they would meet again. "Our Uber is here," he said, looking down at the screen on his iPhone.

Dugard clapped his hands together, and his gleeful yet somewhat unsettling smile widened. "Have a safe flight back to London, my friends. *Ad Omnia Finem.*"

Now that Yinka and Timon had addressed the events of last night; their Uber journey to Dubai International Airport and subsequent flight to Heathrow Airport had been pleasant and entertaining. Yinka now had an easy and playful rapport with Timon. They made fun of Dugard's posh idiosyncrasies, tried to outdo each other when it came to who could come up with the most creative insults about Mancini and reminisced about their two weeks together, travelling across the globe.

At 7.30 pm, Yinka and Timon landed at Heathrow Airport. As soon as Yinka walked out of the plane and through the airport's terminal, her body immediately jerked at the drastic change in temperature. Compared to the Persian heat of Dubai, London was practically the Antarctic.

While waiting to collect their luggage from the conveyor belt in the quiet baggage reclaim area, Yinka and Timon did not say a word to each other. Yinka could feel the tension hanging over them like dark clouds promising rain. Once they collected their suitcases and walked out of the arrivals gate, she knew this was the end of their time together. Unless the universe conspired another convoluted event to bring them together again, it would be a definitive goodbye once they said goodbye to each other.

"You should receive the final payment of three million pounds this week as part of our agreed consultancy fees. I have your bank details, so I'll deposit the money into your account immediately once the funds are available. "

Yinka spoke deliberately in a business tone to Timon to lessen the aching pain of the end of their business partnership. With her suitcase beside her, she stood in front of Timon at Heathrow Airport's lobby, which was busy with activity. Timon was holding onto his big Gucci suitcase and was facing her. There was a look of regret on his face as he softened his eyes at her. At the start of this mission, Yinka would never have imagined that saying goodbye to Timon once it was over would feel like a tragic breakup.

"That sounds good to me. Getting paid handsomely for your expertise is the best kind of appreciation in the world."

Yinka chuckled. "For you, I know it is." She let out a long sigh. "It's been...a journey, Timon. Thank you for everything. And all the best with the wedding and life as a married man." She raised her left hand for Timon to shake.

Timon held onto Yinka's outstretched hand and shook it delicately as if it were a feather, but he did not let go. He squeezed her hand gently. "Thanks, Yinka. And I hope you've obtained whatever this whole Afchain investment means to you."

"I did."

The more Timon smiled at Yinka, a pained smile, the more she could tell he was finding this whole farewell as tricky as she was.

"And I hope you build that school in your village and become a mother one day. Your boyfriend is a very lucky man. I hope he realises that. Even with all your stubborn sophistication." Timon threw her one of his boyish grins.

Yinka muffled a laugh. "I was waiting for that."

"And don't forget, there's more to you than just your body and beauty, Yinka. Don't let those be the only things that define you."

Yinka felt a burst of emotion rise through her chest like an expanding bubble floating upwards, but she managed to burst it. She breathed out heavily, composing herself. "I won't."

Still holding her left hand, Timon raised it to his lips and kissed it tenderly. "I don't know any Latin, but I know how to say goodbye in Yoruba at least. *O dabọ*."

A light laugh escaped Yinka's mouth. "That pronunciation wasn't too bad. Well, goodbye, Timon. Again, thanks for everything."

After finally letting go of her hand, Timon nodded at her curtly, turned around, and walked away from her. She watched him as he reached the lift some feet away and pressed one of the buttons. Timon stepped inside when the lift doors opened and then turned around to look back at Yinka. He gave her a final wave, regret colouring his dark eyes. Feeling deeply saddened, Yinka waved back. The lift doors closed shut.

And like that, Timon was out of her life.

As Yinka thought back to that electrifying kiss she had shared with Timon, her lips formed an involuntary smile. In another life, if the universe had plotted their paths differently, she and Timon could have been something more than friends. But Yinka had a life, and Timon had his. It was impossible to align them. Now, what she had to look forward to was being reunited with her friends and Oge, her only and one true love.

Yinka pulled her smartphone from her leather jacket and called Montana's number.

"Hey, Monty, I've arrived at Heathrow. Are you here yet?"

"Yep, I just pulled up at the car park, babe," Montana said in her bubbly and warmly familiar voice. "And I've got a major update to share. Josh has received a video message from Oge's kidnappers. They will release him to us tomorrow and send us the location of where he'll be. We did it. Oge is finally coming home, Yinks."

PART SIX

BETRAYAL OF THE HEART

49

Kojo's last meeting with Federica was a day ago in Dubai. In the evening, she had visited his hotel to deliver the mini recording camera she had planted in Mancini's room.

"I put myself in harm's way to do this," Federica said, handing Kojo the black box with the recording device inside. "Fortunately, I retrieved the device this morning while he showered. Then I left. Never to return."

"Thank you, Federica. I cannot appreciate you enough for what you have done for me," Kojo said, holding the black box.

"I did not do it for you; I did it for me," Federica said. She gripped a light pink, medium-sized Antler Clifton suitcase in Kojo's hotel room doorway. "I have informed Silvio that our marriage is over, and I am flying back to Milan this evening to pack the rest of my belongings. Then I will meet my daughter and her boyfriend in Monte Carlo."

Kojo stepped forward and gently placed his hands on Federica's shoulders. "And us? Do you still wish to see me again?"

Federica did not immediately respond. Cruelly, for she must have sensed the longing in Kojo's voice, she let the question hang in the air. Kojo felt her delayed answer was an axe waiting to drop down on his neck and cut it clean.

After what felt like an eternity, Federica stared deeply into Kojo's dark eyes, searching for something inside his iris, and sighed. "I am starting the next chapter of my life, and I have fought hard for this moment to be free of my vile husband finally. And I do not wish to begin this new phase entertaining men who lie to me."

Kojo nodded stiffly, feeling his heart sink like copper in an ocean. "I understand," he said in a low voice.

"But, if I listen to my heart, I know I have grown close to you," Federica continued. Her eyes had warmed now. "I would like to keep seeing you and attempt to build a relationship with you, but I will not wait for you indefinitely. So you have a month to complete your mission, and then you can come and find me in Monte Carlo. That is if you care for me like you say you do."

Kojo smiled at her, feeling relieved that there was still a chance they could continue the romantic journey they had started. "I care for you. And that is coming from my heart."

"Then you will come and find me when your mission is done. One month. Never contact me again if I do not hear from you after that."

Kojo nodded, and then, to his surprise, Federica leaned forward and gave him a tender kiss. At that moment, he desperately wanted to take her to his bed, gently strip her of her clothing and make love to her in this Dubai heat, but he knew better than that.

After the kiss, Federica stepped back. Now, her mouth had curved into a cheeky grin. "Before I go, I have one final thing to say to you."

"You have my ears, Federica."

"I wish you hadn't told me your name was Steven Hartlett. It's such a bland name. Kojo is much better."

And with those final words, Federica had left Kojo's hotel room.

* * *

Twenty-four hours after leaving Dubai, Kojo was back at MI6 headquarters. He sat on the leather sofa in Tiwa's cylinder-shaped, reinforced steel underground office. In front of him, his superior sat cross-legged on the leather swivel chair in complete silence. Her dark hair was in a braided bun, and her golden earrings, the shape of the African continent, dangled from her ears as she flipped a silver biro between her fingers. She was in deep thought.

Kojo sighed and leaned back on the leather sofa. "You're keeping me in suspense here, Tiwa. So what are your thoughts on the Mancini recordings?"

Tiwa darted her eyes to Kojo now. She smiled at him. "The work you've done in Dubai has been outstanding. You've outdone yourself, Kojo. The information on these recordings is hugely promising. We're one step closer to incriminating Dugard and bringing down The Cable."

"I told you I wouldn't let you down," Kojo said, sitting up and grinning at her.

But Tiwa was not exaggerating about the significance of the Mancini recordings. Even Kojo had not expected such crucial details when he had sat down in front of his laptop back in Dubai thirty minutes after Federica had left, a cold Guinness can in his hand, as he downloaded the video files by connecting the micro recording camera to his laptop via Bluetooth.

The video footage of Mancini's meeting, in grayscale HD so it resembled security footage, was about ten minutes long. On the laptop screen, Kojo saw Mobolagi Bankole and Abdul Kazeem Mustafa standing with Silvio Mancini in his room. All three men were facing a widescreen television perched on a metal stand. To Kojo's surprise, Emiko Shinoda's face was on the television screen. She was having a Zoom conference call with the three men.

"Dugard has always been the biggest fool among us," Mobolagi said to the group, with a sneering grin on his long and dark brown face as he spoke in his solid Nigerian accent, accentuating his every word with a noticeable intonation and rhythm. "For the many years we have worked with him, he has been over-ambitious in his attempts to have his fingers in any Nigerian infrastructure project, which shows great promise. He seems to forget that his family name holds no sway in post-colonial Nigeria." Mobolagi chuckled to himself as if sharing a private joke. "But what he is attempting to do with this Afchain company is bold even for him. He went to such lengths to deceive us and pretend he had no stake in it, acting as if he was merely introducing us to the company. Worse still, he drags my son into this duplicitous game of his, attempting to make an even greater fool of me."

"Dugard's actions do not surprise me," Mancini said, looking at Mobolagi. "The English do not build anything. They steal, and if they can't, they make sure they are reaping the rewards through shady contracts that conceal their criminality. An English man will smile at you while holding the dagger to kill you behind his back."

"You talk like you're not European, Mancini," Mustafa said, sneering at the Italian as he turned to him. "Europeans built their power by carving distant lands and reaping their resources. Italy is no different. If my history is correct, Italians colonised much of East Africa."

"Gentlemen, I wasn't aware I had been invited to a history lesson on African colonisation," Emiko said from the television screen, her voice impatient. "Let us focus, please. Through our corporate spies, which we placed at Afchain's headquarters in Abuja, we have verified that Dugard owns a sixty per cent stake in the company through a shell company

he set up in the Cayman Islands under an alias. He purposefully did not divulge this information to us, going against the
rules of our multilateral partnership. Duard bypassed us,
knowing we wouldn't agree to invest our client's money into
crypto. Now, he has obtained investment from us to speed up
Afchain's development. Mobolagi, you ordered us to invest in
Afchain, knowing that Dugard had a majority stake in it.
Why?"

"Because, Emiko, I want Dugard to be under the impression that he has deceived us successfully so we can confront
him when the time is right." Mobolagi frowned, now looking
agitated. "Dugard's investment of our client's money into the
UK market has been providing low returns for some time
now. The Cable was formed to be a reliable network where
our clients could invest and conceal their profits in our
respective countries. But Dugard has been nothing more than
dead weight, and it is time to cut him loose. Permanently."

"And how, Mobolagi, do you suppose we do that?"
Mustafa asked him, eyes narrowed.

Mobolagi shrugged his shoulders. "We will kill him, of
course." He had uttered the deadly sentence so nonchalantly
that Kojo had known then that Mobolagi was a very
dangerous man who had most certainly ordered hits on
people before.

"And how exactly are we going to kill such a prominent
English businessman?" said Mancini.

Mobolagi turned to Mancini and bent his dark lips into a
sneer. "He will meet his end at the African Tech Summit in
Lagos in three weeks."

"You want to kill Dugard in Nigeria?" Emiko said,
sounding startled by the suggestion.

"If you recall, we have all agreed to attend the summit,"
Mobolagi said. "We will host a private meeting with Dugard,
and we will all attend. In that meeting, we will confront
Dugard about his deception regarding Afchain, force him to

sign over all of his stake in the company and then he'll be escorted out into a vehicle which will be involved in a staged violent robbery resulting in Dugard's untimely death."

"And what of your son and the woman he was with? His business partner?" Emiko said, a slight concern in her voice. "What about them?"

"They're inconsequential," Mobolagi said. "I suspect, from how Dugard introduced them to us, that they are not even aware they were Dugard's pawns all this time to obtain investment for Afchain."

"So we are still going to retain our investment in Afchain?" Emiko said. "I thought you did not trust blockchain technology or crypto?"

"You ask the right questions just like your mother always used to; God rest her soul," Mobolagi said, smiling at Emiko. "I am not too familiar with the crypto world, but I see the opportunities it provides. The crypto industry is not regulated, especially in African countries, so it can be useful for concealing our clients' money. My son is not wrong. Afchain is a worthwhile investment, but not with Dugard at its helm. So we shall remove him from the equation."

At that point, the meeting in Mancini's room ended. The rest of the secret video recording was of Mancini inviting several prostitutes into his room. Kojo had turned off the footage once Mancini's sexual frivolities began. Federica had not been exaggerating about her now ex-husband. The man was a piece of work.

"So we now have compelling evidence that The Cable exists, and we know its members," Tiwa said, looking at Kojo as she continued to flip her silver pen between her fingers. "The question now is what MI6's next move should be?"

Kojo leaned back against the sofa and stroked his chin. "Well, we need to stop Dugard from being killed at the African Tech Summit so we can extradite him to the UK to face criminal charges of money laundering and racketeering.

Secondly, we need to record this meeting that Mobolagi will be hosting with Dugard and the other members of The Cable at the African Tech Summit. By recording that meeting, we will have enough irrefutable intelligence to bring down this criminal organisation for good."

Tiwa hummed; she sounded uncertain. "It would be risky, Kojo. I agree that recording that meeting will strengthen the intelligence you've already collected. But, at the same time, Dugard's life will be in danger. We'd need to record enough of the meeting to get the information we need but also stop Dugard from being killed."

"I know, and that's why we're going to have to work with the Nigerian State Security to pull off an operation of this scale," Kojo said, looking straight at Tiwa."

Tiwa chuckled. "From what I know of Nigeria's State Security, they won't be so easily cooperative with MI6, especially if Mobolagi Bankole has already bribed them all. But you're right; we'd need to engage with them to pull this off."

Kojo scratched the side of his forehead. "We need to be a fly on the wall in that private meeting happening at this African Tech Summit. I do have an idea. We could have a spy infiltrate Mobolaji's inner circle and place themselves within the meeting."

"A spy?" Tiwa said, raising her eyebrows in surprise. She broke into a knowing smirk as she shook her head at Kojo. "Why do I feel you already have someone in mind?"

"Yep, Mobolaji's son. Our crypto wonder boy."

"Mr Bakare? You really think so?"

"There must be a reason why he was working alongside Miss Saraki to help her secure investment for Afchain. From the other recording I have, from when I bugged their hotel rooms in Tokyo, I learned that Miss Saraki was on a mission to secure investment for Afchain to free her kidnapped boyfriend. Miss Saraki and her team specifically recruited Mr Bakare to help them accomplish this. I want to know how

Miss Saraki convinced him to work for them. What do they have on him? Once I find that out, we can coerce Mr Bakare to spy on his father for us and get himself a seat in that private meeting at the African Tech Summit."

Tiwa stopped flicking her pen and placed it on her worktable. She leaned back against her swivel chair and narrowed her eyes at Kojo. "It sounds a little flimsy, Kojo if I am being honest. But I have no alternative strategy so we'll run with yours. Find out how and why Miss Saraki and her team recruited Mr Bakare. Once you have the information, let's bring him in. If it comes to light that Mr Bakare has got himself into some unpleasant business, then we can exploit him."

50

A STRONG GUST of wind blew against Yinka's face, whipping her braids against her face like tentacles.

Yinka and the rest of the Robin Hoods stood in a sprawling, grassy airfield on a cloudy and brisk afternoon. They were in the English countryside of Windsor, located in the historic Berkshire in southeastern England. Through an encrypted message sent to Joshua's mobile a day ago, Oge's kidnappers had instructed them to come to this exact location. Here, Oge would be released safely to them when he arrived by plane.

Yinka created some warmth for herself by rubbing her hands together. Her teeth chattered at this low temperature, even in her white parka coat. Looming in the far distance in front of her, surrounded by tall, English oak trees, was a medieval, fifteenth-century manor that Yinka and the team knew, from their research, was called Crafton Manor, and it was a grade 1 listed building owned by a family that was part of the English nobility. But why they were meeting Oge's abductors at gentrified land remained unclear to Yinka and the others. It was another one of the many oddities surrounding this entire saga. Thankfully, it would soon be over.

"It's bloody cold, mate," Jaali said as he came to stand next to Yinka. He was also dressed in a parka coat, as were the other Robin Hoods still sitting inside the white rented minivan Montana had driven from London. "How are you feeling, Yinks?"

"I am feeling good," Yinka said, smiling at Jaali. "I am just glad this ordeal is finally over, and we'll have Oge back with us."

"Yeah, it's been a wild ride for sure. More so for you since you were the one jet setting all over the world convincing rich people to give you money for a company none of us give a shit about," Jaali said, elbowing Yinka playfully on her left rib. He put his hands inside his coat pockets. "It's also a sign from God that now is the right time for us to leave this life. We've become so notorious that we're now on dangerous people's radar. People who have the resources, expertise and technology to stage a whole kidnapping of one our own and blackmail us to carry out these kinds of operations for them. The Robin Hoods have to disband for good after this."

Yinka nodded. "You're right. Even thieves need to know when it's time to retire. We've had a great run."

Jaali's lips curved into a smirk. "Yeah, we have. I am ready to be a father and a husband to Monty. Lead a normal life."

Yinka nodded. "I am right there with you, Jaali."

Joshua had stepped out of the minivan along with Montanna and Kisi. All three walked over to where Yinka and Jaali stood in the field.

"Look up in the sky," Joshua said, his right hand across his forehead as he squinted his eyes and looked at the thick, grey clouds. "I can see an aircraft approaching."

Indeed, when Yinka raised her head and peered at the thick and grey blobs of cloud against the dull sky, she could make out the silhouette of an aircraft hovering through the air as it sliced through the overcast. As the plane began its gradual descent, approaching the expansive grass field, the details of the aircraft became clearer. The jet's white and blue body paint and its eagle-shaped, streamlined fuselage were now apparent to the naked eye. Yinka felt her heartbeat rise when the recognition dawned on her. *Isn't that Dugard's private jet?*

The aircraft landed with a thud on the grass field a few metres away from where Yinka and the others were standing. It sped forward for a minute, flattening the grass with its tyres before gradually slowing to a crawl. The aircraft then steadily rotated, as if parking in a bay, before it stopped, and the loud sound of the plane's turbines died out.

Montanna came to stand beside Yinka. She placed a hand on Yinka's left shoulder. "Let's go get your man, Yinks."

Together, Yinka and the Robin Hoods trotted towards the grounded business jet. The closer Yinka got to the aircraft, the more confident she felt it was the same private jet that belonged to Dugard. But her suspicions were overshadowed by the fact that she was about to be reunited with Oge. As she approached the plane, the anticipation increased Yinka's heart rate, and she could feel tingles on her skin.

The main passenger door near the plane's tail suddenly extended outwards, revealing a flight of stairs attached to the door.

Oge emerged from the rear of the plane, standing on top of the airstair. Considering his ordeal, he looked healthy and surprisingly unharmed, wearing an unbuttoned black trench coat, brown combat trousers and matching boots. Curiously, these were not the same clothes he had worn during his abduction in Berlin. His cornrows were still the colour of cinnamon, his long stubble beard looked noticeably thicker, and the permeant, dark pink scar running down the side of his left face still gave him the tantalising edge of a hardened freedom fighter.

Propelled by a pure and overwhelming rush of emotion, Yinka ran towards Oge as he walked down the metal steps and onto the field. She almost floored him as she flung herself over Oge, not caring how over-dramatic it looked. Streams of tears poured from her eyes.

"I have missed you so much, my love," Yinka said tenderly, resting her head on Oge's warm and hard chest. She needed to hear his heartbeat, breathe in his natural smell and feel the contours of his torso. It was not a dream. He was truly back with her.

Yinka pulled herself away from Oge and took in his lips before he could even speak to her. Those beautiful, moist, supple, and weighty lips sent a wave of longing through her body as she kissed him repeatedly and desperately, as if she were fearful someone would take him away from her again. It was Oge who, with some resistance from Yinka, eventually untangled their mouths.

"I have missed you too, Coffee Bean," Oge said faintly. "Missed every piece of you."

Jaali, Montana, Joshua, and Kisi gathered around Yinka and Oge in a semicircle. Yinka wrapped her hands around Oge's waist as he looked at the team warmly.

"I am so happy to see all of you," Oge said, beaming at the others. "Thank you for what you've done for me."

"Mate, we're family," Jaali said, punching Oge lightly on his left shoulder. "We were always going to do whatever it took to rescue your big, light-skinned head."

Oge chuckled. "I knew I could count on all of you."

"These people didn't harm you, did they?" Montanna said, with the tone of a worried mother.

"Nah, his pretty boy looks are still intact," Kisi said, chuckling.

"It is truly a relief to see you are alive and well," Joshua said, nodding as he adjusted his glasses. "We were uncertain of what your kidnappers would do to you while they held you captive."

The familiar voice of a well-spoken English man penetrated Yinka's euphoria.

"It's so wonderful to meet the infamous Robin Hoods finally," Dugard said. "By the way, how do you find my new English countryside estate? I just purchased it."

Not believing her eyes, Yinka watched as Dugard, wearing a grey three-piece suit, descended from the airstairs. She felt like she was looking at someone who had risen from the dead. Following Dugard down the metal stairs were three men with ruby player builds and dressed in combat gear. They had Glock 19 pistols hoisted into black leather harnesses around their multi-functional tactical vests. Two of the men were bold, with thick necks and flat noses. But the third man, who was grinning, had a blonde man bun, green eyes and a silver tooth. Yinka immediately realised he was Oge's primary abductor, who had called himself Bobby when he had contacted Yinka and her team about the Afchain mission.

"Nice to finally meet you lot in person," Bobby said in that heavy and snide cockney accent. "And I gotta say, I love the whole reunion going on. Isn't it just lovely when family is reunited?"

"That is enough of your chattering, Bobby," Dugard said, impatience creeping into his voice. He now stood before Yinka, Oge, and the others, and Bobby and the two other mercenaries stood behind Dugard. A big smile formed on Dugard's face as his eyes travelled to Yinka and rested on her. "I told you, Yinka, that we would see each other again. Of course, I had purposefully omitted how soon. I had to see the surprise look on your face. And I must say, I was not disappointed."

"So it was *you*," Yinka began, glaring at Dugard, her anger rising steadily. "You were the one who abducted my boyfriend? You were the employer your bulldog-looking thug was referring to."

"Oi, come on. There's no need to throw insults," Bobby interjected with an exaggerated frown.

"You coerced us into securing investment for Afchain?" Yinka trembled now, furious at Dugard's deception but not entirely surprised, as she had grown suspicious of him. She was still holding onto Oge, who remained deathly silent.

"You deceitful bastard," Kisi said, her eyes throwing daggers as she narrowed them at Dugard, who remained smiling at them without uttering a word. "All this time, you were assisting us when it was you who had kidnapped our friend and thrown us into this whole ordeal."

Dugard started to snicker as if he were in on some private joke. "My dear lady, I did not kidnap anyone. Funny as this may sound, but your boyfriend, your leader, kidnapped himself. Isn't that right, *Oge?*"

Yinka shook her head at Dugard's unexpected revelation, which scrambled her thinking. She looked up at Oge. He was looking away from her now, and his light brown face seemed to have gone chalk-white as he stared hard at Dugard.

"Oge, bruv, what's this posh prick on about?" Jaali said, stepping forward as Montana pulled him back. "The fuck he means you kidnapped yourself?"

Oge let out a heavy sigh, raising his chest. He closed his eyes, shook his head several times as if he were suffering from a severe migraine, and then raised his head back up again, opening his eyes, now with a steely glaze.

"I was never kidnapped. The whole abduction in Berlin was staged. By me and Dugard."

Yinka's arms unclasped from Oge's waist and flopped to her side as if they suddenly had no bones. She stumbled back from her boyfriend, her brain in a mess of confusion and shock, her heartbeat racing. "Wha---what do you mean your abduction was staged?" Yinka looked at Oge, shaking her head, trying to make sense of the madness she was hearing. Oge stared at her, his eyes conveying no emotion.

"Why would you do this, Oge?" Joshua said, his voice a mix of hurt and horror as his eyes widened in bewilderment behind his spectacles.

"For the past year and a half, we have been systematically targeting every member of the Bankole empire," Oge said, his voice in an even and matter-of-fact tone as his eyes lingered over Yinka and the team. "We integrated into their professional and personal lives and exploited our position to blackmail that poisonous family. But I didn't make us target the Bankoles just because of their widespread corruption in Nigeria. I wanted to cripple the Bankole bloodline as much as possible before I severed its head permanently."

"You want to kill Mobolagi Bankole?" Kisi said, raising her eyebrows. "Why?"

"Because he murdered my mother."

51

THE REVELATION ROCKED YINKA. She placed her hands over her mouth.

To this day, Yinka could still clearly recall eighteen years ago in Abeokuta, the village in Nigeria where she and Oge had both grown up together, when a letter bomb had killed Oge's mother. Oge, who had been standing in front of his mother when the makeshift bomb detonated, had sustained severe burns to his chest and face.

Around the same time as the incident, Yinka's father was battling cancer. While she was supporting him, she still visited Oge's bedside every day for almost six months at the Abeokuta State Hospital as he lay in the hospital bed screaming and crying in agony and pain. It took several operations and skin grafts before Oge would fully heal and recover from the deep burns on his skin sustained in the explosion. Now, the only evidence of Oge's tragic childhood was the long scar stretching down from the left side of his forehead.

"How do you know it was Mobolagi who killed your mother?" Yinka said her voice straining under the weight of emotions she was wrestling with. "You told me you could not remember the face of the man who gave you the letter bomb."

"Those black diamond rings Mobolagi wears on each of his fingers," Oge said, through gritted teeth, "were the same rings worn in the same way by the man who gave me the letter bomb to deliver to my mother. I could never forget how distinct they were. I noticed it when I interviewed Mobolagi years ago as a young journalist in Lagos." Oge snarled. "He did not recognise me as a grown man, but I knew then, without a shred of doubt, that I had finally discovered who my mother's killer was." Oge's voice sounded like it was on the cliff edge, about to fall into a fierce rage, but he had pulled it back.

"So then why all of this…this fake abduction plot? Why this mission to get investment for Afchain?" Montanna said, her face scrunched in confusion.

"If I may interject," Dugard said, cutting through the emotionally tense revelations heating the atmosphere. Yinka and everyone else on the windy field turned to face the English aristocrat.

"Three years ago, your leader over here," Dugard gestured to Oge, "had used his considerable journalistic investigative skills to discover that I was helping Mobolagi Bankole launder various funds from several of his criminal activities in Nigeria and those of his politician friends, and investing these ill-gotten proceeds into various investment assets in the UK. Whether it was buying properties in Knightsbridge, purchasing stocks in FTSE 100 companies or other viable investments, I was cleaning dirty Nigerian money by concealing it and washing it through the legitimacy and the complexity of the British economy. A very naughty business that could get me in quite the spot of trouble should someone bring attention to my activities."

"But rather than expose my business affairs with Mobolagi and others, we struck a deal." Dugard looked at Oge and smiled as if he had won a personal victory. "I would get your leader close to Mobolagi, who is notoriously difficult, practically impossible, to access if you're not in his carefully selected circle. You could not get to him even with all your deception and espionage talents. But I would only provide this unfettered access to Mobolagi on the condition that Oge raised nine million investment for Afchain from three business associates of mine."

"And what does Afchain have to do with you?" Joshua said, glaring at Dugard.

"I practically own it," Dugard said, his lips twisting into a snarky smile. "As I am sure Yinka knows all too well now, cryptocurrencies are a revolutionary approach to money. No central bank or government governs them. Crypto frees money from the few elites' control and gives it back to the people. It is something Nigeria desperately needs."

"You are fabricating a lie," Joshua said, disgust thick in his voice. "You want to use this Afchain technology to launder money into Nigeria. Cryptocurrency is still unregulated, especially in West Africa, so your fraudulent activities would go unnoticed. You are treating Nigeria as a mere dumping ground for your criminal enterprise."

Dugard huffed dismissively and then laughed mockingly at Joshua. "Please, boy. Nigeria is a cesspool of corruption already. The country's dismal economy runs on dishonesty and bribery as its fuel. It was a much more prosperous nation governed by great Englishmen like my grandfather. Independence from British rule was a curse to Nigeria, not a gift." He shrugged his shoulders. "Anyway, in recent years, my business associates' trust in my investment opportunities has lessened because Mobolaji influenced them. He no longer has faith in me, and neither do the others. If I had personally pitched Afchain to them, they would never invest, especially if they knew my stake in the company. So, I needed Afchain to be sold to them as a profitable investment opportunity from a third party."

"Oge convinced me that all of you, his team of Robin Hoods, could do it, and I merely provided some assistance along the way to ensure we received the full investment." Dugard's smile stretched as he looked directly at Yinka. "And thanks to you and Mr Bakare's brilliant teamwork, the mission succeeded."

"But why bring Timon into all this?" Yinka said, shaking her head. She was overwhelmed by all these revelations, especially that Oge had made such an inconceivable effort to deceive her and the rest of the team.

"Timon?" Oge said, raising his eyebrows at Yinka, surprised by her question. "Mobolaji's son? Why do you care, Coffee Bean?"

"Just tell me, Oge. You owe us all complete honesty now. And don't call me Coffee Bean."

Oge looked at Yinka briefly, studying her, and then he sighed. "I spent years learning all I could about Mobolaji when I knew it was him who murdered my mother. Through my research, I discovered the existence of Timon Bakare, the love child he had fathered with one of his housemaids in the late 80s with whom he had a short affair," Oge said, speaking to Yinka directly. "Although Mobolaji makes no public mention of the secret son who lives in London, I had unearthed evidence to suggest he had a fondness for him. It so happens one of Dugard's relatives works at Timon's hedge fund, so we bribed him to convince Timon to take on an unsavoury investor named Musa Jirongo."

"Musa Jirongo? Isn't that the Kenyan arms dealer who recently fled his native country after facing charges of selling illegal weapons to Somali terrorists?" Joshua said.

"That's right, and I can tell you're the most well-informed one on this team," Dugard said. "Like his father, Timon proved to be someone who would do anything for money, even work with someone as callous as Musa Jirongo, a former client of mine. So once my relative at Timon's hedge fund secretly informed us of the crypto companies Timon was investing Musa's money into, I used my considerable network in the crypto space to pay a few very talented Nigerian hackers to destabilise those crypto companies with a significant hack. Inevitably, Timon ended up losing a lot of Musa's money as a result of these hacks. And believe me, Musa Jirongo is not a man whose money you want to squander."

"The hack gave Timon the incentive to work with you because we knew he now needed the money you were offering him to pay back Musa Jirongo," Oge said, his eyes still on Yinka. "Seeing as he is a specialist in crypto, it just made sense to recruit him. It was icing on the cake that he was Mobolagi's son, as it was another way for me to exact revenge on a member of the Bankole family. Even though he's not directly involved with them, he is still Mobolagi's blood. And his favourite son."

Yinka felt nauseated by all this duplicity, but she had a stronger concern now. "But will Timon receive the final payment for helping us?" she said, not caring to conceal the deep worry shaking her voice.

Oge glared at Yinka. "What does it matter?"

"Answer my bloody question, Oge!"

Oge let out an impatient sigh. "No, he won't receive the money."

Yinka put her hands over her mouth, sinking into an even deeper state of shock. "So…so what happens to Timon if he can't pay back this Kenyan arms dealer?"

Dugard responded in his eloquent voice. "Unfortunately, Yinka. Timon is a dead man."

Yinka's tears crept out of her eyes involuntarily as she stepped further away from Oge, shaking her head at him. Oge merely looked at her, his face completely blank, as if he were a machine and not a man of flesh and blood—not the man she had loved most of her life. Montanna walked forward and hugged Yinka from behind.

"How could you betray us like this, bro?" Jaali said, his fists curled and teeth clenched. "We're supposed to be family."

"Exactly, after everything we've done together over the years," Kisi said defiantly. "We followed you on this journey to give back to the poor, but you're just as bad as the people we steal from."

"You're full of shit, Kisi. All of you are," Oge said, his voice filled with surprising revulsion. "The main reason you all joined me after you graduated from your fancy London university was because I showed you how we could line our pockets by blackmailing African criminals in fancy suits who drove nice cars and had comfortable government positions. You did it for the money, even if we gave some of it to the less fortunate. Yes, we became close over the years and cared for each other like family, but the promise of big returns initially attracted you to my cause. None of you truly cared about battling corruption in Africa."

"So you used our love… my love…for you, to manipulate us into carrying out this ridiculous mission to secure investment for some dodgy crypto company so you could gain access to Mobolagi?" Yinka said, choking on her words as the pain of Oge's deception burrowed into her. Montana continued to console her by rubbing her shoulders. "Do you know I could have been raped, Oge? I put myself in harm's way because I would do anything to save the man I love. Yet all this time, you were never in trouble. How could you do this?"

"I did all this because you were all losing your drive and resolve for the cause," Oge said, his eyes hovering over Yinka and the rest of the team. "It was clear none of you had the same passion for this anymore. You wanted normal lives now. So, if I had come to you honestly from the beginning, none of you would have supported this. Staging my kidnapping renewed your focus and made you all driven again. And it worked."

"You're out of your mind, Oge", Jaali said. "We're thieves, not killers. And you've manipulated us so that you can kill Mobolagi Bankole. But we won't help you do that. It ends here for us."

"Oh, I think you will," came Bobby's voice, which had been so quiet up until now. Yinka and the others jerked their heads towards him, almost forgetting he was also on the field with the two other armed mercenaries. He had unholstered his Glock 19 and was now pointing the handgun at Yinka and the rest of the Robin Hoods.

Yinka turned away from the Cockney-accented mercenary to face Oge. "What's the meaning of this?"

For the first time since being reunited with her and the others, Oge's expression softened, and he regarded Yinka with sad regret. "Dugard has informed me that Mobolagi has invited him to a private meeting at the African Technology Summit happening in Lagos in three weeks."

Dugard walked away from his henchmen to look at Yinka and the others properly. His smile, which Yinka had once found charming, was now sinister and mocking. "Mobolagi would never let me in that meeting with my security," he said, talking to Yinka and the others. "So you and your team will use your considerable talents in infiltration and surveillance to sneak my hired men and Oge into the African Tech Summit event. I know where the meeting will be taking place, so Oge and my men will interrupt it and put a bullet in our dear friend Mobolagi's head."

"So you're just going to kill Mobolagi in cold blood once you're in that meeting room at the event? Is that it, Oge. That's the big plan?" Kisi said, looking at Oge as if he had gone mad.

"Yes, I am going to assassinate him." Oge's voice was eerily detached. "Consider this our final mission. When I have killed Mobolagi, you can all go your separate ways. The Robin Hoods will disband." Oge then rested his dark brown eyes on Yinka. "Please cooperate because I don't want anything bad to happen to you, Coffee Bean," he said, his cold voice revealing a slight desperation. He shifted his eyes away from Yinka to regard the others. "I know I've deceived you all. And I don't expect you to forgive me. But this had to be done. There was no other way I could get close to Mobolagi."

Oge looked back at Yinka, and she once again saw the deep regret swimming through his eyes. "Coffee Bean, I am sorry for betraying your heart and the trust that you gave to me. But everything I've done is for a righteous cause. Our parents spent their whole lives fighting corruption in Nigeria by writing about it and never won the war. They changed nothing. So this is the only way. Through violence."

"You keep telling yourself that, Oge. How could you do this to those who love you so much?" Yinka shook her head, feeling the stinging tears soaking her cheeks as she grappled with Oge's immense betrayal but also with the fact that Timon's life was in danger. And she could do nothing to save him.

It was then that Yinka realised her true feelings for Timon. She loved him, but she would never get the chance to tell him because he would be dead.

52

ORISA SMOTHERED Timon with kisses and hugs when he picked her up from her mother's flat in Wembley in his Porshe after leaving Heathrow Airport. When she answered the door, Timon bit his lip in eager lust, enthralled by how attractive Oria looked in her skin-tight, high-waist denim leggings pulled up to her curvy hips and wearing a white crop top showing off her toned midriff.

The first thought that came to Timon's mind when Orisa jumped on him as he stood at the doorway and then proceeded to cling to him like a cat, kissing and sucking his neck, was that he couldn't wait to have sex with her back at his Battersea penthouse.

A few hours later, Timon's lustful thoughts had become reality. That night in the master room, he made longing and intensely physical love to Orisa on his comfortable, king-sized bed. Gripped by an intense craving for her body, since he had not had sex for two whole weeks, he had temporarily forgotten about Yinka and the monumental outer-body sensation of the kiss he had shared with her in Dubai.

Yet as Timon laid next to Orisa five minutes after they had both climaxed - Orisa riding him to ejaculation with so much wild enthusiasm her head had flung back as if she were galloping on horseback - Yinka glided soothingly and effortlessly into Timon's thoughts. That kiss they had shared in Dubai, that kiss which felt like the purest physical experience he had ever had with a woman - and Timon had many experiences of kissing women to compare to - tingled on the epidermis of his lips, sweet and satisfying.

"I bet you've missed that, haven't you, boo?" Orisa said, rolling over to him and resting her mid-sized, caramel-coloured breasts against his bare chest.

"I did miss you, Yinka," Timon said, his mind not in the present moment but floating in a fantasy of its own as he gazed at the white ceiling.

"What'd you call me?" Orisa said, her acrylic nails already starting to enclose Timon's skin as she looked pointedly at him, eyes already ablaze with rising rage.

Realising his slip of the tongue caused by his stubborn intrusive thoughts, Timon shook his head and chuckled nervously, attempting to make light of his foolish slip-up. "Nothing, baby. My brain isn't thinking straight after that last round," he said, grinning at her. "I think you fucked the brains out of me."

For a few seconds, Orisa went deathly silent. Her eyes narrowed as she peered into Timon. Already, Timon was bracing himself for a night of drama, desperate apologies and pleading for forgiveness since he had just called his fiancée another woman's name post-sex, but, much to Timon's inner sigh of relief, Orisa's expression softened, and her lips curved into a naughty grin.

"Well, my handsome and wealthy fiancé, I don't think the night is over. I have been starved of sex for too long, and I am ravenous. So you better reboot your brain because we're going another round."

As Timon rolled over and climbed on top of Orisa, her eyes misty with lust as she spread her legs for him to enter her, he summoned all his discipline to rid thoughts of Yinka from his mind.

* * *

The following morning, as Timon drove his Porsche to Canary Wharf to meet Chikezie and Russell at their office, thoughts of Yinka remained submerged in his head.

When he turned on the radio in his car to BBC Radio 1xtra and Tems' 'Free Mind' was serendipitously the next song on the radio DJ's playlist, Timon's lips curved into a smile, and instantly all his feelings about Yinka came flooding over him like a burst dam: how she enjoyed reading, her sharp and inquisitive mind, her fierce stubbornness, her superb cooking and her arresting beauty. Yinka had somehow found his way into his heart, and Timon would need to rinse her out. He was getting married to Orisa, and he could not have another woman occupying the space in his heart that was supposed to belong to her.

"So when are these people going to pay you the rest of the funds, T?" Russell said.

Timon was now at the Level 39 office. He sat on the swivel chair in the glass conference room with Russell and Chikezie.

"Before we left each other at Heathrow Airport, she said I'd receive the rest of the three million this week. So by Friday at the latest, I should have the rest of the money in my account, and I'll wire it straight to Musa."

"That is a big fucking relief, mate," Russell said, dragging his right hand down his face. "Because I've been stressed the fuck out. Musa's bloody henchmen are still monitoring my Fulham flat daily."

Chikezie huffed, scowling at Russell. "You think you've got it bad? I have a wife and a daughter, and I've got Musa's men driving down our street every other hour. On several occasions, I've had to lie to my wife that it was nothing so she wouldn't call the police." Visibly stressed, Chikezie massaged his forehead before looking at Timon. "T, you're one hundred percent certain this Yinka lady will pay you the rest of the money?"

"She'll pay, don't stress, Kez," Timon said, confident that Yinka would come through. "I trust her. Completely."

* * *

On Thursday evening, three days after the meeting with Russell and Chikezie, Timon collected his mother from the care home and drove to Halstead, a small leafy town in Braintree, Essex, where the venue for his impending wedding to Orisa would take place at a lavish private estate. Naturally, Timon covered eighty per cent of the wedding costs. And it was far from cheap.

As soon as he arrived at the estate with his mother - the first time they had both visited the venue - Timon quickly understood why the price tag for renting out the estate was astronomical. The mansion before his eyes, which Orisa had solely chosen, looked like it had been carved out of Buckingham Palace and transported to this part of Essex.

Timon walked across the cleanly cut, fresh green field with his mother by his side, the mansion looming ahead. Together, they made a beeline for Orisa, who was standing beside her slim and tall mother, dressed in a traditional Nigerian gown.

Suddenly, Timon's heart began to race. At that moment, the reality of marrying Orisa tightened around him like metal chains. Wasn't he supposed to feel happy he would be her husband?

"Good afternoon, Ma," Orisa said, curtseying to Timon's mother, a gesture of respect in Yoruba culture. "It's good to see you again."

"And you too, Elizabeth," Iyenemi said, smiling warmly at Orisa." You look lovely."

Orisa already looked deeply uncomfortable as she gave Timon's mother a strained smile, clearly annoyed that his mother had called her by the wrong name. But she made an effort with her for once, hooked her arm underneath Iyenemi's, and took her to her mother.

Timon watched as his mother, and Orisa strolled over to embrace Orisa's mother. But instead of joining them, Timon stayed rooted on the spot. He stared at the grand mansion before him, with its dove-white façade and diversity of large square windows evenly spaced out. Something did not feel right.

"Why are you standing there like you've never seen a big mansion before?" Orisa said cheerfully, and it oddly irritated Timon as she walked over to him. She hooked her right arm underneath Timon's left. "Come on, my future husband. The wedding planner is already inside to show us and our mothers around the mansion. I have so many ideas and concepts about how we can decorate the interior for the wedding."

As Timon was pulled towards the grand estate by his fiancée, a powerful epiphany suddenly overcame him and illuminated his brain like lights switching on after a power outage. He could not marry Orisa because she did not have his heart. She never really did.

Timon was going to call the wedding off.

53

WHERE THE FUCK IS THE REST OF MY
MONEY. I AM GETTING VERY, VERY
PISSED OFF RIGHT NOW. AND YOU
SHOULD BE LOSING A LOT OF SLEEP
KNOWING THIS.

TIMON RECEIVED the threatening text from Musa Jirongo late
Friday afternoon.

He had left his Canary Wharf office and was driving past
Battersea Park, returning to his penthouse, when the text
flashed on his phone attached to the Porsche's dashboard.
Timon read the threatening text message in Musa's unset-
tlingly high-pitched voice, with that Kenyan accent that gave
his speech its distinctively East African cadence.

To calm the arms deader down, Timon tried to call Musa
to assure him that the money would be with him by the end
of the day, but he did not answer. Feeling pressured, Timon
sent Musa a grovelling text, promising him the money would
be in his account by Sunday. But even Timon was starting to
harbour some doubts. *Why hadn't Yinka paid the rest of the
money by now?*

When Timon had entered his penthouse, he gave Orisa a

quick peck on the lips. She was enjoying her soft life sitting on the sofa, her feet up, and eyes glued to her iPhone and barely watching the Netflix documentary about a serial killer she had put on. Timon retreated to the master bedroom. Once inside, he closed the door and scrolled through his contacts on his phone to Yinka's number. He called her twice, and it went to voicemail each time. Timon had decided to text her. After rewriting the copy of the text several times, he finally pressed send.

```
Hey Yinka, I hope you're doing
well. I wanted to confirm with
you again when I can expect the
rest of the money, as I have not
received it yet. I hope to hear
from you soon. Thx. Timon.
```

After sending the text, Timon sat on his bed and watched the screen on his Samsung for several minutes, eagerly waiting for Yinka's text. After ten minutes, he realised he would not get a response. *Maybe she's busy or preoccupied,* Timon told himself as he stood up and chucked his phone onto the bed. *She's going to pay you the rest of the money. She wouldn't lie to you. Not after everything you've been through together. The trust you had built with each other. That kiss you shared.*

Reassured, not letting the thought that Yinka could betray him stew in his mind, Timon undid his tie, removed his shoes, replaced them with his velvet slippers, and walked out of his room to spend time with Orisa.

As the afternoon stretched into the evening, Timon found himself sitting next to Orisa on the living room sofa in front of the silver, widescreen television. She had ordered some Thai food an hour earlier. As Timon sat beside her, eating some stir-fried noodles from a white deli box, he knew now was the time to tell Orisa that he wanted to cancel the wedding.

Throughout the day in the office, Timon occupied his

thoughts with how he should broach the topic with her. Having dated Orisa for a year and a half now, Timon expected a lot of insults, tears, more insults, followed by even more tears when he told her he was having second thoughts about their relationship so he could no longer proceed with the wedding. From what his mother had taught him, Timon knew that as a man, you owed a woman your honesty and truth, even if it meant bruising her pride and shattering her heart. And as a man, you just had to deal with that fallout. In the long term, it was better to live in your truth than live a lie, especially when it came to something as life-changing as marriage.

Timon placed his now empty deli box on the glass table before him. He breathed a heavy sigh, mentally preparing himself, and turned his whole body to face Orisa. She was dressed in black leggings and wearing one of his Billionaire Boys Club hoodies, the one in white. It was the first item of clothing she wore when she first slept over. *How cruelly poetic she had to be wearing that hoodie this evening.* Timon cleared his throat.

"Orisa...I need to tell you something important," Timon said softly and calmly, looking at her light brown face.

Orisa turned to face him, a string of noddle dangling out of her lips which she sucked into her mouth like a snake's tongue. She smiled at him innocently. "What's up, boo?"

"We need to call off the wedding. I don't know if I am ready for this." The words had flown from Timon's mouth like a kamikaze plane.

Orisa looked flabbergasted, as if someone had thrown a bucket of cold water over her. With her hands now trembling, she placed her stir-fried noodles on the glass table, then looked at Timon as if he had just sentenced her to an early death.

"Timon...what are you saying? You don't want to get married?"

"I don't."

"Why…why this sudden change?"

Before Timon could respond to Orisa, he heard his Samsung Galaxy ringing in the master bedroom. Using the fact that someone was calling him as an excuse to stall the difficult conversation he knew would have to continue eventually, Timon leapt from the sofa, hoping it was Yinka calling him, and headed to the main bedroom, leaving Orisa, who sat frozen on the couch, her face in total bewilderment.

Unfortunately, the evening was only going to get worse. When Timon answered Chikezie's call, he heard pure terror in his best friend's voice. In their decade-long friendship, Timon had never heard Chikezie sound so terrified.

"Thirty minutes ago, I pulled up outside my house with my wife and daughter after coming back from shopping, and I saw Musa's men break into my house," Chikezie said. He spoke frantically and sounded out of breath. "I saw them holding guns, bro. If I had arrived home earlier…" Chikezie became too emotional to complete the sentence. "That was too close, man."

"Fuck," Timon said, feeling his heart pound against his chest. "Where are you now?"

"I've just checked myself and my family into a Premier Inn in Brentwood. I have also tried to call Russell to warn him, but he's turned his phone off." Chikezie's breathing was loud and heavy down the line. "We have to call the police now because this has gotten out of hand. But T, right now, you need to take Orisa, leave your apartment and stay in a hotel till the police are involved. You're in real danger."

Timon went into panic mode after the chilling call with Chikezie ended. There was no time to overthink. All he knew now was that Musa and his men were most likely on their way to his apartment to kill him potentially, and God knows what they would do to Orisa. Worse, he did not know if they were an hour or five minutes away. But it didn't matter. He needed to get out of this apartment. Now.

Timon hurried back into the living room. At the sight of him, Orisa stood up from the sofa. Her cheeks were soaked, and her eyes were puffy and red. She had been crying.

"Timon…," she said, sniffing and hiccupping as she placed two hands against her chest. "I…I understand what you mean. Look…I have also been having some doubts about us…"

"We need to get out here right now, Orisa," Timon said in a blunt tone as he walked past her to the kitchen to locate the keys to his Porsche. Their conversation regarding the future of their relationship would have to be postponed. Now, a far more pressing matter was at hand—their survival.

Orisa frowned and placed both her hands on her hips. "Don't be so rude," she said, her anger bubbling beneath her voice. "We need to have *this talk*. Timon, can you stop looking for whatever you're looking for in the kitchen and face me!"

"Did you not hear what I said, Orisa!?" Timon shouted, spinning around to glare at her, now gripping the car fob key. "We have to leave. Right now!" Timon could hear the piercing panic and fear coursing through his voice, and Orisa had also detected it because she was looking at him with grave concern.

"What's going on?"

Timon hurried out of the kitchen towards Orisa and placed his hands on her shoulders. He looked her dead in the eyes. "Listen to me. A very dangerous man is after me, who wants to kill me possibly, and he is on his way to this apartment. So we must go."

Orisa stepped back from Timon and shook her head. Fear and confusion twisted her pretty and innocent face. "Who is after you? And why do they want to kill you? What have you done?"

Timon ran his hands over his low-cut, trimmed hair in

frustration. *Why wouldn't she listen?* "Orisa, I promise I'll answer all your questions later. But we need to get a move on."

"But where are we going? What about my clothes and my jewellery? I haven't even finished eating my stir fry."

Timon was in awe, and not in an impressed way, by Orisa's apathetic reaction to the gravity of their situation. "Orisa, are you serious right now? I just told you that someone is heading over here to potentially murder me and maybe even do you harm as well, and you're talking about finishing your noodles and your clothes and your jewellery. Are you hearing yourself?"

"Excuse me, I am still hungry. And yes, my clothes and jewellery are very important to me. There are Swarovski diamonds and two Gucci handbags in our bedroom. They are thousands of pounds in value."

Timon did not even get a chance to lose his patience with Orisa. Two loud knocks on the front door interrupted their conversation. They immediately stopped bickering and turned to the white front panel door a few feet away to their right.

Suddenly, everything about the apartment became eerily still except the noises from the Netflix serial killer documentary playing on the widescreen television. The sound of Timon and Orisa's breathing filled the silence.

"Orisa…we need to hide in the bedroom," Timon said, his voice low, reaching for her left hand. His throat was dry, and his tongue felt like sandpaper. "He's here."

Orisa let out a high-pitched scream. Timon pushed her and himself to the ground as the booming sound of three gunshots rang in their ears. Bullets splintered the frame of the wooden front door, whizzing through the air and breaking a vase of flowers, tearing through the sofa, causing one of the cushions to explode into a heap of wool, and shattering a part of the panoramic window surrounding the top-floor penthouse. The crashing sound of a million shards of glass plummeting to the floor filled Timon's ears and threw him into a frenzy of confusion and fear.

A smell, similar to the smoke from fireworks , settled in the room when the shooting stopped. Even though Timon's ears were ringing as he lay on his stomach on the floor, Orisa beside him with her hands over her ears and tears now pouring from her eyes, he heard the front door creak open, followed by the sound of boots and shoes stepping onto the laminate surface of the penthouse's living room. Then came Musa Jirongo's voice.

"Get off the bloody floor, Mr London Money. No man with any respect will let another man stand over him." Musa laughed, sounding like a deranged hyena.

Shaking, Timon slowly got to his feet. Orisa, who was visibly petrified, remained on the floor with her hands over her ears and her eyes shut tight. Timon bent down and helped her get to her feet. Once they were both standing, Orisa's eyes remained closed, and she shook on the spot, but Timon faced Musa with open eyes.

Still sporting bantu knots and wearing his round spectacles, the Kenyan arms dealer was dressed in a fitted, dark green suit with a double-breasted jacket and a yellow shirt matching his monk strap shoes. His two muscular and tall goons, whose names Timon had forgotten, stood slightly behind him, one on his left and the other on his right. In his left hand, Musa was holding an ink black Beretta handgun, which he was tapping against his crouch. It was the same gun he had pointed at Timon weeks ago in the lobby of the apartment.

"Look at how all of this shit has escalated," Musa said, in a voice so calm he might as well have been talking to Timon at a restaurant. "I have messed up your front door, ruined your couch and smashed one of your expensive windows with bullets. And this is a lovely home, Mr London Money. I take no pleasure in destroying beautiful things."

"Musa...look...I completely understand that you're unhappy right now," Timon began, carefully choosing every word he uttered, "but we don't need to result to all of this. We can come to an agreement."

Musa shook his head and sighed as if deeply disappointed in Timon. "I know you Nigerians like to be tricky and sneaky, but I am a Kenyan man. The slippery ways of Nigerians do not work on me. We had a deal, Timon. A very clear and reasonable agreement regarding the repayment of my money. Do I tell lies?"

"Musa look..."

"Am I lying? Answer me." Musa's voice was firmer now. He continued to tap the Bretta against his crouch.

"No, you're not."

"So why didn't you honour our deal, man?" Musa shook his head at Timon again. He then let out another exasperated sigh. "I have trusted you twice now, Timon. Firstly, I trusted you to invest some of my money into crypto, and then you lost all of it. Then I trust you to return all my money you lost, and I gave you three weeks, a very reasonable and gracious amount of time, and then you only pay some of it back. Like, what is this? I am a clown to you? A fool?"

"Of course not, Musa. I have the utmost respect for you. I can pay you the rest of the money. Just give me a bit more time."

"No, no, no, no! "Musa said, stamping his feet on the floor. "I have given you enough fucking chances. I no longer like your vibe, Mr London Money, or shall I say, Mr Lose My Money. And now, I am going to have to be an asshole and punish you." Musa lifted the Beretta from his lap and raised it towards Orisa.

As Timon reached for Orisa to push her out of harm's way, one of Musa's henchmen sprung towards him with surprising speed. He threw his huge hands on Timon's shoulders and pulled him away from her.

"Get off me!"

"Timon!" Orisa shrieked. She dared open her eyes. When she saw the gun pointed at her, she began to sob, her legs shaking as she raised both her hands in the air.

"Don't do this, Musa," Timon pleaded, tears now edging from his eyes as he struggled to break free from the grip of Musa's henchman, who had him in a firm headlock. "I am pleading with you for more time to get the rest of the money."

"I am afraid I don't have any more time to give you," Musa said, the barrel of the Beretta steadily aimed at Orisa. "I told you what would happen if you did not pay me back on time. Be thankful that I am going to show you a little mercy and not stick my gun up your girlfriend's ass as I originally promised if you failed to repay me. Instead, I'll just put a bullet in her head. Gruesome, yes, but much less humiliating."

"Timon…" Orisa whimpered, now looking at Timon desperately. Her mouth was trembling, and her tears fell onto her snivelling lips as snot poured from both her nostrils. "Please, don't make him kill me."

"I am begging you, Musa. Don't harm her." Timon was crying now. Still, he struggled but could not escape the bulging forearm around his neck. "She has nothing to do with any of this. It's between me and you."

When Timon realised that Musa would shoot Orisa no matter his pleas, it was enough for him to summon all the strength he had. He elbowed Musa's goon hard in his gut, causing the brute to stumble back and yelp in pain.

Now free, Timon threw himself at Orisa, grabbing her by the waist to pull her to the floor.

At the same time, Musa pulled the trigger.

54

WHEN KOJO DISCOVERED the concierge knocked unconscious and sprawled on the floor, his face badly beaten but still breathing, he immediately retrieved his MI6-issued Glock 19 pistol tucked inside a holster underneath his grey overcoat. He walked to one of the elevators.

As an MI6 intelligence officer, Kojo had an extraordinary privilege offered to only a few employed by Britain's intelligence agency. He had a license to kill—not indiscriminately. But his line of work sometimes brought him into dangerous situations—this exact moment being one of them.

Timon's address at the Lombard Wharf riverside apartments in Battersea, flat 124, was easy to locate by leveraging MI6's multiple connections to government and local departments.

With his pistol by his side, Kojo jabbed his finger on the elevator console to take him to the 27th floor. When the elevator came down, Kojo entered it, and the metal doors closed shut. Over the mechanic hum of the lift, as it ascended to the near top of the building, Kojo could hear his own loud breathing, heavy with adrenaline. What he thought would be a simple and routine questioning of a potential asset now looked like it would be far more complicated and threatening. Although he wouldn't know for sure until he reached the 27th floor, Kojo's seasoned gut feeling told him that whoever had attacked the concierge in the lobby was somehow connected to Timon.

The lift doors slid open as soon as the elevator reached the 27th floor. Kojo inhaled a deep breath and exhaled slowly. Nerves still tingling, he stepped out of the elevator. The empty corridor before him had white painted walls and vinyl flooring, and all flats had the same white wooden doors.

Following the information on the signage pinned to the walls with directions to flats 120-124, Kojo walked along the corridor before turning down a path on his left. With his right hand, he gripped the handle of his Glock 19, and his index finger was already inside the trigger guard, hovering over the trigger.

One of the first lessons in handling a firearm Kojo was taught when he was a Royal Marines commando in the British army in his 20s and 30s, being one of the few black soldiers to achieve that distinction, was to always keep a grip on your weapon high and tight. There should be no spaces between your flesh and the gun when you grip it. It was crucial for handling the forceful recoil from the gun a shooter would feel after discharging a bullet or a series of rounds.

Kojo took another right turn down to another corridor. Timon's apartment was at the end of the passageway, about 25 metres away. But that wasn't all Kojo saw. Three men stood before the apartment door, their backs to him.

He stepped back, resting on his boots' heels so as not to make a sound with the sole of his shoes. Now, he stood behind the end of the wall and leaned out slightly to get a good view of the adjacent corridor where Timon's apartment was. He wanted to get a good look at the men from a distance. Although Kojo could only see the back of the men, he could tell that the more petite man looked around 5" 7, wore a seaweed green suit, and was flanked on each side by two tall men in black suits with broad, muscular shoulders. Something told Kojo that these gentlemen were not Jehovah's Witnesses delivering the Good News.

One of the three men, the shorter man in a green suit, began firing bullets into the wooden front door of the apartment. The sound of bullets discharging, of wood splintering and then glass shattering, engulfed Kojo's ears, but he did not flinch or loosen his grip on his weapon. The rattling of bullets discharging from a firearm was not strange to Kojo's battlefield-seasoned ears.

The shooting lasted for maybe five seconds before ceasing. Still peering from the corner of the wall, Kojo watched the three men step into Timon's apartment. Whatever they were about to do next, one thing was clear – Timon's life was in danger.

Kojo slid away from the corner of the wall and scuttled quickly to the side of the wall in the other corridor that led to Timon's apartment. Now positioned in what was known as the weaver stance - a common two-handed technique for shooting firearms - Kojo slowly advanced towards Timon's now bullet-riddled apartment with his feet in a sort of boxing stance, with his right foot slightly in front of his left, his shoulders rolled over, and his pistol extended forward, gripped by both his hands.

As he quietly approached the apartment, Kojo could see through the doorway and hear the tense conversation inside. A man with a noticeable African accent talked about "not having any more time to give", and then Kojo listened to a man with a London accent pleading. It was most certainly Timon.

Now less than seven metres away from the bullet-riddled apartment, Kojo could see inside. One of the broad-shouldered men who had stood outside the flat minutes ago was now gripping Timon in a headlock. Standing about three feet away from Timon was a petite, young black woman in a white hoodie and black leggings with shoulder length, curly hair and light brown skin. She had raised her hands in the air and was shaking and sobbing uncontrollably as the man in the green suit raised his Beretta at her. The other broad-shouldered man in a suit watched everything from the side with an expressionless face.

Then, all hell erupted.

Timon broke free from the headlock he was in and threw himself at the girl in the hoodie, flinging her to the floor. Musa's gun went off with a loud bang, and Kojo immediately sprung into fight mode, announcing his arrival.

"Guns down now!"

Kojo's Royal Marine Commando training kicked in. His senses suddenly dialled to eleven. The brute in the suit, who had restrained Timon before he broke free, flicked his left hand back, reaching for something inside his blazer. Kojo never gave the man a chance to withdraw his weapon. He pressed the trigger on his Glock 19, instantly feeling the force of the recoil charge through his hands like a jolt up his arms and his shoulders as the bullet discharged from the gun's barrel. The big man in the suit dropped to the floor with a thud.

Kojo had swiftly stepped into the apartment, his forearms never dropping below eye level. He pulled the trigger again. The other big man, who had been standing on the lefthand side of the petite black man in the green suit, screamed in pain as he tumbled to the ground, rolling on the floor in agony and clutching his thigh where the bullet from Kojo's gun had penetrated.

Moans from the two fallen men filled the living room as the bullets lodged inside their flesh. Kojo was now inhaling deep, heavy breaths, and his brow was sweaty. Adrenaline was surging through him now as he stood face to face with the man in the green suit and yellow shirt whose hair was twisted into black knots so it looked like mushrooms of hair were growing out of his head.

The green-suited man gawked at Kojo, his eyes wide behind his circular-rimmed spectacles, shell-shocked by the speed with which Kojo had made quick work of his men. Still, the man was gripping his black Beretta, with the barrel now aimed at Kojo. He had an unsteady grip.

"Put the fucking gun down," Kojo demanded, his Glock 19 fully trained on the man's chest as Kojo slowly circled him.

The man, whose glasses looked steamy from sweat, followed Kojo's movement with his Beretta, which remained unsteady in his shaking hand. "Go fuck yourself, man," the man spat. His voice reminded Kojo of the Somalian pirates who had hijacked a boat in a film he had watched a while ago starring Tom Hanks.

"I won't repeat myself. Put your gun down."

It was a quick flash, but Kojo instantly recognised that look on the green-suited man's face. He had seen it in enemy combatants and suicide bombers during his tours in Afghanistan and Iraq. It was a look which communicated a total commitment to kill. That same look now gleamed in man's eyes beneath his glasses like a twinkle promising certain death. Kojo did not hesitate. He squeezed the trigger before the man could squeeze his.

The discharged bullet from Kojo's pistol hit the man in the sternum, just under his neck. With a choking sound, the man staggered back, his glasses dropping from his face. The Beretta slipped from his hands and fell to the floor as he grabbed his now profusely bleeding neck with both his hands. Then his eyes drew back, and he collapsed, smacking his head on the floor. The yellow shirt underneath the man's blazer turned the colour of red wine, and his body ceased all movement. He was dead.

It was the sound of a woman moaning in excruciating pain that snapped Kojo out of his shock of having just killed a man, something he had not done in a long time. The black jumper he wore underneath his overcoat felt drenched in sweat, and now he could feel the ache in his shoulder blades from raising his gun for so long. He dropped his arms down, his nose catching a solid whiff of gunpowder and turned around to look at where the sound of the moaning woman had come from.

Occupied with not getting himself shot, Kojo had not realised that Timon had dragged the woman in the white hoodie to a marble island in the kitchen during the whole ruckus. The woman was on the floor, slipping in and out of consciousness as her head rested on Timon's lap. Timon himself was sobbing as he caressed the woman's cheeks, begging her to stay awake. A growing patch of red was expanding across the woman's white hoodie like spilt ink. She had been shot.

Kojo hurried over to Timon. The woman had now lost all consciousness from the heavy loss of blood. Timon looked up at him, his mouth trembling, shaking his head as tears poured from his eyes, but Kojo ignored him. Instead, he knelt, picked up the woman's right hand and placed his thumb on her wrist to check her pulse. It was weak but still beating. She would survive if they got her into an ambulance right now.

"She's alive, but she has suffered a bullet wound to her right shoulder," Kojo said without addressing Timon directly. He stood up, retrieved his phone from his overcoat and dialled 999.

"I have an emergency. I am at the Lombard Wharf apartments in Battersea at flat 124. There is a woman who has been shot; she is in critical condition and needs urgent medical attention. There are also three men with bullet wounds. Two are in critical condition. One deceased. There is a man in the lobby who has been attacked but has no life-threatening injuries. Please get here as quickly as possible with an ambulance. Thank you."

After ending the call to the police, Kojo looked back at Timon. He was cradling the woman's head on his lap. He then looked up at Kojo again. Recognition flashed on his face.

"I... I've seen you before," Timon said, his voice weak. He was suffering from severe shock following the dramatic events that had just transpired minutes ago. "You were at... you were there, weren't you? At Mancini's yacht party in Sardinia?"

"You've got a good memory, Mr Bakare," Kojo said, staring at Timon, unsmiling. "My name is Kojo Owusu Harrington. I am an intelligence officer for MI6. As soon as the emergency services arrive, you will be detained for questioning regarding the nature of your associations with Sir Richard Dugard and your involvement in Afchain." Kojo then surveyed the bloody and destructive scene of death, bullets and wounded bodies spread before him in the fancy penthouse.

"And I must say, Mr Bakare, it looks like you've got yourself into a heap of trouble, haven't you?"

55

WHEN THE EMERGENCY services arrived and dozens of Metropolitan police officers descended on Timon's penthouse apartment, both Kojo and Timon were arrested and taken into custody. The woman who had sustained a bullet wound to the shoulder, who Kojo would later learn was Timon's fiancée, was placed on a stretcher, as were the two other men Kojo had shot. The man in the green suit with the outlandish hair, whose life Kojo had taken, remained spread out like an eagle on the apartment floor, his Beretta and glasses beside him, as the forensics team inspected his lifeless body.

For the four hours Kojo spent in the cell at the Lavender Hill police station, he slept. The intensity of the shoot-out in Timon's apartment and the rush of adrenaline—a sensation he had not experienced since he had retired from the Royal Marines—made his whole body feel drained of energy.

At around 4 am, after MI6 had contacted the police station and verified his identity, Kojo was released from jail without any charges. He was picked up by an unmarked black Vauxhall Corsa and driven back to his studio apartment in Clapham Common.

Once inside his flat, Kojo had removed all his clothing,

except his boxers, and collapsed onto his bed. Immediately, he had sunk into a deep sleep, his dreams punctuated by images of making love to Federica and the face of the man he had killed hours ago. He had no clue how long he had slept until a wet sensation on his nose stirred him, and he realised Felix, his pet cat, was licking his face.

"Yes, I am getting up. I appreciate the wet wake-up call, Felix," Kojo said as he sat on the edge of his single bed and tried to gather his thoughts.

Saving as much as he could on MI6's modest salary, Kojo eventually afforded a mortgage on a studio flat overlooking Clapham Common. The studio's interior was sparse - a physical representation of Kojo's life - with yellow walls, a British flag rug in the living area, a standard kitchen, and a small television. He had a single photo of his white English family pinned to the front door.

As Kojo stood from his bed and stretched, the dramatic events from yesterday evening engulfed his mind like a mental explosion. Suddenly, he was out of his stupor and focused. He went over to the wooden desk of drawers beside his bed and picked up his Samsung Galaxy lying on top of it. He had several missed calls from Ravi, the personal assistant to the Chief of MI6. When Kojo saw that it was 2.50 pm from the screen on his phone, he gasped. He had been knocked out for almost twelve hours.

The doorbell rang. Kojo put his smartphone back down and walked to the front door, Felix trailing behind him. He pressed the intercom to hear who had rung his doorbell outside.

"Who is it?"

"It's Ravi, sir. Please let me in. I have a lot to update you on."

* * *

Twenty minutes later, after taking a quick shower and getting dressed, Kojo sat in the passenger seat of another unmarked black Vauxhall Corsa. Ravi sat beside him, legs crossed. They were heading to MI6's headquarters in Vauxhall for an urgent meeting with Tiwa.

Ravi had brought Kojo a thick, brown ring file which contained a comprehensive report detailing everything about Timon, much of which Kojo already knew and some he did not, and other information related to everyone who had been at Timon's apartment yesterday as well other known associates of his. A man named Chikezie Ejikeme, who was Timon's business partner at Secure The Coin Capital, the amusing company name for Timon's crypto hedge fund, had been arrested by police at a Premier Inn in Essex this morning following an official warrant of arrest from MI6. Timon's other business partner at the hedge fund, Russell Collins, had also been issued an arrest warrant but had conveniently fled the country yesterday afternoon.

But what surprised Kojo the most was the identity of the man he had shot dead back in Timon's apartment. It had been Musa Jirongo, one of East Africa's most notorious arms dealers who had been on the run from his country, facing war crimes. Not only that, from the files Kojo was reading, it appeared that Timon had been using his hedge fund to invest some of Musa's money into various crypto assets. A smile stretched across Kojo's face.

"Well, you certainly seem chirpy considering what you've just been through," Ravi said, curiously side-eyeing Kojo. "Something you read in the files, sir?"

"I've just found the pressure point I needed," Kojo said, nodding and grinning at Ravi. "Did you say Mr Bakare was transferred to an MI6 detention centre?"

Ravid nodded. "Yes, sir. But the chief wants to speak to you urgently before you do anything else." Humorously, Ravi looked from side to side to ensure no one would eavesdrop on their conversation, although only the three of them were in the vehicle, which included the driver. He leaned into Kojo, speaking into his left ear.

"I am giving you a heads up, sir. She's not happy at all that a Kenyan arms dealer has ended up dead on British soil, killed by an MI6 officer. Count your lucky stars; you're good friends. Anyone else would be decommissioned from MI6 effective immediately for the stunt you pulled. But she's still going to have stern words with you."

* * *

Ravi had been right. When Kojo entered Tiwa's office, he found his boss sitting on the edge of her black computer desk with her legs crossed and arms folded. Dressed in a double-breasted navy suit jacket and matching wool stretch trousers, Tiwa looked as stylish as she always did, but the stern frown on her face made Kojo feel like he was about to be repri-manded by the headmistress of a school.

"What the bloody hell, Kojo?" Tiwa said, slapping her hands on her thighs and letting out an exasperated sigh.

Kojo sat on the leather sofa, as always, during their meetings.

"I gave you a simple assignment to confront Mr Bakare for questioning. So imagine my surprise when I get a call at midnight that a fugitive Kenyan arms dealer has been murdered on British soil by an MI6 officer, and then it's all over the BBC and Sky News. That is not how I wanted to start my Friday. Now thanks to your trigger finger, I've been in meetings since 7 am, getting an absolute bollocking from everyone, least of all the Foreign Secretary ."

"Look Tiwa, I sympathise with all the bureaucratic bullshit politics you have to put up with, but I know you've been debriefed by the police following yesterday's incident at Mr Bakare's apartment," Kojo said, his arms now spread across the sofa. "How could I have known that Musa Jirongo, of all people, would be at Timon's apartment with two killers and about to murder him and his fiancée? I entered a highly charged situation where the threat to my life and Timon's was substantial, and so I had to exercise my license to kill."

Tiwa sighed, closed her eyes and massaged her forehead with her left hand. "I know you had no choice, which is the only leverage I had to stop you from being decommissioned from MI6. You should be thankful to God it worked. The Foreign Secretary wanted your head on a platter this morning." She then opened her eyes, looked at Kojo, and gave him a cheeky grin he wasn't expecting. "On the bright side, you single-handedly managed to embarrass MI5. The fact that a renegade East African arms dealer had entered the UK undetected and MI6 had got to him first, even if by mere chance, has MI5 blushing with its tail between its legs."

"You see," Kojo said, leaning back on the sofa and curving his mouth into a smile as he looked at Tiwa, "at least I helped you score some political points."

Tiwa chuckled, shaking her head at Kojo, amused. She unfolded her arms, now in better spirits. "Well, we've got our man now, safe and sound, thanks to you." She stood from her desk, walked up to Kojo, and touched his shoulder. There was a tender look on her dark brown face. "Now, as your friend, not your superior, how are you feeling? I should have asked that first; I am sorry. From the police debrief I read, what happened in Mr Bakare's apartment sounded like a harrowing experience. It must have been terrifying. Walking straight into danger like that. Killing a man."

Kojo rested his left hand on the hand Tiwa had placed on his shoulder. Although he did not need to hear her words, he was grateful for them. Then briefly, at that moment, Kojo greatly longed for Federica's presence. "It wasn't easy at all, but don't forget that before I was the best intelligence officer in this crazy circus, I was a soldier. A very deadly one."

"I know that, but how are you feeling? Mental health good?"

"I've had a good night's sleep. That's all my mental health needs."

Tiwa nodded and removed her hand from Kojo's shoulder.

"So where's Mr Bakare being held now?" Kojo asked.

"Initially, Police detained him at Lavender Police Station after the incident at his penthouse, but he has now been trans-ferred to one of our specialist detention centres in Harmondsworth."

"Well, let's not keep our crypto investor waiting. It's time Mr Bakare atoned for his sins."

14-year-old Timon Bakare felt like the ship's captain who had lost his crew mates. He had been betrayed, and now, he was being expelled from school permanently.

Head bowed, eyes still blurry from the waterworks he had pulled earlier, Timon plodded alongside his mother in the quiet school corridor. Wearing her beige waistcoat and headscarf, his mother could barely look at him.

Twenty minutes earlier, Timon's mother had kept shaking her head, her face contorted in shock and shame, during the emergency parent meeting organised by Mr Rice, his now former school's head-teacher. He had played video footage of Timon, his girlfriend, DeDe, and three other friends breaking the law as they drank alcohol and smoked cigarettes in an empty classroom they had sneaked into after school.

The other parents present, all of West African descent, also gaped at the footage in disbelief. DeDe's dad, a tall and square-jawed Igbo man, had the aura of a strict Nigerian father who would give his daughter a taste of his belt when they got home. Timon would have preferred lashings to the deep look of shame his mother pierced into him with her hooded eyes as Mr Rice ended the footage.

"Now I have to find you a new school," Iyenemi Bakare said, her voice cracking. "You know I already feel pressured to keep the salon open. Why would you bring me additional stress? O fe pa mi?"

"Mummy, I am sorry," Timon said, a lump in his throat.

But Timon's mother raised her hand, gesturing him to seal his mouth. "Be quiet. You have brought shame on me today. And yourself."

Those words had caused more pain to Timon than any leather belt tearing into his skin could have done. Tears ran down his cheeks as he gripped his schoolbag and looked down at the corridor with classrooms on each side. Somehow, it all seemed unreal that this was the last time he would ever walk down these corridors or be in these classrooms. All the friends he had made. Memories he had built. Gone.

When he reached the playground, walking slightly behind his mother as they headed to the car park, he saw Yinka Saraki, with her dark skin and ponytail. She was standing by the green railings in the playground. He could feel his anger, like a volcano on the verge of erupting, as he locked eyes with the wicked girl who had tricked and betrayed Timon and his friends.

Yinka lifted her left hand and waved goodbye at Timon, her pink lips curved into the snarliest grin.

Timon's last memory of Kingsford Comprehensive, before he walked out of those school gates forever, was of Yinka savouring her moment of victory with her deceitful smile. The wicked girl had fooled him and his friends even though they had followed her orders. Yinka had never intended to keep her promise not to show the incriminating footage to the headteacher. In the end, she had gotten the last laugh.

56

Timon had lost all track of time.

The troubling events of the last twenty-four hours ate away at his mind as he sat in a metal chair in front of a steel desk in a concrete and windowless room. Two other metal chairs were vacant on the opposite side of the desk. Only the dangling lightbulb above him provided a faint light in this gloomy setting.

The only other person in the square room was a tall, white police officer who stood in the corner by the door. This officer had taken Timon from his second cell he was transferred to in the morning in a white van. When Timon inquired why he was moved to a new location, the officer was vague, saying that Timon would be interviewed but did not state by whom. Everything that was happening felt surreal, like some terrible hallucination from eating some mushrooms in Amsterdam, but Timon was too emotionally and physically drained to try and make sense of it all right now.

Tried as he might block it out, he kept reliving the moment when Orisa's head laid on his lap as a pool of her blood - he had never seen so much blood in his life - began to spread across her hoodie like running dark paint. When the police had taken him into custody, the first thing Timon had done was wash his bloodstained hands in the toilet sink at the station, Orisa's blood washing down the sinkhole. Mercifully, the prison staff gave him a plain white t-shirt to wear so he wouldn't have to sleep in Orisa's dried blood. Tears crept at the edges of Timon's eyes and trickled down his brown cheeks in single droplets.

What had happened to Orisa and the danger he had put his loved ones in were the consequences of his greed. He knew that. Chikezie had warned him, on multiple occasions, not to allow Musa Jirongo to become an investor in their hedge fund. Musa, who Timon had last seen sprawled out and probably dead on his apartment floor, had been a man who traded in the illicit sales of arms to terrorists in Somalia. But Timon had ignored that fact, seeing it as irrelevant to his goal of securing the bag and growing the size of his hedge fund. And to what end? Only for Orisa to end up in hospital with a bullet wound, for Chikezie to have to hide his family in a hotel for protection, and God knows what had happened to Russell.

Then there was Yinka Saraki. Timon clenched his fists as her dark-skinned face, beautiful as it was deceitful, burned in his memory like someone pressing a hot iron against his skin. The bitch had betrayed him. Again. Just like she had done at school all those years ago when she had first ruined his life. Now, as an adult, she had pulled the same trick on him and sealed his fate again. But what made Yinka's deception worse this time was that Timon had genuinely grown to trust her, and, even more painfully, he had fallen in love with her. But she had played him like a sucker. Timon's mouth twisted into a sadistic smile. Yinka Saraki was a true bitch in every sense of the word. A woman who could take a man's heart and squeeze all blood from it. And she'd kiss you while slowly killing you. Some day, somehow, Timon would exact his brutal revenge on her.

The sound of the door opening snapped Timon out of his dark thoughts. He looked up and saw MI6 officer Kojo walk into the room with his tall, well-built frame and clean-shaven head. He wore a long grey coat, a black jumper, and matching boots.

Following behind Kojo was a black woman dressed in a sharp navy blue suit. She looked around her mid-forties but kept herself in shape. Her black hair was raised in a braided bun, and her facial features—thick lips and a slightly wide nose instead of a pointy one—plus her general aura made Timon confident that she was Nigerian.

"Thanks, Jason. We'll take it from," the Nigerian lady said to the police officer standing guard. She spoke in a very eloquent British accent that was softly authoritative. Timon could tell the Nigerian woman was not only highly educated by how she sounded but was also in a position of power from how she carried herself.

The police officer left the room as Kojo and the Nigerian woman pulled out the metal chairs from the desk and sat opposite Timon. While the Nigerian woman looked sympathetic as she regarded him, Kojo stared at Timon with a nonchalant, almost pitiful expression.

Until now, Timon had never been arrested or had many dealings with the authorities, apart from one time the police cautioned him when he had thrown a wild house party during his student days at Cambridge or when the police had stopped him in his Porsche on two occasions. But he knew enough about police procedurals from films and television shows he sometimes watched to understand that he was about to be interrogated.

"Firstly, it's nice to meet you, Timon," said the Nigerian woman, giving Timon a warm smile. "My name is Tiwa Akintola. I am the chief of the Secret Intelligence Service, or MI6, as you probably know it." She then tipped her head at Kojo. "I believe you've met Kojo. He is a senior intelligence officer who works under me. Firstly, how are you feeling?"

"Well, after the hell I've just been through in the last 24 hours or so, I can't say I am feeling chirpy," Timon said, looking around the room. He then shifted his eyes to Kojo directly. "My fian...the girl shot in my apartment. How is she doing?"

Tiwa answered Timon's question while Kojo continued to stare at him silently. "She's receiving medical treatment at King's College Hospital. You'll be pleased to know that she's stable and will recover."

Timon gripped his chest and breathed a sigh of relief. "Thank God."

"But when she's well enough, we'll have to unfortunately detain her for questioning," Tiwa said.

"Detain her for questioning?" Timon said, jolted to alarm after hearing such an authoritative and severe phrase, especially coming from the mouth of the person in charge of one of the UK's most prominent intelligence agencies. "Why does she need to be questioned? Look, I want a lawyer."

Kojo burst into laughter, his howling reverberating across the sparse, greyish room. "Listen, Top Boy."

Timon glared at Kojo. "Don't call me Top Boy."

"I'll call you whatever I please," Kojo said in a frank voice. The older man narrowed his dark eyes at Timon with such seriousness that Timon immediately held his tongue. The MI6 officer was intimidating.

"Now you listen to me carefully, *Top Boy*. Getting a lawyer is not going to do you a world of good. In fact, speaking to a lawyer in your current position is the last thing you want right now, considering the crimes you've committed."

"Crimes?"

Kojo let out another deep laugh and turned to look at Tiwa incredulously as if he had just heard someone say something so idiotic. "He said 'crimes' with such surprise as if he hasn't been knowingly investing money for a fugitive arms dealer. Can you believe this man?"

"Look, Timon," Tiwa said, her eyes as soft and welcoming as her gentle voice, which Timon knew was a mere pretence as the 'good cop' in this interrogation, "we have enough evidence that shows you and your two other business partners at your hedge fund were investing blood money, which belonged to the now deceased illegal arms dealer, Musa Jirongo, into various crypto assets. We've already arrested and detained Mr Ejikeme."

Timon felt his heart sink. *What have I done?* How could he have allowed this to all get so out of hand? "What...what about Russell Collins, my other business partner? Has he been arrested?"

"He fled the country yesterday afternoon, Timon," Tiwa said regretfully.

"Fled the country?" Timon said, shaking his head. He began to feel a pulsating headache and massaged his forehead. Nothing was making sense.

"So let's recap, shall we," Kojo said, a playfulness in his voice as if he were enjoying Timon's torment. "You've been laundering money for a wanted arms dealer through crypto investments; then this same arms dealer would have killed you and your girlfriend if I had not come to your apartment. Now your girlfriend is recovering in hospital from a gunshot wound, one of your business partners is in custody, and the other one has absconded from the country just as your whole world was collapsing in on itself. I'll be completely candid with you, Top Boy; you are knee-deep in some foul-smelling shit."

"Yeah, I can see that. I don't need clarity from *you*," Timon said, glaring at Kojo, already growing impatient with the man's condescending tone. "So what do you want from me then? What's the purpose of this interrogation since you know so much about me already?

"Now you're asking the right questions", Kojo said, grinning smugly at Timon. "Firstly, I want to know why Musa Jirongo stormed into your flat, ready to put you and your girlfriend in an early grave. And don't lie to us, Top Boy. You don't want to sink into an even deeper pool of shit than you're already in."

Timon let out a profoundly regretful sigh. "I lost five million pounds of Musa's money…"

"Blood money," Kojo interrupted with a hiss to his voice. "He made his fortune dealing and selling death, and he is responsible for the killings of thousands of Kenyans and Somalians, and all this time, you were making him even richer to fatten your own pockets. But, sorry, I interrupted. Do go on."

Timon sighed impatiently and grunted, although the weight of the M16 officer's words clawed at his conscience. "Ok, yes, I lost five million pounds of Musa's *blood* money. Are you happy?" Timon sucked his teeth. "My hedge fund was investing Musa's money into a few promising crypto assets until those crypto companies suffered a serious hack, which resulted in Musa's investments getting completely wiped out. I had an agreement to pay Musa back the money, and I had already returned two million back to him, but I could not pay the other three million."

"And why was that?" Kojo said, leaning slightly forward in his chair.

"The person who was supposed to give me the rest of the money never did."

"I am assuming this person is Yinka Saraki?" Kojo's mouth twisted into a self-pleasing smile when he noticed Timon's eyes widened in surprise. "I see now. She offered you the money you needed to pay back Musa, so that's why you were working with her."

"Wait, you know about Yinka?"

"We know much about you and your business relationships, Top Boy. Yinka and her team recruited you as a crypto consultant to secure nine million in investment from a select group of private bankers for Afchain, the crypto company majority owned by your friend, Sir Richard Dugard."

Timon felt like an idiot in the room. "Wait, what? Dugard has a majority stake in Afchain?"

Kojo nodded with a mocking grin. "Yep, that's right. And I am going to hazard a guess that you didn't even know that the only reason Yinka was trying to secure investment for Afchain was to guarantee the release of her kidnapped boyfriend."

"Her boyfriend was kidnapped?" Timon's head was spinning from all these startling revelations. Still, as Timon digested this new information about Yinka's motivations, her actions throughout their two-week globe-trotting mission began to make more sense.

Now it was Timon's turn to get a one-up on his interrogators. "In case you don't know, Yinka and her team call themselves the Robin Hoods. They steal from business people and politicians in Africa through blackmail and extortion. Yinka uses her sexuality to seduce and trick men."

"Like what she did to you then?" Kojo said, shaking his head at Timon. "From the start, she was not telling you the whole truth. She manipulated you to help her secure investment for Afchain so she could save her boyfriend's life. And as soon as you had fulfilled your purpose, she ultimately betrayed you, practically leaving you for dead. Those are the actions of a dangerous woman."

Timon bowed his head as Kojo's words stung his pride. As much as Timon couldn't stand the MI6 officer, he wasn't wrong about Yinka or about Musa's money being blood money.

"Look, Timon," came Tiwa's reassuring voice again, "you've been unknowingly caught up in an international conspiracy. Dugard has been on MI6's radar for a while, and we have confirmed that he is part of a clandestine global network of corrupt private bankers known as The Cable. They all work together to launder criminal money into each other's respective countries. We suspect Afchain is just a front for Dugard to clean dirty money through a crypto exchange. And, as you know, Dugard is an associate of your father's, who we're also monitoring now."

Timon rose slightly from his chair and stared wide-eyed at Tiwa. "MI6 has been monitoring my father?"

Tiwa nodded. "That's correct. Your father, Dugard, Silvio Mancini, Emiko Shinoda and Abdul Mufasa Kazeem are all part of this criminal network. But Dugard has gone behind their backs and deceived them into investing in Afchain without them knowing he has a majority stake in the company. You and Miss Saraki were merely proxies in Dugard's plans, to make it seem as if he had no connection to Afchain to the other members of The Cable."

Kojo grinned at Timon. "However, your father has discovered Dugard's deception, and let's just say he isn't too happy."

"So then, why did Yinka and her team target me?" Timon said, looking at both Tiwa and Kojo. "Was it because of my crypto specialism or because I am Mobolaji's son? Would that even matter? Could she have somehow known I would need the money she offered me because I was in debt to Musa?"

"Who knows? It might be a combination of all those reasons," Kojo said, shrugging his shoulders. "But it doesn't matter. What does, though, is how we move forward. How do you get yourself out of this pickle? Let's be honest now. Laundering money for a terrorist arms trader breaks all sorts of financial conduct regulations and laws. You'd be looking at a hefty prison sentence, which goes for your two business partners. It's all looking rather grim for you right now, isn't it, Top Boy?"

So this was their play, Timon thought, narrowing his eyes at

Kojo, who winked at him, knowing he had him. *They were going to use him. But for what?*

"So what's the deal you're offering me here?"

"You catch on quick, Top Boy. Now I understand why you're one of the few black boys from inner-city London who made it into Cambridge." It was a backhanded compliment. Timon could tell Kojo was not a fan of him.

"Two weeks from now, your father is organising a private meeting at the African Tech Summit with the other members of The Cable. The summit is taking place in Lagos," Tiwa said, speaking to Timon. "Dugard has been invited to the meeting, along with your father and the rest of The Cable members. They will confront Dugard about his duplicity regarding Afchain, force him to sign over all his stake in the company so they can take control of the technology and then have him murdered."

"Jesus," Timon said, shaking his head incredulously. "My father is going to have Dugard killed?" Although Timon did not have any emotional connection to his father, learning that his old man was conspiring to murder someone was a lot to digest. "Alright, so…so what do you want me to do?"

"We want you to leverage your relationship with your father and get yourself in that private meeting at the African Tech Summit. We're going to implant a microscopic camera on you so you'll be recording the whole meeting before it is interrupted by Nigerian security forces who MI6 will be cooperating with. We'll then extradite Dugard to the UK to face his crimes and use the meeting recording as our final piece of evidence we need to bring down The Cable entirely."

Timon was sweating now. He wiped his brow. "And I assume if I refuse to be your pawn, I'll face prosecution for my financial crimes?"

Tiwa nodded, but she had a sympathetic look on her face. Oddly enough, she reminded Timon a little of his mother if she were much younger. "Yes, Timon, that's correct. But if you work with us and succeed, you will be pardoned for your financial crimes and we will extend that grace to Mr Ejikeme. Your other business partner, Russell Collins, we are still suspicious about his involvement in all this."

"And since you'd be assisting MI6, we have a duty of care to protect you," Kojo said, although that did not sound too convincing to Timon.

Whatever he decided, Timon knew he was fucked either way. The current predicament he found himself in was of his own making. If only he had heeded Chikezie's warning about Musa. Timon sighed regretfully and nodded, resolved to his fate. "Ok, I'll do it."

Kojo clapped his hands triumphantly, his lips curved in a smug smirk. "You've done the right thing because the way I see it, I saved your life, Top Boy. And so now your life belongs to me, to MI6. And you will be our spy in Lagos."

PART SEVEN

SPIES IN LAGOS

57

LEKKI PHASE 1, located on the Lekki peninsula, west of the upscale Victoria Island and Ikoyi, was the epitome of high-end living in Lagos for Nigeria's wealthiest citizens. It was also a haven for some of Nigeria's most corrupt and scrupulous politicians and businesspeople.

The Robin Hoods had blackmailed and extorted money from several residents in the Lekki Phase 1 neighbourhood, so it was only natural that Dugard had rented a five-bedroom, ultra-modern duplex there. Here, the Robin Hoods were being held under armed house arrest by Dugard's mercenaries.

Two days ago, Yinka and the team, including Oge, had left Dugard's manor in the English countryside on Dugard's private jet and flown to Lagos with Dugard's henchmen. Dugard had stayed behind in England as he had some errands but would be flying to Nigeria in a week to attend the two-day African Tech Summit.

After having their phones and bank cards confiscated as soon as they touched down in Lagos, Yinka and the others were driven to Dugard's rented property and immediately set to work laying out a detailed plan of how Oge and the British mercenaries would covertly infiltrate the Nigeria National Theatre, the venue for the African Tech Summitt, and kill Mobolaji Bankole when he hosted a private meeting with Dugard.

To Yinka and the other Robin Hoods, Oge's and Dugard's plot to assassinate Mobolaji was beyond madness. Still, when they heard Bobby and the two mercenaries walk through the house's corridors with their heavy boots and guns held firmly against their chest, they knew they had no choice but to comply.

The 'central murder room' was the nickname Jaali had given to the room in the house where Yinka and the others had spent two days planning the mission's pragmatics. Currently, all of them were in the room apart from Oge. Joshua was sitting by a wooden dinner table in the white-marbled room, two laptops in front of him. He was looking at some schematics of the Nigeria National Theatre that Kisi had procured from an older and hopelessly in love Igbo businessman living in Lagos, whose construction company had helped with the recent building renovations.

Jaali and Montana were both sitting on a leather sofa, looking down at a map of Surulere sprawled on the floor. Surulere was a province in Lagos where the Nigeria National Theatre was situated. Pen marks had been scribbled across the map as Jaali and Montana figured out the best getaway routes by car for Oge and the British mercenaries once they had assassinated Mobolaji, which would be no easy feat in a city as congested as Lagos.

Kisi was pacing around the room, calling anonymously from a burner phone. She was attempting to bribe a police officer in the Lagos Police Command, who she had briefly dated, to provide her with some police uniforms for Oge and the mercenaries to wear so they would not draw any attention to themselves once they were inside the venue. The Robin Hoods were doing what they had been doing successfully for years, but only now were their skills being used to plan an execution instead of extortion.

Yinka had spent the past two days contacting a few of the street boys she had befriended around mainland Lagos over the years, locally known as 'area boys' who acted as her eyes and ears on the ground. For a bribe - anything even slightly valuable was never free in Nigeria - the Lagos area boys would provide Yinka with local intelligence on potentially corrupt police officers, dodgy business people, deceitful professionals and amoral civil servants who could be black-mailed or bribed for the correct fee. Yinka had been trying to find out if someone could sneak them into the African Tech Summit, but there had yet to be any promising leads. Stressed, Yinka walked out of the room where the team was working and stood by the glass balcony.

The heat from the scorching sun pressed against Yinka's dark skin. Having grown up and spent much of her life in Nigeria, she was used to the scorching tongue of the sun. Stretching before her eyes, she saw the main road with kapok trees lining the concrete pedestrian. The streets were built well in this affluent part of Lagos, with no cracking or decaying sidewalks. The neighbourhood featured other detached luxury apartments and flats spread around the area, protected by tall railings or gates. Some of the houses were only half built, with only the foundation of the building set on the pot of brown land. These half-built homes looked like they had not been paid attention to for a while, but Yinka was not surprised. Half-finished buildings were a common sight in Lagos, a city that was perpetually under construction.

Yinka looked over the parapet to find Oge on the front porch, wearing green combat trousers and a black vest. He was smoking a cigarette. For no particular reason, Yinka could see; he was looking at the steel and black gate surrounding the compound. Knowing him, he was in one of his contemplative and brooding moods.

Since Oge had revealed his deception to her and the team, Yinka had not spoken to him. She was unable to even look at him. Wisely, Oge avoided her on Dugard's jet, giving her the space he knew she would need. Yinka exhaled heavily. No more avoiding difficult conversations. She would need to speak to Oge privately and try to talk him out of this insanity.

Yinka turned around and walked away from the balcony.

"And just where do you think you're going, my sweet, dark chocolate lady?" Bobby said as he stood before the doorway, blocking Yinka's exit to the front porch. He folded his arms over his broad chest. The tall and stocky English brute wore combat shorts and a white vest with his Glock 19 pistol tucked inside a waistband holster.

Yinka narrowed her eyes at him. "I don't care that you carry a weapon; if you call me a sweet and dark chocolate lady again, *oyinbo*, I will make you swallow your teeth and then excrete them out painfully from your pink asshole."

"Fuck me, you lot ain't got no manners, have ya?"

"Get the hell out of my way."

Bobby stepped forward. A couple of inches taller than Yinka, he glared down at her, his lips curved into a snarl. "I don't know what an *Ohandbo* is, but I don't like being called nicknames, love."

"Read my face carefully. Does it look like I care what you like or dislike?"

"Enough," Oge's deep voice commanded. He stood behind Bobby, about three inches shorter than the English mercenary. "She's allowed to come outside, alright. We're holding her captive, but she's not in prison."

Yinka strutted past Bobby, ignoring the loud, dismissive grunt he made as she went past him. *Idiotic goat*, Yinka thought to herself as she followed Oge to the front porch.

A mosquito buzzed past Yinka as she and Oge stopped on the bright green lawn. After taking a final pull of his cigarette, Oge threw it on the ground, squashed it with his feet, and finally looked at Yinka. Although the roguish charm she had fallen in love with was still there, Oge's eyes seemed hollow now, as if he hadn't slept properly in a while. It was clear the drastic choices he had made had taken a toll on him.

"I thought you would be giving me the silent treatment for the rest of my days," Oge said dryly, with a weak smile. "I know you, Coffee Bean. It will take a lot of work for me to earn your trust back. I accept that."

Yinka steeled herself and pushed back the threatening tears with the power of pure stubbornness. She took Oge's left hand tenderly into her own. "Oge, this is madness. Look at what you're doing. You are forcing the team, literally at gunpoint, to help you murder a man. We are thieves. We steal money. Not lives."

"Well, maybe it's time to be more than a thief," Oge said, raising his voice and curling his right hand into a fist. "And Mobolaji Bankole is not just *a man*. He's *the man* who killed my mother. Every time he breathes, it is an insult to my mother's memory but also a curse to Nigeria. His life has gone on long enough."

Yinka flung her hand out of Oge's palm. Now, she could feel her earlier pity for him give way to desperate anger. "You're not a killer!"

"Yes, I am, and you know I am. Or have you forgotten that I murdered my white English father with my bare hands?"

Yinka stepped back from Oge, her heart beating fast as her emotions rose. It was true that Oge was a killer. She remembered nine years ago, two days after she had graduated, Oge finally came to visit her in London. She recalled feeling speechless in her rented apartment in Camden, which she shared with the other Robin Hoods who were graduates then and not yet the thieves they would become when Oge had told her how he had murdered his father.

"I have told you the story. My father, a British army soldier stationed in Nigeria in the late 80s, had fancied my mother and given her a child. He won her heart, but all that time, he had a wife and two kids back in England." Oge scrunched his face in disgust. "I was only three months old when he abruptly left Nigeria and deserted my mother, leaving her alone to raise me." Oge's eyes had gone glacial as the red mist lingered within them. "He left and never looked back. And when I finally tracked down my old man years later, living by himself in Brighton after his wife had divorced him and his children had abandoned him, he had wanted nothing to do with me. I was just some unwanted result of some meaning-less fling he had with an African woman, is what he told me, verbatim. So I snuck into his house and strangled him in his sleep. Not because he hurt me but because he hurt my mother."

"But killing your father did not rid you of the trauma and hurt he caused you and your mother, Oge. If you kill Mobo-laji, it won't ease the pain of your mother's murder either." Yinka hoped she was getting through to him. "And corrup-tion in Nigeria won't end with Mobolaji's death."

Oge shook his head and looked away from Yinka into the far distance. "Back in Germany, you told me on that balcony that we were just professional thieves, and you were right. Throughout these years, all we have done is steal from the corrupt, give some of the money we've stolen back to the less fortunate and then make ourselves rich with the rest of the money we stole. We're cowards as well. But I am done with all that." Oge looked at Yinka again, and she was struck by the fierceness of his eyes, like a forest blazing with fire. "As much I hated him, my father was a decorated soldier. My mother named me Ogedengbe, after the famous Yoruba warrior, Ogendengbe of Iilesa, who fought for the Yoruba clan against Ibadan in the Kiriji War. I am a warrior, not a thief, so it is time I started behaving like one. That is why I will kill every corrupt man and woman in this country. And my vendetta starts with Mobolaji Bankole."

"But Dugard is corrupt, and yet you are working alongside him. You can't think this Afchain company of his will do any good for ordinary Nigerians."

Oge sighed. "Dugard is a slimy foreigner who has been working with Mobolaji for years, helping him launder criminal money from Nigeria into the UK and vice-versa. Afchain is nothing more than a money laundering scheme. Like most foreign entities, Dugard exploits Nigeria. I know this. But he sees Mobolaji as an enemy, so an enemy of my enemy is useful. In the short term."

"And what about us? What about our relationship in the short term and the long term?" Yinka smacked her left hand against her chest, frustrated that she was not making any breakthrough. "Our future together? A family, kids, you know, a normal life? Don't you even want that with me?"

Oge's eyes softened. There was now a sorrowful, borderline pitying look on his face as if he were about to tell a young child that their pet dog had died. "I love you. You're the only woman who will ever have my heart; you know that. But I will be honest with you, Coffee Bean, my war against corruption in this country, which is my sole purpose, is more important than our relationship. It's more important than having a family with you. And always was."

Yinka shook her head in despair, feeling that everything she had based her life on had now crumbled before her eyes. "But I gave everything to you," Yinka said, her voice a painful and pleading cry as her eyes began to water. "I put my life on hold for you. I set aside all I ever wanted, children and a family, to serve your mission. And *this*….this is how you break your promise to me?"

"I never promised you anything, and you knew who I had

become when I reunited with you in London. But you ignored what your eyes were showing you about me, and instead, you let your heart paint a romanticised idea of me. You tricked yourself into believing I was still that little boy in our village. But that boy died when he saw his mother perish before his eyes." Oge hardened his facial features as he looked deeply at Yinka. "You deluded yourself into loving me as a fantasy because you closed your eyes to who I was in reality. A killer."

Tears, hot and stinging, trickled down Yinka's cheeks. Oge's word tore into the limbs of her soul and mauled it to pieces. Now she realised, with terrible clarity, that she had wasted so many of her youthful years with a man whose purpose had never aligned with hers. And it had been evident that Oge would never make her his wife or give her children. Yet, like some lovesick puppy, she had mindlessly stayed by his side, behaving like his pet as she wilfully used her body to serve his purpose. It was painfully, horribly clear to Yinka now that her relationship with Oge had turned to dust in this moment. Unsalvageable. As Yinka mourned the death of their relationship, she heard Bobby's voice as he approached them on the front lawn.

"Oi, you two need to come inside. There's something you need to see on the telly."

58

WHEN YINKA and Oge followed Bobby into the white marble living room, Jaali, Montana, Kisi, and Joshua were also present. They stood in an arch around the widescreen television built inside one of the living room walls. Whatever was on the television, they watched it with a deep interest. Yinka went to stand next to Montana while Oge watched the screen but stood a few feet away from the group, no longer their trusted leader and friend but a pariah.

A female news anchor, wearing an Ankara blouse, was speaking about a high-profile killing in London. Yinka gasped when she realised that the news anchor was talking about Musa Jirango, the man who was supposed to have killed Timon.

"Authorities have now confirmed that the deceased man killed in a shooting at an apartment in Battersea two days ago was 47-year-old Musa Jirango. He was a Kenyan arms dealer who was, at the time of his death, a fugitive from his native country and wanted by the Kenyan government for illegally trading weapons with Somali terrorists. The authorities have refused to publicly name who killed Musa Jirango and why exactly he was at the property. Residents

living in the million pound apartments in one of the most affluent
parts of London heard several gunshots in the evening at around 7
pm. It is alleged that the apartment belonged to a 30-year-old man
living there with his fiancée, but the UK government has said the
incident's details are sensitive. They will not be releasing any
further information at this time."

It took a few minutes for Yinka to digest the news report
as her mind scrambled to various conclusions. Did Musa's
death mean Timon was alive? Who had killed Musa and
why? If Timon was alive, where would he be now?

"Do you think Timon is alive?" Jaali said, turning away
from the television and looking at the faces of the group,
saying aloud what everyone was thinking. "It sounded like
Musa Jirango was gunned down in his apartment, and Timon
doesn't strike me as a man capable of shooting someone
dead."

"Taking an educated guess, I'd say he is alive. The news
report did not mention other casualties apart from Musa
Jirango," Joshua said, adjusting his glasses. "But, curiously,
the UK government won't divulge any more information
about the incident—only confirm Musa's death."

"It doesn't affect our mission if Mobolaji's son is alive or
not," Oge said, his voice firm as he scanned the faces of
everyone in the room. "He no longer matters."

"But he does matter," Yinka said firmly, staring at Oge and
feeling a new coldness toward him. "He knows about us and
what we do after figuring it out when I was travelling with
him. What if the police in the UK have him in custody?"

Oge shrugged. "He's in London, and we're here in Lagos. I
don't see how what he knows could affect us."

"Musa Jirango being killed in Timon's flat and the UK
government keeping very tight-lipped about the whole incident cannot just be a coincidence. Think about it. Dugard
planted Musa to become one of Timon's clients so Timon

would eventually choose to work with us when he lost Musa's money. Wasn't that part of your whole scheme with Dugard?" It took all of Yinka's discipline not to chuckle mockingly at Oge as he looked at her blankly as she spoke. "For all we know, the UK government could have been monitoring Dugard's or even Musa's movements. If Timon has been arrested and detained for questioning, he could say something about Dugard to the authorities, and Dugard could end up detained in the UK. That would impact your mission to assassinate Mobolaji."

"That's a fair point," Kisi said, nodding at Yinka.

Oge glanced at Bobby who shrugged his shoulders. He looked back at Yinka. "Fine then. We must find out if Mobolaji's love child is alive."

"And the easiest way to do that is for me to contact him," Yinka said, hoping that her desperate hope for Timon's wellbeing did not come through in her voice. "I'll need my phone back."

"You're getting ahead of yourself. What makes you so sure he will respond if you contact him?" Oge said, narrowing his eyes at Yinka. "After all, you did not pay him the rest of the money for his part in securing investment for Afchain. Musa was definitely at Timon's flat to murder him. If he is alive, he wouldn't trust you now."

"He probably doesn't trust me, but all we know now is that Musa is dead. We don't know if Timon is, and I know, even if he hates me, he'll respond if I contact him. And if he does, then at least we know he isn't dead, and then we can decide how we proceed."

With a deathly silence, Oge studied Yinka, his dark eyes probing her face, trying to read the secrets of her heart. In the end, he relented and sighed. "Ok, I'll give your phone back, but only yours. Call him or message him. If you hear back from him, let me know immediately. Promise me, Coffee Bean?"

For the first time, Yinka felt a kind of repulsion when Oge called her by the nickname he had given her when they were childhood lovers. She nodded at him stiffly, "I promise."

It had also been the first time Yinka had lied to Oge.

And it would not be her last.

59

BEING A CITY MAN, it was only fitting that Timon's first experience of Nigeria should be in Lagos. But not even London prepared you for a city like this.

The heat from the sun, stuffy and suffocating, had made Timon feel like he had walked into a city built inside a steam room with no ventilation as he exited the plane with Kojo at the Murtala Muhammed International Airport. But he reassured himself that he would soon get used to the temperature. After all, not too long ago, Timon stayed in Dubai for seven days. That part of the world was practically a desert.

But what Timon would not be able to get used to was the traffic in Lagos. It was unlike anything he had ever experienced, even as a Londoner. After Kojo had ordered an Uber from the airport - both of them had to pay the short and dark-skinned taxi driver an extra fee for their luggage, cash in hand, something Timon had never done in any other part of the world he had been to - they had spent almost two hours trapped in traffic that crept forward at a snail's pace.

Even now, as Timon stood by the window in his room at the Citiheight Hotel in Ikeja, the capital city of Lagos state, dressed in denim jeans and a brown T-shirt, he watched from the window as a winding stretch of cars and yellow minibuses horned and tooted on the busy and noisy highway outside the hotel, thick smog of fumes rising from the many battered road vehicles. Just outside the hotel, Timon could hear the hum of the generator supplying electricity to the building, something he would never see in London.

Lagos was an assault on your senses. Men on mopeds and yellow, engine-powered tricycles whizzed and swerved through the gaps in traffic. Timon noticed older women wearing colourful blouses, similar to what his mother some-times wore, balancing wooden bowls on their heads so effort-lessly it looked like a magic trick as they strolled through the crowded streets. Hawkers, some topless and wearing sandals, stood at the edge of the roads, loudly advertising their goods to the slow-moving vehicles caught in traffic while young boys, in battered vests and dusty footwear, tapped on driver windows, clearly trying to make a quick buck. Like London, Lagos was a city where everyone was on the move. But Lagos seemed even more tense; its population even more possessed by the spirit of survival at all costs.

The knock on his room door ejected Timon from his thoughts. He took his head out of the window and faced the interior of his room. With its creamy white walls, wooden laminated floor, and small television attached to the front wall, the hotel room was perfectly functional but unimpres-sive compared to the lush hotels he had stayed at in Sardinia and Tokyo. It did not matter, though, as Timon would only spend the night here.

Timon walked over to the wooden door and opened it to find Kojo standing in the doorway. The MI6 officer wore a loose-fitting white T-shirt showcasing his thick forearms and round biceps. He was also wearing brown khaki trousers and black military boots. In his left hand, he held a black briefcase.

Timon let out an agitated sigh. He was not in the mood to

speak to Kojo after the seven-hour flight from London to Lagos and the two more hours to reach their hotel because of the dismal traffic. But Kojo did not notice that Timon was tired. He certainly didn't care if he had as he casually let himself into the room. Timon rolled his eyes and closed the door after him.

"How does being in Nigeria for the first time feel, Top Boy?" Kojo said, now standing in the middle of the room.

"What'd you want me to say? It's boiling and noisy," Timon said bluntly, shrugging his shoulders and standing by the bed. "And if you keep calling me Top Boy, I'll start addressing you as Uncle. I mean, you're in your sixties, right? You were probably born in Ghana in the late 50s or something."

Kojo laughed but shook his head disapprovingly at Timon. "I am forty-five, and I look quite young for my age. And I wasn't born in Ghana. I was born in England and adopted by a white English family from Oxfordshire, for your knowledge."

Timon raised his eyebrows at Kojo, momentarily surprised by this insight into the MI6 officer's life. It explained why he had a slightly posh accent. He hadn't grown up in inner-city London sounding like Hugh Grant. "Well, you still look like an African uncle, old man. Those muscles don't make you look any younger, mate."

Kojo chuckled and took a heavy step forward, and Timon instantly reacted by stepping back, feeling intimidated. The memory of Kojo making quick work of Musa's men back at his Battersea apartment and then offing Musa by shooting him dead with a single bullet flashed in Timon's mind. Maybe he better keep his mouth shut.

"You can take the piss out of me all you want, *Top Boy*," Kojo said, smirking at Timon, "but let me remind you that the trajectory of your life now depends on the successful completion of your mission here in Lagos. So if I were you, I'd drop the ageist jokes, engage that Cambridge-educated brain of yours and listen very carefully to what I am about to tell you."

Timon knew when it was time to take matters seriously. He nodded stiffly at Kojo.

"Smart man," Kojo said, flicking a toothy grin at Timon. He then walked over to the single bed and placed the black briefcase on the mattress.

Timon watched with silent intrigue as Kojo unlocked the latches on the briefcase. When he pulled the front case back,Timon was underwhelmed by its contents: a small black box was inside and a silver watch.

"Now listen very carefully," Kojo said, looking at Timon. "What you're looking at in this briefcase is millions of pounds of state-of-the-art intelligence-gathering technology."

"Really?" Timon said, dismissively waving his left hand at what he saw inside the briefcase. "A watch and a black box?"

Kojo narrowed his eyes at Timon. "That watch doesn't just tell the time. It has a built-in camera, and when you press the crown, it instantly takes high-res photos of wherever the face of the watch is facing. You understand?"

Timon raised his left thumb, and Kojo shook his head.

"Inside that black box is a microscopic recording device and video camera, the size of a tiny button and built with a synthetic material, which enables it to attach to almost any surface. Using these devices, you are to spy on your father, gather as much information as you can about his business operations and be present at the private meeting he is having with Dugard at the African Tech Summit. When you're inside that meeting, you need to plant the microscopic camera in the room or on yourself so I can view what's happening in the meeting from my end. This part is incredibly important. Do you understand?"

"How am I supposed to get into this private meeting? It's not like my father has invited me to it."

"You'll have to figure that out. You're a Cambridge graduate, aren't you? But I don't care how you do it, Top Boy. You know your mission, and I've given you the tools to help you accomplish it."

Kojo closed the briefcase. "You have my number, so call me privately if you have anything significant to update me on."

Timon looked at the briefcase on the bed with the million pounds worth of spy tech and then back at Kojo. "I haven't done any of this spy business before. What advice can you give me?"

Kojo regarded Timon silently for a moment. He then curved his lips into a small smile. "The most effective spies earn the trust of those they spy on. So earn your father's trust."

"But I barely know the man and don't like him very much either."

Kojo shrugged. "You may not be fond of him, but he's fond of you if he has agreed for you to stay at his big house indefinitely. He wants to get to know his son from England, who he never really raised. He's regretful and wants to compensate for lost time, so you should exploit that. It's what a good spy would do." Kojo looked at his watch and then back at Timon. "I need to leave, but before I do, I wanted you to know that we've been investigating Russell Collins, your business partner who absconded abroad, and we believe he might have some relationship with Dugard. But you needn't worry about that right now. I am just updating you. "

Before Timon could ask further questions, Kojo turned his back to him, walked to the front door, opened it, and left the room, closing it behind him without saying goodbye. *Prick*, Timon thought.

Now, Timon stood silently in the room. The metal-air conditioning unit on the wall was humming loudly, and the noises of the honking vehicles stuck in the Lagos traffic outside reverberated in his ears. He looked at the briefcase on the bed and shook his head.

Of the random detours in life Timon expected to happen - he accepted that the universe would always throw you a curveball once in a while - being blackmailed by MI6 to spy on his father in Nigeria was a plot twist he could never have predicted.

* * *

The next day, on a humid afternoon, Mobolaji Bankole arrived at the hotel to collect Timon.

But his father's arrival came with the type of fanfare one would expect from the country's president. Three black Audi SUVs had parked outside the hotel. Three men, dressed in black dashikis and wearing black fila caps, had entered Timon's room. One of them carried Timon's two suitcases while the other two men escorted Timon outside.

As one of the men opened the back door to one of the SUVs for Timon to enter, he noticed an earpiece in the man's ear. If there was one thing Timon had already learned about his father, it was that he took his protection very seriously.

When Timon climbed into the back of the SUV, his father was sitting on the left-hand side of the backseat, reading a newspaper. Mobolaji wore a tailored brown dashiki, matching trousers, and polished black brogues. He wore his distinct golden rings with black gems on each finger. The black cane he used to support himself, with the golden lion head, was resting against the door on his left side. Timon also noticed the watch around his father's left wrist. It was a gold Rolex Day-Date watch, similar to the one Timon owned but a more expensive model.

Mobolaji folded the newspaper, placed it on his lap and turned his head to face Timon. His dark brown lips stretched into a smile across his long, slightly saggy face. "Welcome to

Lagos, my son, and I am so overjoyed that you are here," he said in his heavy Nigerian accent. "When you called me two days ago, saying you were visiting Nigeria for a holiday, I was touched you had contacted me. It is by the grace of God that we are reunited again." He stretched out both of his arms, beckoning Timon to hug him. For a second, Timon hesitated, but he remembered what Kojo had told him:

The most effective spies gain the trust of those they are spying on. So earn your father's trust.

Timon leaned forward and embraced his father. The gesture was awkward, considering the last time Timon had put his hands on his father, it had been violent.

"Please excuse all of the security," Mobolaji said, easing back into the leather seat after the hug. "You wouldn't know this, but I was shot a year ago by an angry protestor, and the bullet entered my thigh, hence the cane I use now. In a country like Nigeria, my son, you will soon learn that those of us who have worked hard and built wealth for ourselves attract much jealousy and contempt. But God will punish those with envy in their hearts."

Timon was unsure how to respond to his father's words, so he nodded stiffly.

Five minutes later, the three SUVs had departed the hotel and joined the motorway. Although there was still traffic, mercifully, it was not as punishing as it had been yesterday. Still, Lagos was as busy as ever, and Timon looked through the window and observed the fullness of life in the city. Now, he noticed many of the buildings in this part of Lagos looked derelict, with peeling paint on their façade, rusting tin roofs, and shabby sidewalks covered in dust or rubble. At times, Timon felt like he was driving through a shanty town. It was evident that poverty was rife here.

Mobolaji's voice made Timon look away from the window. "I know you have been here less than a day, my son, but what do you think of Lagos so far?"

"It's busy," Timon said, looking at his father as he spoke. "It is like London, but people's energy here is more…"

"Frantic?" Mobolaji said, his thick, dark brown lips curving into a knowing grin.

Timon nodded. "Yeah, that's exactly the word I'd use."

Mobolaji chuckled. "My son, let me tell you something. I was born in Lagos, and I've spent my whole life here. Your grandfather, who you resemble so much, by the way, opened one of the first banks in Lagos, and he was one of the first Yoruba bank governors to provide loans to Nigerians to start businesses. Since then, Lagos has been a city of continuous growth and change. It never stays the same because it is not a stagnant place. There is no time to stand still here because this city will swallow you whole if you do."

Timon nodded at his father's words, considering them. "Well, you've done very well for yourself…Dad." The word 'Dad' felt strange on Timon's lips, like experimenting with a new lip moisturiser.

Mobolaji gave Timon a warm smile. "I have, but through hard work, my son. Many Nigerians do not want to work hard in this country. Shortcuts to great wealth are what they desire either through thievery, bribery or, in many cases, carrying out murderous rituals as if their satanic idols will reward them with treasures for their human sacrifices. But they are fools and crabs in a bucket. Many Nigerians do not understand that money does not come to you because you pray for it at church or mosque. No, you must go out and seek your fortune. When you find it, you pray for God to order your steps so that you can make the smart moves to grow what you have. That is how I built my wealth, son."

Timon nodded, impressed not only by his father's wisdom but also by his way of speaking which was considered and thoughtful, like a sage.

Throughout the rest of the car journey through Lagos' mainland, Mobolaji pointed out certain aspects of Lagos life to Timon, such as the yellow minibuses he kept seeing around, sometimes with people hanging precariously from the doors. These were transport buses called Danfos. The yellow-coloured tricycles that whizzed through traffic were called Keke. The more his father told him about Lagos life, the more captivating the city became.

The SUVs drove across a long, winding bridge called the Third Mainland Bridge, which connected mainland Lagos to Lagos Island. Timon was awestruck by the stunning views of the Lagos Lagoon, its dark waters catching the sun's light so it sparkled. He also glimpsed the poverty that seeped through Lagos when he saw, from the comfort of the SUV he was in, the waterfront settlements built on the lagoon, surrounded by wooden canoes. It was by some miracle that the wooden homes, built on stilts over the water and with straws or rusting steel panel for roofs, had not crumbled into the river. Timon was impressed by the ingenuity of those river settlers and recognised how privileged he was not to have to endure such a hard life.

Once they had entered Lagos Island, Timon noticed that traffic congestion had significantly reduced. Also, everything on the island felt more relaxed and smooth compared to the cacophony of noise on the mainland. The busy chaos still characterised this part of Lagos, but it felt more manageable on the island. The further inward they drove, the landscape and buildings began to take on a more modern and polished appearance. He noticed several glistening skyscrapers on Lagos Island that would not feel out of place in London.

By the time they arrived at a place on Lagos Island, humorously called Banana Island because of how it curved at the edge of the island, Timon felt like he had entered Nigeria's answer to Beverley Hills. Here, gated mansions, many of which were three storeys tall and built with ultra-modern and sleek architecture, lined the streets. Lush, perfectly trimmed bushes and tall palm trees decorated the pavements, and the sidewalks did not have cracks or rubble, nor did the roads have any potholes. Although Timon saw many properties still under construction and the area felt relatively unpopulated compared to the rest of Lagos, he knew instantly that here was where the one per cent of Lagosians dwelled and dined.

All three Audi SUVs pulled up outside a detached cream-coloured mansion with black railings fenced around the entire property. In the middle of the front porch was a magnificent fountain with a chalk-white statue of an angel, surrounded by a lawn of grass and black lampposts. Several men dressed in black dashikis were patrolling the perimeter of the extravagant mansion. Timon noticed the men had rifles slung over their shoulders.

Mobolaji turned to face Timon, stretched out his right hand and placed it on Timon's right shoulder. The golden rings he wore on each finger, with dark gems embedded inside, twinkled.

"Welcome to my not-so-humble abode, son. The rest of my family are currently at work, but I shall introduce you to them once they return this evening. Afterwards, we will commemorate your visit with a grand feast."

60

THE BANKOLE PALACE, the unofficial name for Mobolaji's luxury property, was an extravagant seven-bedroom, detached mansion. At 7000 square feet of space, it was the largest residential home Timon had ever stepped foot in.

After being escorted into the property by his father, flanked by security guards, Timon's first reaction was to stand in the marble-floored reception and marvel at the sheer scale of his father's house. He gawked at the long, golden spiral staircase in front of him that led to the second floor of the property, and he felt blinded by the mansion's interior, primarily glossed in gold so it dazzled your eyes. The walls were covered in a snow-white paint with golden ornamental plastering, as were the decorative fluted pilasters, which stood like ancient Roman columns. The Bankole family lived as if they came from royalty.

Two young black girls, wearing long black kaftans, had taken Timon's two suitcases from one of the SUVs and brought them inside. Another young black girl with a pretty heart-shaped face and big eyes, who looked about eighteen, walked up to Timon with a smile. To his surprise, she gave him a curtsy as if he were a royal prince.

"Sah, please let me take you to your room," the house girl said in a soft but strong Nigerian accent, which painfully but fleetingly brought back memories of Yinka to the front of Timon's mind.

"This is Tinuke, one of my brightest house girls," Mobolaji said, who had now come to stand next to Timon. He was balancing on his crane, which he leaned on with his left arm. "She will attend to your every need during your stay. When she takes you to your room, you will see some folded garments on your bed tailored for you. In your wardrobe, you will find other clothes. I am sure you will like them as it is the fashion of young Nigerian men." Mobolaji patted Timon on the shoulder. "Have a shower and relax for a few hours. Tinuke will be outside your room should you need anything in the meantime. I must attend to some business matters now, but when dinner is ready to be served, Tinuke will bring you to the dining hall to meet the family." Mobolaji then gave Timon a warm smile. "*Your family.*"

After Mobolaji departed, Timon followed Tinuke up the spiral staircase. She led him down an eloquent corridor with the same white walls and golden ornaments as the reception. The corridor smelt of lavender, and as Timon followed the house girl, who occasionally looked at him and gave him a shy smile, he felt like he was in a high-end hotel in Mayfair rather than a family home. Tinuke stopped in front of a white door with a golden handle. She took a key from her pocket, unlocked the door, and turned to face Timon.

"I have cleaned the room and laid the bed. You will find the finest selection of creams, soaps and perfumes in the bathroom," Tinuke said. Her tone was so mechanically formal; it was as if she had learned how to speak this way by watching how butlers spoke in Downtown Abbey, but then she added her Nigerian twist. "Should you need anything else, sah, you only have to ask me or any other house girls or boys, and we shall endeavour to make it possible ."

"Thank you," Timon said, smiling at her, but Tinuke only nodded as if it was against the law for her to show him too much affection.

Timon entered the room, shutting the door behind him, and took in the sight before him. The room was so spacious it felt like a luxury studio apartment. The plastered walls were dark gold. At the front of the room, there was a king-sized bed with a golden canopy, white covers, and dark brown velvet pillows. A folded, short-sleeved black dashiki and trousers lay on the mattress. By the side of the bed, Timon saw black Versace slippers.

It took Timon thirty minutes to wash himself in the golden shower inside the marble-tiled bathroom, cream himself with cocoa butter, and put on the dashiki set his father had bought. Once he had slipped into his comfortable slippers, Timon spent the next few hours watching Netflix documentaries and catching up on the news on the 65-inch flat-screen television in the room. Afterwards, he went to sleep for two hours.

At around 6 p.m., there was a knock on the bedroom door. When Timon went to answer it, he saw Tinuke standing by the doorway, her hands by her lap and a friendly, if stiff, smile on her face.

"Good evening, sah. The rest of the Bankole family have arrived and are seated at the dinner table in the dining hall. Your father has requested your presence."

61

WHEN TINUKE FINALLY LED TIMON TO the dining hall, he felt like he had entered a banquet. Like the rest of Mobolaji's mansion, the stately dining room boasted golden decorations on the white walls, deluxe plastering, and gold-painted window panels. A chandelier, the size of an orbital satellite and decorated with glistening diamonds, hung from the ceiling.

Seven people, including Mobolagi, were seated in golden chairs around the long, light brown dining table, which had a polished ceramic finish and sterling silver cutlery neatly placed on white cloths.

Mobolaji, now wearing a white tunic, took his position at the front of the dining table with four men and three women of various ages, all seated around him. As soon as everyone at the table realised Timon and the house girl had entered the dining hall, they all turned to look at Timon. He immediately noticed that the oldest woman, with a light complexion and wearing a white blouse, who sat closest to Mobolaji, regarded Timon with barely disguised contempt.

"Everyone, I would like you all to welcome my son, Timon," Mobolaji said, extending his arms outwards like the chief of a tribe. "He is one of my children, like five of you sitting here at this table, so please treat him with the same kindness and love we all show each other in this family. *Se o ye?*"

Apart from his father, all the faces looking at Timon gave him either a suspicious or curious look. Still, none of them questioned the family patriarch, and all nodded in silent agreement.

As he stood in front of the table, Timon felt naked. He cleared his throat. "It is nice to meet all of you, and I look forward to getting to know you all over the coming days." He hadn't felt like an outsider since his days as a Cambridge undergraduate.

"Take a seat, my son. Our chefs will be serving dinner shortly."

Timon sat in a vacant seat on the left side of the dining table at the edge. Tinuke silently dismissed herself and left the hall.

A young woman with short hair, possibly in her late twenties, sat beside Timon. She resembled Mobolaji so much, right down to his long face. The woman, who must have been his half-sister, wore a Gucci bandanna, a long-sleeved brown sweater with the Prada logo at the centre, and hooped diamond earrings. She turned her head to look at Timon and gave him a genuinely friendly smile.

The warmth his half-sister showed him was absent from the much older man sitting opposite Timon. He looked like he was in his very early 50s. He was dressed in a dashiki similar to Timon's but with a crimson hue and wore a matching fila. The man had a big, fleshy nose like the snout of a hog, a thick neck, and a round, paunchy figure. He gave Timon a very unfriendly stare.

While everyone waited for the chefs to serve the food, Timon spent the next five minutes summarising his education and what he did for a living. Everyone around the table listened attentively, but no one asked him any questions.

Tired of hearing himself speak, Timon was grateful when the chefs, in white t-shirts and blue aprons, and some house girls and boys began bringing an assortment of dishes to the table.

As they set down the pots and trays of food, Timon realised it was primarily Nigerian food. There was a silver tray of dark orange jollof rice, with its smoky aroma, a few plates of pounded yam dough served with vegetable egusi stew, a tray of crisply cooked golden brown dough shaped into balls known as *puff puff*, which Timon's mother had made for him on occasions during his childhood. The chefs also brought a plate of akara, a fried black eyes peas cake, a bowl with oven-cooked chicken drumsticks, a tray filled with bean pudding called *moi moi* and a variety of drinks such as Coca-Cola, Supermalt, bottles of wine and Guinness. The whole length of the table had enough food to feed three families with leftovers.

"Before we serve ourselves, let us give thanks to God almighty," Mobolaji said, looking across everyone sitting before him at the dining table. He closed his eyes and bowed his head. Everyone around the table copied Mobolaji like a domino effect. Timon, who hadn't prayed over dinner since he was a teenager living with his mother, closed his eyes and bowed.

"Our Father, the last two years have been a truly testing time for our family," Mobolaji began. "Nearly everyone sitting at this table has endured a personal and humiliating attack by a dastardly group of criminals who call themselves 'The Robin Hoods' but who are nothing more than crooks who exploit those of us who have worked hard for our wealth so that they can line their own pockets. They are not a righteous group as some claim."

Timon flinched in surprise. Surely, his father could not be

referring to anyone other than Yinka and her team of thieves? Now, it made sense. The Robin Hoods had targeted Timon because he was Mobolaji's son, and they were going after every family member. He felt a rising anger as he realised how deep Yinka's deception went and how much she had toyed with him.

"But we have endured despite the public scrutiny our family has been dragged through," Mobolaji continued. "And by God's grace, we will all pull through this dark period in the saga of this great family. Amen."

A collective 'amen' from all members of the Bankole family echoed in Timon's ears. With prayers over, everyone's eyes flicked open. They tantalisingly surveyed the buffet before them, ready to fill their plates and stomachs, but Mobolaji still had more to say.

"Before we feast, I would like to introduce Timon to the Bankole dynasty," Mobolaji said, flashing his pristine white teeth at Timon. "If you do not mind, my son?"

"Sure. I've introduced myself."

Mobolaji nodded, looking pleased with Timon's response. "Well, let me start with my wonderful wife, Angelica Bankole." He gestured at the woman in the white blouse seated next to him, who narrowed her dark eyes at Timon, unsmiling. "She is an editor for the largest lifestyle magazine in Nigeria and the mother of my wonderful daughter, Eniola, who you sit next to."

Timon turned to look at Eniola, who smiled at him, and he shook her hand.

"Before I met Angelica, I was married to my late wife, Taiwo, who passed away almost thirty five years ago. May her soul rest in perfect peace. But she gifted me four wonderful children who have become accomplished adults." Mobolaji beamed at the four adults sitting close to each other on the right of the dining table. "Firstly, there is my eldest, Adekunle. He is the CEO of Nigeria's internationally lauded private healthcare hospitals." The older man with a big nose who sat opposite Timon nodded curtly but did not smile at Timon. "Sitting next to him is my second son, Oluwaseun. He is one of the best-performing lawyers in Lagos and has a thriving legal practice. Beside him is Mikel, the chief financial officer for one of Nigeria's leading IT software companies. And last, but by no means the least, my eldest daughter, Moryao, is currently the first female governor for the Central Bank of Nigeria." Mobolaji clapped his hands, beaming with pride at Timon. "As I am sure you've realised for yourself, excellence is a common thread in this family."

Timon nodded, genuinely impressed by his half-siblings' accomplishments. Like Timon himself, they were all over-achievers.

With the family introductions over, the Bankole family began to fill their plates with large helpings of food. Timon had gone for the jollof rice, chicken drum sticks and some suya. The food was delectable, particularly the exemplary cooked spicy suya.

The Bankoles lived a life so incredibly comfortable that, as he ate his delicious food, Timon thought back to the settlers living on the Lagos lagoon, who probably survived on not even a third of the food on the dining table. Poverty existed everywhere, even in London, but the disparity was less substantial than in Nigeria.

Timon looked up at his father, who was secretly an international criminal who had made his fortune with dirty money. Tried as he might to deny it, Timon realised he was no different. The realisation made him feel ashamed of himself.

* * *

"I hope that wasn't all too overwhelming for you, my son," Mobolaji said as he poured Macallan scotch whiskey into a double old-fashioned tumbler. "I have a huge and accomplished family, as you can now attest to. We can be intim-idating."

Timon took the glass of scotch his father handed him and admired the décor of the study. After dinner, Mobolaji had invited Timon to his private library for a chat.

Surrounded by the dark brown walls and oak-carved bookshelves, Timon felt like he had been transported back to his student days at Cambridge when he had spent countless hours studying and writing essays with Chikezie and Russell at Trinity College library. Framed pictures of famous leaders such as Martin Luther King Jr, Nelson Mandela, and, oddly enough, even Winston Churchill hung from the walls.

Mobolaji stood by a chestnut executive desk in front of a broad, square window that offered an impressive view of the mansion's expansive garden with its vast lap pool and stone fountain.

"It wasn't so bad, and it was nice of you to introduce me to your family. I never knew you were married twice or had that many children," Timon said. He took a sip of the scotch and held the alcohol in his tongue for a few moments before letting it wash down his throat. It was intense but quality scotch, with the various flours tingling satisfyingly on his tongue. "My mother never spoke much about you, and I never cared to do research. I just knew you were a powerful man in Nigeria."

Mobolaji nodded, his dark eyes seeming to flash with pained regret. He smiled shyly at Timon. "Your mother did not have kind words to say when she spoke of me?"

"You know that she did not," Timon said, now feeling a sense of irritation beginning to replace some of the budding respect he was starting to develop for his old man. "Do you know she's sick? She has mild Alzeihemer's disease, and I was the one who paid for her to be cared for at one of the best care homes in England. I did that for her because no one else would. Certainly not you." Even when Timon spoke the last sentence, he instantly regretted letting his emotions get the better of him. He was supposed to gain his father's trust, not subject him to judgment, but Timon could not help it. For most of his life, he had built a healthy dislike, bordering on contempt, towards his father, and these deeply entrenched feelings could not just be flicked away despite what was at stake.

Mobolaji sighed deeply and sipped his scotch. "I am sorry to hear about your mother's sickness. I did not know."

"Why did you abandon her?" Timon was running on emotions now; he knew it but could no longer reign it in. Perhaps it was the scotch.

"I owe you the truth and nothing less," Mobolaji said, levelling his dark and dreary eyes on Timon. "Your mother was a housemaid here and was close to my late first wife. When my first wife passed away in '85, your mother comforted me, and we fell in love, but..." Mobolaji shook his head. "I could not marry her because she was a village woman, and I don't say that to be disparaging. However, it would have raised eyebrows at that time in Nigeria, especially considering my business and political ambitions. When I met my second wife, Angelica, your mother had fallen pregnant, but she outright refused to get rid of the child, being a devout Christian woman, and I was not going to force her. But I told her I could not look after her because I had agreed to marry Angelica, who came from money and had strong political ties. So I forced your mother to go and live in the UK, to be out of the picture, not to bring embarrassment to myself, but I would send her money to help raise you. And I hope you're aware that I fulfilled that promise."

"Yeah, I know you did," Timon said, turning his head away from his father. As painful as it was to hear his father say that he had abandoned his mother to protect his political capital, Timon at least appreciated his father's transparency.

"I want you to understand that I do regret pressuring your

mother to leave Nigeria and treating you both as an afterthought for many years. I was a young and ambitious man back then—also a very selfish one." Mobolaji walked up to Timon and placed his right hand on Timon's left shoulder. "But God has brought you back to me, my son. Now, all my children are with me."

Timon nodded and felt touched by his father's words. He then yawned loudly, covering his mouth.

Mobolaji chuckled. " It has been a long day. Rest, as I am sure you will be tired after such a big meal. We will have plenty of time to catch up as father and son."

* * *

After the heartfelt tete-a-tete with his father, Timon followed Tinuke, who led him back to his room. Curiously, when he arrived on the second floor, he was greeted by Angelica Bankole standing in front of his room door.

Timon estimated she was in her mid-50s with defined cheekbones, full dark lips, a Nubian nose and deep set eyes. Her black weave reached her shoulders, and she wore dark red lipstick. At her age, Angelica had a sort of elder stateswoman beauty. Timon could tell she would have been jaw-droppingly stunning in her youth.

As Timon walked closer to Angelia with Tinuke beside him, he saw the sternness in Angelica's eyes as she levelled them at Timon. His father's second wife would not be his friend in this family.

"Leave us," Angelica said directly to the housegirl as Timon came to a halt, standing three feet away.

"Yes, Ma," Tinuke said. The house girl curtsied to Timon before turning on her heels, walking briskly down the corridors and disappearing from view as she descended the spiral staircase.

Timon curved his lips into a tight smile. "Is there a problem, auntie?"

Angelica snorted. "I will be candid with you, Timon. Your presence in my home unsettles me," she said, her eyes pressing into Timon like poisonous fangs. "Your mother was merely my husband's brief concubine, a pet actually, whom he banished to England when he grew bored of her. And I know you never wanted anything to do with your father. Now, suddenly, you are here, trying to win his favour. So what is it? Are you after his money? Do you desire to be included in his will?"

Timon raised his chin at Angelica to let her know he was not intimidated by her questioning. "With all due respect, auntie, my relationship with my father does not affect you. I met my father in Dubai during a business presentation I had given, as I am sure he told you, and he offered me his number. I came to Nigeria for some business but felt, in my heart, that I should spend some time with my father while I am here. And just so we're clear, *auntie*, I do not need my father's money. I have built my wealth just like everyone else in the family."

Angelica scoffed, and now her lips twisted into a contemptuous scowl. "*Family?* Do not fool yourself, young man. You are not family. And despite what my husband says, do not think you are one of us. You are an outsider."

"Are you finished? I want to go to bed now." Timon looked at Angelia straight in the eye and held her gaze.

Sucking her teeth loudly, Angelia stepped aside, and Timon opened the door to his room.

"Goodnight, auntie," Timon said, closing the door on Angelica before she could respond.

Timon leaned against the door and clenched his teeth. Although enraged that his father's second wife had spoken ill of his mother, Timon knew better than to retaliate. Frustrated, Timon massaged his forehead.

Gaining his father's trust so that he could somehow worm his way into his meeting with Dugard at the Africa Tech Summit a week from now would be challenging. And now Timon faced another obstacle: his father's distrustful wife. He dragged his hands down his face.

"How the hell did I get myself into all this drama?"

And it was only going to get more complicated.

62

TIMON RECEIVED the unexpected text from Yinka on Sunday morning.

At the time, Timon joined the rest of the Bankole family in the lush garden of their mansion on a relaxing Sunday afternoon after attending Sunday service at the grand Cathedral Church of Christ with them. After the service, Mobolaji and his two other sons, Oluwaseun and Mikel, departed to attend important business meetings.

Eniola was swimming in the pool while Moryao was sipping a cocktail by the pool with AirPods in her ears. Angelica was reading a Vogue magazine as she relaxed on one of the rattan sun lounger beds.

As Timon sat on one of the sunbeds, he noticed his father's wife occasionally looked away from her magazine and stared at him. Her dark eyes would narrow, transparently hostile, before she returned to her magazine.

Timon ignored her intimidation games and scrolled through the news on his Samsung Galaxy. Then, his smartphone made a ping sound, alerting him of a text message. Yinka's name popped up on the screen.

Jolted by her unexpected text, Timon almost dropped his

phone in the pool when he saw her name. Breathing heavily and with trembling hands, Timon was about to open Yinka's text before he was interrupted.

"*Ṣe o sọ ede Yoruba?*" Adekunle Bankole said. The eldest of Mobolaji's children had set his round and large frame down on the sun lounger bed right next to Timon's, his heavyset frame sinking the mattress under the middle-aged man's weight. His round belly stretched out his black dashiki.

Timon shook his head. "I don't know what you're asking me. I don't understand Yoruba very well, sorry."

Adekunle laughed, his face doused in mockery. "Well, isn't that something?" he said, shaking his big head at Timon. "My youngest half-brother from big London does not even understand his father's language. With your Cambridge degree, you should learn to speak and understand Yoruba, Mr English."

Timon could only respond to Adekunle's ridicule with a soft and awkward chuckle. "I will learn in time," he said, giving Adekunle a far-from brotherly smile.

"See that you do," Adekunle said, staring coldly at Timon. "Now, I have come here to ask you something. And you will answer me truthfully."

Timon raised his eyebrows. Was he about to be subjected to another hostile interrogation by another family member? He placed his Samsung Galaxy in the left pocket in his trousers and sat up straight. "What do you want to ask me?"

"My father told me that when he met you in Dubai, where you gave a presentation about some Nigerian crypto company, you were with a young Nigerian woman. Her name was Yinka Saraki. She was dark-skinned, had braided hair, and was very attractive. However, I can find no record of her at all. She's not on LinkedIn or even registered as an employee at Afchain. So, who is she, and what is your relationship with her?"

Timon shook his head, trying to keep his face passive. "Why do you want to know?"

"Answer my question."

The seriousness that flashed over Adekunle's eyes instantly told Timon that Yinka and her team of Robin Hoods had wronged this man in the past. If Timon hadn't been working for MI6 to spy on his father, he would have given Adekunle the complete truth. However, given the desperate circumstances he found himself in, revealing that he had unknowingly been working with the group that had targeted and humiliated the Bankole family would do little to help his cause.

"I am as much in the dark about her as you are," Timon said, shrugging his shoulders. "She employed me as a crypto consultant to help her gain investment for Afchain. I believe she worked for Afchain as a contractor, but that is all I know. She told me nothing about her personal life."

For what felt like a long time, Adekunle silently stared at Timon, his eyes holding Timon's gaze as he searched them to find any signs of dishonesty in Timon's response. But Timon was unnerved and looked back at Adekunle nonchalantly.

Finally, Adekunle abated. "Very well," he said, and the big man with his round and protruding stomach laboriously lifted himself from the sunbed. "But if she contacts you again, you will let me know. Understand?"

Timon nodded. "Of course."

* * *

With his heart racing, Timon shut the bedroom door and retrieved his Samsung Galaxy from his pocket. After his eldest half-brother's interrogation by the pool, Timon knew he could not risk responding to Yinka's texts near any Bankole family member. Now that he was alone, Timon opened the message Yinka had sent him:

> Please tell me you're okay. I
> know about everything.

For a minute, Timon could only stare at Yinka's brief text message on the screen. It was not the message he was expecting from her. Then again, he wasn't even sure what he expected from her as he did not believe he would hear from her again. Once Timon had calmed his nerves and focused his mind, he typed his careful response:

```
I am surprised you're contacting
me. You lied to me. Again. I was
almost killed because you did
not fulfil your end of our deal.
What do you want from me now?
```

Timon sent the message. Within two minutes, his Samsung Galaxy made the short notification sound, like a space beep, notifying him of a new text message. Knowing it was from Yinka, Timon opened the message in a rush, heart racing:

```
I want to explain why I did not
send the rest of the money but I
wanted to know if you were okay
first. Like I said, I know about
everything that happened to you.
Where are you now?
```

Timon messaged back:

```
I am in Lagos
```

A minute later came Yinka's reply:

```
Why? Where are you staying?
```

Before responding, Timon thought about how much he should divulge to Yinka. Despite the oddly concerned tone of her texts, he would be a fool to trust her unquestioningly after everything that had happened. At the same time, based on what he knew about Yinka's behaviour, there must be some crucial reason she had contacted him again, or else why bother? After several drafts, Timon sent his sparse reply:

> I am staying with my father and
> his family

Yinka's reply was slower than her previous texts. Timon looked at the phone screen in anticipation. Why was it taking longer for her to reply? After five minutes, his smartphone made that little notification sound again. Timon opened Yinka's message:

> There is going to be an attempt
> on your father's life. You might
> be in danger as well. Dugard has
> been behind everything. I need
> to speak with you urgently, but
> I can't call you. I am being
> watched. When can you meet me in
> person?

63

It did not take Timon long to realise that the house girls were spying on him. He knew his father's wife had ordered them to do it.

The first time Timon had noticed it was after he had read Yinka's troubling texts and opened his room door to find Tinuke standing right outside. Although she had said she was checking to see if he was okay as he had left the garden abruptly, Timon knew the house girl was lying and had been trying to eavesdrop.

Later that evening, as Timon sat in the exquisite living room with Eniola, the only member of the Bankole family who seemed keen to start a relationship with him and asked him many questions about his life in London, from the side of his eye, he caught Angelica talking, in a severe manner, to another house girl in the doorway that connected to the living room. It had been brief, but Timon saw the house girl flick her eyes at Timon and give him a curious look before shifting her eyes back onto Angelica.

At that moment, Timon understood that calling Kojo to discuss Yinka's troubling message was out of the question.

However, the severity of Yinka's shocking text required a proper conversation with the MI6 officer, not text messages.

Late that night, while lying in his bed in the darkness of his room, the stillness only broken by the faint buzz of mosquitos, Timon messaged Kojo, saying he needed to meet with him urgently in person. Thankfully, the MI6 officer did not ask further questions and told Timon to meet him at the intersection of Breadfruit Street and Balogun Street at the Balogun Market tomorrow at 11 am. The location was thirty minutes from The Bankole Place. Timon agreed to meet him there.

* * *

"Balogun market is one of the most hectic places on Lagos Island," Mobolaji told Timon the following day during breakfast.

Timon, Eniola, Angelica and Mobolaji sat around the dining table in the grand dining hall. Several baskets, filled with pastries, from croissants to apricot danishes, were spread out across the dining table by the house girls, as were boxes of cereal and milk. It was 9 am, and the absent members of the Bankole family had already departed for their lucrative jobs. Timon, dressed in a cream-coloured dashiki with matching trousers, sat next to Eniola. Across the dining table sat his father and his wife, who peered over the newspaper she was reading and narrowed her eyes at Timon.

"My father is right, Timon," Eniola said, who was dressed in a brown Gucci tracksuit and had taken a day off at her magazine publishing house. "Even to us native Lagosians, Balogun Market can be treacherous. You are a British foreigner with money. The market traders and area boys will smell the overseas wealth on you like perfume and strip you naked." Eniola chuckled, grabbing a croissant and placing it on her plate.

"If I may ask, what business do you have in Balogun Market?" Angelia said, placing the newspaper she had been reading down on the dining table. She picked up the white mug beside her and sipped her tea. "Lagos Island has other places for shopping which are safer and less chaotic than Balogun Market. So why there specifically?" She eyed him, suspicion colouring her face.

"An old business partner of mine insisted we meet there to catch up as he is also visiting Lagos."

Mobolaji clapped his hands in delight. "Invite him here! Any associate of yours is welcome into my home."

"No, he wouldn't like that," Timon said, raising his left hand in protest. "He dislikes being a guest where he does not know the hosts personally. He's a peculiar man in that way."

"Well, if you must go to Balogun Market, two of our security guards will escort you," Angelica said, holding her cup of tea and giving Timon a crooked smile.

"I could not agree more with my darling wife," Mobolaji said. He got close to her and kissed her cheek. At the gesture, Angelica tittered like a schoolgirl, and Mobolaji turned his attention back to Timon. "Two of my best boys will chaperone you. That shouldn't be a problem, should it, my son?"

Timon curved his lips into a tight smile. "No problem at all. Thank you, Dad."

* * *

An hour and a half later, Timon stepped out of the black Audi SUV and onto Balogun Street, the start of the two-kilometre market at the centre of Lagos Island. This part of the market was less busy but every corner was lined with squalid, makeshift stores selling various fabrics, accessories, electronics, hair weaves and fresh food. Ordinary Nigerians, many dressed plainly and with no-nonsense and stern expressions on their faces, strolled through the concrete street littered with heaps of rubbish. Others sat in the raised pavement blocks, conversing in what sounded like Yoruba, pidgin English and some other dialect alien to Timon's ears. As a black police jeep drove by, Timon's ears picked up the noise cluster, from voices to car horns, roaring deeper into the expansive market.

Samuel and Ibrahim, the two security guards tasked with escorting Timon around the market, stood behind him. Samuel was tall and skinny, while Ibrahim was short and stout, with three deep, vertical scars on his dark cheeks. Together, they looked like a comical duo as Timon turned around to address them. Just from their dull faces, he could tell the two men were well-trained and not on any nonsense.

Timon clapped his hands, beaming at them. They stared back at him with no readable expression. "Listen, my guys, you don't need to follow me into the market. I will talk to my friend for a few minutes, and then I can meet you back here."

Samuel and Ibrahim glanced at each other, and, to Timon's surprise, they burst into hysterics.

"Na so? Abeg, London boy dey play," Samuel said, his firm Nigerian accent accentuating his pidgin English. "He will meet us back here? Make you no vex me."

Ibrahim chuckled, elbowing Samuel playfully on the rib. They then engaged in their shared cackling again, much to Timon's impatience, for he knew he was the subject of their ridicule. Once their laughter had ceased, Ibrahim regarded Timon with a straight face. "No, sah. We take you to market. We follow instructions. Got it?"

Timon relented with a sigh. "Okay, fine."

He began walking deeper into the market with the two security guards trailing behind him as the barrage of noises from traders, shoppers, and hagglers became louder. He followed the rusty street signs nailed to lampposts that told him where Breadfruit Street was located and where the MI6 officer was waiting for him.

64

DRESSED IN BROWN KHAKI SHORTS, a short-sleeved white shirt, and sporting black aviator sunglasses, Kojo had arrived at Balogun Market fifteen minutes ago.

He was standing by one of the rusted railings outside a tall, derelict building and was away from much of the sweeping market's hustle, bustle, and sheer claustrophobia. Still, the ramshackle quality of the whole place firmly remained. Bin bags, broken bottles and even old clothes littered the brown, concrete streets. There seemed to be endless construction work everywhere, and the smell of diesel and petrol issuing from the exhaust pipes of old vehicles, mopeds and yellow minibuses engulfed the place.

A few locals gave Kojo curious glances, from the women balancing baskets of water bottles on their heads to a few young and unemployed men sitting on the pavements. Despite having a dark complexion, something about Kojo marked him as a westerner to local Nigerians. Of course, he was Ghanaian by way of ethnic origin.

Many years ago, after he had finished his tour in Iraq, Kojo had travelled to Accra to visit his dying mother one final time, the woman who had given him up for adoption to a white English family. She had been too poor to raise him by herself in the UK, especially when his father had succumbed to the harsh realities of England in the seventies and killed himself. However, she also did not want Kojo to live impoverished in Accra. Giving him up for adoption was the best way Kojo's mother had felt she could show him love; well, that is what she had told Kojo when she was an old and withered lady clinging to the handles of life.

During his brief stay in Accra, Kojo had felt like a disconnected outsider looking in. Now, in Lagos, he felt even more detached, as if he were an observer in a land where he should have some spiritual or sentimental connection.

The sight of Timon was walking down the street towards him snapped Kojo out of his rumination. Two dark-skinned men were walking behind Timon: one tall and slim, the other short and stout and both dressed in brown combat trousers and green vests. Kojo walked away from the fence and approached Timon, who looked at him with a concerned face. Kojo threw his arms flamboyantly around Timon in a tight embrace.

"Timon, my fondest student, it is so good to see you again," Kojo said, stepping back as he gripped Timon's shoulders and inspected him. "You are looking well, my old friend."

"Erm…yeah, you too," Timon said, his mouth morphing into an awkward smile.

Kojo turned his attention to the two men standing behind Timon. "I would like to speak to my old student about private matters related to my family and business. It won't be long. Is that okay, gentlemen?"

The two men nodded stiffly, clearly intimidated by Kojo's muscular frame, well-spoken English, and authoritative accent.

"Thank you. We'll be down the street."

"So what is so urgent and sensitive that we couldn't have

made this meeting a call, Top Boy?" Kojo asked Timon. They had both walked a few metres down Balogun Street before turning a corner into a small alleyway so they could speak privately.

"I have people spying on me, alright," Timon said, looking behind his back to the busy street.

Kojo raised his eyebrows. "Who's spying on you?"

"My father's wife has suspicions about my sudden reappearance in my father's life, and she has the house girls spying on me. And that's not the only headache I am dealing with. My eldest half-brother was questioning me about Yinka Saraki yesterday. He's been trying to find out who she is. Did you know that Yinka and her team have been targeting the Bankole family by stealing money from them through blackmail? That's probably why Yinka hired me and then betrayed me. And she's why I needed to speak to you urgently."

"Why is she suddenly so important?"

Kojo noticed Timon become tense and suddenly looking visibly distressed. A minuscule part of Kojo felt some pity that Timon was in this difficult predicament. However, the rest of Kojo intensely disliked the crypto hedge fund manager. Timon had invested money from a known terrorist arms dealer into crypto assets to line his pockets. Kojo could not respect a man who sold his morals for profit.

"Yinka sent me a text message yesterday. Look what she wrote." Timon reached into his trouser pockets and pulled out a Samsung Galaxy phone. He fiddled with it briefly before handing the phone to Kojo.

"Read the texts she sent me and tell me what we do next."

Kojo removed his aviator shades and read the correspondence between Timon and Yinka. He widened his eyes in shock at Yinka's bombshell revelation in the last text. He handed Timon's smartphone back to him. He then stroked his chin, contemplating this new and very troubling intelligence.

"Well, what do we do with this new information?" Timon

said, the desperation loud in his voice. "Dugard planning to murder my father is something you and your boss failed to mention. I thought it was the other way round?"

"Engage that Cambridge degree brain of yours, Top Boy; I did not know about Dugard's plot to have your father killed," Kojo said, shaking his head. "If what Yinka is saying is true, and I can't fathom why she would lie, then it complicates our mission here in Lagos. However, I need further context before deciding on the appropriate action." Kojo exhaled deeply. "I know it might be difficult for you, but you'll have to find a way to meet Yinka in person. Can you do that?"

Timon shook his head in frustration, placing one hand on his left hip and another massaging his left temple. After a few seconds of grunting, he nodded. "Yeah, I think I know a way I can meet her in person without looking suspicious."

"Excellent," Kojo said. "Once you've agreed on a time and place for the meeting, message me the details. I want to be present during your little reunion with the dangerous woman who betrayed you."

65

TRUDGING along the muddy and wet road, the grey 2018 Toyota Corolla pulled up just outside the Landmark Centre on Victoria Island. Oge, who was driving the vehicle, switched off the engine. Yinka sat beside him in the passenger seat. This evening, she dressed like she was ready to party all night in Lagos in a bright orange, solid halter top, blue belted shorts with a tropical print, and her Louis Vuitton handbag over her shoulder. But Yinka was not going clubbing; she needed to look the part for where she was going.

Victoria Island was Lagos' version of Miami, although less glamorous. It was the ultimate destination for partying and shopping for many wealthy millennials and Gen Z Lagosians. Many famous Western brands, such as the Hard Rock Café on Landmark Boulevard, were imported here. Landmark Beach was ten minutes away on foot. Last night, while discreetly texting Timon, Yinka had agreed to meet him inside the Truth Beach Club.

Oge, dressed in a plain black t-shirt and matching shorts, turned to face Yinka. He looked uncomfortable as he shook his head at her. "I still think I should come with you," he said.

"We discussed this already. Timon doesn't know who you

are, which will make him panic," Yinka said. Outside, she saw a police jeep drive past the Toyota and two men pushing a wheelbarrow towards one of the building sites in the area. "As you know already, he doesn't trust me now. I am lucky he even agreed to meet up with me, so I can't have you turning up by my side." She held Oge's gaze as she spoke, using his affection for her to conceal her true motives.

Oge pressed his lips together as he searched Yinka's face, weighing her up. As long as she had known him, Oge always assessed a situation carefully, patiently, and logically. It was why he had successfully led the Robin Hoods to blackmail dozens of corrupt African businessmen, women, and politicians for nine years and ensured they eluded capture each time. But he still had a soft spot for her in his heart, and Yinka would exploit it like he had done to her.

"I know it's important for us to find out why Timon is now in Nigeria, and I understand why he is sceptical about you calling him," Oge finally said after a minute of silence. "But can I still *trust you*, Coffee Bean? After everything, can I still count on your *loyalty*?"

Yinka leaned forward and gave Oge a deep kiss on his lips. She did it with vigour and passion, just like he had taught her when he had educated her on how to seduce men. When she pulled back, Oge stared at her, his face more trusting. "You hurt me, but I have had time to think about everything. And I still believe in your cause, my love. You still have my heart. My loyalty. Despite everything. Whatever happens, I am with you to the end."

It surprised Yinka how easy it was to lie to him now, to deceive him. But Oge had played with her emotions, abused her love for him, and even put her in danger. She was hurt now, and vengeful.

"Okay," Oge said with a relenting sigh. "Find out why he's in Lagos and what happened with him and Musa in London. Dugard is flying into Nigeria tomorrow to assess our progress and wants to know as much as possible. When your meeting with Timon ends, I'll still be here in the car, so head back here."

Yinka nodded, then gave Oge a quick smile before opening the passenger door and stepping out into the dark and wet evening.

After walking down the concrete slope towards Landmark Beach and then plodding across the sandy coast, the shores were calm in the warm evening; Yinka stopped right in front of the white, block-shaped two-story building. Truth Beach Club.

The venue was already in full swing. Nigerian men in their early twenties and some as old as their late fifties strolled into the club. Many of the younger men, and even some of the uncles with round stomachs, wore designer tops and expensive trainers and had glistening chains around their necks or diamond studs in their ears. The Nigerian girls, with their designer bags over their shoulders like Yinka, were dressed in either shorts or tight jeans with a designer top. Some ladies had arrived in nothing but bikinis with a sarong wrapped around their waists. On the open rooftop of the club, a DJ was busy on the decks, blasting out one of Burna Boy's global hit records.

In better days, Yinka, Oge and the rest of the Robin Hoods had partied at the Truth Beach Club all night, usually after they had successfully stolen a lot of dirty money from an unsuspecting African politician or businessman. They would buy cocktails and open a bottle of Moët or vintage Dom Pérignon, celebrating their spoils. Yinka sighed regretfully, not only because she missed those days but also because she had shamefully celebrated being nothing but a thief. Sometimes, she wondered what her father would think of her as he watched from beyond the grave and observed the dishonest life his daughter had chosen to lead.

Yinka closed her eyes to refocus and steady her nerves.

Knowing Timon was inside the club and she would be reunited with him electrified her skin and made her heart race. She could not wait to see him again; she had been thinking about him often since he had responded to her text, overjoyed that he was alive and well. But she also expected him to reproach her. Even hate her. In his eyes, she had betrayed him, and in a way, she had. But Yinka hoped that Timon would understand why she did what she had done after explaining everything. Whether it would be enough to gain his trust back, Yinka was not sure. But she would soon find out.

Sauntering behind two young and beautiful Nigerian couples, Yinka entered the Truth Beach Club, her heart thumping hard with nerves.

66

UNDER DIFFERENT CIRCUMSTANCES, Timon would have been enjoying himself immensely with Eniola and her rich friends at the Truth Beach Club this evening.

Sitting in one of the comfortable private booths on the beach that Eniola had rented for her entourage, Timon watched as fashionably dressed Lagosians, wearing the latest designer clothes and expensive watches, dominated the dancefloor with their fancy footwork and swung their hips to the popular Afrobeats songs blasting from the speakers. Buckets filled with alcohol, from Moët to Chivas Regal, were brought to all the booths by the bar staff. Even now, a bucket filled with expensive champagne was placed on the table inside Eniola's booth, along with two platters of suya, French fries, fried plantain and chicken wings.

Giddy with excitement in her yellow bikini top and shorts as she sat beside Timon, Eniola stretched out her hands and lifted a bottle of Moët from the bucket. She corked it open herself, causing rapturous applauses from her friends sitting around the booth. She then poured champagne into everyone's wine glasses.

"So, how does the party life in Lagos compare to London?"

Eniola asked Timon. She had filled Timon's wine glass to the top, and the champagne overflowed like a waterfall.

"People party way harder here than back in London," Timon said, picking up his wine glass.

As Timon pressed his lips against the rim of the glass to take a sip of champagne, he caught Kojo from across the club, standing by the bar. He wore black sandals, white shorts, and a plain brown dashiki. Although the MI6 agent wore his aviator glasses, Timon could tell he was judging him as he shook his head. Timon scoffed. Given the immense pressure he was under, it wasn't a crime for him to let loose a little. Any moment now, Yinka would step into this establishment, and Timon would have to confront her, coming face to face with the woman who almost got him killed. He was not entirely sure how he would react when he saw her. But he knew he needed to keep calm and composed. Too much was at stake.

"Yo, London boy, why the long face, *oga?*" said Tunde, a music producer in Lagos with long dreadlocks and a pierced nose. He was Eniola's boyfriend and spoke in a humorous fusion of Nigerian and American accents. "This is how we rich Lagosians turn up, bro."

Timon chuckled and grinned at Tunde. "I am enjoying myself, man. I just have a lot on my mind."

"Look around you, oga. You are seeing some of the finest Naija babes in Lagos. How can you even be thinking of stress right now?"

As Timon opened his mouth to respond jokingly to Tunde, he saw Yinka stroll into the club. Everything around him seemed to move slowly and blur into the background at that moment. His heart skipped in his chest as he gawked at Yinka's slim and curvy body seductively covered in a sleeveless orange top and blue belted shorts with orange print designs of tropical trees. She had kept her braided shoulder-length hair and her dark complexion married magnificently with her bright attire. Timon experienced an intense longing for her for perhaps a few seconds until his brain sharply reminded him of her betrayal. Now, her beauty stung. Timon clenched his teeth and the brief euphoria of seeing her again dissolved into bitterness.

Yinka stopped just before the main dancefloor and scanned the venue. When her eyes rested on Eniola's booth and she found Timon's eyes still staring at her, she clutched the straps of her handbag, now looking weary. She then nodded to her right, gesturing for Timon to follow her.

"Guys, I am going to the toilet," Timon said, who had already begun to stand up from his seat in the booth.

"Is everything okay?" Eniola said, sounding worried. "You've been quiet."

"Yeah, I am good. I'll be back soon. Please don't wait for me, though. You all keep drinking up."

As he approached Yinka, Timon glanced at Kojo, who was still leaning by the bar, doing his best to be inconspicuous. Timon nodded at him, and Kojo nodded back, immediately understanding what was happening.

Timon followed Yinka out of the Truth Beach Club and onto the private beach without saying a word to her. The gritty sand spread into his Gucci sandals as he walked behind Yinka. She led them further away from the venue until the music faded into a distant hum.

After five minutes of silently walking, Yinka stopped and turned to face Timon. Only the two of them were this far out into the private beach in the gloom of the darkening sky and cool air. The fluorescent lights emitting from the private villas across the beach illuminated their faces, and, for a split second, Timon mentally teleported back to the BLU sky lounge in Dubai, where he and Yinka had shared that incredible kiss.

"Timon…I am so relieved you're okay," Yinka said, her voice softer with a quiet joy that Timon had not expected. "I know everything about you and Musa Jirongo. I saw the news about the incident in your apartment. Is your fiancée okay? How did you survive?"

Anger trickled up Timon's spine, and he chuckled bitterly. "She's not my fiancée anymore." Timon then shook his head, immediately realising how ridiculous it was that he had revealed that information right now. He glared at Yinka. "Listen, I almost got killed, and my now ex-fiancée is in hospital with a bullet wound," Timon said, lifting his upper lip at Yinka. "Because you didn't pay me the other half of the money as we agreed, you put my life and the people I care about in danger."

"Believe me, it was not my fault you did not receive the rest of the money, Timon," Yinka said, her voice quivering. "I was lied to and I never knew the safety of your life and your loved ones depended on you receiving all the money."

Timon sucked his teeth bitterly. "You're lying. All this time, you've been setting me up, Yinka, just like you did at school all those years ago."

"I swear to you, Timon, I did not set you up. Not this time."

Timon could hear the pleading in her voice, but was it genuine, or was she trying to take him for a sucker again?

"You never told me you needed the money because you were in debt to Musa Jirongo. All I knew when I approached you in London was that you'd need the money I was offering, nothing else. Oge, my boyfriend…" Yinka let out a regretful sigh. "Well, my ex-boyfriend now and Dugard set up this whole Afchain business and orchestrated your involvement with Musa Jirongo. They worked together to manipulate me, my team, and you into helping them gain investment for Afchain."

Timon shook his head, now lost in a haze of confusion. "You're not with Oge anymore?" he said, surprisingly pleased to hear this development. Once again, Timon shook his head.

Get a grip, mate. "And what do you mean your ex-boyfriend and Dugard orchestrated my involvement with Musa Jirongo? How? Why?"

"Yes, please do elaborate."

Kojo's unexpected interruption caused Timon and Yinka to jolt as if Kojo were a ghostly spirit that had materialised from the darkness.

The MI6 officer was casually strolling towards Timon and Yinka, hands in the pockets of his shorts. He stopped a couple of inches away from where they stood. "By the way, it's a pleasure to finally meet you, Miss Saraki. My name is Kojo. I know a lot about you; paradoxically, I know almost nothing about you. You're certainly a woman full of mysteries and complexities."

Yinka scrunched her face in confusion at Kojo's intrusion and then looked back at Timon, raising her eyebrows at him. "Who is this man? A friend of yours?"

"He's with me, but he's not a friend," Timon said, narrowing his eyes at Kojo, who chuckled at Timon's remark, unbothered. "He works for MI6, you know, the British secret service. And he's the one who killed Musa Jirongo...and saved my life."

"Despite how Timon feels about me, and he's right, we're not friends, but even he knows I did save his life," Kojo said playfully. Timon got the impression all this entertained Kojo. "And as repayment to me and also for his crime of illegally laundering money for the late Mr Jirongo, your former business partner here has agreed to be an agent for MI6 and spy on his father."

Yinka shook her head in confused shock and looked at Timon wide-eyed. "Why are you spying on your father?" Her face showed such genuine care for his wellbeing that Timon's rage towards her cooled down slightly. But before he could respond, Kojo had already opened his mouth.

"The reasons why he is spying on his father does not

concern you at this moment, Miss Saraki," Kojo said in his authoritative voice. "You sent Timon a message saying that Dugard was making an attempt on Mobolaji Bankole's life. That's very serious. So how about you enlighten us on what Dugard plans to do and why?"

Yinka narrowed her eyes at Kojo, scrutinising him. "I thought I recognised your face. You were at Silvio Mancini's boat party in Sardinia, right?"

"Yes, I was, but that is irrelevant. You need to start talking, Miss Saraki. Right now."

Timon could see that Yinka was not fond of being spoken to so bluntly. Despite the intensity of their group conversation, Timon grinned when he saw a flash of her stubbornness, that quietly fierce side to her that he secretly adored. Again, Timon shook his head in disbelief. *Are you serious right now? Get a grip*.

Timon nodded stiffly at Yinka. "Tell him everything."

Yinka pressed her lips together and gave Timon a solemn look. She nodded. "Okay, then."

For the next ten minutes, Yinka revealed new shocking revelations to Timon. All this time, Dugard had been the one who had engineered it so that Timon would take on Musa Jirongo as an investor in his hedge fund. It had also been Dugard, using his extensive network of hackers in Nigeria he had paid generously, to cause several security breaches in the crypto companies Timon had invested Musa's money into, creating the scenario where Timon would be in debt to Musa and so would have no choice but to accept Yinka's crypto consultant job offer. Even more outlandishly, Yinka's ex-boyfriend had faked his kidnapping to galvanise Yinka and her team to secure investment for Afchain, which was majority-owned by Dugard. In return, Dugard would let Oge get close enough to assassinate Mobolaji. And now, Yinka and her team were under armed house arrest on Lagos Island by Dugard's hired thugs and Yinka's ex-boyfriend as they planned Mobolaji's assassination at the African Tech Summit in five days.

"But why does your ex-boyfriend want to kill my father?" Timon said. His brain scrambled to process everything after Yinka finished her exhaustive explanation.

"Because your father murdered his mother," Yinka said.

Timon rubbed his forehead, now throbbing with this frenzy of bombshells. "Killed his mother? How can your ex-boyfriend be so sure my father did it?"

"Oge's mother, who was also my auntie, was killed by a letter bomb that was handed to Oge when he was just twelve years old, and it exploded when his mother opened it in front of him." Yinka let out a rueful sigh. "The man who had given Oge that package with the explosives inside wore nine golden rings with…"

"Black stones in each ring," Timon said, finishing Yinka's sentence in a faint voice as the distinct rings his father wore on his fingers flashed in his mind. He now felt lightheaded as the truly callous actions of his father began to sink in, especially now that he had started to grow fond of him slowly. How could he be the son of such a despicable man?

Yinka massaged her forehead. Timon could see that she, like him, was under a crushing weight of pressure. Suddenly, he wanted to comfort her, but he wasn't sure if he had forgiven her despite everything she had divulged.

"So Dugard is planning to have your ex-lover murder Mobolaji at their private meeting at the African Tech Summit, and Mobolaji is also planning to have Dugard murdered at that very same meeting," Kojo said, shaking his head at the lunacy of it all. He chuckled. "I can't see anyone taking notes in that meeting."

"I assume you have intelligence which confirms Mobolaji's plans to kill Dugard?" Yinka said, addressing Kojo directly.

"Smart woman," Kojo said, winking at Yinka. "I see why you like her, Top Boy."

Timon gave Kojo a side-eye. "What are you talking about, man?"

"Anyway," Kojo said, half chuckling, "This private meeting at the African Tech Summit could end up being quite the bloody mess. Literally."

"Exactly, so I should warn my father despite what he's done," Timon said, staring at Kojo. "I should tell him to call off the private meeting with Dugard at the summit since his life is in danger now."

Kojo glared at Timon. "You will do no such thing, understand? That meeting must go ahead because Mobolaji, Dugard and the other members of The Cable will be present. They will incriminate themselves when they confront Dugard about Afchain. And you," Kojo dabbed his finger at Timon, "will need to be in that meeting and wearing that mini recording camera to capture everything. With that footage, MI6 can bring down Dugard and this whole international money laundering network led by your father."

"But knowing what we know now, my life will be in danger if I attend that meeting," Timon said, raising his voice as he took one step towards Kojo, ignoring the man's size and his lethal skillset. "I am going to be in a room where two people are going to try and kill each other. I am like a rabbit in the middle of wolves." Timon grimaced at Kojo. "Doesn't my life mean nothing to you? Aren't you supposed to look out for my wellbeing? Or is your mission everything, and I am just…just collateral damage?"

"Don't be so overdramatic, Top Boy," Kojo said, grinning at a fuming Timon. "MI6 has a duty of care to protect its spies. As your handler, I will do exactly that. With this new information that Miss Saraki has provided, I can convince the Nigerian State Security Service to provide me with trained officers who will swarm into the meeting before the situation escalates. You just need to wear that mini camera when you're in there." Kojo narrowed his eyes at Timon. "And from the sounds of it, you still haven't convinced your father to invite you to that meeting. What's taking so long?"

Timon walked away from Kojo, ignoring him, and sighed stressfully as he stood facing the beachfront. From behind him, he heard Kojo address Yinka.

"I am curious. Why did you give us this information? Why put yourself at greater risk?"

Upon hearing the question, Timon turned to face Yinka, intrigued to hear her response.

"Because it's the right thing to do," Yinka said after a moment of silence. "Mobolaji is a vile man who deserves to be punished for his crimes, but I don't condone murder. It's not what me or my team do. We steal, not kill." Yinka turned away from Kojo and looked at Timon, her eyes slightly watery. "And also...I owe you, Timon. I put your life in danger, and I am sorry about that. This is me trying to make amends to you."

Admittedly, Yinka's words had touched Timon, but her deception was still lodged in his heart, and he still couldn't trust or forgive her completely.

Kojo stepped towards Yinka. "Right now, you're inside Dugard's inner circle?"

Yinka nodded. "That's correct, Mr super agent."

Kojo chuckled. "Very funny. From what I understand, you and your people are fighting against corruption in Nigeria. Well, now you're in a position to bring down both Dugard and Mobolaji, who are using Nigeria as a dumping ground for criminalised money from around the world. Do you want to fight corruption? Then help me bring down Mobolaji's organisation."

"What do you want me to do?"

"I'll give you my number, and you can message me when it is convenient, of course, about anything Dugard is planning. On the day of the African Tech Summit, when you can, you'll inform me of any significant developments in Dugard's operation to assassinate Mobolaji."

"I'll do my best. By the way, Dugard will be arriving in Lagos tomorrow."

"Well, that's good to know." Kojo smiled at Yinka. "See, you're being useful already."

Yinka pulled out her phone as Kojo gave her his number. Timon watched Yinka save his contact details.

"So what will you tell Dugard and your ex-boyfriend?" Kojo said, speaking to Yinka. "I assume they know you've met with Timon, or you wouldn't be here."

Yinka shrugged her shoulders. "I'll think of something. I've spent the last nine years lying and stealing for a living. I know how to lie when I need to."

"Alright, well, I am going to leave you two now as I have a crucial meeting in Abuja tomorrow afternoon, so I have a flight to catch." Kojo turned his head to Timon. "Remember your objective, Top Boy. You have to be in that meeting."

Timon and Yinka watched as Kojo treaded away from them and crossed the beach, heading back to the club. Soon, he became a mere speck consumed by the twinkling lights from the buildings across the seafront.

Turning his attention away from Kojo, Timon levelled his eyes on Yinka. She looked stunning this evening, and his eyes could not peel away from her even if he tried, despite the conflicting emotions wrestling inside of him.

"Looks like we've both been played, huh," Timon chuckled.

Yinka smirked bashfully. "Even us super smart Nigerians fall for tricks once in a while. No one is perfect." She gave Timon those soft and warm eyes again. "But I didn't play you, Timon. Not this time."

"But you didn't tell me the whole truth either. You let me believe you were recruiting me solely for my crypto expertise when you knew I needed the money. You hid your true motives for seeking investment into Afchain from me."

"That's true; I won't deny any of that," Yinka said, nodding with remorse. "And I am sorry I wasn't completely honest with you. I deceived you only because I thought my ex-boyfriend's life was in danger, but it never was. He played me for a fool, too."

"But now your ex-boyfriend wants to kill my father. And with good reason, to be honest. So, whose side are you on, Yinka? My side or his? Or will you deceive me again? By your admission, you're a professional liar. You've been doing it long enough."

To Timon's surprise, Yinka stepped forward, placed her right hand behind Timon's head, pulled him towards her and connected with his lips.

The kiss was even more explosive than the one in Dubai, and Timon felt a wave of euphoric pleasure surge through him. Ravenously, Timon pulled Yinka into him by her waist and kissed her deeply and longingly, stroking her braids, then gripping her thighs and feeling her breasts press against his chest. The kiss carried a convincing power that melted Timon's coldness towards Yinka. Never had he desired a woman as much as he yearned for Yinka at this moment, their lips and bodies entwined.

Before their very physical display of affection escalated into tearing each other's clothes off and having sex right on the beach, which would have been inappropriate - no matter how much they both wanted it and needed it - Yinka pulled away from Timon. He was now breathless as he licked his lips, feeling like he had just awakened from a blissful dream.

Yinka stared deeply into Timon's eyes. "I've spent almost a decade deceiving people and allowing myself to be a sexual pet for a man I loved. I have used my body to blackmail, embezzle and steal money. All for him. But now I am making my own choices influenced by no one but myself and my truth." Yinka took Timon's hands into her own. "I am choosing you, Timon. Not because I have to. But because I want to. This is my truth."

Timon searched Yinka's dark eyes. Although a part of his brain was telling him to distrust her words, disregard her sweet voice and dispel his fondness for her, he could also hear what his heart was screaming at him. It was loud. He decided to listen to it.

"And I am choosing to forgive you, Yinka. Not because I have to. But because I want to. That is my truth."

Yinka stole another quick kiss. Timon wished it hadn't been so brief.

"I need to go now, Timon. I don't know when I'll see you again, but everything will be alright. Somehow."

"I am not religious, but I pray you're right."

Yinka chuckled. "Neither am I, but I'll be praying too. Two non-religious people praying has to be very powerful."

"Yeah, definitely," Timon said with a quiet laugh.

Yinka let go of Timon's hands, gave him a sad smile and walked away.

For a while, Timon just watched as Yinka trekked up the beach. Life was funny. At school, he had bullied Yinka due to his immaturity and insecurity. Yet, against all odds, he had fallen deeply in love with her years later and under the most unexpected circumstances. Even the way she walked now, striding ahead with her head high and handbag at her side, and despite the gravity of the situation they were both in, she was still more determined and ferocious than any woman he had ever known.

So long as Yinka was on his side, Timon knew he would get through this ordeal. Maybe, and he was praying to God now, there was even a future for them. One with four kids, a big house, and Yinka's school for girls. A beautiful and honest life. And all this mess with a dodgy crypto startup, international money laundering operations, spies, assassinations, and a vengeful ex-boyfriend would be a distant memory.

67

"So Musa Jirongo was gunned down by a government agent?" Oge said. He stood before Yinka in the marble living room of Dugard's rented apartment in Lekki Phase 1.

Fifteen hours had passed since Yinka had been with Timon and the MI6 agent at Landmark Beach. It was now 11 am the following day, and Yinka was providing an update on her rendezvous with Timon to Oge, Bobby, and Dugard, who had arrived in Lagos three hours ago. She was mixing fact with fiction to create the most believable lie.

Yinka nodded at Oge. "Timon told me that Musa had violently arrived at his flat, with the intended aim to have him killed for not delivering the full payment he owed him, but Musa had was gunned down by some UK national security agent who had been spying on Musa as soon as he entered the UK." Yinka kept her tone of voice even and relaxed.

"Let's say I even buy that explanation of Musa's untimely demise; why exactly has Timon come to Nigeria?" Dugard said. He was sitting on a black leather sofa, dressed in one of his spiffy three-piece suits, and had his legs crossed. He was eating an apple and had his crystal blue eyes levelled at Yinka the whole time.

"He wanted to get away from the ordeal he experienced in London," Yinka said, speaking to Dugard directly as Oge and Bobby stood some feet before her. "From what little he would share with me, after the events in London, he decided to come to Lagos to relax and reached out to his father."

"And how did you convince him to tell you all this?" Dugard said. He took another bite of his apple, crunching loudly as his eyes never strayed from Yinka's face. "Surely, he would feel betrayed by you?"

"I told him the rest of the money I intended to give him as part of our deal never came into my account and that I was tricked. I put on some fake tears. He bought it."

Dugard pressed his lips together and hummed. He took another bite of his apple and chewed loudly before swallowing. "You know, I observed your interactions very closely during our trips around the world when you two were securing investment for Afchain. I could tell you two had grown particularly *close*."

Yinka could feel Oge's eyes on her as she frowned at Dugard, but she kept calm. "We established a strong working relationship, yes. We had to. You and Oge made it mandatory to recruit him as our crypto specialist. He wouldn't have been my first choice. Or second."

Dugard twisted his lips into a sneer. "How can we be so sure, Yinka, that your working relationship with him has not evolved into something more… *intimate*?"

Yinka sucked her teeth loudly and turned to face Oge. He had a passive look, but his eyes glinted with a slight scepticism. "Do you believe what I am saying? I have no loyalties to Mobolaji's son. I barely know him."

Oge did not regard Yinka but stared at Dugard, who smiled mockingly at them both.

As the tension in the room heightened and Yinka felt the

beginnings of nervousness, Oge relented with a sigh. "I trust her, Dugard. Okay."

"Very well, she's your girlfriend, of course," Dugard said. He took a final bite of his apple, left the chewed and disfigured remnants on the armchair, and stood up. "But word of advice, young man, I wouldn't always put my faith in a woman's loyalty. Take it from me. I was divorced three times. A woman will confess her love to you and sign your death warrant the next day, especially the beautiful ones."

"I am praying a bird shits on your suit," Yinka said, scowling at Dugard.

"Anyway, how far are we coming along?" Oge said, ignoring Yinka and Dugard's squabble. He turned to face Yinka. "Is all we need in place?"

Yinka nodded. "Pretty much. The team has procured a Lagos State police uniform and the fake police ID I'll be using. Joshua has just purchased the tactical earplugs we will all be wearing to communicate with each other, and we finally have a getaway van. It should fit all of us, even that ogre standing over there and his ugly friends." Yinka smirked contemptuously at Bobby.

The English mercenary sniggered, his massive arms folded across his chest. "Shit, will anything nice about me ever come out of your mouth?"

"We've also managed to get hold of two Berettas from some of the Lagos area boys I know," Yinka continued, ignoring Bobby. "Montana and Jaali have planned the best escape route from the venue, and Joshua and Kisi will be monitoring the event from their laptops inside the getaway van. Joshua has access to cameras strategically placed within the venue by one of the event organisers we bribed."

"Most impressive," Dugard said, nodding curtly at Yinka. He then turned to Oge. "You weren't exaggerating when you first told me your team is world-class professionals at this."

"We'll meticulously go over the logistics again today," Oge

said, speaking directly to Yinka and Bobby. "Armed security will be present at the event, so we'll need to enter the theatre undetected, locate and enter the meeting room, assassinate Mobolaji, and get out quickly and smoothly. I want to avoid any armed conflict with security or police."

"I'll leave all that to you," Dugard said, who had stood from the sofa and began to leave the room with Bobby following behind. He reached the doorway, stopped and turned to speak to Oge. "I have given you the location where Mobolaji will be hosting the private meeting with our business associates and me. This is as close as I can get you to him and, more in your favour, Mobolagi won't have his personal security with him. The rest is now on you, so consider my side of our bargain honoured." With those final words, Dugard departed the living room with Booby.

Now, Yinka and Oge stood alone in the living room. The silence between them hung heavy and loud in the air. Yinka looked at Oge. He dipped into one of the pockets in his combat trousers and pulled out a cigarette.

"So you're smoking whenever you want now?" Yinka said, giving him a weak smile. "I thought it was only after sex?"

Oge shrugged his shoulders. He placed the cigarette in his mouth and lit it with a transparent disposable lighter before pocketing it. "When Mobolaji is no longer breathing, then I'll quit smoking for good." Oge then gave her that boyish smile that had once sent tingles through her whole body. "That's a promise I will keep for you, Coffee Bean."

Yinka choked back tears in that moment. She suddenly felt the weight of her deception to Oge. Even though she no longer tethered her heart to his, she still cared for him deeply. They had too much history for her feelings to evaporate overnight. "Oge," Yinka said softly as she walked over to him. She touched his left shoulder and stroked it tenderly. "It's not too late to turn away from all this. Me, you, Monty, Jaali and

Johsua can sneak out of here tonight. We still care about you even after everything."

Oge took a long pull on his cigarette, blew a thin haze of smoke over Yinka's head and looked at her with cold eyes. "You know I don't do things halfway, Coffee Bean. I am seeing this through to the end. Mobolaji will be dead in four days. And then my mother's spirit can finally rest knowing her son has avenged her."

Without saying another word to her, Oge walked away.

* * *

"Your British government is always sticking its Pinocchio nose in the affairs of its former African colonies," Colonel Mohammed Salisu said to Kojo in his harsh Nigerian accent as he sat on the brown sofa, legs crossed, in the office of the British High Commission in Abuja.

The Colonel wore green military regalia decorated with several medals and had a red military beret on his head. He had three vertical tribal marks on each of his cheeks. "And now you come here to Abuja with your big British balls, asking me to help you bring down one of the most powerful men in Nigeria. So I must ask you. Are you a brainless baboon?"

Three hours ago, Kojo had taken plane from the Murtala Muhammed International Airport in Lagos to the Nnamdi Azikiwe International Airport in Abuja. As soon as he arrived in Abuja - now the official capital of Nigeria and the country's political backbone - a government official collected him from the airport and drove him to the British High Commission building in Abuja's Central Business District.

The purpose of Kojo's visit was to meet with Colonel Mohammed Salisu, the 55-year-old Director-General of the State Security Service, Nigeria's equivalent to MI5, and Susanna Jenkins, a petite white English woman in her late forties with dark blonde hair and a full fringe who served as the British High Commissioner to Nigeria.

"Colonel, with all due respect, there is no need to say all that," Susanna said in her private school-educated English voice. "Britain and Nigeria are friends and close allies. Everything we do together is for the mutual benefit of our countries."

Colonel Mohammed Salisu was well respected among Nigeria's defence community. He had served as a high-ranking officer in the Nigerian Army for over two decades before taking up the most senior post in Nigeria's State Security Service, which he had maintained for a decade, surviving four Nigerian presidents to become the longest-serving Director-General of the State Security Service since its conception in 1986. Unfortunately for Kojo, such a track record meant the Colonel liked to puff his chest and possessed an ego the size of an air balloon.

Mohammed sniggered. "Spare me the rehearsed speech, Madame Jenkins. Your honourable friend here is proposing that I approve of an operation to arrest Mobolaji Bankole, one of the most well-connected men in Nigeria, and Sir Richard Dugard, who, I might add, once served as the British Higher Commissioner himself and won much favour with Nigeria's elite. The president will not approve an operation to arrest them on Nigerian soil."

"So even though I've told you, with proven intelligence, that Bankole and Dugard are both involved in an international money laundering network which funnels criminalised money into Nigeria's economy, you will stand back and do absolutely nothing?" Kojo was disgusted by the spineless behaviour of many of Nigeria's security agencies. They were unwilling to act against crime or corruption if it went against their own self-interests because many of its high-ranking personnel were complicit in it themselves. But Kojo had expected this. He still had his ace up his sleeve.

SECURE THE BAG | NOT THE HEART

"Unfortunately, Mr Owusu-Harrington, these are the cards I have been dealt," Mohammed said, leaning back on the sofa. His dark pink lips stretched in a self-serving grin. "In Nigeria, one does not bite the hand that feeds them until that hand stops bringing the right portion of food."

Susanna shook her head and looked up at Kojo with a deflated face, unsure what to do next.

Kojo nodded and smiled at Mohammed. "But what if you led an operation instead to save Bankole's life and apprehend the leader of the Robin Hoods?"

Mohammed jolted up on the sofa. He leaned forward, his eyes levelled on Mobolaji. "What are you babbling about?"

"I currently have two valuable spies on the ground. One is very close to Mobolaji, and the other is close to Dugard. I've learnt from the asset closest to Dugard that he is working with the man who has led a series of blackmailing campaigns against many Nigerian politicians and elites. The leader of 'The Robin Hoods' as your media has dubbed them."

"And why would Dugard and the leader of the Robin Hoods be working together?"

"Because the leader of the Robin Hoods intends to assassinate Mobolaji Bankole at the African Tech Summit at a private meeting between Bankole, Dugard and their business associates. He believes Mobolaji was responsible for his mother's death. Why else do you think every member of the Bankole family has fallen foul of this group? The killing of the family patriarch is the endgame. As for Dugard, he has some business grudge against Mobolaji, so he wants him out of the picture."

Mohammed leaned back on the sofa, shaking his head in shock. "Well, that is quite something," he said, nodding. "Quite something, indeed."

Kojo knew he had him now and continued. "Imagine if Dugard and the leader of the Robin Hoods succeed in assassinating Bankole. I gave you the intelligence to stop it, but you did not act. If this was to be made public, how would that look on your celebrated record, Colonel?"

Mohammed launched from the sofa and squared up to Kojo. The Colonel was two inches smaller than Kojo, but he was equally broad-shouldered and carried a good amount of muscle himself. "You slimy bastard," Mohammed said, his lips curved into a twisted smile. "You Ghanaians have always been sneaky."

Kojo smiled back at Mohammed, holding his gaze. "I was not raised in Ghana or by a Ghanaian family. But my birth mother and father were Ghanaian, so I suppose you're right. I am sneaky."

"Colonel, I would take this new intelligence very seriously," Susanna said. Mohammed turned away from Kojo to look at her. "If you stop Mobolaji Bankole from being murdered and apprehend the leader of the Robin Hoods, it will reflect very well on you."

Mohammed turned back to look at Kojo. "And your intelligence is indisputable?"

Kojo nodded. "As solid as chopped yam."

"So then why should I not contact Mobolaji Bankole right now and inform him that his life is in danger and he should cancel the meeting at the African Tech Summit?"

"You can do that, but then you wouldn't capture the leader of the Robin Hoods. I am offering you two trophies here, Colonel. Are you only going to settle for one?"

Mohammed chuckled and shook his head. "Okay, fine, you've managed to sway me. I will still need to get clearance from the President but I should be able to have a group of armed agents present at the African Tech Summit. However, the aim is to protect Mobolaji Bankole and apprehend the leader of the Robin Hoods. Your British government can do whatever it wants with Dugard."

"That works for me," Kojo said, looking at Susanna and giving her a wink before turning back to Mohammed. "But you'll have to let me lead most of the operation, Colonel. It's going to be a very tense and delicate situation in that meeting. If your men make the wrong move, the operation can implode in our faces."

"If that is how you want it, then fine," Mohammed said, giving Kojo a cold stare. "But your intelligence better hold up, and there should be no surprises. I want my trophies."

68

THE MURKY AND still waters of the Lagos lagoon reflected the sombre greyness of the sky as Timon stood facing forward at the bow cockpit of his father's high-performance cabin cruiser.

Looking into the peninsula, he saw great white pelicans and smaller birds gliding on the horizon. Although the cabin cruiser was some way out into the lagoon, Timon could still see, if he squinted, the sandy Landmark Beach where he had reunited with Yinka the previous night. As she entered his thoughts, he felt that insatiable desire to physically be with her tighten around him like a warm blanket on a freezing night. As troubled as his mind was, thoughts of Yinka had found a space in his head, bringing some peace to his stressed mind like a scented candle.

Yet, not even thoughts of Yinka could soothe what she had told him about his father. Mobolaji had murdered someone's mother. Since learning of this terrible act, Timon had avoided his father at the Bankole Palace, opting to stay in his room as he wrestled with the truth of his father's homicidal nature. But he had been unable to avoid his father for so long.

Earlier this morning, Mobolaji unexpectedly visited Timon

while he lay in bed. Dressed casually in a navy Hugo Boss T-shirt and white trousers, Mobolaji had come into Timon's room and asked him to join him on his cabin cruiser. It would be just the two of them. Although something had felt off about his father's request, Timon had agreed because he had no reason to refuse.

But Timon's suspicions were confirmed when he arrived on the white and sleek cabin cruiser to see his father's two most trusted security guards, Ibrahim and Samuel, armed with rifles, patrolling the boat's starboard. Although his father had told him not to worry, knowing now that his father was capable of murder, his words provided no comfort to Timon.

Now, the cabin cruiser had sailed quite a considerable distance from the Lagos mainland and floated in the lagoon with its engine turned off.

"So, how are you finding your first time in Nigeria, my son?" Mobolaji said, snapping Timon out of his thoughts as his father approached him, supporting himself with his black cane with the golden lion head.

Dressed in a black dashiki outfit, Timon turned away from the mass of water and looked at his father. His eyes went to the golden rings on his father's fingers with their black, embedded gems. Timon then looked at his father, hoping his voice would not betray his nervousness. "It's been enjoyable so far, Dad. Eniola showed me a good time last night at the club."

Mobolaji chuckled as he nodded. "I am not surprised. My daughter is the self-proclaimed party queen of Lagos. She enjoys her father's wealth but makes her own money too. She is the Lagos Kim Kardashian, as she often tells me."

Timon let out an uneasy chuckle. He briefly looked over his father's head. Ibrahim and Samuel stood at the stern of the boat, their rifles slung over their shoulders. Although Timon had no way of truly knowing, he strongly suspected those weapons weren't on display as an intimidating deterrent. They were loaded.

After a moment of silence, Mobolaji spoke again. "Did you meet anyone last night at the beach?" His father's voice was relaxed, but Timon detected the quiver of menace crawling underneath it.

"Why do you ask?" Timon said. A droplet of sweat fell on the side of his head. Despite Nigeria always being hot, Timon suddenly felt even more heated.

"I will be completely transparent with you, my son. My wife does not trust you, you see," Mobolaji said. He was no longer facing Timon but looking out into the dreary lagoon. "She thinks your sudden arrival and reaching out to me, given our prolonged estrangement, is suspicious. She believes you have an ulterior motive for being here in Lagos. My wife is a sharp woman, but she is still a woman, so she's naturally suspicious, as women can sometimes be, irrationally or otherwise. But, as a smart husband should, I should still investigate her suspicions."

"You don't trust me?" Timon said. He glanced nervously at the armed guards and then looked back at his father, who was still facing the mass of water and not looking at him.

"You haven't answered my question, *Timon*," Mobolaji said, calling Timon by his name for the first time since Timon had been with him in Lagos. It sent a tingle of fear down Timon's spine. "Did you meet anyone last night on the beach?"

It was clear that somehow, his father knew he had left the Truth Beach Club yesterday to meet with people on Landmark Beach. But how much more did he know? There was no way of knowing, but Timon knew that his life now rested on him playing this right. He needed to craft the perfect lie—and quickly.

"I met with my two business partners: the one I mentioned previously who is visiting Lagos from England, and the woman who was with me in Dubai, Yinka Saraki. The consultant for Afchain." Timon kept his voice as even as possible. "I was updating them about me and you. Your wife is not wrong; I contacted you for a reason. As you know, in Dubai, Yinka and I acted on behalf of Afchain to secure investment. But it turned out Dugard owned a majority stake in Afchain, which he never disclosed. My business partners and I were never reimbursed for our efforts and have been unable to contact Dugard. He no longer answers my calls or my emails."

Timon let out a sigh, feigning regret. "So I travelled to Lagos to reach out to you and spend some time with you in the hope that, after I had asked, you would be able to put me in contact with Dugard so I could confront him as to why he has not paid me or business partners for successfully securing the investment and why he withheld the fact that he has a majority stake in Afchain. I apologise for not being completely honest from the start."

Mobolaji nodded slowly, and he had a thoughtful expression on his long and droopy face. Timon could feel more and more droplets of sweat run down his forehead as the deathly silence stretched. He was on a boat with two armed men. If he wanted to kill him now and throw his bullet-riddled body overboard, his father could do it. Nobody would be none the wiser—a perfect murder.

"Thank you for your honesty, my son," Mobolaji finally said, sending a wave of relief through Timon. "When Eniola told me she had seen you speaking with two people on Landmark Beach yesterday night, plus my wife's suspicions, you understand why I had to confront you in this manner." Mobolaji then turned his head to face Timon. His dark eyes were a void of blackness. "I have many enemies in Nigeria, my son. So I must always question everyone near me, even those I call family."

Timon nodded. "I understand, Dad. As someone who has

also built considerable wealth, I can never be too trusting of everyone around me. Wealth brings false smiles."

Mobolaji grinned knowingly and nodded. "It seems like we are both dealing with an English rat. Dugard has lied to me as well, you know, as well to the investors you secured investment from, about his ties to Afchain. My father always told me: 'The mouth of a liar does not bleed.' When dealing with Westerners, especially the English, one must always have a degree of healthy scepticism, my son."

Mobolaji looked away from Timon to face the lagoon again. "If I told you that I built all my vast wealth by investing the money of many of Nigeria's most powerful and corrupt for profitable returns, what would you think of me?"

Upon hearing this, Timon again realised how similar he was to his father. And he hated himself for it. They shared the same craving for money and status and would do almost anything to have both. But Timon would never go as far as directly killing another human being. His mother raised him better than that.

"I invest the money from high net worth people into valuable crypto assets," Timon said, staring out into the waters. "Some of them have done terrible things to obtain their wealth, but you told me, Dad, you don't pray for money to come to you; you go and find it. And when you do, you grow it to make wealth for yourself. Where money comes from is not important; it is what you do with it that matters." Timon knew he no longer believed in that, but he would say what he had to do to secure his father's trust.

Mobolaji chuckled. "Some would say we behave like typical, corrupt Nigerians. But corruption is not unique to Nigeria or Africa like the bias Western media will have the world believe. Everywhere in the developed world, if there is a way to make a lot of money, people will exploit it. And if there is a way to hold on to a lot of money, the elite will exploit it. And how do the elite do this? With corruption. When power and money share the same bed, they will always give birth to corruption. Not just in Nigeria. Not just in Africa. In all nations of this world. The simple truth is money is the universal language of the corrupt. The root of all evil." Mobolaji curved his lips into a small but wicked smile. "For some, money is even the language of their heart."

Mobolaji turned away from the lagoon, gave Timon a warm smile and placed his right hand on Timon's shoulders. "Thank you for being honest with me, my son. We will deal with Dugard's treachery together. Are you aware of the African Technology Summit in Lagos four days from now?"

Timon shook his head. "No, I wasn't aware," he lied.

"It is the biggest technology conference held annually across different African countries, and this is the first year Nigeria has hosted the event. I am sponsoring it through my various businesses. Dugard and a few associates of mine, who you've met already, will be attending the summit and we have scheduled a private meeting with Dugard to confront him about his stake in Afchain, which he hid from us. I would like you to join me in that meeting so you can also air your grievances with him."

Timon placed his left hand on the hand his father rested on his shoulder. "Thank you, Dad. I appreciate that."

Mobolaji gave Timon a heartfelt smile and beamed with pride. Despite knowing what his father was capable of, Timon would be lying if he said he did not feel a little fond of his father now.

"Of all my children, I am most proud of you. You know why?"

"No, why?"

"Because you're a true self-made man. Raised only by your mother, you went to Cambridge, built your hedge fund and obtained wealth without my help. My other children, dear to my heart as they are, have been handed everything to them because they carry my last name. But you, you do not have my last name, but you are more like me than any of my other children. You are my true heir, son. And I love you."

Timon could not stop the involuntary tears from sliding down his eyes. Hearing his father validate him for the first time, acknowledge his accomplishments, and tell him he loved him moved him dearly. Yet Timon was also actively lying to his father's face. For a moment, Timon considered warning his father about Dugard's plot to assassinate him at the African Tech Summit meeting, but he decided against it.

"I love you too, Dad."

Mobolaji squeezed Timon's shoulder and smiled. "Let us return to the house, my son. The chefs are cooking ikokore and fried snails with pepper sauce. It is some of Nigeria's finest and most expensive delicacies—the food of the wealthy."

69

Hundreds of attendees worldwide poured into the National Theatre, Nigeria, for the three-day African Tech Summit. The white concrete theatre resembled a football stadium, with a curved, dome-shaped structure that evoked the shape of a military hat, fitting as the landmark came into existence in 1976, constructed during the military regime of Olusegun Obasanjo.

The National Theatre, Nigeria, covered around 23,000 square metres of grassland and stood tall at 31 metres. The main hall could seat 5,000 people, with a state-of-the-art banquet hall which could fit 1,500. There were two exhibition halls, two cinema halls, a marquee, a VIP lounge and even a roof garden. The facilities were fully air-conditioned with reliable sound systems and interactive video conference call capabilities. As one of Nigeria's most prominent cultural landmarks, the government paraded the venue as a beacon for celebrating the rich arts and culture of the nation - making it the perfect venue for the first African Technology Summit in Nigeria.

Over 2,000 tickets had been sold for the event, attracting leading venture capitalists, superstar investors from Silicon

Valley and global players in the world of technology to the heart of West Africa. Across three days, the summit would feature dozens of keynotes from well-known tech founders and entrepreneurs and over one hundred booths, from fintech companies to virtual reality startups, all promising to transform Africa with the infinite possibilities of technology.

Yinka stood by the corner of the main hall. She was dressed in the uniform of the Lagos State police—a blue shirt, black trousers, and a black beret on her head. With her fake ID and police garb, it had been relatively easy for Yinka to walk straight into the theatre without resistance. Now, she surveyed the busy hall.

Hundreds of men and women congregated around the hundred or so booths set up across the exhibition hall. Some guests wore traditional agbada and dashikis, but others opted for more European-styled suits, shirts, blouses, blazers, and pencil skirts. A massive Microsoft stand was in the middle of the hall, with a 3D display of the African continent projected onto the roof.

While the atmosphere evoked the sense that attendees were glimpsing the futuristic Nigeria of tomorrow, Yinka focused on keeping her eyes out for Mobolaji, Dugard and Timon. Her sultry kiss with Timon on Landmark Beach still tingled on her lips and tongue. She shook her head. *Remain focused.*

A tactical earplug was slotted into Yinka's left ear, enabling her to communicate with Oge, the rest of the team and Dugard's mercenaries via a radio frequency set up by Joshua from the black getaway van parked a mile away from the theatre. Presently, they were all inside the truck. The Robin Hoods were monitoring live footage of the venue from three laptops. Now, Yinka could hear the radio earpiece cackle in her ears.

"Hey, Yinks, Jaali here," came Jaali's voice from the earpiece. "You good?"

"I am good, Jaali," Yinka said quietly, turning away from the passing guests and the other police officers so they wouldn't notice her speaking. "Is there any visual on Dugard?"

"Yeah, he just entered the venue and is going to the auditorum on the second floor where Mobolaji is watching a keynote. Make your way there in about fifteen minutes."

"Got it."

"Coffee Bean," came Oge's voice from the earpiece. "Remember, as soon as Dugard has met with Mobolaji and the others, and they start making their way to the meeting room, you'll need to hurry to the utility room on the basement floor and open the fire door exit where the fire door alarm is disabled. As you're dressed as a police officer, no one should question you."

"I know, and I am clear on everything. We've gone over the plan numerous times."

"I know. You got this."

Yinka sighed, emotionally distraught that Oge still casually called her by the nickname he had given her when they were lovers, without knowing she no longer felt the same way about him. She massaged her forehead, rubbing away any intrusive and unhelpful thoughts so she could focus on what she needed to do. At some point, she would also need to message the MI6 officer to let him know when Oge and the English mercenaries had entered the building. So much was at stake. Yinka had been in many tense situations before, but this particular mission ramped up her anxiety and stress levels to critical levels. Seducing men was one thing, but executing an assassination was a whole different kettle of fish.

Now walking briskly through the crowd of delegates who marvelled at the holographic display of Africa on the ceiling, Yinka made her way to the elevator to take her to the second floor. As she got to the lift and pressed a button on the elevator's control panel, she turned to her right. Her eyes widened in surprise.

Emiko Shinoda, dressed in a black and gold kente print blouse, which suited her, was heading towards her. She was conversing with a Nigerian man in a blue agbada and wearing a black fila cap. Behind her was her brother, Jin, dressed in a pink dashiki, who was speaking to a pretty Nigerian woman and laughing. Recalling the instant connection she had shared with Emiko back in Tokyo, a strong urge to protect the young Japanese woman came over her.

As Emiko came into proximity, Yinka turned away from the lift and tapped Emiko on the shoulder as she walked past. Emiko and the older Nigerian man she had been speaking to stopped. Her brother and the lady had walked on for a few seconds longer before looking back and stopping, eyebrows raised in confusion as to why Emiko had suddenly stopped walking.

"Is there a problem?" Emiko said, giving Yinka a bemused stare.

Yinka leaned her head forward and murmured into Emiko's ear. "It's me, Yinka. You're in danger. We need to talk discreetly."

Emiko pulled back, but tactfully, she displayed no shock at what Yinka had just told her. Calmly, she turned to the Nigerian man, her brother, and the young Nigerian lady he was with. "I am going to talk to this police officer quickly, so please go to the cinema hall without me. I'll find you."

"Is everything okay, Emiko?" Jin said, looking at Yinka's face and narrowing his eyes suspiciously.

"Everything is fine, Jin. Follow Esther and Mr Ojukwu, okay."

After Emiko's company had departed, she quietly followed Yinka down through the hall until they reached the women's toilets and entered it together. Luckily, the white stone lavatory was empty. They stood by one of the cubicles, facing each other.

"Yinka, this is quite the surprise," Emiko said, shaking her head as she looked at Yinka with a tender familiarity as if reunited with an old friend. "Why are you dressed as a police officer?"

"Emiko, I don't have much time to explain everything," Yinka said, ignoring her pounding heart. "But there will be an attempt at Mobolaji Bankole's life at the meeting he has organised with you, Dugard, and the others. It's all part of Dugard's plan."

"What?" Emiko said, her jaw dropping in shock. "But Mobolaji is also planning to have…"

"Dugard killed after the meeting, I know." Yinka put her hands on Emiko's shoulders. "Look, MI6 are monitoring you and the rest of your business associates. They know you're all part of Mobolaji's international money laundering network that funnels criminals' funds into the UK and your respective countries. If you attend that meeting, you'll be potentially incriminating yourself or, worse, seriously harmed."

Emiko pressed her lips together and mused at Yinka. "If you know I am a criminal like the others then why are you helping me?"

"Because you tried to warn me, Emiko. I know you don't want to do this, but you do it because of your father's legacy. But it doesn't have to be your path for the rest of your life. We women can change our paths. We don't need to follow men's beliefs. Look, I have lived a dishonest life, too, Emiko. I've been a thief and a liar for almost ten years, and I lived that way for a man I loved. But not anymore. I am choosing a new way to live my life as a woman and giving you a chance to change your path, too. Woman to woman."

For a moment, Emiko stood facing Yinka, her eyes contemplative as she looked at the stone floor. Her small lips curved into a smile, and she looked up at Yinka. "Thank you,

Yinka, for warning me. I won't attend the meeting. But what about you?"

"I have to be in that meeting to stop my ex-boyfriend and Dugard from assassinating Mobolaji," Yinka said.

Emiko raised her eyebrows. "Your ex-boyfriend?"

"It's all too lengthy to explain, but you should leave soon, Emiko."

"Okay," Emiko said, nodding. "But whatever you plan on doing, be careful, Yinka."

70

ALTHOUGH TIMON HAD BEEN on edge since arriving at the African Tech Summit, continuously looking at the small, microscopic camera he had pinned on the collar of his gold-coloured dashiki to ensure it had not fallen off; he still managed to be impressed by just how well organised the event was.

Contrary to what some might expect about a tech conference in Nigeria, the summit looked and felt as grandiloquent and awe-inspiring as any of the dozens of glitzy tech events Timon had attended worldwide. Unfortunately, given his circumstances, Timon could not take it all in. After all, he was in the middle of a dangerous mission.

Fifteen minutes ago, Mobolaji, dressed in a glorious golden agbada three-piece suit with a matching fila hat, had re-introduced Timon to Mancini, Mustafa and Dugard. Everyone's handshakes and smiles were nothing but pure performances. Despite conspiring to have one another killed, Mobolaji and Dugard had even embraced, giving each other a friendly pat on the back.

"How is Yinka?" Mancini said after releasing his tight grip on Timon's right hand. "I still think of that rich, dark and arresting beauty she possesses. She is a woman of astounding talents."

When Timon noticed Mancini licking his teeth, his light brown eyes glinting with something sinister, he had to restrain himself, or he would have broken Mancini's Botox jaw immediately. Instead, through clenched teeth, he had said, "She's doing fine. Should I see her again, I'll tell her you send your regards."

"It is so wonderful to see you again, Timon," Dugard said, extending his right hand. "And much sooner than I would have expected. But at least you're in good health."

Now privy to Dugard's machinations to have him killed by Musa Jirongo, Timon shook the English aristocrat's hand with a deliberately aggressive grip. He smiled satisfyingly as Dugard winced in pain and withdrew his hand, glaring at Timon.

With the re-introductions over, Timon took a seat beside his father in the dome-shaped auditorium. Dugard, Mancini, and Mustafa sat in the same row with them. A young Nigerian man in his early twenties gave a spirited thirty-minute presentation about a future Nigeria that would finally fulfil its potential on the international stage by investing in technology to unlock new industries and revenue streams for the country, which would lessen its dependence on oil. Timon desperately wanted to believe him.

While Timon watched the presentation, Mobolaji placed his hand on Timon's left shoulder and leaned towards him. "Nigeria will be in good hands if we continue to educate our youth. Hopefully, one day, we can even attract talented Nigerians in the diaspora, like yourself, to return home. There is much fruit to grow here, my son. We simply need to fertilise the soil."

After the presentation in the hall had concluded, everyone stood up from their chairs. Some followed the crowd, leaving the hall, while others stayed and conversed. Mobolaji, with

Timon by his side, was now facing Dugard, Mancini and Mustafa. "Gentleman, let us head to the meeting room upstairs. We have much to discuss."

Dugard nodded. "Yes, please. I am famished, though, I must say."

Mobolaji gave Dugard a tight smile. "Dugard, you and your undisciplined stomach. But don't fret, my English friend. We will have some salad and cold potatoes waiting for you after the meeting—the finest of English delicacies."

Mancini and Mustafa began to laugh at Dugard's expense, the latter now looking flustered as his face went bright pink. An older Nigerian man wearing a blue agbada came over to Mobolaji. He whispered something in his ear, and Timon saw his father grimace in annoyance.

"Unfortunately, Miss Shinoda will not be joining us," Mobolaji announced. "No worries. Gentlemen, let us proceed to the meeting room."

As Timon followed Mobolaji and the others out of the hall, he felt someone watching him. He turned to his left, and standing by one of the exits further down the hall was a dark-skinned female police officer wearing a beret hat low over her head. The officer's heart-shaped pink lips, almond-shaped eyes, and button nose gave away her identity. It was Yinka. Timon almost tripped as he stopped to stare at her, his heart pounding.

"My son, why have you stopped?" Mobolaji said, tapping Timon on the shoulder. "Are you okay? You look stunned."

Timon quickly regained his composure and smiled at his father. "I am fine, Dad. I thought I saw someone I knew."

When Timon looked back at the exit, Yinka was gone.

* * *

Inside one of the small meeting rooms at the National Theatre, Nigeria, stood an elite security squad on standby, awaiting orders. These men were the best-armed officers Nigeria's State Security Service had to offer. All of them were wearing black tactical gear from head to toe, with the letters 'DSS' printed on their bullet-proof vests and helmets. Some wore balaclavas, enhancing their deadly mystique. The soldiers gripped IWI Tavour assault rifles as they paced around the room with itchy trigger fingers.

Kojo, also dressed in tactical gear, sat on a wooden chair beside Mohammed Salisu, who wore the same combat gear. While Kojo had no rifle, he had slotted his reliable Glock 19 handgun into a holster around his waist. Mohammed Salisu had slung his assault rifle over his right shoulder.

The atmosphere in the room was tense. Kojo could feel it. During his days in the British army, when he had waited behind enemy lines with his fellow soldiers, ready to storm a village to raid out insurgents in some Middle Eastern village in the mountains, he had experienced this same feeling of suffocating anticipation. But operations like this, with lives at stake, were successful when you did not let the adrenaline and pressure get to your head. One had to remain calm, collected and disciplined.

In front of Kojo and Mohammed, a laptop was perched on a wooden table. From the screen, they were watching live greyscale footage from the mini camera that Timon had attached to his collar.

Despite harbouring very little goodwill towards him, Kojo was grudgingly impressed by Timon's pertinacity and resourcefulness. He had managed to get a seat at Mobolaji's meeting, not letting the pressure and gravity of the mission get to him. He had proven himself a capable spy.

Kojo watched on the screen as Dugard, Mustafa, and Mancini sat around the long boat-shaped conference table. Dugard sat alone on the left while Mancini and Dugard sat three chairs apart on the right side of the table. Curiously, Kojo noticed that Emiko Shinoda was absent.

Due to the position where Timon had attached the microscopic camera, Kojo could not see Mobolaji. Still, it did not matter so long as the recording captured Mobolagi's voice during the meeting.

"How long will we sit here like lame ducks watching these men talk?" Mohammed said, looking at Kojo. "And I don't see any sign of the leader of the Robin Hoods or any threat in that room."

Kojo gave Mohammed a sidelong glance. "The meeting has just started. As I told you, Colonel, I have an asset within Dugard's circle who is helping the leader of the Robin Hoods organise the operation to assassinate Mobolaji. This asset will text me when the leader of the Robin Hoods and Dugard's mercenaries have entered the venue. But before we storm in, I need to get enough footage and recording of the meeting. That was our deal, if you recall?"

Mohammed sucked his teeth. "This is crazy, you know that?"

Kojo ignored him as he felt his phone vibrate. He took his phone out of one of the many pockets in his combat trousers and unlocked it. There was a message from Yinka:

They are inside.

71

As soon as Yinka saw Mobolaji, Timon, and the others leave the auditorium, she hurried out into the corridor with the other attendees. She felt a jolt of pleasure when she had seen Timon, who looked disarmingly handsome in that golden dashiki outfit. However, Yinka had no time to swoon over him. Now, she had to execute the second most crucial element of the operation.

Passing hurriedly through a crowd of people talking in the hallway, Yinka made her way to one of the elevators. As soon as she was in front of one, she pressed the button on the access control panel for the basement floor. About five people poured out of the elevator when the lift doors opened. Yinka nodded curtly to them as she stepped into the elevator. When the doors closed, she heard the cackle from the tactical earplug.

"What's your location, Coffee Bean?" Oge said. "Should we leave the van now and get into position?"

"Yes, leave now and quickly. I'll be in the basement in three minutes."

The lift reached the basement floor and opened to a dimly lit concrete corridor with a slight draft and a damp smell, like being in a storage room. Yinka stepped out of the lift. One of the venue staff, a young man in his early twenties, was pushing a wheelie bin as he made a beeline to the elevator. As soon he saw Yinka, the young man stopped pushing the wheelie bin.

"Are you supposed to be down here?" the young man said, his eyebrows raised at Yinka.

"You are talking to a police officer like that?" Yinka said firmly, scowling at the young man. She sucked her teeth loudly. "What is your name so I can report you immediately to your superior."

"Sorry, Ma," the boy now said, panic colouring his thin, dark-skinned face. "I don't know...I don't know what I was thinking..."

"Get out of my face. And make your way upstairs." Yinka narrowed her eyes menacingly at the boy.

"Yes, Ma. Sorry."

After the boy, with his head bowed, entered the elevator with the wheelie bin, and she heard the elevator doors close and began to ascend; she continued her brisk walk through the corridor. Anyone could come to the basement anytime, and she may not pull off her intimidation tactics again. Now, she sprinted through the concrete corridor, her footsteps echoing. As she made her way to the fire exit door, she lifted her finger to her right ear and pressed a button on the tactical earplug.

"Are they in position?" Yinka said, who was now a few feet away from the fire exit door.

Montanna's voice responded in her ear. "They're in position, Yinks. Be careful, please, and get back here as soon as this nasty business ends."

Once Yinka had reached the fire exit door, she stood before it. She dipped her hand into her left pocket, took out her smartphone and quickly found the MI6 agent's number. After sending him a short text, she put the phone back in her pocket and placed her hands against the panic bar. She pushed the fire exit door open.

As if they were about to engage in a raid, Oge, Bobby, and the two other English mercenaries stormed inside. All four men wore brown army tactical gear and black cashmere balaclavas. Bobby and the two mercenaries held rifles, but Oge held a silver Beretta 92 in his right hand. The four of them stood in front of Yinka. The three mercenaries kept turning their heads in every direction, and their twitchy energy gave Yinka the impression that they had just popped pills and downed them with cans of Red Bull.

Holding a black carrier bag in his left hand, Oge pulled out a black balaclava, precisely like the one he wore, and handed it to Yinka. She took it from him and immediately wore it over her face; it felt itchy. Oge then handed Yinka a black Beretta from the carrier bag. She felt the weight of the deadly weapon as soon as she took it from him.

"The gun is loaded already. You remember how to use a firearm, right?" Oge said, his voice slightly muffled through the balaclava. "It's been a while since I taught you how to shoot."

" I remember," Yinka said, speaking through the fabric of the balaclava.

"You don't have to be there when I do this, Coffee Bean. You can leave now if you want. I would understand."

"Like I told you, my love, I am with you to the end."

"Oi, you two, stop fucking doing romance," Bobby said, standing between the two other mercenaries with his rifle over his shoulder. "We gotta move it."

Oge nodded at Yinka and began to hurry down the corridor towards the elevator, Bobby and the two other mercenaries following suit. With the cold steel of the Beretta pressed against her palm as she gripped it, Yinka followed the men to the elevator.

* * *

Timon felt like his nerves would cause his heart to explode as he sat in the warm, bland-looking meeting room. The walls were faded white, a tall filing cabinet stood near the front of the room, and the air conditioning unit on the wall hummed loudly. As his father began to speak, Timon tried to stay relaxed. Kojo had said he would protect him. MI6 owed him a duty of care. But how much did Timon trust that? It did not matter now anyway, as Timon was already sitting in this deadly meeting. For now, at least, the meeting had not descended into a bloodbath.

"I will get straight to the purpose of this meeting," Mobolaji said, scanning the faces of the other three men in the room. "We're here to discuss you, Dugard. Or, more specifically, your duplicity."

Dugard widened his eyes, looking utterly bamboozled at Mobolaji's statement. The man was a good actor. He looked at both Mancini and Mustafa with a puzzled expression. They both stared back at him with blank faces. He then turned to Mobolaji. "I beg your pardon. How dare you speak to me in that way, Mobolaji."

"Will you continue insulting us with this pantomime, Richard?" Mustafa said, dressed in his white thawab robes and a chequered keffiyeh. "We know about your eighty per cent stake in Afchain that you purchased through one of your fictitious companies registered in the Cayman Islands."

Timon watched as Dugard leaned back in his chair, now looking oddly relaxed, even entertained. His straight lips had curved into a self-serving smile. "Well, you men have certainly been doing your due diligence. However, I was under the impression that our joint enterprise was built on a foundation of trust."

Mobolaji grimaced and sucked his teeth. His Nigerian

accent sounded deeper now, harsher. "How dare you talk of trust. Did you think you could invest in a Nigerian tech company under my nose, but I wouldn't find out? You knew we would not put our client's money behind another one of your investment proposals since your performance has been poor over the last few years. Your investments in our client's money have proven unprofitable. Knowing we have little faith in you, you go behind our backs. You even used my son," Mobolaji gestured to Timon, "to convince me and the others sitting around this table to invest in a company you practically own."

Dugard began to laugh. "What can I say, Mobolaji? I was desperate."

"You was foolish and overambitious as always," Mancini said, shaking his head at Dugard. "But this Afchain crypto company does show a lot of promise. Our clients' money can be funnelled through it, so for once, you may have been on to something. So, it's not a bad investment. Isn't that right, Timon?"

Timon, who was not expecting Mancini to address him, looked at the Italian banker and nodded stiffly. The tension was too heavy, and Timon could not trust himself enough to speak.

"We will continue to invest in Afchain and oversee its development as the platform readies its launch," Mustafa said, clasping his hands together.

"But you will not be at the helm of it, Dugard," Mobolaji said, narrowing his eyes at the English aristocrat. "You will willingly forfeit your shares in Afchain to us."

To the shock of everyone in the room, Dugard howled in laughter, his head rolling back in hysterics as he clutched his rubs. "Now that is rich, Mobolaji," Dugard said, wiping a non-existent tear from his left eye. He narrowed his eyes into slits. "Forfeit my shares, you say? And should I be non-compliant?"

Timon looked at his father. Mobolaji's lips had curved into

a sinister grin. "Then you'll be leaving Nigeria in a coffin, my dear friend."

"Threatening to kill an English aristocrat," Dugard said, shaking his head and mockingly waggling his left index figure at Mobolaji. "You've got even bolder in your old age, my friend. But hold that thought; I have a message on my phone."

Mobolaji raised his eyebrows and flared his nostrils. "Do you not understand the severity of the situation here?"

But Dugard was no longer paying attention to Mobolaji; he had pulled out his smartphone. Whatever he was reading on the screen pleased him because a wide, toothy smile formed on Dugard's face. He calmly placed his phone in his pocket, looked at Mobolaji and shook his head. "I think you're the one that will be ending up in a coffin, my old friend."

Mobolaji did not get the opportunity to swear bitterly at Dugard's insolence.

The door of the meeting room swung open.

Four men, dressed in mud-brown combat gear, black bala-clavas over their faces, and holding firearms, marched into the room. A woman, wearing a police uniform and balaclava over her face, also stepped inside with the armed men.

Mustafa instantly stood up. "What is the meaning of this!" he shouted, but one of the armed men pointed his rifle at him. Mustafa clenched his fists but immediately sat down.

Timon clutched his chest, his heart palpitations behaving like steel drums, and he breathed in and out in quick intakes of breath. As three armed men stood behind Mustafa and Mancini, Timon noticed the woman in the police uniform holding a Beretta. She was standing next to the fourth armed intruder, who stood at the front of the conference table, facing Mobolaji.

Timon looked into the eyes of the policewoman through the slits of her mask. The recognition smacked him in the face. It was Yinka. The man she stood beside, who had a smaller and more athletic physique than the other armed men, raised his glinting silver Beretta and aimed it at Mobolaji. There was no mistake about it; Timon knew it was Yinka's ex-boyfriend, Oge—the man who had come to seek his vengeance.

* * *

"The leader of the Robin Hoods has entered the meeting room! We have to go inside now!" Mohammed said, launching from his chair. "Men get ready; we're going in."

"Will you wait," Kojo said, launching from his chair and grabbing Mohammed by the wrist. The colonel flung Kojo's hand away.

"Enough of this," Mohammed spat, a vein popping on his left temple. "Mobolaji is in danger."

"You go in there, storming in with your men; you could set off a shootout. There are civilians here, for God's sake."

Mohammed, who had been fuming seconds ago, began to relax slightly. He looked at the laptop screen, where a man in a balaclava aimed a silver Beretta at Mobolaji's head. "Three minutes, then we're storming in there. I don't care."

Kojo sat back down, now watching the monitor screen with intensity. "Fine, let me see what is said. He hasn't immediately shot Mobolaji."

Mohammed sucked his teeth. "Three minutes, Ghanaian."

72

Yinka stood beside Oge, aiming her Beretta at the men around the boat-shaped conference table. As she observed the faces of the men she recognised, Yinka found it surreal knowing she had been delivering an investor presentation for a crypto company when she had last stood in front of this same group of wealthy men. Yet now, she was standing before them with a gun aimed at their heads, and they did not even know it was her, well, apart from Dugard and Timon, who would have surely realised it was her underneath the balaclava.

Dugard's lips curved into a toothy, triumphant smile. He began to clap as he stood from his swivel chair and looked at the faces of Mobolaji, Mancini and Mustafa, who remained frozen in their seats, their eyes darting from the armed men in the room to Dugard.

"You underestimated me, Mobolaji," Dugard said, speaking directly to Mobolaji now, who glared at Dugard defiantly. "How dare you think you can outsmart me!" Dugard suddenly shouted, causing Yinka to jerk. He banged his right fist on the polished wooden table. "To think you're better than me! Ludicrous! I started this joint enterprise. I created this modern network that allowed our corrupt clients to clean their money through the UK, Nigeria, Italy, or Japan through our investments, a novel concept which grew our wealth tenfold. I did that, not you, Mobolaji. Yet, you became the de facto leader over time as I lost my influence."

Having worked himself up a sweat, Dugard took a handkerchief from his blazer's pocket and wiped the sweat on his brow. He straightened his suit jacket. "But now the power scales will again tip back in my favour." Dugard curled his lips into a sneer and pointed his right finger at Oge. "You're reckoning is at hand, Mobolaji. Your past has caught up with you."

Dugard then turned to Oge. "The floor is yours."

Yinka watched as Oge remained silent for a moment, his gun trained at Mobolaji, who stared back at him with narrow eyes and pursed lips. She looked at Timon, whose eyes darted from the gun in Oge's hand and then back at Yinka. But she was not going to do anything. Not yet.

After a minute of grim silence, Oge finally spoke. "I have waited a long time to be in this exact position," he said in a measured tone but one dripping with menace. "The most beautiful dreams I've had over the years have been me imagining this very moment. But this is no dream for you, Mobolaji Bankole. I am your worst nightmare. Do you know who I am?"

Mobolaji raised his eyebrows incredulously and casually shrugged his shoulders. Despite a gun in his face, Mobolaji seemed unperturbed. "How can I possibly know who you are wearing a mask over your face?"

To Yinka's shock, Oge removed his balaclava with his free hand and dropped it onto the conference table. "How about now? Recognise me? It was you who gave me this permanent scar on the left side of my face." Oge dragged the butt of his gun along the lines of his facial disfigurement.

Mobolaji shook his head and looked at Oge like he should

be locked up in an asylum. "Nigeria is a big country, young man. It has over 200 million people, and you expect me to recognise your face? And I would remember if I gave a man a scar like the one you have."

Oge began to cackle, and Yinka could see the red mist in his eyes, which was thicker than she had ever seen. He looked deranged. "That's good, that's very good, Mobolaji. Okay, let me narrow it down for you to make it easier. Eighteen years ago, there was a talented Nigerian journalist, a woman. She had been investigating you for several years. She planned to expose this whole international crime ring you are involved in and had evidence that you had invested a lot of Nigeria's government funds into other investments around the world to line yourself and your criminal friends' pockets. She had enough evidence to put you and your cronies behind bars for decades."

"And when you discovered she was about to publish this exposé, and she refused to be intimidated by your threats, you drove over to her house and gave her young son a parcel to deliver. A parcel that contained a small, crude bomb."

Yinka saw the dreadful recognition in Mobolaji's eyes now. All the colour seemed to drain from the man's dark brown face, and he no longer looked so unbothered. Now Mobolaji's bottom lip quivered, and for the first time since Yinka and the others had stormed into the room, Mobolaji realised he was potentially looking at the face of his grim reaper.

"You...you are the boy?" Mobolaji said softly, his voice faint as a whisper. Then, almost maddeningly, he cackled. "Her boy. I had forgotten about her boy."

"That day, you had called me a good son," Oge said, tears creeping at the edges of his eyes. "And like any good son, I have come to avenge my mother today."

"Will you kill him already," Dugard interrupted. He

slammed his hand on the table. "What are you waiting for? This is the man who took your mother from you."

To Yinka's surprise, Oge took one step forward, his gun still trained on Mobolaji, and then he pointed it at Dugard. Immediately, Dugard contorted his face in ferocious anger.

"Have you lost your mind, boy!? Who do you think you're pointing that gun at?" Dugard then flung his head at Bobby and the two other mercenaries. "Kill Mobolaji and then kill this boy. Now!"

Yinka looked from Oge, who was pointing the gun at Dugard, then at Bobby and the two mercenaries on the left side of the room. She was confused as to what was happening. Then, to Yinka's disbelief, Bobby shrugged his shoulders.

"Hey, Richard, mate, it's not personal or anything," Bobby said, in his cockney accent, "but he's been paying us more than you, so… he's technically our boss, not you."

Dugard stumbled back in shock, his jaw hanging in disbelief as he slowly turned to face Oge with horrified eyes.

"You're scum, Dugard. A filthy coloniser," Oge spat, his Beretta now aimed at Dugard's forehead. "You think Africans are below you. Well, you're about to meet your maker by the hands of one."

Dugard raised his hands in the air. "No, wait…!"

Yinka stumbled back in horror and shock as Oge's gun went off with a loud bang, and Dugard immediately dropped onto the floor like a sack of rice. The shot rang loudly in her ears and reverberated across the room.

Now acting on pure adrenaline, Yinka raised her Beretta at Oge. "Enough!"

Bobby and the two other mercenaries raised their rifles at Yinka, ready to shoot her. Then, in almost perfect unison, Yinka heard Timon and Oge scream.

"Don't shoot her!"

Oge, who had looked stunned for a moment when Yinka had pointed her gun at him, suddenly faced Timon, who had launched himself from his seat, his face filled with fear and his forehead moist with sweat. Yinka could see the realisation dawn on Oge's face as he slowly turned around face at her.

"You betrayed me for the son of the man who murdered my mother, Coffee Bean?" Oge sounded utterly heartbroken.

Tears slid down Yinka's cheeks as she shook her head."You betrayed me first."

Then, the door of the meeting room burst open again.

Within seconds, everybody was ducking under a hail of gunfire.

73

When Yinka's ex-boyfriend shot Dugard dead, the bullet hitting the English aristocrat square in the forehead and dropping him dead immediately, Kojo knew then that the entire operation had gone to shit. It was no longer under his control.

"Men, move now!" Mohammed screamed from the top of his lungs.

Staring silently at the laptop screen, stunned into shock, Kojo heard Mohammed and the State Security Service forces storm out of the room, boots stamping against the floor and the sound of magazines loading into rifles.

Kojo's brief paralysis lasted less than a quarter of a minute, and he instantly snapped back into the moment. Dugard was dead. Kojo had a new mission now: protect Timon and Yinka.

As he rushed out of the room, Kojo unholstered the loaded Glock 19 from his utility belt. He was heading to war.

* * *

When Timon saw the meeting room door burst open and a flurry of men dressed in SWAT-like combat gear burst inside, he immediately grabbed his father and pulled him onto the floor. He wasn't sure who fired the first shot, but once the first shot went off, all Timon could hear were the popping sounds of bullets and shattered glass as he lay on his stomach on the floor, his father covering his ears beside him. Then, a loud bang of a cabinet falling to the floor reverberated in the room. The only thought that came to Timon as the chaos ensured around him was to get out of the room rather than lay here waiting for a bullet to find him and his father.

As he looked up from the floor, he saw another entrance at the back of the room. He grabbed his father's arm and pulled him up so he was on his knees.

"We have to run to that door now. I'll support you."

Mobolaji nodded, his forehead shiny with sweat and his small dark eyes glinting with fear. Timon lifted his father from the floor, supporting him with his arm as if he were a wounded soldier and dragged him to the front door as he blocked out the sounds of gunfire. Just as they reached the door and Timon kicked it open, a bullet whizzed by. Mobolaji howled in pain, and they both stumbled out of the room, a trail of blood already forming on the floor.

Yinka had thrown herself onto the ground on the opposite side of the room as Oge and the mercenaries immediately began firing at the armed soldiers that had burst into the meeting room. She had dropped her Beretta, which had now slid underneath one of the swivel chairs. She crawled hurriedly to it, the sound of gunfire exploding in her ears and above her head. Then she heard the loud bang of something hitting the floor. When she reached her gun, she saw Timon on the floor with his father, hands over their heads, as the bullets slashed the air like metal wasps.

Sweating as her heart drummed against her chest and breathing heavily, Yinka reached for her Beretta, stood up slightly, crouching, and looked over the conference tab. Oge, Bobby, and the two mercenaries were now at the other end of the meeting room, ducking behind swivel chairs as they exchanged fire with the Nigeria State Security Service armed forces, who had fortified themselves with the toppled metal cabinet.

As she crouched on the side of the conference table, Yinka noticed the MI6 agent exchanging gunfire from behind the cabinet. He was dressed in black tactical gear and firing a Glock 19. Shaking, Yinka turned her head to look over to the right side of the conference table. She saw Mancini slumped over on his chair, his head on the conference table. He was not moving. Only when she saw a line of blood trickle from his forehead did she realise the Italian banker had been shot dead, caught in the crossfire. In the corner of the room, Yinka saw Mustafa curled up with his knees raised to his face, blocking his ears as the gunfire rained.

Now caught in this deadly shootout, Yinka decided to keep crouching by the side of the conference table. When she turned back to check on Timon, she could not believe what he was doing. He was dragging his father towards the back door. Everything happened fast. She saw Oge look in their direction, and just as Timon kicked the door down and dragged his father through, Oge fired a shot at them. She heard someone scream; it sounded like Mobolaji, but she couldn't be sure. Oge then ran after them, narrowly missing being shot himself.

Ignoring every part of her which told her to stay where she was, Yinka hurried towards the back door, stepping over Dugard's corpse as she remained in the crouching stance, gripping her Beretta with both her trembling hands.

· · ·

After firing God knows how many rounds, Kojo finally managed to take down one of the men firing at them from the opposite side of the meeting room. It had been the biggest brute, the one with the blonde man bun, and he dropped to the floor with a thud. In the corner of the room, Kojo saw Timon pull his father upwards and drag him towards the back door of the meeting room. *What is he doing?* Kojo thought, shocked.

Yinka's ex-boyfriend, with his surprisingly boyish light brown face with brown cornrows, turned towards the direction of the back door and shot at Timon and his father. The bullet hit Mobolaji Bankole in the rib. Then he ran after them. Moments later, Kojo saw a policewoman in a balaclava, crouching, go after all three men.

"Colonel, cover me," Kojo said, loading a fresh magazine into his Glock 19.

Mohammed, who had been exchanging gunfire, was now leaning against the dropped filing cabinet like a soldier in the trenches. He nodded at Kojo. "You better move quick, Ghanaian."

Kojo did not need to be told twice and sprang forward, moving with rapid steps as he ducked behind the table, hands over his head as the sounds of gunfire continued to cackle in the room like dozens of fireworks going off simultaneously.

When Kojo reached the corridor, he was met with pandemonium. A few people had started to run down the hallway, screaming at the sound of gunshots coming from the meeting room war zone he had just escaped. In front of him, about 150 yards away, Kojo saw Timon hoisting his father up by his chest as they sluggishly made their way to the elevator, his father limping and leaving a trail of dark blood on the floor.

Then Kojo saw Yinka's ex-boyfriend marching towards them, his silver Beretta aimed at the two of them. The policewoman in the balaclava, who Kojo now realised must be Yinka, shouted at him.

"It's over, Oge!"

Oge was momentarily distracted as he stopped dead in his tracks and looked wide-eyed at Yinka, who stood behind him. Now was Kojo's opportunity. He fired his gun but missed Yinka's ex-boyfriend by some mark, the bullet instead ricocheting off a wall, destroying one of the roof lightbulbs.

Immediately, Oge flung his body in the direction of where the shot had come from, glared at Kojo and aimed his Beretta at him.

Before Kojo had a chance to fire his gun again, he heard the gunshot ring in his ears, immediately followed by an intense and sharp pain which shot down his right arm as if someone was continuously stabbing him with a sharp needle. He dropped his gun, stumbled back and then collapsed against the wall in agonising pain. Even before he put his hands on his shoulder and felt the slippery and warm blood gushing from his left shoulder, he knew Oge had shot him.

Oge quickly reloaded his Beretta and raised it again at Kojo. He was ready to pull the trigger again. For Kojo, time froze as he looked at death in the hollow barrel of that silver gun. An image or maybe a memory of Federica lying beside him on a soft bed materialised before him, radiant and heavenly. Kojo would die today, and the last thing he would remember would be her face.

But death would not greet him today.

As Oge tightened his finger around the trigger, Timon, whose dying father lay slumped by the elevator, tackled Oge to the floor.

Yinka had been about to fire a warning shot at Oge for him to stop after he had shot the MI6 agent in the shoulder, and it looked like he was about to shoot him again. But she had never got the chance to.

Timon rugby tackled Oge onto the floor.

Now, the two men were fighting on the ground, violently wrestling each other as they tried to reach for the Beretta that had fallen out of Oge's hand.

Standing a few feet from the two tussling men, Yinka raised her gun, but she knew she would never pull the trigger. She decided she would kick Oge's Beretta out of reach, but before she could even take a step, Oge gained the upper advantage over Timon and gave him a hard right hook to his nose. Blood exploded from his nostrils and he rolled on the floor, moaning in pain.

Oge struggled to his feet, panting heavily, and picked up his Beretta. He turned around and aimed the gun at Timon, who was now shielding his bloody nose with his two hands. He looked up at Oge as he lay on the floor, wide-eyed with frozen fear as he stared at the barrel of Oge's gun.

Yinka raised her gun at Oge for the second time, ignoring the hot tears clouding her vision. "Oge, please. Stop!"

Oge abruptly turned away from Timon to face Yinka, his gun now raised at her. She saw sweat dripping down his forehead and over the facial scar that ran down the left side of his face. Maybe it had been Yinka's tears or her pleading voice, but the murderous delirium that had gripped him seemed to fall away in that moment. Now, he looked exhausted and distraught. Yinka had never seen him look so regretful and broken. The red mist left his eyes. Now, they were dark brown. Lowering his gun and panting heavily, he looked at Yinka gravely.

"Coffee Bean…I am so sorry."

Several gunshots in quick succession rang in Yinka's ear. She saw Oge's eyes go to the back of his head and thick streams of blood pour from his mouth. The silver Beretta dropped from his now limp fingers. Several bullets had penetrated his upper torso, and blood stains were already soaking his combat gear. Oge fell to his knees and then crumpled onto the floor. He was dead.

Yinka looked to her right, where the gunshots had come from. Two hundred yards away, a Nigerian State Security Service officer had his assault rifle aimed forward as he released his finger from the trigger. The man who had fired the fatal shots had three tribal marks on each cheek. Now other Nigerian State Security Service forces, who had been involved in the shootout in the meeting room earlier, were now running towards him.

There was a cackle in Yinka's right ear, and then Joshua's voice came from the earplug.

"Get out of there, Yinka. Head to the van. We need to go. Now!"

Stunned, unable to even think, Yinka took one last look at Oge's body slumped on the floor. A pool of blood was now forming around his bullet-riddled corpse. She then looked at Timon. He was in a fetal position, but she could hear his faint moans.

Then Yinka turned away from the death and carnage.

And she ran.

PART EIGHT

SECURE HER HEART

74

ONE WEEK after the events in Lagos, Timon stood on Southwark Bridge, overlooking the shimmering, blackened waters of the River Thames on a chilly London evening.

Wearing a black leather jacket, grey chinos, black boots, and leather gloves, Timon observed the passing cars and Londoners walking past him on the sidewalk in their characteristically unbothered fashion.

Timon checked his Rolex. It was 8 p.m. He looked down at the collar of his coat to see the tiny black spec attached to it. The microscopic camera was firmly in place.

When Timon looked up and stared down the bridge, he saw Russell strolling towards him with his mop of dark brown hair. He wore a long brown coat, a navy blue jumper, denim Levi jeans, and black boots. Bags were underneath his blue eyes. While his dashing English good looks were still intact, Russell looked rougher, as if he had rapidly aged by a decade overnight.

Timon and Russell embraced on the bridge, patting each other on the back.

"Shit, T, my guy, you don't know how happy I am to know that you're alright," Russell said, stepping back from

Timon. "Fuck me, man. Everything went so left, so quickly. I heard about that shootout in your apartment, and I couldn't sleep for days. Thought you was...you know..."

Timon wanted to knock Russell out and toss him into the River Thames, but he remembered what he was here to do. Besides, Timon wasn't a killer. He wasn't his late father. "I get it, Russell."

"How's Kez, man? I haven't phoned him yet since I flew back to London. He's good, yeah?"

Timon nodded, looking at Russell blankly. "Yeah, he's good. I am seeing him tomorrow." He then exhaled heavily. "Why did you do it, Russell? And be honest with me, bro. You owe me that, at least, after everything that's happened."

Russell regarded Timon for a moment. His face had gone pale. He looked over the bridge to the Thames stretching out into the bank and St Paul's Cathedral looming in the distance. Russell sighed heavily. He shook his head with a grimace. "How much do you know?"

"I know quite a bit, bro. But start from the beginning."

Russell nodded. "Look, my uncle, Sir Richard Dugard, was a super-wealthy British banker. He approached me when I met him on holiday in Johannesburg two years ago. He knew from my father that I had started a crypto hedge fund, our hedge fund, and introduced me to Musa Jirongo. Like I knew Musa was a dodgy guy from the get-go; come on, he sells..." Russell smirked sadistically, "Sorry, he sold bloody weapons to Somalian terrorists, but I thought fuck it, he has a shit load of money that our hedge fund needs." Russell now turned to look at Timon. "And don't forget, T, you were the one who said it didn't matter how our clients made their money. All that mattered was that they had lots of money for us to invest. Secure the bag no matter what. Remember that?"

"Yeah, I did say that, but what I never said was that you should engage in insider trading, did I? You started telling Dugard what crypto investments we were making for Musa, giving him all that confidential information, which your uncle then used to specifically target and hack those crypto companies we'd invested Musa's money into so we'd end up losing his money. Why did you do it, Russell?"

Russell heaved his chest, sighing once more and shacked his head again. "My uncle gave me £10,000 each time I shared information about our crypto investments for Musa."

"But you were already making big enough money with our hedge fund? And your family is minted. How can you need more money?"

Russell chuckled. "Come on, bro. You, of all people, should know that there is no such thing as having too much money. I thought my uncle was trying to get revenge on Musa; that's why he wanted to know where we were investing his money. I didn't expect my uncle to somehow hack into those crypto companies we'd invested Musa's money into. When he told me what he had done, he told me to relax, gave me an additional £20,000 to keep quiet, and said everything would be alright. Then, he called me one day, saying I needed to leave the country immediately because I was in danger."

"And you didn't bother to alert me or Kez."

Russell shook his head again, and his eyes dropped to the ground with shame. "T, I was panicking and on edge. I just booked a plane ticket and fucked off to Greece. Over there, I heard on the news that Musa was killed in your apartment. Then I later learned my uncle was shot dead by some lunatic at a tech summit in Nigeria." Rusell sighed and punched the palm of his left hand in frustration. "My uncle was into some deep shit, and I should have refused his money from the start and never got us involved with Musa."

Timon sighed regrettably and placed his hand on Russell's left shoulder. "Yeah, you should have refused your uncle's money. Greed got the better of you. Got the better of me as well. But no bad deed goes unpunished, Russell."

Russell looked at Timon and gave him a puzzling look. "What are you on about?"

"I have been recording you, bro, in real-time. The police are going to be here any second now. Sorry, bro."

Russell's eyes widened in shock, and he pushed Timon lightly on the chest, spun around and sprinted down the bridge. But he barely got to ten yards before three Vauxhall Astra police cars swerved onto the bridge, their sirens blaring. Two police officers, one male and one female, sprang out of the police cars, chased after Russell and flung him to the ground.

As Timon watched a now uncontrollably sobbing Russell be handcuffed and dragged to a police car by the two officers, he heard footsteps from behind him. He turned around to see Kojo approaching. The MI6 officer had his left arm in a white cast hanging from a sling and was dressed in brown trousers, a black jumper, and a long grey overcoat hanging over his hulking frame.

"Is it ok if I keep this mini recording camera?" Timon said, grinning at Kojo. "Could come in handy if I ever need to spy on an unfaithful girlfriend."

"If you've got ten million quid to spare, contact MI6." Kojo smiled at Timon.

Timon stood still as Kojo extracted the small device from his collar with a metal toothpick. A smartly dressed woman approached them, holding a small case in her left hand. Kojo placed the miniature device inside the case, and the woman nodded curtly at him, closed the case shut, and walked off. Kojo stood beside Timon now as they both watched Russell sit inside one of the police cars, handcuffed and head bowed, as its wailing sirens threw spinning blue lasers over the bridge.

"That was an excellent performance," Kojo said. "You're not too bad at being a field agent. Seeing as you're out of a job now, there could be a new career at MI6 if you're interested. We need more diversity at that circus anyway."

Timon chuckled. "Thanks for the offer, but no, I am good. I have been in the middle of two shootouts in three weeks, and I swear I've started seeing my hairline recede already. MI6? I don't need that stress in my life."

"Fair enough, not everyone's built for it. So what's next for you, then? You can't exactly go back to managing rich people's money anytime soon."

"I know," Timon said. He watched the police cars speed off down the bridge, their loud sirens becoming fainter the further down the road they travelled. "I'm not sure what I'm going to do next, to be honest with you."

"Well, whatever you decide to do, just make sure it's legal, please. No more working with African arms dealers—or any arms dealers, for that matter."

Timon chuckled. "Of course. I am done with all that."

"And thank you, Timon."

Shocked to hear Kojo's gratitude and to be called by his actual name for once, Timon turned to face the MI6 agent. "Wow, you're calling me by the name my mother gave me."

Kojo half-chuckled. "Well, you've earned my respect. You did a brave thing back there in Lagos. You saved my life. I'll be completely transparent with you. I initially thought you were just a rich prick who had no morals or principles and only cared about making money, but you showed me there's more to you."

"You saved my life first, so I thought it fair to return the favour. Even we rich pricks show gratitude." Timon winked at Kojo and extended his left hand. "Take care, uncle. Maybe think about retiring, yeah?"

Grinning, Kojo gave Timon a firm handshake. "You know, maybe I just might. You look after yourself, Timon. Go and live an honest life."

* * *

"A week ago from today, well-respected British businessman and former diplomat to Nigeria, 65-year-old Sir Richard Dugard, was shot dead in Lagos during the assassination of Mobolagi Bankole, the 73-year-old private banker to many of Nigeria's upper class as well as a respected businessman. The shocking murders, which have rocked Nigeria and Britain, took place in a violent shootout at The National Nigeria Theatre during the first day of the African Technology Summit. The international event, attracting many of the world's leading tech companies and entrepreneurs, was held in Nigeria for the first time."

"Other casualties include Silvio Mancini, the 63-year-old Italian private banker and film financier well-known in Italy's film industry and Hollywood circles. At the time of his death, he was being investigated for alleged links to the Sicilian Mafia as well as a string of sexual harassment allegations. Bobby O'Hare, a 38-year-old English mercenary for hire, was also killed in the shootout along with two of his associates, 42-year-old James Hornby and 35-year-old Frank Dune. It is believed that all three English mercenaries had played critical roles in the assassination of Mobolagi Bankole."

"A seventh causality of the shooting, thought to be the mastermind behind the assassination, is 30-year-old Ogedengbe Akindoju. Nigeria's State Security Service forces gunned him down. Ogedengbe or 'Oge', as some former colleagues knew him, had been a former reporter for the Lagos Tribune but had quit the newspaper ten years ago and disappeared into obscurity until now."

"Ogedengbe's late mother, Bisi Akindoju, had been a celebrated journalist in Nigeria, renowned for her groundbreaking reporting into corruption within the highest ranks of Nigeria's political and business class. Tragically, she was murdered 18 years ago, at the age of 35, when a letter bomb delivered to her home killed her. The case remains a cold one. The Nigerian authorities have not given any statement to establish if the murder of Bisi Akindoju was the motive

that drove Ogedengbe Akindoju to carry out one of the highest-profile assassinations that Nigeria has seen in recent times.

Colonel Mohammed Salisu, Director-General of Nigeria's State Security Service, gave an official statement today in Abuja, Aso Drive:

"It is very early days in our investigation of this tragic incident that took place at what was supposed to be a celebration of Africa and the role of technology in enriching the lives of Nigerians. Fortunately, the Nigerian State Security, under my leadership, responded quickly and neutralised the threats, resulting in no civilian casualties outside of the seven officially reported."

"Ogedengbe Akindoku and his team of so-called Robin Hoods had been involved in a series of extortion and blackmail campaigns in Nigeria and other West African countries for several years now, targeting wealthy individuals and politicians. Fortunately, he is no longer a threat. While his co-conspirators remain at large, we are confident these thieves will be deterred from carrying out any further attacks following the death of their ring leader. But of course, we will remain vigilant."

"We are continuing to cooperate very closely with the British High Commission and our intelligence and security agency counterparts in the UK and Italy to establish all of the facts of this heinous and tragic incident. We will have more to update in due course, but for now, we ask you to respect the privacy of the families of the deceased. Thank you."

Chikezie changed the news channel as soon as the BBC News reporter had concluded the news report.

With a glass of Hennessy and coke in both their hands, Timon and Chikezie sat on the leather sofa inside the living room of Chikezie's home in Essex. For the past few days, Timon had been staying at his best friend's house while his Battersea apartment, still riddled with bullet holes and blood-stained floors, was still being treated as a crime scene by forensic experts. Timon wasn't even sure if his insurance covered crazy Kenyan arms dealers arriving unannounced at your home and shooting up the place.

"Bloody hell, T," Chikezie said, reclining on the sofa. He took a swig of his Hennessey. "I can't even imagine what you've just been through. You were caught right in the middle of some conspiracy to assassinate one of Nigeria's most well-known businessmen and bankers. And he was your father all this time. Why'd you keep it secret?"

"For most of my life, I didn't care about my Dad, Kez," Timon said, shrugging. "Even when he physically came to see me for the first time when I graduated, I wanted nothing to do with him. And now I know he's a murderer, too." Although Kojo had advised him to keep what he knew about Mobolagi and The Cable confidential, Timon had told Chikezie everything that happened in Lagos and why Musa Jirongo had come after them in the first place. He trusted Chikezie with his life, so he trusted him to keep all this between them. "And I am sure the crimes my late father had committed will come to light publicly soon." Timon breathed a heavy sigh. "But, if I am being honest, I am not even sure how I feel about my father's death. I did grow closer to him when I stayed with him in Lagos." Timon took a swig of his Hennessey.

"Are you going to go to his funeral?"

Before he returned to London, Timon had been informed by his half-sister Eniola that there would be a state funeral for his father at the Cathedral Church of Christ in Lagos Marina in three days. Timon had not yet decided if he wanted to meet the rest of the Bankole family face-to-face.

It was a secret he would take with him to the grave, but Timon knew he could have warned his father about the impending attempt on his life. If he had, Mobolagi would be alive today. But Timon had decided to do nothing. Now, his father had left behind a widowed wife and adult children who had loved him dearly. Timon had his father's blood on his hands, but it was not the blood of a saint, far from it.

"I am not sure yet, Kez. Right now, my life is like a plane flying in some random airspace with the pilot having no clue where to land. I can't even relaunch our hedge fund or get a job in any finance position because we've been barred from the industry for three years as part of this plea deal with the FCA for laundering Musa Jirongo's money. Then there is Orisa."

"What about her?"

Timon turned his head to look at Chikezie. "Shit has been so crazy, I haven't even had a chance to update you, have I? I called the wedding off, Kez."

Chikezie widened his eyes in surprise. "Damn, you are saying fuck it to everything," he said, chuckling. "I thought you were in love with Orisa?"

Timon shook his head. "I thought I loved her, too. Then I met someone else and realised she was not the one for me. But I owe her an apology—for everything."

Chikezie nodded and took a sip of his brandy. "You also owe her the truth, T. I know who the other woman is. You don't need to tell me. It's Yinka, right?"

Timon jerked his head back in surprise. A wide smile stretched across Chikezie's face.

"Bro, I have known you for ten years now. You think I can't tell when you're in love. You had this glow about you whenever you spoke about Yinka after returning from Dubai. You have never smiled like that whenever you have spoken about Orisa." Chikezie gave Timon a cheeky smirk. "From school enemies to falling in love. It's cute."

"You're a dickhead, you know that?" Timon said, shaking his head as he muffled a laugh.

"You aren't denying it, though."

Timon sighed. "I don't even know where she is, Kez. After that crazy shootout at the tech summit in Lagos, when I looked up from the floor, with my broken nose and Yinka's now dead ex-boyfriend sprayed out on the floor across me, she was gone. I tried to call her, but her phone number was already disabled." Timon shook his head, despondent. "After everything she's just been through, she won't be in the right mental state to hear about my feelings for her anyway."

"Fair enough," Chikezie said, looking at Timon. "But if you love someone, you should let them know. But right now, you must tell Orisa what's in your heart. You owe her that."

"I know."

Timon and Chikezie's conversation was interrupted by Chikezie's five-year-old daughter, Susanna, rushing into the living room and throwing herself onto Chikezie's lap.

"Daddy, Daddy, you said you'd play with me," Susanna said, bouncing on the spot like a child who had just injected candy into their veins.

"Yes, yes, I am coming," Chikezie said, slowly getting to his feet. "As for me, T, I am going to use this free time to spend it with my family. Fortunately, I have enough money saved that I don't need to work for three years anyway. Now I can enjoy the real treasures in life, like spending time with this hyperactive princess of mine." Chikezie bent down and pinched his daughter's cheeks. Timon smiled.

As Chikezie followed his daughter up the stairs to her room, Timon leaned back against the sofa. The brandy helped relax his mind as he contemplated the right path to take in this new wilderness he found himself in as a 30-year-old man.

But Timon had told himself one thing: money would not be the only motivation that guided his life decisions, as it always had before.

75

When Timon walked into Orisa's room at King's College Hospital to visit her, holding a box of expensive chocolates from Fortnum & Mason and a bouquet, he wasn't even sure if there was more space in the room to set his flowers down. She had turned her room into a garden.

It turned out that Orisa getting shot had done sensational numbers for her social media channels. From her hospital bed, she had started her vlogging series *'Surviving The Bullet: The Visual Journey of a black independent woman'* where she talked about the experience of being shot, shrewdly linking it back to violence against black women. The vlogs had been so successful she had managed to land a lucrative television deal from it. She had told Timon all this as he caught up with her by her hospital bed. When securing the bag, Timon had to give Orisa her dues. How many people could turn a traumatic experience such as getting shot by a mad man into a television deal?

On his way to see Orisa, Timon had contemplated how much he should divulge about everything he'd been through in the past weeks. Not wanting to run the risk of her sharing confidential MI6 intel - Timon did have the same level of trust in her ability to keep her mouth shut that he had with Chikezie - he had decided to say only what was already in the public domain, elaborated slightly on specific details and omitted anything to do with MI6, international money laundering networks, the Robin Hoods and Yinka. But he spoke to her about his father and his involvement with Musa.

"I wish you'd told me all this, Timon," Orisa said, looking at him from her hospital bed as he sat in a wooden armchair beside her. She wore a blue patient gown, and her left arm was in a sling similar to Kojo's. A television was attached to the front wall before her hospital bed. It was currently showing one of her favourite reality dating shows. "But you never tell me much about yourself. You never said anything about your work or past throughout our relationship."

Timon looked at her, contrite in his feelings, and nodded. He noticed that she was still wearing the engagement ring. "I should have been more open with you about my life. But I didn't think you'd..."

"...be interested," Orisa said, giving him a knowing smile. "I know you don't think I am smart enough for you, Timon. I always felt like I was just the shiny girlfriend on your arm— another trophy like your Porshe and your penthouse." There was no sarcasm in her tone when she spoke, and Timon sensed that Orisa was not talking to him from a bitter place. He was surprised by her level of self-awareness.

"You like shopping, fancy dinners, and luxury holidays," Timon said, smiling at her and himself as he remembered some of the best moments of their relationship. "And you're only 23, so you're focused on what you enjoy. But after a while, I felt like I wanted more, you know? To settle down properly. And if I married you, Orisa, would you want to have a family with me so soon?"

Orisa stared hard at Timon, blinking a few times as she pondered his question, and then she looked away from him to face the wall. "Honestly? I don't even want kids. I can barely stand my nephews. Maybe I am too selfish and focused on my influencer career right now. But does that make me unworthy to be someone's wife?" Her voice cracked a little.

"No, it doesn't make you unworthy. The right man for you wouldn't care if you don't want kids later in life or never."

Orisa turned her head away from the wall to look at Timon. "But you're not the right man for me, are you, boo boo?"

Timon sighed heavily and shook his head at Orisa, looking at her ruefully. "No, I am not."

It was difficult for Timon to watch the single tear trickle down Orisa's left cheek. She looked away from him, dabbed at her eyes and composed herself. Then she turned to look at Timon with a tight smile. "Well, it's good we called off our engagement now instead of getting married and going through some bitter divorce in six months. I am an Igbo girl, so I don't play about my money. I would have taken you to the cleaners." She laughed, but Timon could detect she was using her sarcasm to mask the pain she was feeling, knowing their relationship would record its time of death in this hospital room.

Timon chuckled, but it was of sorrow, not joy. Breakups were always painful, more so when they were amicable. "I have no doubt. You're a businesswoman first. It's all about that bag, right?"

Orisa nodded, smiling at him, but there was a subtle sadness. "You know me, boo boo; gotta secure the bag at all costs. "

Timon could sense his time to leave was approaching. "And for what's it worth, since I've put you through so much, I mean, you got shot because of me, you can keep the engagement ring."

Orisa lifted her finger where the sparkling ring twinkled. "Oh, you thought I was going to give this back? Oh, please. I will pawn this and use the money to fund my next four holiday trips to the Caribbean."

Smiling, Timon stood from the armchair and gently took Orisa's left hand into his own. "Thanks for all the amazing times, Orisa. We'll always have those, and I am a subscriber to all of your YouTube channels, so I'll check in once in a while to see what you're up to; no doubt it's something exciting. Go and conquer this world and be all you're meant to be."

This time, Orisa could not hold back the tears as they ran down her face. "Thank you....Timon," she said through quiet sobs. "You look after yourself, and please stay out of trouble."

Timon bent over her hospital bed and tenderly kissed Orisa on the forehead. "I will."

After waving goodbye to his ex-fiancée, Timon left the private hospital room. He still had another visit to make.

* * *

As always, Timon found his mother in the garden at the Loveday Abbey Road care home in Maida Vale, tending to the plants.

When they had lived together in Canning Town, Iyenemi Bakare had no interest in gardening. But the way Timon saw it, now that his mother did not have to run a busy salon business while also raising a son all by herself and keeping a roof over their heads, she now had the free time in her later years to live life purely for leisure, rather than for survival. She deserved it, and Timon was glad he was able to do this for her. Fortunately, Timon had enough savings to pay for her to stay here for another year until he had to send her to a less expensive care home now that he wouldn't be earning the vast sums of money he had previously earned. But at least she had the experience of living next to the Queen.

"My son, my sweet boy, you are finally putting on some

weight," Iyenemi said as she embraced Timon. She was wearing a floral apron and holding a water can. "Does your wife cook for you now?"

"No, Mum. She doesn't cook, and she's not my wife. We called the wedding off."

"Oh," Iyenemi said, raising her eyebrows at Timon with a perplexed expression. "But I was at your wedding last week. Your father came down from Nigeria."

Timon heaved his chest, feeling the swell of emotion that almost pushed tears from his eyes. "Mum, there was no wedding. And my father did not come."

"Oh, well, that's a shame, but I could see you were not so sure about her. A mother always knows. I hope she's doing ok?"

"Yeah, she'll be fine. It was a mutual breakup."

As Timon observed his mother for a moment, who had now bent down to water a collection of shrubs, he contemplated if he should tell her that he had met his father in Nigeria and had stayed in his big mansion with his second wife and met his half-siblings. Should he explain how he had witnessed his father shot by the man whose mother he had murdered with a letter bomb? Timon decided he would not mention any of it. Those were his burdens to shoulder, not his mother's.

"Mum, can I ask you a question?"

"You can ask me anything you want, my handsome boy."

"Do you still remember much about my father?"

Iyenemi stopped tending to the plants, rose to her feet and turned to look at Timon. She gave him a pensive look. "I remember some things about him, yes. He is a very respected and powerful man in Nigeria. His ambitious spirit made him magnetic."

Timon nodded solemnly as his mind briefly flashed back to the moments he had shared with his late father in Lagos. "But do I remind you of him?"

Now, his mother gave him a knowing smile. "Some of him is in you, yes. You are ambitious, like he is. And hardworking, like he is. But you have one thing your father never had?"

Timon moved closer towards his mother, intrigued. "What was that?"

"You have a great deal of love for people inside of you. Your father did not always have that. You get that from mummy."

Timon chuckled, but it was a painful laugh, and now he felt tears at the edge of his eyes. "To be honest, I have fallen short of the kind of man you expect me to be, Mum. I haven't been a good man."

Iyenemi rested her aged, dark eyes on Timon. She his left hand, caressed it and gave him a mother's kind gaze. "Whatever you've done, my handsome son, I know you are a good man. We all lose our way sometimes; you only need to find the right path again. And repent for your sins."

"Yeah," Timon said, sniffing as he dabbed the tears away with his left wrist. "Mum, there's someone in Nigeria—a woman from my childhood whom I met again as an adult. I have fallen in love with her, but I don't know if I should tell her about it because she's in pain. She's suffered a terrible loss."

Iyenemi stared intensely at her son. "What does your heart tell you?"

"That I should tell her I love her."

Iyenemi smiled. "Well, there's your answer, my sweet boy. Go and find her and tell her you love her. All you can do is see what happens and respect whatever she says. At least she'll know what your heart feels for her."

76

Kojo took a large gulp of his ice-cold Corona beer as he sat on the nouveau-style terrace at the Café de Paris in Monte Carlo.

From here, on a bright and warm afternoon, the sun caressing his skin, Kojo had a marvellous view of the beautiful spectacle of the Monte Carlo casino. If he were not currently on a Zoom call with the chief of MI6, he would watch the high rollers step out of their Ferraris and Jaguars as they entered the casino, their wealth glowing like an aura around them, the same way the sun shines on a nice day such as this.

"You'll be pleased to know, and in no small part to your efforts, that we've now dismantled The Cable's entire network," Tiwa said from the laptop screen. She was sitting in her office back at MI6's HQ.

Kojo shifted his bum in his chair, careful not to move his left arm too much, which was still inside the sling. Getting shot was such a physical inconvenience. "Well, that's good to know," he said, nodding at Tiwa. "It's unfortunate about the deaths of Dugard, Mancini and Mobolagi. The whole mission ended up a bloody mess, in my opinion."

"Yes, we could have done without the bodies, but at least we have Mustafa and Emiko alive, the last remaining members of The Cable. Mustafa denies all allegations of being part of any money laundering network. Still, Emiko has proven to be more cooperative and is currently providing us with names of the various criminal entities across the globe that had their money tied up with The Cable. As a result, she'll probably escape a severe sentence, but the young lady has her work cut out for her if she wants to change her family's reputation."

"Well, at least she's begun righting her family's wrongs, and everyone deserves a chance to start again." Kojo took another swig of his beer. "What about Afchain, the big crypto platform supposed to change finance in West Africa?"

"Its development was shut down," Tiwa said. "Once it was made public that criminal proceeds had funded the Nigerian tech company, it was quickly dismantled and lost all of its legitimate investors. It's a shame that the technology was being built partly for money laundering purposes, as it could have changed the lives of millions of Nigerians."

Kojo sighed. "See, that's the problem with technology. It's never built solely for the greater good of the people. There always needs to be a profit made on it. And the need to make money always invites corruption. It's a shame about Afchain, but the world continues to spin, and we move on."

Tiwa nodded, and then she gave Kojo a disheartening look. "And speaking of moving on, there's the matter of you handing in your resignation." She smiled playfully at Kojo. "I am surprised you are quitting MI6. If I recall correctly, you loved keeping busy protecting your Queen and country and taking out the villains in the big bad world. What's changed?"

Kojo chuckled and shrugged his shoulders. "When I got shot in Lagos and saw the barrel of a gun staring at me, as cliché as it sounds, I did see my life flash before my eyes." Kojo laughed. "Can you believe that? It took seconds away from being shot to death for me to finally have the epiphany that maybe I do want to be in a relationship. And I don't want to die alone with my cat."

Tiwa cackled. "Well, you're a very stubborn man. It would always take something extremely drastic for you to commit to someone. And I think I can hazard a good guess as to who the lucky woman is." She gave Kojo a knowing wink.

"Well, she's recently become a widow, so my timing couldn't have been better."

Tiwa shook her head, and she smiled at Kojo. "I am going to miss that inappropriate humour of yours."

"I'll send you a postcard." Kojo then pressed his lips together and smiled sadly at his former boss. "Don't forget how great you are. MI6 are lucky to have you running the show."

"Thank you," Tiwa said, smiling warmly at Kojo. "And thank you for your service to MI6 and your country. Now go and enjoy your retirement, you middle-aged man."

Once the Zoom call ended, Kojo closed the laptop. He then unzipped the leather laptop bag beside one of the table legs and placed the laptop inside. As soon as he closed it, he saw Federica in all her radiant Italian beauty by the terrace doorway.

Dressed in a white, sleeveless maxi dress that softly flared out at the bottom, with a golden neck choker, and brown sandals, Federica waved at Kojo, sending him the most effulgent smile a woman had ever given him. Since meeting her on that fateful day in Sardinia on her now-dead husband's yacht, Kojo had never seen Federica look so free, so jubilant. He intended to not only add to her happiness but maintain it.

Holding his laptop bag in his left hand, Kojo walked up to Federica and gave her a full kiss, feeling re-energised instantly by the texture of her moist lips.

Frederica pulled back and inspected him. "You know, *amore mio*, had you arrived here a day later, I would not be standing before you. I almost didn't think you would make it."

Kojo gave her a playful smile. "Well, I wanted to keep you in suspense."

Federica laughed and kissed him again. "Come, let us go. I can't wait to introduce you to my daughter and her boyfriend. They are waiting for us by the pier."

"Federica, quick question."

"Yes?"

Kojo scratched the back of his head, giving her a slightly embarrassed smile. "Do you know where I can buy cat food around here? I brought my cat, Felix. He's back at my hotel. I couldn't leave him behind in London. He's been too loyal to me."

* * *

As Timon sat in the black taxi that drove over the bumpy granite roads in Abeokuta, southwest Nigeria, he looked out the window. Giant boulders, rocky hills, shops and houses made from wood and concrete with tin roofs, sandy roads, and low-rise concrete commercial buildings and bungalows with fading, brownish paint characterised this part of Nigeria.

Already, Timon could tell that this part of Nigeria would be vastly different from the relentlessness of Lagos. Admittedly, he was a little intimidated being in this part of Nigeria by himself, which he could tell lacked the modern amenities you would find on Lagos Island. But Timon would push past his anxiousness and be brave. No matter what, somehow, he would find Yinka. Timon's gut feeling told him that coming to Yinka's childhood home was the most logical place to start searching for her.

He looked away from the window and sat back in the uncomfortable taxi seat. The driver had driven Timon all the way from his hotel in Lagos Island, where he had been staying for two days, to Abeokuta, which was more than 80 kilometres by car. Throughout the long car journey, Timon had been reflecting on his father's state funeral, which had taken place yesterday. After much consideration, Timon had decided to attend in the end. It had been a surreal and sobering experience.

His father's funeral had been the first time Timon had attended a funeral for someone directly related to him. The inside of the cathedral had been packed to the brim with people, nearly all from the business and political class of Nigeria, to pay their respects to Mobolagi Bankole, who lay in the majestic golden casket. Dressed in regal white robes, as light as the clouds against the blue summer skies, Mobolagi looked like he was in a peaceful sleep, with his hands placed on his lap and each of his rings, with their black stones, left untouched on each of his fingers to be buried with him.

Timon had stood with his half-siblings and Angelica Bankole at the front of the cathedral during the church service. Because Mobolagi had not died for natural reasons, his funeral was not one of celebration but of mourning, and the family's clothes reflected that as they had all worn black. Timon had worn a black, long-sleeved dashiki similar to his older half-brothers. His two half-sisters had dressed in black blouses with black headwraps. Angelia, sobbing throughout the service, had worn a black blouse with red leather gloves. She had been clutching a matching Louis Vuitton handbag. Not once did his father's widow acknowledge Timon's presence.

After the church service, Timon hugged Eniola, who was in such inconsolable tears that he felt tremendous guilt. He had said nothing to his half-brothers, who treated him with the same air of indifference as their stepmother.

Before leaving the cathedral, Timon had gone up to his father's coffin alone and looked down at his corpse. He had no tears for him. But Timon had no hate for him either. His father, ambitious and powerful as he had been in life, had been consumed by greed and corruption and had done anything to keep hold of the power and wealth he had obtained, even going so far as murdering an innocent woman —a mother. The universe had responded in kind, and karma had come to exact its vengeance. Timon now saw his father's death as a stark reminder and warning. Never sacrifice all human decency for the pursuit of riches.

"We are here, sah."

Timon's thoughts about his father evaporated when the taxi driver announced their arrival at Timon's hotel. He gave the taxi driver 200,000 naira in cash, which the taxi driver counted carefully, each paper note stretching the man's mouth into a bigger and bigger smile. After helping Timon with his single piece of luggage, a plain suitcase, as Timon knew dragging around one of his Louis Vuitton or Gucci suitcases in a remote city in Nigeria would attract unwanted local attention, the driver immediately got into his taxi and sped off down the dusty granite road.

Timon's sighed heavily, looking up at the hotel where he would stay for the week. From the outside, The Cesar's Court Hotel & Suites looked pleasant with a convincingly modern facade with beige walls, brown tiled roofs and small windows. Dragging his suitcase behind him, Timon made his way to the hotel. After checking in, he planned to order some jollof rice with suya meat and then sleep. Tomorrow, he would begin his search for Yinka.

For his first three days in Abeokuta, Timon made no progress in his quest to locate Yinka. With her phone number disabled, plus the fact she had no digital footprint and he had no pictures of her, Timon knew he might as well have been looking for a ghost. Nonetheless, he had travelled here to find her, so he would at least give it a good go. While Abeokuta was not as sprawling as Lagos, it was not small either. One of the guests staying at the hotel had told Timon that he was in the biggest city in Ogun state. Finding Yinka would be more complex than Timon first realised.

Timon hired a private driver, an Igbo man named Okonkwo, to get around the city. He was built like a wrestler and was not one for small talk. When Timon asked him if he knew a woman named Yinka Saraki, Okonkwo shrugged.

"You, this British boy, there are millions of women in this state," Okonkwo said in a harsh and heavy Nigerian accent. "Na wa o! If it is not my wife, sister, auntie or cousin, how can you expect me to know this woman you are searching for?"

Timon paid Okonkwo a generous day rate to drive him around Abeokuta. At the start of his search for Yinka, Timon had been driven to mostly shopping malls and street markets, hoping to spot Yinka among the crowd of women in African print blouses who walked along the rocky sidewalks, roamed the markets or moved through the city, getting on with their day. But he did not see her among them. Timon had even ventured into some shopping malls, asking people walking past, street merchants and shopkeepers, if they knew a woman named Yinka Saraki. Some shook their heads while others gave him an angry stare, annoyed that he was disturbing their day, asking them about some woman.

By the third day, Timon felt he had made a mistake coming to Abeokuta. He knew his plan to find Yinka had no logic, and he had acted out of pure emotion. To distract himself from the painful realisation that it might be impossible to find Yinka in this city with just her first and last name and that he was probably out of his depth, he decided to be a tourist.

On Wednesday afternoon, Okonkwo had driven Timon to the Olumo Rock tourist centre. According to one of the hotel clerks Timon had spoken to, Olumo Rock was the city's star attraction and a must-see experience for anyone visiting.

Located in the heart of Abeokuta, the mountain stood at 137 metres above sea level, almost half the height of the Eiffel Tower. Before it became one of Nigeria's most popular tourist destinations, Olumo Rock had protected the Egba Yoruba people during periods of war in the early 19th century. From the accounts of locals Timon had spoken to, if you were to reach the apex of the rock mountain, an awe-inspiring panoramic view of the whole city was your reward.

Dressed in white shorts, a plain brown dashiki, and white Nike Airforce One trainers, Timon began to climb the famous rock mountain, walking across the stone steps carved into the grey, rocky surface. Feeling adventurous, Timon did not follow any tourist guide, opting to explore the mountain himself. Thankfully, there weren't many tourists today, so Timon used the lifts and bridges to ascend the rock, feeling like he was in his own Indiana Jones film.

As Timon climbed further up, he used some of the smaller rocks as footholds to reach a new part of the fortress. He marvelled at the enormous stone boulders and thick branches growing and twisting around the rock as he squeezed through narrow caverns and climbed steel ladders.

At one point in his quest to reach the top of Olumo Rock, Timon stopped and bought some water from a food stall to quench himself from the heat, as he was now sweating from the physical labour. He was surprised and then fascinated to find some people had built settlements here, their quaint homes painted in different colours, with drawings of animal spirits and Yoruba writings carved into the walls that Timon did not understand. One day, he would need to learn to read and speak Yoruba fluently.

It took twenty minutes for Timon to reach the peak of Olumo Rock. Tired and sweaty, feeling the moist underneath his armpits, he felt a great swell of accomplishment and a sort of spiritual awakening by reaching the top of the rock. The sight that greeted Timon when he reached the pinnacle of the mountain took his breath away.

And it wasn't only the view.

A young woman was sitting on top of one of the boulders near the mountain's edge with her legs folded, her hands in her lap, and her eyes closed. It took Timon only seconds to know who she was. He could hardly believe his eyes.

Yinka's hair was no longer braided, and for the first time, he saw her natural dark hair in a small, curly afro. She wore a dark orange Kentre print dress with a matching hair band wrap, and her dark brown skin tone looked even more earthly and rich in this natural environment, like the shells of the purest coffee beans.

Feeling an almost overwhelming swell of joy in his chest, Timon climbed onto the boulder and called out Yinka's name.

77

Yinka had many memories scattered throughout her childhood of climbing to the top of Olumo Rock. The first time she had ventured here, she was six years old, and her father had taken her shortly after her mother had passed away. Since it was such a long time ago, the details of that day came in blurry fragments, like shards from a broken window. Still, the feeling she had experienced, breathing the crisp air as she gazed upon the city, her father holding her hand, was cemented in her memory.

The second time Yinka visited the top of the Olumo Rock was when she was thirteen years old. It was the start of the new school year. Mr Akedu, her school teacher, had taken a class of sixteen schoolchildren up the mountain, including herself and Oge. Yinka could never forget that day because it was the first time Oge held her hand, and it lasted for only a few seconds before Oge let go so their classmates wouldn't notice. Later, during that same trip, she and Oge secretly left their classmates and behind one of the tall trees they shared their first kiss. The beginnings of their intense and longing romance.

Yinka dabbed at her eyes, feeling the stinging sensation

that threatened tears. Since escaping with her life from that nightmarish experience at the African Tech Summit, the memory of Oge and now his death attacked her mind like hornets, stabbing relentlessly at her heart with their stingers. She could still remember being inside the getaway van as it sped away and how she had howled like a wounded animal once the adrenaline had left her body when the realisation fully dawned on her that Oge was gone forever.

For the past three weeks, she had struggled to sleep at her auntie's bungalow near the Oke Sokori Mosque. The bungalow once belonged to her father, but her auntie bought it when she moved back to Nigeria after living in east London for fifteen years. Throughout the night, flashes of Oge's crumpled and bullet-ridden body plagued Yinka every time she shut her eyes. Kisi and Montanna, who were staying nearby with Joshua and Jaali at a rented apartment, had come over at night and consoled her as she mourned Oge's death.

The Robin Hoods, now officially disbanded, were laying low in Abeokuta following Mobolaji's highly publicised assassination. To cope with her grief, Yinka had been coming to the Olumo Rock every day since arriving in Abeokuta. She came here just to be alone and away from everyone—just her mind and her spirit. Oge was gone. Violently killed. And she felt a tremendous guilt that she had not done more to save him.

So when Yinka heard Timon's voice call her name, she thought it was her imagination playing tricks with her. Then she heard his voice again. Had her grief driven her mad? She turned her head to where Timon's voice came from, and her heart leapt in her chest.

There he was, Timon, standing before her in the flesh. He was staring at Yinka, his eyes wide with wonder as if he were an explorer who had stumbled upon the greatest treasure.

Now, with her heart racing, Yinka slowly got to her feet, but she did not run to Timon and embrace him. After the initial shock of seeing him, Yinka's next thought was that she did not want him to be here.

"What...what are you doing here, Timon?" Yinka's voice sounded thin, like a piece of dwindling string.

"I came to find you, Yinka," Timon said, his voice trepid and shy.

"Where are you staying?"

"I am staying at the Cesar's Court Hotel."

Yinka shook her head. She felt lightheaded and confused. "Why would you come and find me? What do you want from me?"

Now, Yinka watched as Timon took one step towards her, his eyes glistening with affection and longing. The look on Timon's face intimidated and even scared her, for a part of her knew what he might say, and she wasn't sure she wanted to hear it.

"I am so sorry about Oge," Timon said, his eyes on her and his voice tinged with an honest vulnerability. "I can't imagine your pain, but I want to help you through it, Yinka. Because in my heart...I know...I know that I love you."

The declaration from Timon had felt like a gust of wind that threatened to blow Yinka off the cliff. She shook her head in denial. "No, no you don't."

"I really do, Yinka, and I had to tell you because you've captured my heart. My old life is no more. My business is gone, and I broke up with my fiancée because I never truly loved her. And when I think about what I want to do next, what I want the next chapter of my life to look like, and who I want it to be with, it's you. It's only you."

Timon took another step forward. "I want to stay here in Nigeria with you and help you build your school for girls and then build a big house and have children with you. I want to marry you and be the most caring and loving husband I can be. I want the next chapter of my life and every chapter after that to be good and wholesome, and I want to do that with you. Only you."

Yinka stared at Timon as he gazed at her with eyes raging with raw passion. A complex entanglement of emotions tightened around her. There was the joy of hearing Timon's admission of his love for her, pain because she still held onto Oge's memory, and fear of not knowing what a future with Timon might look like. The only man she had ever given her heart to was Oge.

"Timon...I...what do I say?"

Timon hurried towards her now, took her hands and raised them to his chest. The feeling of his fingers between hers sent a tingle of comfort that travelled quickly to her chest. "Do you love me, Yinka? Let's start there. Back in Lagos, on the beach, you said you chose me. Do you still feel that way?"

Yinka looked deeply into Timon's dark eyes. She was drawn to them, lost in that mesmerising and remarkable blackness. Slowly, she began to allow herself to feel Timon's all-encompassing desire to love her and to trust it. Like a creaking door, she could sense her heart beginning to open and give space for Timon's love for her. Then, Oge's dead and bloodied corpse intruded into her thoughts. And just like that, the door to her heart slammed shut.

Yinka flung her hands away from Timon's grasp. She took a step back, shaking her head at him. Rejecting his love. Burning tears ran down her cheeks.

"It doesn't matter if I love you or not, Timon. It would be an insult to Oge's memory to be with you. You're the son of the man who killed his mother."

"I am not my father, Yinka. You know that. I want to be nothing like him."

"But your father is still the reason why Oge is dead." Yinka began to sob, and she clutched her chest. Timon made a move towards her, but she glared at him fiercely. "Stay away from me." Timon did not take another step. "Please go back to London. Rip me from your heart. Forget about me forever. That is what I want from you. To forget me."

Timon's eyes looked watery, but no tears emerged. He looked to the sky for a moment and then back at Yinka and seemed resolved to Yinka's decision, but she saw the hurt in his eyes. He nodded solemnly. "If that's what you want, then I'll respect that. I wish you all the best, Yinka. I hope you find peace one day. And I could never forget you, even if I tried to."

Silently, Yinka watched as Timon turned around, climbed down from the boulder and walked down the iron steps built into the edges of the rock until she could no longer see him. Timon was gone.

Overcome with grief, Yinka burst into tears and slowly crumbled to her knees.

* * *

The evening descended on Abeokuta.

At the Orange Lounge & Bar opposite the Ashkash petrol station, multicoloured bulbs hung from strings attached to branches in the outdoor bar. As a live band played a rendition of a popular JuJu music track from the famous King Sunny Ade, the light from the bulbs bounced off the orange-painted concrete walls and tables, creating a relaxing ambience in the busy venue.

Yinka, Montana, Jaali, Kisi, and Joshua huddled around a wooden table at the back of the outdoor bar. A circle tray lined with ten tequila shots, two for each of them, was set on the table. They each picked up a shot glass and suspended it before them.

"Cheers to the end of the Robin Hoods," Jaali said, raising his shot glass the highest, "and to the start of our new lives as normal and law-abiding civilians making an honest living."

They necked their shots and slammed the glasses on the table.

"This concoction burns my throat," Joshua said, wincing. "I will never understand the logic of paying for an alcoholic beverage that is not only unpleasant but can cause a variety of health issues."

Kisi rolled her eyes, Montana laughed, and Jaali facepalmed. Yinka smirked weakly, trying her best to get into a celebratory mood but unable to muster the spirit.

"I am going to miss you, Engineer," Jaali said. "I think I'll name my son after you." Jaali, sitting next to Montana, bent down and kissed Montana's stomach.

"It would be an honour."

"He's joking, Joshua," Kisi said dryly.

Everyone around the table burst into cheerful laughter as Joshua flung his arms in the air, although he had a smirk on his face. Yinka couldn't laugh. She couldn't even imitate the action of laughing. Instead, she just looked at the tray with the shot glasses, her face blank.

Timon's visit weighed heavily on her mind. He had travelled from London to tell her that he loved her. The more Yinka thought about Timon's gesture, the more she felt she was about to lose someone special from her life. Someone placed their hand on Yinka's left shoulder. She looked up, and saw that it was Montana. Her round and bright eyes considered Yinka with a sisterly kindness.

"Yinks, if staying in your auntie's house over here is going to be a bit much, you can come to stay with Jaali and me for some time in London," Montana said, beaming at her. "We have a spare room in our new home till the baby arrives."

"Thanks, Monty," Yinka said, smiling weakly at her. "But I think I should stay in Abeokuta with my auntie. She's really missed me. I'll help her renovate the house and start building the school. I have more than enough money to do both now."

"I think I am going to buy a villa in Miami and just live a

perpetual hot girl summer," Kisi said, placing a toothpick in her mouth. "Maybe date a bunch of basketball players till I am bored."

"I am heading back to London to get a normal IT job where I don't need to breach security cameras and hack encrypted messages," Joshua said. "I think I am better suited to the civilian life."

"Guys, we had a good run and now we gotta leave the life of thieves behind," Jaali said. "And despite how he treated us in the end, we still owe it to Oge for inspiring us and leading us in this crazy chapter of our lives. So, let's make a toast to our late leader. Our brother. Our friend. We forgive him and honour his memory."

Everyone picked up their second shot glass from the tray.

"To Oge," Jaali said.

"To Oge," everyone replied in unison, knocking back their shots.

Yinka wasn't sure what possessed her to tell the group at that moment; maybe the second tequila shot loosened her tongue, but she felt she could no longer keep it to herself. "Timon came to see me today when I was meditating at the top of Olumo Rock." Immediately, all eyes fell on her.

"Timon? As in crypto boy?" Kisi said, raising her eyebrows.

Yina nodded. "Yeah, him. And he came from London to tell me that he loves me, wants to marry me, help build my school, and give me children."

Everyone around the table looked at each other, confused by Yinka's sudden revelation. Montana, sitting opposite Yinka, leaned forward. "But you love him too, don't you?"

Yinka couldn't help but smile weakly, feeling the tears creep to the edge of her eyes. "You can tell?"

Montanna placed both her hands over Yinka's resting on the table. "I am your best friend, babe. I could sense something was different with you when you came back from

Dubai. And it wasn't to do with the fact that Oge would be set free. You looked so sad as well. Like you knew you would never see someone you cared deeply about again. I knew it was Timon."

"Wait a sec, yeah. When did you catch feelings for him?" Jaali said, shaking his head as he looked at Yinka incredulously. "I thought you couldn't stand the guy because of how he treated you at school?"

"Love is a funny thing," Kisi said, chuckling. "It can start in the most unexpected places. Also, it's kinda hot that enemies to lovers romance."

"How love functions is more confusing than quantum physics," Joshua said, rolling his eyes.

Yinka sighed with regret. "I told him to return to London and forget about me."

"Why?" Montana said.

"What do you mean why?" Yinka said, looking at Montana with raised eyebrows as if the reason was obvious. "His father killed Oge's mother."

"Yeah, and his father is *dead*, by the way," Kisi said. "Correct me if I am wrong, but he barely even spoke to his pops, right? Mobolagi abandoned him and his mum before he was even born, is what you told us."

"I know that, but that's not the point. I would be disrespecting Oge's memory if I go and be with Timon."

"Yinks, listen to me because I am about to spit some real facts," Jaali said, his arms now folded. "I loved Oge, man. He was my bro. But he made his own choices, and he chose to deceive us all because hatred and revenge had consumed him. And I don't say that to judge him because I don't know what I'd do in his shoes, but his desire for revenge is what got him killed, let's be real. Not you. And he is no longer here now, but you are, Yinks. I've watched you live the last nine years of your life for him, so how about you start living your life now for yourself? If you want to honour his memory, choose to be happy. That's what I know Oge would have wanted for you in the end."

Jaali's words seemed to grab Yinka by the collar of her dress and shake her violently out of her self-pity and self-loathing. Tears, which felt like a release, trickled down her cheeks. "Thank you, Jaali. Honestly."

"You don't have to thank me, my sister." Jaali winked at her.

"And just to add, I can't believe Timon came all the way from London to Abeokuta just to declare his love for you," Kisi said. She began clapping her hands. "How many black men in this day and age would be so intentional in wanting to be with a woman and do a grand gesture like that? Not many, I tell you."

"Exactly, it took this one," Montana slapped Jaali playfully on the shoulder, "ten years to propose to me."

"Oi!" Jaali said, giving Montana a mock disapproving side-eye. "I must be absolutely sure before committing my whole life to a woman. The wrong decision can be hazardous, you know."

Montana stuck her tongue out playfully at her fiancée and then faced Yinka. "So where's Timon now?"

"He told me he's staying at Cesar's Court Hotel."

Montana gave Yinka a steely and determined gaze. "Fantastic. We'll both head there first thing in the morning. We're gonna get your man, Yinks."

78

"Mr Bakare has left the hotel," said the hotel receptionist to Yinka and Montana. They stood at the golden-tiled reception desk in the Cesar's Court Hotel. It was 10 am.

"Can you please tell me how long ago he left?" Yinka said, putting her hands on the desk.

If Timon had left hours ago and was already at Murtala Mohammed Airport, then there would have been no way for her to contact him. His number had been in her old phone, which she had since destroyed to avoid any risk of being detected by Nigeria's intelligence agencies.

The receptionist, a pretty lady with a light brown complexion who wore too much foundation and had too much red lipstick, gave Yinka a false smile. "If you can be patient, I can check."

Yinka did her best to stop herself from sucking her teeth and gave Montana a slide eye. The receptionist opened the logbook. After five minutes of casually flipping back and forth through the logbook, Yinka suspected the receptionist was deliberately slow, she finally stopped on a page. "It looks like Mr Bakare checked out about fifteen minutes ago. He left for Murtala Muhammed Airport with one of our local drivers."

"What car did he leave in?"

The receptionist raised her thin eyebrows at Yinka. "And why do you want to know that information?"

"Please, my sister. *Abeg, O.*"

The receptionist rolled her eyes. Yinka wished she could pluck out the receptionist's eyebrows with tweezers.

The receptionist was now tapping a biro on her head, thinking. "He left with Okonkwo, our local chaperone. He drives a dark green Honda Accord."

"*Oṣeun,*" Yinka said to the receptionist, then she turned to face Montana. "He only left fifteen minutes ago, so we still have time to catch him."

"Great, let's get in the car."

Five minutes later, with Montana in the driver's seat and Yinka sitting beside her, they were speeding down the bumpy, brownish granite road in the silver Toyota High-lander they had been renting since staying in Abeokuta.

As Montana drove past the concrete bungalows and the few people who strolled on the dusty sidewalks, Yinka noticed a church up ahead, painted green, although the paint was peeling off, and it had a rusty tin roof sloping down. Seeing the church jogged a memory from a long time ago, of herself and Oge passing it on their way home after school. It was the last time they were both happy and innocent children. Yinka caught herself smiling at the memory and knew that was the version of Oge she would remember and cherish.

"I can see a dark green Honda Accord just ahead," Montana said, pointing at the windshield.

Yina looked ahead, and Montana was right. Trudging along the rocky road was a green Honda Accord ahead of them. A man was sitting alone in the backseat of the car. Yinka would recognise the back of that big head anywhere.

"Blast your horn, Monty, so that the driver will stop."

Montana pressed her horn and did so several times. Yet the green Honda Accord continued down the road unabated. "These stubborn drivers," Montanna said, sucking her teeth.

Yinka shrugged her shoulders. "We'll just have to block his path."

Montana turned to look at Yinka and gave her a playful smirk before flicking her eyes back on the road. She pulled the lever in the gearbox to a higher gear and pressed on the accelerator pedal. The Toyota Highlander shot forward, and Yinka gripped the side of her headrest. As their car shot past the Honda Accord, Yinka turned to her left to see Okonkwo, the driver, who was a big man, glare at her and Montana from the window.

With an impressive showcase of her driving skills, Montana steered the car sharply to the left and hit the brakes hard. Yinka jerked forward, her seatbelt stopping her from flying through the windshield as the car suddenly stopped in the middle of the granite road.

Okonkwo had exited his vehicle now and was shouting all manner of colourful obscenities at Yinka and Montana as they sat in the car. They both unlocked their seat belts.

"This is going to be fun," Montana said.

Yinka and Montana stepped out of the car and cautiously walked towards the increasingly irate Okonkwo.

"*Ma binu*, sah," Yinka said, raising her hands in the air. "We wanted you to stop when we sounded the horn, but you did not."

"Se omugo ni o?" Okonkwo said harshly, in his loud Nigerian accent. "Why would I just stop because you are beeping your horn? *Eediots*."

"Yinka? What are you doing here?"

Yinka looked past Okonkwo's massive head to see that Timon had stepped out of the car. He was wearing denim jeans with a white dashiki top. White really suited him.

SECURE THE BAG | NOT THE HEART

Okonkwo snapped his head back at Timon. "So this is the Yinka woman you have been looking for, eh, British boy?"

"Yeah," Timon said, taking three short steps forward. "I had already found her, but she's come to find me now." His eyes lingered on Yinka, never looking away from her.

Yinka raised her head at him, pretending to be unbothered even though her heart wanted to fly out of her chest. "I did come to find you. It seems like we keep finding each other."

Okonkwo kept turning his head from Timon to Yinka, completely baffled by what was going on. Montanna strode towards him and pulled him away.

"Come now, uncle, let us not get in the way," Montanna said, pulling Okonkwo by his sleeve who was following her. She winked at Yinka as she walked past and gave her a reassuring smile.

"You gave me a nickname when we were in Tokyo," Yinka said, all her attention on Timon. She was maybe eight feet away from him. "Do you remember what it was?"

Timon chuckled. "Yeah, I do. I called you Miss Stubbornly Sophisticated."

Yinka nodded. "Yeah, and you were right. Sometimes, I am too stubborn and too sophisticated that I get in my way. I get in my head too much. When all I need to do is just listen to my heart sometimes."

Timon gave her a soft smile. "I am in the same boat as you. But you know how it is: following your heart is not easy for highly talented Nigerians like ourselves. We're brainy people—too intelligent for our own good."

Yinka let out a short laugh and took one step towards Timon. "You flew from London to tell me you loved me. You then asked me if I loved you back, but I didn't give you an answer, did I?"

Timon shook his head playfully. "Nope, you didn't. It's a bit rude, to be honest."

Yinka bit her lip, grinning. "I agree, so I came to find you so I could give you my answer. Do you want to know what it is?"

Timon took one step towards her. His eyes were expanding with joy. "I am all ears," he said.

"I love you, Timon. And I want to spend the next chapter of my life with you and all the chapters after that."

Timon did not take a single step this time but ran to her, took Yinka into his arms and lifted her in her orange kente print dress. With her legs wrapped around his waist, as Timon supported her by holding her from her bottom, she gave him a kiss that came straight from a place deep within the fountains of her soul. She poured all her love into him and could feel Timon give all himself to her. For a minute, they just let their lips enjoy the taste of each other as they lusted and delighted in the pleasurable and sensual physicality of one another. Then Timon carefully placed Yinka on the ground, and they stared at each other, breathless and lightheaded.

Timon's eyes lit up as he gazed in awe at her as if he were staring at the meaning of life itself, which made Yinka know she could feel secure with him. She anticipated the first time they would make love to one another, which would be very soon. If the eruption of pleasure they felt from simply kissing each other were anything to go by, sex would be an out-of-body experience. She looked forward to the rest of her life with him.

Yinka placed her hand tenderly on Timon's left cheek. "You have secured my heart, Timon."

"And you have secured mine, Yinka, and it will always be yours."

ACKNOWLEDGMENTS

'Secure The Bag, Not The Heart' is now the fourth novel I have self-published as an independent black British author through my publishing company 'Urban Intellectual Books'. As with any undertaking, especially one as daunting, challenging and exciting as writing a novel, I could not have brought this book into the world without the help of some fantastic people.

First and foremost, I have to thank my younger brother and sister. As they will attest, I can be an annoying older brother, and often, despite being the eldest, I behave like the youngest in our trio. But, this book would not have materialised without my siblings' support, both financially and creatively. So thank you so much, Seun and Tinuke, for everything you do for your silly brother. I love you both, and I promise always to show you love tenfold back. And yes, I'll also learn to be less annoying.

Secondly, I must thank my wonderful parents for their generosity and patience. My parents are the hardest-working people I know, and I am everything I am in this world because of how they raised me. When times have been tough, and I have had many tough times while I was writing this novel, my parents' support, financially as well as emotionally, really got me through these difficult periods. I owe it to you, Mum and Dad, to live an honest and respectable life.

'Secure The Bag, Not The Heart' is a love letter to James Bond and the espionage genre in general. So it is only fitting to thank the late Ian Fleming (28 May 1908 - 12 August 1964), the famous English writer who created James Bond. From a young age, I fell in with Fleming's fictional MI6 agent and his thrilling missions in the brilliant stories Fleming wrote and the world-renowned film adaptations. I must also reference John le Carré (19 October 1931 - 12 December 2020), another brilliant writer in the espionage genre, from whom I drew much inspiration for my novel. It has been so fun writing in the espionage genre that I will certainly be returning to this world again and revisiting some of the characters in this story, but that is down the line.

Lastly, I want to thank all my fans and everyone who has purchased the novel. I write stories so they can be read and enjoyed, and without readers, I don't know what I'd do with myself, so thank you for reading my work. You give me purpose.

REVIEW REQUEST

Book reviews are incredibly important for writers, especially for self-published authors. Reviews increase word-of-mouth and help generate sales, both good and bad.

Please write a review of my novel on GoodReads (scannable QPR below) or Amazon. It can be a great or scathing review - all reviews are welcome!

Thank you so much.

SCAN TO LEAVE BOOK REVIEW

DO YOU WANT TO BE A PUBLISHED AUTHOR?

Are you a young and inspiring writer who doesn't know the first thing about publishing or how to get your book out into the world?

Don't worry—it's all good. As someone who has been in the self-publishing world for several years, I am happy to help you accomplish your book publishing goals.

If you're interested in publishing a novel or want to book me for writing and speaking events, don't hesitate to get in touch with me at:

Email: urbanintellectualbooks@gmail.com

Mobile: 07908073815